"TERRY McMILLAN STANDS AS A LITERARY BESSIE SMITH."
—*The Toronto Star*

Praise for Terry McMillan and her novels

How Stella Got Her Groove Back

"The novel sparkles." —*Chicago Tribune*

"The dialogue is true, the storytelling witty."
—*The Philadelphia Inquirer*

"Entertaining. . . . If you're looking for some angst-free fiction with a West Indian setting, leave Jamaica Kincaid and Toni Morrison on the shelf and pack this brash, sparkling fairy tale." —*Boston Herald*

"McMillan's fans will rejoice in the book's funky, romantic exuberance." —*The Miami Herald*

"Told in McMillan's vintage home-girl prose, scattered with expletives, potshots at men, and plenty of soul-stirring, toe-curling sex. . . . McMillan also demonstrates her virtuosity with witty, spicy, and fast-paced dialogue."
—*The Seattle Times*

"Terry McMillan is the only novelist I have ever read who makes me glad to be a woman."—*The Washington Post Book World*

"Spicy and overtly frank." —*New York Daily News*

continued . . .

JUN 17

CH

Disappearing Acts

"Hot and electric . . . a love story waiting to explode."
—*The New York Times Book Review*

"If Ntozake Shange, Jane Austen, and Danielle Steel collaborated on a novel of manners . . . [*Disappearing Acts*] might be the result." —*The New Yorker*

"A funny, earthy novel. . . . With eloquence and style, McMillan gives her work a voice that is her own, one tough enough to speak across class and color lines, daring enough to make a statement about our country and our times." —*Newsday*

"A get-out-your-handkerchiefs love story. Unflinchingly realistic . . . warm and natural." —*USA Today*

"*Disappearing Acts* contains something increasingly rare in books or film today: a full-blown, sophisticated love affair between two African-American adults . . . McMillan has created two real and believable characters . . . complex and true." —*The Denver Post*

continued . . .

"A delicious family saga . . . poignant yet hilarious . . . an affecting and life-affirming read . . . [which] constantly surprises as it enlightens. A triumph."   —*Los Angeles Times*

"Moving and memorable."   —*The New York Times Book Review*

"[A] slam dunk of a novel . . . this book is a gift."
—*Newsday*

"A touching and funny portrait."   —*People*

"Nobody does it better . . . sassy, inventive, humorous, and wise. She can make me laugh out loud, but she is just as capable of moving me to tears. . . . *A Day Late and a Dollar Short* embodies McMillan's belief in romantic love as the most profound expression of one's humanity."
—*The Toronto Star*

Waiting to Exhale

"With relationships between African-American men and women in the spotlight as never before, here comes McMillan's report from the front . . . bawdy, vibrant, deliciously readable. A novel that hits so many exposed nerves is sure to be a conversation piece. It has heart and pizzazz and even, yes, the sweet smell of a breakthrough book."   —*Kirkus Reviews*

Also by Terry McMillan

Mama

Disappearing Acts

*Breaking Ice: An Anthology of Contemporary
African-American Fiction (editor)*

Waiting to Exhale

A Day Late and a Dollar Short

The Interruption of Everything

HOW STELLA GOT HER GROOVE BACK

TERRY McMILLAN

 NEW AMERICAN LIBRARY

New American Library
Published by New American Library, a division of
Penguin Group (USA) Inc., 375 Hudson Street,
New York, New York 10014, USA
Penguin Group (Canada), 90 Eglinton Avenue East, Suite 700, Toronto,
Ontario M4P 2Y3, Canada (a division of Pearson Penguin Canada Inc.)
Penguin Books Ltd., 80 Strand, London WC2R 0RL, England
Penguin Ireland, 25 St. Stephen's Green, Dublin 2,
Ireland (a division of Penguin Books Ltd.)
Penguin Group (Australia), 250 Camberwell Road, Camberwell, Victoria 3124,
Australia (a division of Pearson Australia Group Pty. Ltd.)
Penguin Books India Pvt. Ltd., 11 Community Centre, Panchsheel Park,
New Delhi - 110 017, India
Penguin Group (NZ), cnr Airborne and Rosedale Roads, Albany,
Auckland 1310, New Zealand (a division of Pearson New Zealand Ltd.)
Penguin Books (South Africa) (Pty.) Ltd., 24 Sturdee Avenue,
Rosebank, Johannesburg 2196, South Africa

Penguin Books Ltd., Registered Offices:
80 Strand, London WC2R 0RL, England

Published by New American Library, a division of Penguin Group (USA) Inc. Previously
published in Viking and Signet editions. A portion of this work first appeared in *People*.

First New American Library Printing, January 2004
10 9 8 7 6 5

for Jonathan P.

ACKNOWLEDGMENTS

I am totally grateful to everybody who converged and helped provide me with the time, space, confidence and love to write this book: my son, Solomon, has been my biggest motivator and supporter—I'm glad he's my child and buddy; my agent, Molly Friedrich, for her continued faith and patience over these last few years; my old editor, Dawn Seferian, who I really miss, but also to my new editor, Carole DeSanti, who is so smart and intuitive and really understands authors, which is why I'm glad to have her as my advocate; to my assistant, Judi Fates, for her dedication, hard work and patience; and last, but very much at the top of my list, are my mama, Madeline Tillman, and my very best friend forever, Doris Jean Austin: I miss you both.

AUTHOR'S NOTE

I hadn't planned on going anywhere. All I knew was that as much as I loved my son, I was glad to see him disappear after those doors to Gate 3 closed this morning. Quincy's on his way to Colorado Springs to visit his daddy and now I have the house all to myself. Finally, some peace and quiet. And three whole weeks of it. Of course there are a million things I want to do and now I can do them without being distracted. Without hearing "Mom, can I . . . ?!" every fifteen seconds.

Thank God it's Saturday. And thank God it's summertime. School's out. No more three-day-a-week Little League practice (rain or shine) or those long-ass games. No week-on/week-off revolving carpooling and forgetting it's my week and being afraid to call the parents of the abandoned children who are all standing in the rain for an hour after I forgot them because they are all—including my own son—too dumb to call somebody else. And thank the Lord there's nowhere I have to be: no can't-wait portfolios to review and I don't have to pay attention to any of the four computers in my office, I mean I can actually be off-line for a change and I have no meetings no planes to catch, *nada.*

I've got about a hundred books I've been meaning to read since last year and I figure now I can probably read them all. I've got a house full of trees and straggly vines that need to be transplanted which is what I'm planning to do today but of course when I go out to the garage I have no big pots and just a drop of potting soil and not a single pair of those gloves with the little rubber dots on the fingertips, all of which means I have to go to Home Depot. I hate going to Home Depot because I always end up going down the plant rug toilet or sink aisles when I have enough plants rugs toilets and sinks already. But by the time I get to the checkout I usually have to exchange my cart for one of those flatbed numbers and then I realize I didn't drive the truck so I have to have them put my stuff to the side until I come back and as I'm driving home it occurs to me that they're probably going to switch some of my merchandise and not think I'll notice but by the time I pull the truck up to their automatic doors I'm usually totally pissed at myself for buying all this shit I don't need because despite the fact that I am not a landscaper handywoman or carpenter I have all these useful new tools with which to express my fantasies of do-it-yourselfness and what is really bothering me is that I have most likely spent somewhere in the neighborhood of a thousand bucks which seems to be my going rate here and at Costco and which is also why I am right this minute changing my mind about going today. I'll go tomorrow. With a list and the promise to buy only what's on it.

I look around the house and realize that the house-keeper does a pretty good job—for a sixty-one-year-old Peruvian man—of keeping it clean. He fixes everything that breaks around here, and since he is ultrareligious and I think maybe even a participating Buddhist, out of respect I sort of watch my mouth in my own home. He cleans under and behind everything which is the main reason I have no Saturday morning cleaning to do. I believe from the bottom of my heart that dusting polishing and vacuuming are entirely too tedious never-ending and boring tasks and there are so many other things I would rather be doing which is why I hired Paco in the first place. He is worth the money.

I open all the blinds and notice that the windows are pretty grungy-looking from all the rain we've had here this past spring. Flooding and mud slides wiped out hundreds of homes all over northern California and I felt lucky to be way out here in this boring little valley. I don't do windows which is why I make a mental note to call Of Course We Do Windows first thing on Monday. Paco tried doing them once but he couldn't get up high outside and if he fell and hurt himself I would feel terrible.

I go into the kitchen and make myself a latte and as I stare out into the backyard the first thing I see is Phoenix, our free-from-the-pound chocolate Lab, swimming in our black-bottom pool as if it's his. Then I look over at what is now a storage shed that I was told was once a guest-house and then I turned it into a studio but of course that was when I used to be this creative person and I had energy and a thriving spirit and I would design and conceive and sometimes actually manufacture what I used to call functional sculpture aka handcrafted furniture that people in fact solicited and paid me real money to make for them out of everything from aluminum copper steel wood whatever, but then it became so hard to like pay the rent and then this husband I ended up saying yes to when I should've just said no convinced me that I could use that MBA I got and like combine it with that MFA I also had which of course all by itself was worthless and who could afford this eccentric one-of-a-kind so-called furniture when a normal person could like just go to Thomasville or Levitz or Ikea and of course I didn't know how to mix commerce with art and so I failed at working with my hands. I went with the brain and forged figures inside my economic head and did the total business beat. I have been doing this now for like hell I don't even know how many years but it is another reason why right this minute, looking out at the dog at that clear black water at the little salmon-colored bungalow where I used to pray and dream and invent, I am getting a sudden overwhelming urge to run the vacuum through my mental house and chill out, sit down long enough to smell the cosmos the zinnias the coral bells hell the fucking coffee (which I actually *can* smell right now), so when Quincy comes home I'll be more poised balanced composed than I've been in years. The generic term for it is relaxed. Maybe I can even acquire some of that stuff commonly known as patience that I haven't had in a long time. I'd like to be able to sit down next to my son and watch one of those moronic TV shows that he's always begging me to watch but after a few minutes I always find myself jumping up to do something during the commercials and I repeat this up-and-down business at least five times during a mere half-hour show which means I'm not exactly setting a good example for someone who's always telling her child how he needs to

learn to sit still long enough to give something his undivided attention. All I do when I get up is move things.
Dishes go in the dishwasher. Or they come out. Never-
read magazines newspapers and last week's mail are tossed
into the compactor for crushing. Clothes pulled out of
the washer get pushed into the dryer. Now let's fold. Make
stacks. Everything has to be in its place. Because if I don't
do it, it won't get done.

But I'm tired of jumping up. Tired of running. I would
like to be able to just sit there with my son without moving without wishing I were somewhere else doing something
else without thinking about something else and I'd like to
just hold his hand or put my arm around his narrow
shoulders because I know in a few more years he won't
want me to sit on the couch with him and watch anything
and he probably won't want me to touch him.

I walk from the kitchen into the family room and sit on
the red leather love seat and I look around and see all this
color all these different textures—those golden maple
floors those celery concrete floors these purple plastered
walls that teal suede sofa that black oak pool table that egg-
plant leather floor in my office and this silver slate under
my feet—and I am proud that over the years I have made
my funky little California castle suitable to my needs my
tastes and I have rigged equipped and outfitted it in such
an unorthodox way that it might actually be impossible to
sell even though I am not even thinking of moving anywhere but for some reason today like right this minute I
am feeling imposed upon by all of it as if I went too far
and now all this color all these juxtaposing textures are
backfiring instead of soothing as they always have been

even until just yesterday but not today and as I sit here and watch Phoenix shaking himself dry, I decide that today maybe I should shake myself up a little too.

But how? And where do you start? I look down at the coffee table and notice Quincy forgot the stationery I bought him so he could write to me and his homies while he's away. Maybe *I* should write a few long-overdue letters or something to some folks. That's it! Yeah, I'll write to a few long-lost relatives and to some folks I haven't seen or talked to in ages. Just little notes. Some maybe-you-think-I've-forgotten-you-but-here's-a-gesture-to-let-you-know-I-haven't notes. Hell, I remember when I used to write tons of letters. Now who has time to even call anymore? A lot of times when I do call I'm secretly hoping the person won't be home and that I'll get the answering machine because I know there's something else I could or should be doing that's a helluva lot more productive like washing clothes or doing something in the kitchen but the portable phone is too staticky in the laundry room and kitchen which means I have to stand in one place and talk which is why it's so much easier to leave a two-minute message (if they've got a decent machine) than it is to talk for a half hour or longer, depending on where they fall in your chart of closeness, trying to cover what has happened to you both over the last week month year or two.

I know I'm not alone because I'm forever getting messages from estranged friends and relatives who are pissed because I haven't returned their phone calls from whenever and they say things like, "Girl, I could be dead and you wouldn't know it what kind of fucking friend are you Stella we used to be close did I do something that I don't know about" and I shake my head no or they say we just had a baby or I finally got my divorce and I just wanted you to know that I don't live in Atlanta or Memphis or Los Angeles anymore, and oh by the way, I've got a brand-new grandbaby and did you get the pictures if you did you didn't say nothing about how cute he is and hell, he's got three teeth now or he's walking or in kindergarten and this is the MCI operator with a collect call from BENNIE please press one if you accept and two if you decline and sir the party's not at home and he says okay but can I leave a message anyway and then there is a click and he is just one of my many relatives who call from the penitentiary but then there's hey yeah Stella this is your cousin Rafiki As-Salaam-Alaikum my sister peace be unto you all praises are due to Allah and hey I know you surprised I ain't calling collect but my lady let me use her calling card for a month and you still ain't sent me no pictures of you and I'm still working on my own defense and I was wondering if you could send me fity dollars for some toiletries and such cause my mama ain't been up to see me in over six months she mad at me and my lady ain't got no mo transpo to get way out here and I been in the hole for the past month for something I ain't even did but it's all good and anyway let me know if you can do that and baby, this is your aunt Junie calling and I don't know if you know it or not but Miss Willamae's in the hospital and I know you remember her cause she used to baby-sit you when you was a baby and you know she got cataracts and she had to have that operation finally that she been putting off because of her having all them insurance problems and everythang but you remember her she's Miss Bessie's cousin's sister from her first marriage to Silbert what used to live on the corner of Moak and Fortieth Street, right down the street from Ms. Lucy when she was living and anyway you went to school with her granddaughter but I can't remember her name right now but pray for her even though she's doing much better now and I just wanted to touch base don't get to talk to you much no more and how is Quincy these days? I bet he's tall as you and how old is he now (there is a long pause because she's waiting for an answer) and like a fool I say, "He's eleven and a half, Aunt Junie," but even though you don't stay in touch I want you to know that you both are in my prayers and the Lord is watching over you and I'm gon' call your sisters as soon as I hang up since the rates is low. Love you, baby. I wonder if her machine is gon' get all this and Stella? Did you get this whole message, sugar?

I also don't get very many letters either—maybe five or six a year and that's counting the preaddressed prestamped envelopes I give Quincy when he's away at camp—and shoot, I know at least a thousand people and at least five hundred of them live more than five hundred miles away. Far enough away to write.

It just feels like nothing is the way it used to be anymore and it's not that I'm on some nostalgia trip or anything but I just wonder if I'm feeling like this because I can't believe I'm really forty-fucking-two years old because people tell me all the time I don't look forty-two and to be honest I don't have any immediate plans of really acquiring the *look* if there is a way to look when you're forty-two and I certainly don't feel forty-two even though I don't know how I'm supposed to *feel* being forty-two and what I do know is that I'm not *angry* about being forty-two but it feels like I'm slowly but surely catching up to my mama because she was only forty-two when she died and I'm thinking how is this possible that I could ever be the same age as Mama? I wonder if I could secretly be having a midlife crisis?

Ever since Walter and I split up I guess I have been a little numb. I don't dislike him or hate him for being who he is but I certainly stopped loving him because of it. He bored me to death. Living with him was like living in a museum. It was drafty, full of vast open spaces and slippery floors. He wasn't a bad person, but I just didn't care for his attitudes and later on his principles turned out to be on the opposite end of the spectrum from mine. He wanted me to be just like him. I wanted him to respect our differences. I ended up telling him that he should've married himself, and later that he should try fucking himself. And this is what we basically argued about. Who we were. We never seemed to come to any neutral turf where both of our feelings and positions were acceptable or at least tolerable. We sort of kept this demerit scoreboard for the last eight years, until we ran out of space. He and I both knew that our time was up, so we didn't make a big tadoo about it, we just agreed to stop this before we ended up hating each other.

We were both running on high octane and barely had time for sex anymore and when we did we were both so exhausted the thought of actually being tender and sensuous and playful was not something that even crossed our minds. Or hearts. We just did it to get off, to relieve some of the tension. Some of the stresses and strains of the day that we brought home with us. At times I felt like his prostitute and I'm sure on occasion he probably felt that way too. It got old. And after a few years of this, I started wondering if I'd ever feel any excitement or passion toward him or any man again, and now that it's been a few years since our divorce, I'm pretty much feeling the same way.

Nobody has rocked my world, as the saying goes. Nobody has made my heart flutter like it did when I first met Walter, or even when I fell in love with Chad, and I don't dare go all the way back to high school or college when the world stopped spinning when Nathaniel kissed me. All Dennis did was smile at me and I was like Elvis: all shook up. I didn't know the power of love was so powerful. But I liked it. Liked feeling like I was full of clouds. Like I could probably run a marathon without ever training for it. Like I was "on" something that was causing me to have a continuous flow of energy, making me feel excited about and see beauty in just about everything. I could walk down the street and feel myself grinning and people would look at me and simply grin too. This is when I thought I understood what God intended for us to feel.

But then the bullshit always had to enter the picture and contaminate everything that had been so beautiful. Like where were you and why do you have to do that all the time and how come and when are you and I don't really give a flying fuck if you do but because I felt like it and if you can't handle it tough shit but as much as I wish I could I can't even begin to imagine but just the thought of you don't no not anymore but we could if you weren't so damn stubborn because hell I can't help it if I was and yes you are trying to change me into something that I'm not and want to see how long I can resist this shit want to watch me repel and don't remind me how much we used to have that's the past and it's gone baby live in the here and now and check it out this is getting too thick for me and I'm like sinking somewhere low and my heart weighs a ton here lately and as a matter of fact the mere sight of you being in your presence for any length of time depresses the hell out of me and I don't need this shit who needs this shit so I'm like out of here.

All I know is that I was sort of already using my reserve tank when he left and afterwards being alone took some getting used to. A person can get on your last nerve, drive you to drink, but you still kind of miss their sorry ass after they're gone is what I found out. That empty space he left sort of turned into an ache for a minute, or I should say a few months, maybe even a year. It was like this secret longing I felt to replace the void he left with something or someone else. Only I didn't have the energy. Quincy took up a different kind of space, required a different kind of love. It wasn't until a year and a half ago that I realized I had not felt the warmth of a man's body next to mine, that my lips hadn't trembled, that my breasts hadn't throbbed or between my legs hadn't been wet from anybody's hands except my own, and it made me sad, but I didn't know what to do about it. I was waiting for *him* to knock on the front door, I guess, and just say, Here I am. Your worries are over, baby. I'm here. But there has been no knock. I haven't even bumped into him. Haven't seen him. Haven't walked past him in an airport and felt any current radiate from his body to mine. Not at all. Not anything close.

But it's okay. Because all I know is that marriage wears you out and I'm not sure if I have the energy left for it. All my married friends are mostly miserable. They're just in it because. They started it. Those kids. The money would be all fucked up. Lifestyles would change. Alimony. Child support. And that fucking mortgage and all those cars and visitation and fuck it, let's just stick it out. Some of them don't even sleep together. Some of the men—a lot of the men—are into serious affairs but unfortunately the chicks on the side don't have a clue that most of them have no intention of leaving. The men just need a reprieve. Want to break up the monotony. Smell somebody new. In some cases it's the only way their dicks can get hard and blast off anymore and hell to them it's worth it.

Which is why I have pretty much come to the conclusion that marriage itself is a dead-end institution. I'm not doing it again. All I want is a little companionship. No ring. No "I do till death do us part," because I said that once and we're both still very much alive. Folks expect too much from one another and when you don't won't or can't deliver you fall short and eventually begin to piss the other person off and years go by and the two of you simply tolerate each other. I wasn't born to live like this, and especially with a man. I know God didn't have some master plan where we were supposed to fall in love and then work our asses off to make it work and then it doesn't and then we end up feeling worse longer than we felt good. There's something inherently wrong with this whole notion. It seems like everybody is striving for perfection. The perfect fucking spouse who will make you feel perfect. But I know for a fact that no such person exists. I know for a fact that I am far from perfect, but there have been many instances where I didn't believe that. I fought hard for the right to be right. All I was doing was trying to preserve my right to my own self-image, but I'm here to be whoever I am and if I happen to be a little fucked up then accept me fucked up as I am or leave me the fuck alone. Because if there's ever going to be a change in my behavior or my personality I will do it myself and I don't need you nagging me telling me how fucked up I am because you know what? you're pretty fucked up too.

I don't know how long it's going to take for me not only to fill back up again but to get my engine started. I've been divorced now for almost three years and haven't been on a legitimate date in almost a year even though I have a number to call when I just have to have some even though it's not passionate but purely maintenance-oriented sex and I thank God he's married because I wouldn't want him any other way and these last few months have been tough because he's turned into such a lazy fuck and he's pissed at me for not returning his calls and hiding from him really but I'm tired of having sex with him for the sake of getting off because I have to work too hard and he's started banging me the way he probably bangs his wife, like he's a slug, and I don't like kissing him one bit and I'm at the point now where I just can't do it anymore. Sex should not be cumbersome. And I don't like the idea of searching for love or trying to conjure up passion. Which is probably one reason why it feels like I've lost a lot over these last few years. I know things can never be the way they were (and I wouldn't dare want it back) but there are a few relatively simple things I've stopped doing that I want to put back in my life.

I wish I could call Delilah. But I can't. She'd only been my best friend since college and we only talked on the phone every other day and she was the most brilliant person I ever met and we could talk about anything and she lived all the way in Philly and then last year she decides to surprise me and die suddenly from some stupid liver cancer that she didn't even tell me she had until she was in the fucking hospital and then she was gone the next week and there was a lot of shit we still needed to talk about. A whole lot of stuff. Years and years' worth of stuff. She knew I was going to miss her ass and I *do* miss her black ass and the only way I can make the hurt go away is to do one of two things: pretend that she's still alive and that we're just not on speaking terms, which we went through from time to time, or pretend that she never existed. Trying to do both has required a great deal of effort and imagination and whenever I'm not looking my heart plummets down real low and I can hardly tolerate the longing.

So over these next two weeks I want to try to do some make-Stella-feel-good stuff. Which is why I'm planning to do some things I've been meaning to do but haven't for one reason or another. Mostly because I'm always too busy. Always doing something. Work alone has been kicking my ass. It's been said before, but I'm here to give new meaning to the phrase "I hate my job."

I might actually call up a few old friends and sit in a chair and not roam around the house while I talk but give them my undivided attention, listen to what they have to say, what they've been going through, how they've been feeling. These are people I do care about but now they're just on the B list. My life has gotten too busy. And it's time for me to slow it down.

I will also cook. I used to cook all kinds of interesting and exotic meals, but after Walter left, if Quincy couldn't identify it he didn't even want to try it. A double Big Mac and supersize fries and a nine-piece Chicken McNugget with a medium Sprite and apple pie is his meal of choice. I miss cooking. I miss smelling new smells and stirring new sauces and being surprised by the taste of something different. I will cook. I will make it a habit. I will even make some of those low-fat meals from a few of the fifty or sixty cookbooks I've purchased over the years and have yet to ever open.

For the last two or three years I've been meaning to make a computerized printout of all my relatives' and friends' birthdays and even their kids' and have it printed on a specially made calendar so that each day when I walk into my office all I have to do is look up and see whose birthday is coming up, and their card and maybe even a gift depending on their age and who they were would be a surprise and on time.

I'll also plant some flowers in the front and back yards since I've been reading about the Zen of gardening and how gratifying it can be, and since it's been awhile since I've had sex I'll take whatever form pleasure comes in. At any rate, I've heard that this gardening stuff can relax you and even give you some of those endorphins like people get when they exercise.

This too is something I'd like to improve upon while my son is off to the Rockies with his how-did-I-ever-love-his-lifeless daddy. As it stands now, I am almost ashamed to tell people that I hired a personal trainer who comes to my house three days a week to make me pump and grind and sweat because the bottom line is that I'm lazy and have no willpower and have woken up too many mornings from dreams in which I worked out so strenuously and was truly too beautiful for a woman who'd just turned forty and I put stars like Cher and Tina Turner and Diana Ross to shame but it wasn't until a year later after having a series of such dreams that I realized I had never broken a sweat let alone panted. It has taken me another year to get into the rhythm of working out and there are many mornings when I'd just as soon call in sick, but as a result of my desire to improve my health with the real motive being pure vanity I now am almost in shape although I still have my unfair share of cellulite, but it's not as much as I used to have thank the Lord and I actually do have a number of muscles and my butt is higher and firmer than I ever recall it being but since I'd been paying the health club $105 a month for two years and had actually only been inside to give tours to visiting friends and relatives and inform them that whenever I had the time this is where I usually worked out though the truth was I'd only gone in there to sit in the steam room but since I now have two steam rooms—here and in my cabin at Lake Tahoe—there was really no need to waste my gas driving there so why bother, so last year I admitted to myself that I was bullshitting myself and since I have had a difficult time visualizing myself fat and slovenly and just plain old I decided—like they do in any twelve-step program—to turn myself over to a higher power. Her name is Krystal and she makes Cindy Crawford look like a zero and she only charges fifty dollars an hour. I used to use drugs that cost me more per minute. Which is one reason I could never run for public office. If anyone ever did a background check on me they'd be in for a big shock. But then again, they are always shocked at everybody else's background when they're running for public office, aren't they? No one who has really lived should have a sterling background, in my opinion. My sister Angela is the only baby boomer I know who's never tried any drugs at all. She's missed out on a lot of good shit if you ask me.

But those were the good old days. Times have changed. Twenty years have passed. I am a grown-up. In every sense of the word. I have responsibilities. I am responsible. I am a good mother. I am raising a black male child by myself and trying to be a mother and father and do my very best so that he'll grow up to be a strong proud and confident black man who knows his own worth and value and is not afraid to love and show his feelings and yet he'll be strong as steel on the outside and as soft and sensuous as a cashmere sweater inside. I spend a lot of time being a mother.

I am also a fancy-schmancy analyst for one of the world's largest investment banking institutions and I make a shitload of money and my family is proud of me because I'm the only one who has actually made it to the top but all I know is that it is lonely as hell up here and I don't particularly like it. At this point in my life, I'd settle for being in the middle. My job is dull and boring. I just always assumed that a person could have more than one talent, more than one skill, and you could display as many of them as you had available, but I've learned that this is not necessarily true. It is difficult to be taken seriously if you are an artist, but playing with numbers gets quite a bit of attention. I've also come to realize that the price I'm paying to get paid a lot is a little on the high side. It seems to me that once you get past the two-hundred-thousand-a-year mark you are constantly being appraised and as a result always trying to prove your worth. It wears you out and at the same time no matter what you do or how good you think you are at it, as long as someone ranks higher on that hierarchy than you it makes you expendable. It's too hectic up here and the race is always on. It's always rush hour but I haven't figured out when to put on my blinker because it's safe to change lanes and I'm also not sure which exit I should take to get off this track altogether.

I know there's still room in my life for steel and suede for copper and leather for brass and wood for marble slate glass and material in general, but I just don't know how when or where to put it back in. Mostly because I'm scared. I've always been good at making things that serve a purpose, that perform, that function, but art is so iffy and then there's the mortgage and I'm not sure if I could recapture regain or pick up where I left off, if I'll ever have the guts the chutzpah hell the balls to leave my job.

My divorce and starting all over has taken most of the bite out of me for right now and I don't know exactly how long it's going to take me to get my groove back on as the young kids say. All I know is this: Loss is hard. Starting over is hard. Which is why I'm just trying to get from one day to the next, why I'm on the straight and narrow, and it's probably the reason why most of the time my life is not fun.

Right now I'm tired of thinking about how uneventful my life has been lately and I wish I knew what I could do to put the fizz back into it. How to resurrect myself. How to shoot some vitality into my heart, my mind, this house of soul I live in. I haven't always been dead. I used to live a somewhat exciting life. I used to take chances. I used to do some crazy shit and didn't give a damn because I wasn't hurting anybody. Fifteen years ago my life was interesting because I didn't know where I was going I just knew I was going somewhere. It was exciting because I hadn't arrived anywhere yet. And the journey itself was exhilarating. The detours. The uncertainty. I used to change my mind about things right in the middle of doing the shit. Made mistakes and was woman enough to admit I made them but didn't slay myself for it. It was usually some bullshit that was reversible anyway. Back then I did whatever I felt like doing that gave me pleasure. When did I stop? And why? After or during marriage? Motherhood? My so-called career?

I walk outside for a minute to think about this and when the dog runs up to me with his wet dog-smelling self I pat him on the head and go back into the house. My latte is cold and I step inside my office to pick out a book but out of the thousand or so I have it doesn't seem as if any of them suit my mood. I don't want to read anything too lighthearted or too deep either. I close the door and head back toward the family room because I'm not so sure that I really want to escape my own world. That I want to be engaged.

Part of my problem is that I'm always doing something and if I'm not then I'm looking for something to do. I decide to lie down and take a nap. To simply stop moving. For a change. So I sink into the thick cushions on the red love seat and I close my eyes but the leather is cold against my skin and I'm not exactly exhausted because I haven't exactly exerted any real energy today except what it took to decide on what I was and wasn't going to do.

Without even trying I find myself springing up and decide that I'll watch a little television, something mindless, and it's the one thing I rarely do except maybe by accident like the accident I'm causing right now. I don't even know if I have HBO or Showtime and I'm hoping I do and even though my watch says it's now twenty to one in the afternoon I don't care if I tune in to the middle of a movie because I'm like an intelligent enough woman who should be able to figure out how something started but I guess all I really want is to hear some noise since Quincy's not here making any or maybe I'm just so used to being distracted I need something to stop me from thinking so hard about my own mundane redundant predictable but good little life.

I try three remotes before one works. And as soon as the TV comes on of course there's a commercial and without looking up I hear this melodic baritone voice almost singing "Come to Jamaica" and I swear it seems as if he's talking to me and when I look at the fifty-five-inch screen it is filled with turquoise water and hot white sand and a blazing yellow sun and then a bronzed white man in a flapping white cotton shirt and baggy white linen trousers strolls along the shore and a tanned white woman in a straw hat and sunglasses is stretched out on a chaise longue with a book resting across her chest and they are both holding tall frothy glasses filled with something melon-colored and I think I can smell the papaya juice the pineapple juice and coconut oil and that tropical breeze is whispering in my ear and when I look closer that white woman's legs begin to turn brown and she is wearing my chartreuse bathing suit and my good straw hat and that's my Swatch watch on her wrist and my Revo sunglasses and when I look closer at this woman who now looks like she could be my twin sister I realize it *is* me lying on that chaise on that beach and when that lilting voice once again says "Come to Jamaica," I sit up then stand up and I say to that man, "Why the fuck not?"

"Who're you going with?" Angela asks. She's my younger sister by twenty-one months and she's still about ten years older than me.

"Nobody."

"You can't be serious, Stella."

"I'm very serious."

I can hear her slurping up something. She's always putting something into her big mouth and I guess it's because she's sort of pregnant with twins. "Hold it," she says. "You mean to tell me you're gonna go all the way to a foreign country by yourself?"

"Yes. What's the big deal?"

"Who you gonna do stuff with and what if somebody realizes you're alone and tries to take advantage of you and why do you have to go all the way to Jamaica?"

I knew I shouldn't have told her first. The most outrageous thing Angela's done in years is buy a BMW station wagon. Even though she and her corporate lawyering spouse are in the process of brewing two children they actually went out and bought a completely furnished five-bedroom model home in a semicustom home subdivision which is surrounded by nothing but tract homes and Angela and Kennedy decided to be bold and had the outside repainted a pale gray instead of the other million different shades of gray like every other house in their neighborhood. My sister would be lost without her garage door opener her sprinkler system her trash compactor, and Kennedy'd be disoriented without the landscaper the handyman and I know for a fact that he does not know how to use everyday tools. And like a real fool, Angela cleans her own house since she's in it all day. She likes the predictable. She is truly an all-American girl. But she doesn't watch enough Oprah.

Apparently Angela didn't hear a word Mama said when we were growing up. "Never let a man run the whole show. Never let him know if you're holding the trump card. Never tell him how many men you slept with before him and never ever let him know how much money you got and keep some of your business to yourself cause he'll hold it against you later long after you think he forgot." You think she would've learned after going to the altar once before. But nope. She likes to repeat herself. The first husband (and I can't even hardly remember his name but does it really matter?) caused her to bear a handsome buck whose name I do recall because he is my favorite (well, my only) nephew and he is away at college and well over six feet tall and the only black hockey player I've ever heard of. Evan is twenty. Last I heard he was also smart. He has told me to my face that he thinks Kennedy is a punk but he tries to get along with him because his mom loves the dude. Angela handed her entire soul over to Kennedy for safekeeping when she married him. He is only the second man she has ever slept with. He writes, produces and directs all three acts of their lives on a daily basis and she basically goes along with his program because I truly believe that Angela feels like she's nothing without a man. Unfortunately in her case, it's true. She needs guidance, direction from somebody, and boy does she get it from Kennedy. She doesn't have to think about too much on her own because he takes a scientific mathematical approach toward life in that he's got everything all figured out before the shit even happens. So basically Angela just connects the dots.

She worships her husband. I loved mine. Marriage to her is the end of the rainbow. I wanted it to *be* the rainbow. I wanted each day to be fresh, warm, sprinkled with something redeeming, something that would make me feel good about being here, that this is nice, that the longer I know you the more I like you and as a matter of fact this bond is even getting stronger and it feels good to trust someone and I'm glad you've got my back and you know I've got yours and each morning when I wake up and feel you next to me I am so glad we are here together and when I look at you when I think about you I smile because we both pay attention to each other's needs respect appreciate them and all I know is that I'd like to continue doing this. I think Angela negotiated the terms of her marriage with Kennedy, and being a litigator, he pretty much won.

She's still my sister and I love her like a sister and the main reason I called her first was because she's under the A's on my speed dial and my other sister—Vanessa—is of course way down in the V's.

I am in my car on my way to the mall to buy a few new

bathing suits, a few pairs of sandals, some basic resort wear and a couple of somewhat sexy sundresses.

"First of all, the main reason I'm going to Jamaica is to get away from everything and everybody, so I can lie on the beach and read and chill out without being distracted. If I went with somebody I'd have to negotiate with them about what we're going to do each and every day, and if I don't want to do what they want to do then there'll be tension and I'll spend my vacation compromising and I do enough of that at home and at work and for the first time in years I feel like being totally selfish."

"I think it's ridiculous. Even though I'm four months pregnant and might not be much fun I'd be happy to go with you and you could do whatever you wanted to do."

"I told you I don't want any company."

"When are you leaving?"

"Wednesday."

"Wednesday? Today is already Sunday!"

"I know it. That's why I'm on my way to get some new rags."

"What about Quincy? What if something happens to him while he's with his dad and you're not even in the United States of America?"

"Bite it, Angela. This is the first time I've taken a vacation without Quincy in six years and it's the first time I've done anything this spontaneous in about a hundred. His daddy hasn't exactly jumped over any hurdles trying to get here when Quincy's been sick. I've handled it. Now it's his turn. I'll leave him a number, Angela. Damn. It's also the reason why God invented airplanes. Six hours is all it takes."

"Where exactly are you going?"

"Negril."

"I heard about that place. Nothing but freaks go there."

"That's only one hotel."

"Called Hedonistic or something."

"Yep. But I'm staying right across the street, at the Castle Beach Negril."

"I heard all the beaches are nude down there. That nobody wears any clothes. What are you gonna do? Join in?"

"They have a clothing-optional beach which is completely separate, and hey, if I feel like getting naked, you'll never know, now will you?"

"When did you decide to do all this? I just talked to you a few days ago and you didn't mention anything about needing any vacation. Quincy hasn't even adjusted to the altitude yet and you're already making dust tracks of your own?"

"I'm not listening to you, Angela, okay? After I dropped him off I came home with a gazillion things on my to-do list and it hit me that for the past six summers Quincy has gone to camp for two weeks and all I do is stay home and work my butt off. I also remember when he was born and when I put him down for his nap I'd jump up and start cleaning or something. That's when I remembered Mama's advice about babies: when they take a nap, you take one too otherwise you'll be burned out. So yesterday afternoon I sort of got pissed at myself for trying to do too much all the time and so when this commercial came on TV about Jamaica it was so seductive I called my travel agent immediately and ironically enough she had just come back from Negril herself and she told me that since I was going by myself the classiest place to stay was the

Castle Beach because everything is included—drinks, water sports, meals—and there's no tipping so I told her to book me a first-class ticket as soon as she could like today if possible before I came to my senses and started acting like the responsible adult that I've been for the last twenty years and I told her I didn't care how much the shit cost don't even tell me just put it on my American Express card and I told her I'd pick the tickets up as soon as she called to tell me it was a done deal."

"When are you getting them?"

"They're on my dresser right now."

"What about your passport?"

"My picture's about six years old and I look fabulous if I do say so myself. My hairstyle is weak but I think that was when me and Quincy left Walter at home and went to Australia, remember?"

"Yeah. Don't you think Quincy would like to see Jamaica? Why can't you wait until he gets back?"

"You're not listening to me, Mrs. Cleaver. Read my lips: *I do not want to take my child with me on my vacation.* Did you hear that?"

"Well, you know what they say about those Jamaican men, don't you?"

"What?"

"That they've all got fire hoses for dicks."

"I don't care what size their dicks are! You're not listening to me, Angela. I'm not going down there to get laid. I can get laid any day of the week right here at home. I'm going down there to regroup. I've been living in fifth gear for too long and I need to decompress. That's it in a nutshell. *Comprende?*"

"How long you staying?"

"Nine days."

"Dag, Stella!"

"Look, I'm in the mall parking lot and if I don't talk to you before I leave, I'll call you when I get there."

"You know how expensive it is to call from another country?"

"Then forget it. I'll send you a postcard."

And I hang up. I knew I should've called Vanessa first. She's a lot looser, four years younger than me, still has a fresh attitude and is much more open-minded than your average widow of four years who recently met and has been cavorting with a man old enough to be our father. Apparently J.B. is retired but he worked for years in the sporting goods business so he gives her all the free sneakers and exercise paraphernalia she could ever dream of even though she does not ever walk jog or exercise but takes the stuff because it is free and it's great for her daughter, Chantel, who is only eleven and growing and Vanessa said J.B. who won't tell her what those initials stand for is a recent widower and so they have a lot in common even though all he does is talk about his dead wife and just wants somebody to listen and he wants to show her how to golf and maybe have an occasional dinner like every Friday because since he also has prostate cancer he can't do the nasty which she is grateful for in a sad way but she also said, "Hey, it doesn't cost anything to be nice. And don't *even* think of him as my boyfriend, girl. He's what I call a part-time companion."

I like Vanessa because she is generous, fickle, but full of mucho compassion, and ever since Angela has become mother-bound again she has taken on the job of trying to be our mama. We lost ours twenty years ago when some drunk driver jumped the curb and took her from us and anyway we lost track of our daddy like twenty-five years ago and we don't really care if we ever find him at this point and who's looking but Angela sort of works overtime with her parental posturing and she is making it sound as if I am like asking for her approval to take this vacation. Which I am not.

When I get home I have two messages. The first one's from Vanessa. "Girl, Angela called and told me you're going to Jamaica! How come you didn't call me? Way to go, girl. It's about time your old dead ass did something to liven up your dead-ass life. Way to go. Take plenty of condoms with you and get some from all those young Jamaican boys with big flapping dicks—do one a day if you can handle it, girl—and oooooh I wish I could go with you but Angela said you want to go by yourself and she's such a square and I don't blame you cause this way won't nobody have to be all in your business and you can turn into like a whore and nobody'll ever have to know but call and tell me if you do. Talk to you later. You sure you don't want me to come with you?"

I crack up. Vanessa and I are a lot alike except she's much more outspoken and says whatever comes to her mind and then thinks about it later. She is forever putting her foot in her mouth but that's what I love about her: plus the fact that she really doesn't give a shit. I'm not as impulsive—I at least try to consider the consequences of what I'm doing but even if I'm scared I usually do it anyway because it kind of gives me a rush. This is the main reason why I used to do drugs. There's nothing like a good rush.

Beep. I hear Quincy's tinny prepubescent voice which I'm assuming will change in a short time if and when those hormones ever kick in. On his eleventh birthday he wanted to show me the hair under his arms that he claimed had grown in the night before and as we stood on the upstairs landing and he lifted his elbow up I had to ask him to move into the light which he did and I saw some brownish fuzz and I assumed that's what he was talking about and all I knew was that it smelled kind of skunkish and I suggested he be on friendlier terms with his deodorant. I also decided to take this opportunity to ask if he had hair on any other body parts and he said of course and I asked if I could see an example and he said no way and I said please you don't have to show me your unit although I did want to see if he was going to be as lucky as his daddy. But I didn't want to push the issue but then I heard him say well I'll only show you the top part and I was suddenly in shock because first of all showing me the "top" meant there was something separate and apart from the "bottom" which I hadn't really given much thought to because when he was little it all seemed to be in one little cluster but now there was a top and a bottom so I stood there somewhat afraid and wanting to say forget it but then he was slowly and carefully pulling his pajama bottoms down and I heard him say see and I looked and saw what was unquestionably black hair forming a little triangle against his brown skin and before I could fully absorb what I was seeing I heard the elastic snap against his narrow waist and he said Told you and I heard myself ask How big is your little unit now and he said Big enough, Mom, big enough.

"Mom, this is your loving son Quincy, remember me? Anyway my dad wanted me to call you to remind you that on Tuesday we're leaving for our fishing trip and we won't have a phone for six whole days so you won't be able to talk to your darling son and Dad is so fat now, Ma, you wouldn't believe it if you saw him and last night we were playing Crazy Eights and I couldn't get my legs under the card table because his thighs took up so much space, they were so big and rubbed together and I told him he should start working out and how you have a trainer and how you jog and stuff and how all my friends say how cool you are and he didn't say anything but all I wanna know is how is Phoenix doing? Did you find any more ticks on him you know this is tick season, Mom. I miss him and I miss you even though I just got here. I hope you're having fun without me but not too much fun. I wish my dad had Sega or Super NES but I'm not bored yet I don't think because he tells pretty good jokes. Please call us before Tuesday. I love you. Oh. And I promise to bring you some fish because I'm going to catch lots of them."

I hang up the phone with a grin three miles wide. God, I love that boy! It doesn't surprise me to hear about his dad being bigger because he was on his way to becoming the Pillsbury Doughboy when we split up. All that beer and party-size bags of nachos had caused that middle-aged spread to start chasing after his butt and apparently it finally caught up with him. I decide to call them in the morning and I'll tell the truth: I'm taking a vacation. Got a problem with that?

I can't wait to pack. I went crazy in Macy's, berserk in Nordstrom's, and all I want to know is why don't they have shopping carts in malls? And talk about bathing suits? I think I bought six or seven of them but I can't be sure. And sunglasses. Sexy cotton bras and panties. Cute jogging shorts, tops, leggings. I was totally unable to resist those bright yellow luscious orange sweet pink ensembles in the windows of those specialty boutiques where mostly teenagers and young girls in their twenties with high-performance bodies shop but I went in with a young attitude and bought some of the hottest outfits a woman my age could tolerate because in the so-called misses sections of the major department stores all they had was that senior citizen type resort wear. Those tops are so big and loose they camouflage your breasts. I am very proud of mine and have no intention of hiding them since they still stand at attention when the air hits them. Those so-called T-shirts have Mommie Dearest shoulder pads and rubbery sailboats or starfish or cups and saucers embossed all over the front and I suppose they are also designed to hide your pouchy tummy which I do not have thank the Lord and then those yucky elastic-in-the-waist shorts with the baggy legs that make you look fatter than you may very well really be. Either that or everything is appliquéd with some kind of silver and gold lamé sewn on and even in the shoe department they had tons of those dainty little flat white sandals with clusters of hard fruit or plastic floral arrangements at the toe or they were all pewter and bronze with no heels. All this stuff seemed geared for women over fifty who usually hide under their umbrellas and use number 80 sunblock and wear those cheap straw hats and those loud bathing suits with the flared skirts and they usually have varicose veins and gigantic breasts and they watch children play in the sand or they stare at young women with perfect magazine bodies and remember when they used to look like this and they don't dare look down at their own bodies but instead go back to reading their Harlequin or Fabio romance novels while their husbands ignore them and watch young Swedish German French or Black women's curves rock back and forth along the shore until they're completely out of range. I don't look like their wives yet. I know those days may be coming, but they're not here yet.

A sea of bags covers my bedroom floor and I've opened all the windows as wide as they will go, have the ceiling fan spinning on high, and the whole house is thumping with Montell Jordan's "This Is How We Do It." My son and I actually have some of the same taste in music. I buy some rap but not very much of that gangsta rap because I don't agree with half the shit they're saying and I don't like hearing black women referred to as bitches and ho's and I hate it absolutely hate it when they use the word "niggah" which we have *never* used and I do not allow to be used in our house. I do appreciate some hip-hop, a little SWV TLC Xscape R.Kelly Mary J. Blige Brownstone Boyz II Men Jodeci etc. etc. etc., and Quincy loves those other three young sisters with the bodies I wish I had but I can't think of their names right now oh yeah Salt-N-Pepa. I also like a lot of music by white people, which a lot of my friends don't understand. Quincy loves that rock group

Green Day and Aerosmith and Hootie and the Blowfish and I kind of like them too and I love Seal even though he's African but British and mostly white people buy his music and I love Annie Lennox Diva over and over and Julia Fordham and Sting and hell good music is good music.

It feels like Christmas in the summertime and I'm so excited I almost can't stand it. I've been unwrapping tissue paper from all kinds of beautiful things I hardly remember buying and I've been trying on one thing after another, including each and every bathing suit, and I remind myself to get myself waxed tomorrow after I get my pedicure and fill. I look decent enough in my bathing suits considering I am forty-two and all and I absolutely love these new Wonderbra pads they're putting in this year. I mean I am really vavavooming. I'm standing here admiring myself in the mirror and wondering if when the time comes would I really have the nerve to have any or all of those surgical procedures to improve restore and replenish my youthful image or would I just be like an imitation of myself? I think that's the phone ringing but this music is so loud I'm not sure. I pick it up anyway.

"Oh, you're already partying, I see, huh? Can't you call nobody back?"

"Vanessa, didn't you just leave the message a few minutes ago?"

"Yeah, but why come you couldn't call me back?"

We always change our voices like we're from or been living deep in the hood all our lives, like we're young and hip and not even close to being educated, but this is like our very own special way of expressing our love and endearment toward each other plus deep down inside we don't ever want to forget where we came from, that everybody has not been as lucky as we have in terms of growing up. I mean we did do the projects a long long time ago but then our parents moved us to a nice suburb outside of Chicago where we never witnessed any tragedy except when Daddy left and then when Mama got killed. Most of our relatives still live in the hood and some of them even came right out and told us to our faces that we think we're All That just because we live in predominantly white neighborhoods now. But this is not true. I personally live in a mostly white neighborhood because they have the best schools with the most qualified teachers and I want my son to get the best free education available since my taxes are supposed to cover the shit and besides I don't feel like I have to live in the hood or in an all-black neighborhood to prove how black I am. I don't want to live anywhere close to where they have drive-bys. I don't believe the hype or the stereotype that all black neighborhoods are dangerous and crime-ridden but a whole lot of them are on their way thanks to guns and crack and heroin and no fathers in the house and mothers trying too hard to do it all and failing and then sometimes there is no authority no role models and so respect isn't high on their things-to-do-today list because who has time to like go to church anymore which is one good place to learn about humility and compassion and love, and I'll be honest, I am scared to go some places in the hood and it hurts me because I remember when the hood was the safest place for us to go because we were among our own and it was who we knew we could trust—each other—but times have changed and we are all a threat to each other though I don't get why, but I also don't want to get shot on a whim or get my feelings hurt because I still believe that we are all out here in this knee-deep together. I also don't want my son growing up calling women bitches and ho's and thinking it's cool and he's down and all that and I'd die if he ended up being a victim of gang warfare and all that bullshit because to be honest I want him to understand the streets and all but the shit they learn out there is not exactly the kind of survival skills he'll be needing to get over in college, in America, in the whole wide world.

I go off sometimes and I know it. But I can't help it if I've got an active mind. Yes you can, Stella, now shut up and listen to what your sister's trying to say.

"I just want you to know that I'm proud of you, Sis, for finally doing something spontaneous and doing something for *you*. It's about damn time."

"Thank you, V, thank you. I can't believe I'm doing this."

"Who are *you* telling? But let me ask you something. Can I drive the BMW while you're gone?"

Always wants something. Damn. "Okay, but don't try to put it through a regular car wash and don't drive around on R either, bitch. And don't put any of that generic gas in my car. Only use premium. I'll be able to tell if you didn't. The only catch is could you bring in the mail feed Phoenix and Dr. Dre and change his litter box and their water and maybe drop a few flakes in the fish tank every few days?"

"Ain't no thang. And thanks, Sis. Wild Kingdom'll be under control. Now, have you started packing yet?"

"Have I ever."

"Well, last night things were real slow around here so I went over to my neighbor's house, Cynthia, do you remember her? She's the Mexican chick whose husband won't send her kids back from Alaska and she's gonna have to go to court to get 'em back and shit? Can you believe it? Anyway I told her you were going to Jamaica by yourself and—"

"Vanessa, don't be telling people all my personal business, and especially my whereabouts, girl."

"Look, you don't even know the bitch. Anyway she told me to tell you to pack enough clothes to change at least three times a day because first you have to dress to go to breakfast and then you lay out on the beach and then you change into something for lunch and then again for dinner and then if you party later—and you better party later, bitch—you should change again, into something nasty. But that's four. Make it four. And take a different bathing suit for each day and is your period coming anytime soon?"

"Just had it," I said as I looked down at the rainbow of swimwear lying across my bed.

"Good. She said you should also take some Fleet with you cause you'll probably get bloated and backed up because of the difference in the food and stuff and you probably won't be able to go the first few days cause you'll be so excited and not believe you're on no fucking *island*. Even though she's only been to Cabo San Lucas and Maui she said the tropics is the tropics but anyway you better cross your fingers that you get as lucky as Cynthia, honey, and this other girl at my job who works over in cardiology."

"What are you talking about?"

"Well, Cynthia went to Maui six months ago by herself and met a man on the airplane and he's in the military and he has sent her six airplane tickets in the six months since she's been back. And then the girl in cardiology is a sister and she went to Paradise Island which is supposed to be in the Bahamas or some-damn-where with her mama and daddy—why I don't know—but anyway she was just splashing around in the water minding her own business and met this guy on the beach who turned out to be her scuba-diving instructor and he ended up diving real deep and he also found that black pearl and every day afterwards they were doing something different in the water and honey now they are like totally engaged and shit."

"That's all well and good but I'm not going over to some tropical island hoping or trying to find a husband."

"They weren't *looking* either. That's my point. Just make sure the radar is on though cause you know how you can be: blind as hell cause you always looking up when you should be looking around you."

"Thanks for the sound advice, Ricki. Now I hope you don't mind but I've gotta go. I want to finish packing today."

"What are you telling them at work?"

"Well, summers are our slowest months and hell, I'm telling them I'm going to Jamaica for nine days."

"Okay. I guess that'll work. Nice to know that some of us got it like that."

"I'll talk to you later."

"Wait a minute! What's up with that tired hair? Do something to it, Stella, please. Don't go down there with that nineteen eighties hairstyle. Do something extreme.

Be a little scandalous. Go on over to the hood and get your hair did, girl. Get some of those Jamaican braids or any kind of braids so that when you come out of the water dripping wet you look like those chicks do in the magazines: better than you did when you went in."

I'm laughing now and ironically or coincidentally R.Kelly is singing "Back to the Hood" and I'm thinking maybe Vanessa is onto something and I hear myself say, "Maybe I will."

"Go to Oh My Nappy Hair in Oakland, girl. They'll hook you up."

Which is exactly what I do. It takes ten hours for Fiona who is from Senegal and Dreena who is from Richmond to make me feel beautiful, but this hairstyle also takes about five years off of me which means I'm definitely coming back. These women almost yank my brains out when they grab at least a hundred little braids and pull them into a ponytail on top of my head which I discover gives me sort of an African-Asian look which I wasn't exactly after but when I realize it also works as an instant face-lift I just grit my teeth and keep my mouth shut until they're finished.

Vanessa is totally outdone when she sees me and tells me I look like a real hoochie and I give her the keys to my car. I am so glad that Quincy and Walter aren't home when I call and I simply leave the number of the hotel and all the details. I have a driver pick me up at 8 A.M. and he puts all three pieces of luggage in the back of his Town Car and my eyes are burning because I didn't sleep at all last night and my heart is pounding like crazy when I close my eyes and look out the window of the first-class cabin as we take off and I'm really wondering what might be out there for me. I pray that I'm not going to die up here, because I'm finally doing something for myself, but when I wake up to see that aqua water and an irregular-shaped stretch of green land a thousand feet below and the plane touches down on that runway in Montego Bay and the heat is already swimming up in silver slivers and I am the third person to step off this plane and the force of the sun is already draping itself all over my body and straight through this sundress and I look down and see at least twenty or thirty black men of different shades heights and ages standing at the entrance to Gate 6 and, as I approach them with my braids which seem to be tossing themselves over my shoulders, they all smile at me with those beautiful and chiseled African cheekbones those white white teeth and every size and shape of lips imaginable and one right after another and in unison they carol out to me, "Welcome to Jamaica," and I think for sure that while I slept the plane probably did in fact crash and somehow I have simply landed in heaven.

I t will take almost two hours to drive the fifty-two miles from Montego Bay to Negril and it feels more like I'm on a bucking bronco than in a van. The road is two lanes of meandering pavement that runs parallel to the ocean for long stretches but as it grows darker—pitch black to be exact and it's just seven-thirty—I can no longer see or hear the ocean at all, and folks are appearing out of nowhere on the sides of this road. At least ten times during the first hour I think for sure we are going to hit somebody. A slew of bicyclists taking their lives in their own hands appear to be having a hard time staying on the pavement. The driver is driving like a maniac and he seems to think everything is funny, like when he almost hits a goat that was standing in the middle of the road, or when he asks each of us if we've ever been to Jamaica, then chuckles as if he knows something we don't know. When he honks his horn at folks he chortles, and I will find out later that just about everybody on this part of the island knows everyone else. I'll find out that when you see kids women or men standing on the side of the road walking with an arm extended out like a flag during the daytime nighttime or whenever, they are trying to hitch a ride home and somebody will always stop and give them one until they get to their turnoff. And I will be shocked to learn that women can do this any time of night and still feel safe and nobody ever gets raped or shot or robbed and I'll be thinking that this is how it used to be in America, this is how black people used to treat each other a long time ago when I was a kid, and before I leave I will envy them in more ways than just this.

I am the only black person in my van besides the driver and of the five white couples three are obviously newly-weds and the other two are old and fat and have southern accents and—I am not making this up—are wearing big straw hats. Right after we got on the van at the airport they interviewed me. "Darling, is your husband gonna be joining up with you?" one woman in a hat asked.

"I don't have a husband."

"You mean you're here all by your lonesome?"

"Yep," I said. And I wanted to say, Got a problem with that?

"Aren't you brave," this skinny Barbie-looking woman said. "I'd never dream of traveling anywhere like this alone."

"Why not?" I asked.

"Well, it's so *foreign*," she said.

"And?"

"I'd be afraid."

"Afraid of what?"

"I don't know. Everything."

"Well, watch and see how scared I am when I'm on the beach or at dinner or on the dance floor, okay?"

"And who will you dance with?"

"Whoever asks me or whoever I ask. Maybe him," I said, pointing at her husband.

"He doesn't dance."

"I'm going to try while we're here, honey. I'll dance with you as long as you don't laugh at this stiff Virginian."

I laugh. He laughs. We all laugh and then stare back out into the darkness, each of us wondering how much longer how much further and where oh where the hell is our hotel, because we can't see the twinkle of anything that looks like a resort for miles ahead.

Luckily the driver has on some kind of fabulous reggae music. I can't believe that even though it's only eight o'clock and it's pitch black outside and there are no streetlights, children are playing outside. There are also clusters of old men sitting around makeshift tables made of old boards and doors, playing cards and dominoes. We go around a bend and out of nowhere the van's headlights shine on a group of teenagers just standing around like they're getting ready to do something. Some of them are kissing under heavy trees or sitting on big rocks—there's a head in a lap, a head on a shoulder, and when I see this I remember when and I hurry and turn that little air-conditioner vent so it hits me directly in the face.

The one thing I can't help but notice is that everybody here is black.

Finally, after we've all passed out, the driver honks his horn and yells, "Welcome to the Castle Beach Negril!" I open my eyes and see that the hotel is even prettier than the photo in the brochure.

The white people get out of the van without tipping the driver because of course the ride is supposed to be part of our package but even so I think this is so tacky and downright inconsiderate and when I hand Donovan the driver a brand-new twenty-dollar American bill he nods over and over and says thank you and he gives me a look as if to thank me for showing him some respect. This is like a black thang: You take care of me, I'll take care of you.

Our bags are whisked off and as we all walk toward the lobby I hear loud music coming from outside which is down a long marble ramp that leads somewhere I want to see, and am about to, when we are greeted by two young Jamaican women who offer us a cold wet cloth for our forehead and whatever tropical or regular drink we would like until they get us checked in. I order a virgin piña colada because I don't like the taste of alcohol even when it's camouflaged. Two drinks and I'm drunk anyway, so I stopped trying to get a liquid buzz years ago.

It's now about nine-thirty and when I sit down in my chair I realize I'm beat. But after the young woman who is assigned to me whose name is Abby brings me my frothy white drink with a giant piece of pineapple on it and asks if I'd like to see the rest of the hotel I instantly get a new burst of energy. I follow her down that ramp and can't really believe my eyes. It is like a modern tropical version of *Casablanca*: people are swarming around the dance floor while up on a stage a band is playing something with a funky get-up-and-dance beat and everybody is laughing and clapping and totally oblivious to anything except the music.

Hundreds of white tables with white chairs are mostly filled with suntanned white people dressed colorfully. And then there is the food. A buffet about a mile long is filled with every kind of seafood salad pasta dessert you name it and Abby says follow me and I follow her outside and all I'm thinking as I watch folks partying is that I'm going to like it here and as we approach the deck that leads directly to the beach we walk around the pool and here are more tables and I see smoke and smell barbecue and there are about a hundred people standing in line with plates and everybody looks happy and healthy and folks are feeding each other from fingers and forks and everybody has a drink it seems and they are all waiting for what apparently is prime rib chicken shrimp steak being grilled in front of them. I'm just taking this all in; it turns out to be Jamaica Night. I sip my drink all the way down the pathway that leads to my room and apparently my building which is only two floors is right next to the nude beach. I kind of chuckle when Abby tells me this and she asks if this'll be a problem, and I say, as I've already learned how to say in the last hour: "No problem, mon."

My room is pretty but not as spectacular as the rest of the hotel. I do have a lovely balcony with, no shit, big giant rocks and crashing waves right below like in the movies. There's a ghetto blaster so thank God I brought my Seal and Mary J. Blige among others and I put Seal on immediately and take my clothes off and stand on the balcony and inhale some of this thick moist tropical ocean air and it's real this is so real I made it I didn't die yes I'm really here in Jamaica and I hang up all my clothes and then I take a shower and listen to Seal some more and I put on some pretty white shortie pj's and I lie on my bed and listen to some more Seal and the rolling waves until my body loses me and my mind is clear and soothed and when I open my eyes it is daylight and Seal begins to seduce me all over again. I sit up and realize that yes I'm still here and I call room service and order some coffee and juice which will be here in only ten minutes' time they say and I put on one of my cute peach jogging outfits and look at the clock and it is only 7:30 A.M. which means it's only 5:30 A.M. at home. I should call Quincy but it's too early plus I forgot I can't call him and maybe I should wake up Angela—no, to hell with Angela—and I don't want to bug Vanessa just yet. I now have my gear on and there is a knock on the door and I say thank you and offer a tip but the young black woman refuses to take it. I will find out later how to do this so they will accept it without losing their jobs.

I get my Walkman out and pop Seal inside it. Haven't had enough of him yet. I feel bouncy like I could sort of just fly low but fly nevertheless. This was a smart move, Stella, real smart. I drink my juice in one swallow and am almost too wired to drink my entire cup of coffee, me, Ms. Latte herself.

When I step outside I am amazed at how hot it already is, it has to be in the high eighties, and the humidity is thick but nothing like Chicago, which is where I first went to college and then on to New York where we lived for an incredibly long time until Walter got transferred to a base near Oakland and we moved to Walnut Creek and then I got my job and we moved to this little town called Alamo and then we got divorced and he moved back to Colorado which is where he's from.

I run down the stairs and when I look to the left I see a group of old fat naked white people lying on the chaises and what appears like a family of pink humpback whales on orange air mattresses and when I look a little closer I see at least forty taut breasts whose nipples all point toward the sun and they seem a little incongruous because they certainly don't match the bodies they're attached to. I chuckle and think that there's no fucking way I'd take my clothes off in front of a bunch of old alcoholic-looking white men considering what they used to do to us during slavery and all, which is probably the reason why I'm no darker than I am, and I wouldn't give them the satisfaction of seeing my bare brown body and particularly my cellulite and stretch marks, which only someone dear to me can experience up close.

It all looks different. Everything is green and lush, with giant banana trees lining the asphalt path like a jungle and flowers I've never seen or smelled before. Those fuchsia-colored ones—what are they called?—oh yeah, hibiscus, and I think people eat those don't they and then clumps of yellow and orange and white and I'm thinking my land-scaper could learn something but what I am really beginning to notice for real is that everybody I mean everybody that works here is black. I love this but then again I am already beginning to wonder how much they're getting paid and if they're being exploited like slave labor and making insulting wages because there are so many people working here the grounds are swarming with men in cotton jumpsuits with brooms rakes hedge cutters and I know what it's like in say Mexican hotels and I'm hoping that is not the case here.

I pass the workout room, which is basically outside. There's a serious high-energy funk-pumping aerobics class in progress which a black Mr. Universe-looking guy in a unitard is teaching and I think maybe I shouldn't run today maybe this is where I should be, aerobically speaking. To the left are weights and Nautilus equipment and I'll spend some time in there or Krystal will be able to tell when I get home and we do those stupid lunges and I have no pep in my step or I whine when I have to do pecks or lat pulldowns. I'll be back, I say to myself, and continue down the path toward the gigantic dining room or whatever it's called where I was last night.

These folks do get up early. There are a hundred or more people already lining up and sitting down eating. I have until tenish to eat so I sort of walk by and as I do folks are waving and I'm looking to see if these are the same white people that were on my van but these are different white people and I wave back because I basically like most white people as long as they don't act like Nazis or come across like they're superior or richer or classier or smarter and shit just because they're white.

I walk out by the pool and notice a big wooden armoire filled with towels and I can really see the beach now. It looks even prettier than on my commercial. The sand is for sure white. And damn, the water is like really turquoise, and I walk down toward it, past the boat with all the snorkeling equipment, the big water tricycles with the gigantic wheels, some paddleboats and kayaks and canoes and little sailboats, and there are about five hundred clean white chaise longues all lined up in rows on the beach, some under little fat palm trees, and toward my right the beach stretches and winds for what looks like about two miles before it comes to a point and I guess continues around a cove or something. I would love to run straight into the water but I have my sneakers on.

I start out slowly so I can take everything in. Just as I get my rhythm I almost run smack dab into a cow, which scares the daylights out of me. My heart rate monitor begins to *beep beep beep* informing me that I'm over my target fat-burning zone and then it subsides. Sand crabs scurry into holes as I catapult right over them. In less than ten minutes I am sweating and I realize I forgot to turn my Walkman on but I don't need it because the music is coming out of the ocean and through the air and I'm pushing myself until I realize I can't run any further because a crowd of trees juts out into the water and it's impossible to go around it. On the way back I pass two lovers who are hidden inside a cavern. They are in their bathing suits but still wrapped within each other's arms and kissing so deeply they don't even notice me. It isn't until I pass that I realize how much I envy them. They are in love. And it occurs to me that it's been a long time since I've been in love.

I feel my pace slowing down and then I begin to walk because I am wondering when was the last time I actually said "I love you" to a man and hell, when was the last time someone said it to me? It's been a few years is all I know and although it doesn't make me sad, it causes me to wonder what it might be like to feel it again because I really can't remember right this minute.

By the time I get back to the beach at my hotel the water activities have started and the beach is much more popu-lated. People are dragging boats or getting in boats and there is someone parasailing right over us. Jet Skiers are speeding by, causing turbulent waves which folks seem to love, diving into the plume in this otherwise calm bay, and then one of several Jamaican men says to me, "No snorkeling today for you, mon?"

"Not right now," I say.

"Jogging were you?"

"Yep."

"Keeps you in good shape?"

"I'm trying."

"You looking good, girl."

"Thank you," I say and continue walking.

"Your husband's a lucky man," another says and I smile as I get a towel and dry my face and throw it around my neck and walk into the huge dining room which is now al-most full. I find an empty table and set my Walkman and sunglasses on top and go over to the buffet to get myself some breakfast.

I don't want to be greedy but boy it's hard to know what to choose from since there's so much of everything, and I decide on Belgian waffles and fresh sliced mango. I go back to my seat, smiling hellos at some of the folks from the van last night and a few other friendlies. As I begin to slice my waffles I suddenly smell the most intoxicating scent: a fresh clean citrusy but almost sweet aroma and I can't tell which direction it's coming from but out of the corner of my eye to my left I see a young black man slid-ing his chair under the next table. He is wearing a white baseball cap and some kind of T-shirt and boy are his arms long and hairy and a really deep gold and that's all I can see but he looks like one of those rappers I've seen on MTV but I can't put my finger on which one. I guess he feels me looking at him because he immediately turns to acknowledge me and smiles and nods his head at the same time and says, "Hello," and that's when I bend over and say, "Are you a rapper?"

He blushes and then a broad grin spreads over his handsome face as if I've given him a compliment he doesn't deserve. "No," he says in a soft Jamaican accent and he sort of leans in my direction and that's when I notice that he is entirely too young to be so fine and sexy. His eyebrows are thick and his eyes look Asian and his cheekbones are chiseled and those beautiful thick lips he is using to say "What rapper?" are making it difficult—I can't really take my eyes off how perfect they are—but I hear myself say, "I don't know, you just look like one," and it seems as if his eyes sort of close for a second or two and he hunches his shoulders as if to apologize and says, "I don't rap."

I turn back to the waffles. A young waiter comes to pour more coffee in my cup and I am adding two packages of sugar when I feel someone tap me on the shoulder. When I turn to face him I smell that scent again—now it's more like an ocean breeze with a mist of ruby red grapefruit juice—and I realize it is coming from him. "Are you dining alone?" he asks.

"Yes, I am," I say.

"Would you mind if I joined you?"

Well, how sweet, I think, and say, "No, I don't mind."

He pushes his chair back and stands, picking up his plate, and when I look at him I almost have a stroke. He is wearing baggy brown shorts and has to be at least six three or four and he is lean but his shoulders are wide broad and as he walks toward my table all I can think is Lord Lord Lord some young girl is gonna get lucky as I don't know what if she can snag you. He sits down right across from me and when he looks at me he is looking me directly in the eye. Bold little sucker, isn't he, and I feel a little uncomfortable, to be honest, but I stick my fork inside my waffle which for some reason I don't want now.

"So how are you today?" he asks in his Jamaican accent but it sounds as if it's tinged with a little bit of British. His voice is husky yet soft dreamy and wet kind of smooth and when he speaks it sounds like it's coming from some honest place inside him, you can actually hear it.

"I'm fine. Just came back from a run so I wouldn't get too close to me right now."

"I saw you when you left," he says.

This kind of surprises me. "You did?"

"Yes," he says and once again those eyes are looking right inside me. I wish he would stop this. Sort of. "How long are you here for?"

"Eight days."

"Got in last night, did you?"

"How'd you know?"

"I got here yesterday and I certainly would've noticed you."

"Oh really."

"Really," he says as if he means it.

He is too cute and ought to just stop this little flirting

action right now if that's what he's doing. "What's your name, young man?"

"Winston Shakespeare," he says. "And yours, young lady?"

He is being facetious. "Stella," I say and then think: Did he just say Shakespeare? Yes, he did. And he looks serious. I wonder if this is a common surname in Jamaica. And of course he knows who the guy is. He has to know. But what I'm more curious about is if he relates to understands or enjoys tragedy.

"Nice to meet you, Stella," he says and this time when he smiles he shows off a beautiful set of straight white teeth that've been hiding behind and under those succulent young lips. Stop it, Stella. He's a child. A tall handsome sexy maple-syrup-colored child, but a child nevertheless. Why come they don't come in this make and model in my age group is what I'm wondering.

"Where's your husband?" he asks.

"What makes you think I have a husband?"

"I'm just assuming. Perhaps I shouldn't assume."

"I don't have a husband."

He seems pleased when I say this. But then again maybe it's just my imagination.

"Did you come with your boyfriend?"

"You sure ask a lot of questions."

"Isn't that the only way to get an answer to something you're curious about?"

"Well, of course it is. But why do you want to know?"

"Well, first of all most of the people here are usually couples and most of them are usually white and they're either here to get married or they're on their honeymoon. I thought you might fit in one of those categories."

"Nope," I say and take a sip of my coffee.

He sort of nods his head as if to the beat of some slow music and he then says, "Okay," and he begins to delve into the mountain of confusion that is a mixture of rice eggs hominy and at least five different kinds of meat. As I watch him eat from one pile at a time I am somewhat amazed at how he seems to be savoring each distinct taste and yet he still dabs his mouth with his linen napkin in between bites and slowly returns it to his lap. He also blushes after he puts a little more in his mouth than he should've, and it is clear that he is hungry—he eats like a college student who's come home for the weekend. I am watching him without realizing that I am actually staring but I can't help it because what I see before me is a kind of tenderness and innocence I haven't seen in a man in a long time. It is refreshing and sad at once because he is so young and I am wondering when do men lose this quality? And how do they lose it?

"Are you on vacation?" I ask.

He shakes his head no. Chews and swallows. "I just finished my classes at the university in Kingston and I'm here hoping to land a summer job as a chef's apprentice, something in food preparation or whatever I can get, really. And what about you, where are you from in the States?"

"California."

"Wow," he sings in a very low tone. "California. Where in California?"

"Northern. About forty minutes outside of San Francisco."

"And you like it there?"

"It's okay."

"And what made you come to Jamaica?"

"Now that's a pretty loaded question but it's safe to say that I just really needed a vacation and I figured why not Jamaica?"

"Do you like it so far?"

"Yep. Everyone's really nice."

He is gazing at me again with those dreamy eyes and even though he isn't looking through my jogging top it feels like I am sitting here completely naked and he is admiring me and why he isn't trying to hide the fact is beyond me. I mean I don't get it. What exactly is going on here? I lean forward and spread my fingers against my chest and I say, "How old are you, Winston?"

And he says, "How old do you think I am?"

"Twenty-two, twenty-three at most." His arms are covered with a sheath of curly black hair. The hair on his head is thick and black and shiny and cut close on the sides. His mustache appears to be still growing in but the rest of his face looks like that of a man who shaves on a regular basis. He certainly smells like a man, sounds like a man, and looks like one too.

"I'll be twenty-one on my next birthday."

I nod. God bless the girl who gets to feel those long brown arms around her and those beautiful thick golden lips. Stop it, Stella. Now stop it! "That's nice," I say.

"And you?"

"I'm forty-two."

He puts his fork down. "You're not."

"Oh don't even go there," I say.

"Seriously! You're telling me the truth?"

"I'm forty-two. Why would I lie?"

He's showing me those teeth and shaking his head. And then he looks at me without saying anything and starts nodding his head up and down as if he knows something about me that I don't. "You're being straight with me?"

I nod again.

"You take very good care of yourself, don't you?"

"I don't know. I try. I exercise a little."

"Well, more women should," he says and I feel myself being seduced right here in the middle of this room. This is really starting to get on my nerves. I mean I don't need to be at a breakfast table on my first day here with a twenty-one-year-old boy feeling aroused and what have you, because there is something downright inappropriate about this shit. Sort of.

"Well, look. Winston, is it?"

"Yes. You're leaving already? You haven't even finished your breakfast."

"Well, I ate a little something in my room earlier. And I need to shower and then I'm going to hit the beach and read a little."

He looks as if he wants to ask me something but doesn't exactly know how and then he immediately says, "Are you going to the pajama disco tonight?"

"The what?"

"Well," he says and sort of starts with that sexy blushing business again that is starting to wear me out and I mean like it is kind of driving me a little crazy. "You're supposed to wear bed clothes—you know, something that you sleep in."

"You can't be serious."

"Very. It's fun. I've heard some people get a bit risqué and wild but you can wear whatever you feel comfortable in. The DJ's great. You should come," he says and boy do his eyes have some kind of magic power or what? The way he is looking at me like he is hypnotizing me or something, I don't think I *can* say no. "It should be fun," he says and he is smiling at me again but this isn't one of those regular on-your-face smiles. This young man is smiling about something else. And I'm trying to figure out what it is.

"I don't know about any pajama disco. . . ."

"It's your first night here. What else are you going to do?"

"I don't know. I haven't thought about it yet."

"Come on. I'd love to dance with you."

"Oh, you would, would you?"

"Yes. You look like a good dancer."

"How can you say that and I'm sitting down?"

"I can tell," he says and now he's looking at me like maybe he's in a trance or something. "I can tell."

Is he flirting with me? No. He couldn't be flirting with me. I'm old enough to be his mother! And what could he possibly want from me that he can't get from some young chicks around here, like that fox over there, for instance? On the other hand, he's right. I came here to have some fun, so why not have some? "What time does it start?" I ask.

"About ten. So you'll come?"

"Maybe."

"Would you meet me there?"

"Are you serious?" I ask.

"Why? What's wrong?" He honestly looks perplexed.

"Nothing," I say and feel myself blushing as I stand up. I can see that he's trying not to stare at me and when he stands up I almost lose my breath and this is scandalous just feeling like this over a young boy but as I back away from the table I do hear myself say, "I'll see you tonight, Winston," and he says, "Please don't change your mind. I'm only coming because I want to dance with you," and when I look at him he is doing the smiling stuff at me but this time he has an incredible look of wonder on his face. It is so sweet.

As I begin to walk away I hear him say, "Thank you for letting me join you for breakfast."

All I can do is nod You're welcome, since I am now in a hurry to get out of here because it feels like thousands of eyes are on me and I know they're probably all wondering why I'm not on the nude beach.

Stella, you ought to be ashamed of yourself for getting all shook up over some young boy. I mean really. Get a grip, girl, is what I'm thinking as I walk back to my room, but as I nod and say hello to at least twenty different hotel workers I realize something very profound: I haven't been this aroused on the spot in about three thousand years. It feels like a miracle, because it means I am still alive inside and not dead after all! You may think you've lost it but it's really just lying around dormant, waiting for somebody to come along and reignite those flames you assumed had long since turned to cold white ashes. Apparently the fire is not out. You are not over the fucking hill yet, you can still twitch and flit and flirt. This is great, I think as I run up the steps toward my room, not bothering to peek over at the nudies, and when I put the key in my door, from my tape deck Mary J. Blige is blowing "I'm Goin' Down." I dance on in and as I take off my jogging gear I make a mental note to thank this young man somehow for whatever it is he has done which I hope I'll be able to put my finger on before I leave.

I shower and lay out all seven bathing suits on the bed

and try to picture myself in one in particular. Three of them are two-piece but I feel like a one-piece today for some reason, so I reach for the chartreuse with that magical Wonderbra stuff inside even though I really don't need it but it gives you a real boost in more ways than one so I put this one on and pull all my braids up into a ponytail and I put on some sunglasses and slip into a giant lemon yellow T-shirt that is really a minidress and I grab one of the ten books I brought with me, my Walkman and my suntan lotion, and I'm off.

It is a scorcher. The beach is packed. It's not a very big beach, not like a public beach where there are thousands of people and kids. It's not like that here. First of all there are no children hallelujah because this is an adults-only resort. It is refreshing not to see little ones with their little pails and shovels ruining the shoreline with their big potholes and not to hear their squealing and wailing. I admit their laughter isn't bad but the fact is if you don't hear or see any kids you don't really miss them, at least that's how I feel after lying on my chaise for an hour or so.

I am almost two shades blacker and my skin which is normally an olive brown is getting a little reddish glow to it and I am feeling very tropical already. I would like to get as dark as possible because I've always wished I'd been born blacker, so black that I am almost Godiva-edible like the proud Africans I love to look at in my big photography books on the coffee table at home.

I am sweating and need something cool to drink and as I look around the beach I see a young woman with short braids and a tray full of drinks heading my way. I scan the entire beach to see if I can spot Winston but I don't see

him and I turn to look toward the swimming pool and because of his height I should be able to see him but I don't.
I drink the second of what will turn out to be probably
close to forty or fifty virgin piña coladas over the next
eight days and then gallop into the water which is nowhere
near cold and I am really freaked when I see a school of at
least a hundred tiny silver fish swimming around my ankles. I begin to run, looking down in the water to see if
they're following me but they're not so I head on out
toward the deep part and dive under.

I feel like a mermaid or something as I come up for air
and go back and forth below until I'm tired. I'm grateful
I spent the money and got human hair instead of that fake
stuff like Vanessa did. When she went swimming, she said,
she felt like she was sinking to the bottom because those
fucking braids weighed a ton when they got wet. As I walk
back toward the shore I look over at the snorkeling boat
heading out. I've been told about the clothing-optional
cruise that leaves every day at eleven but I'm not going on
that cruise, not even considering it. Volleyball, which
starts every day at eleven too, is more my speed. And even
though I'm afraid of heights I'm vowing to try parasailing
before I leave this island and maybe water-skiing and for
sure snorkeling, but I have no desire whatsoever to scuba
dive. I don't want to go that deep.

I drink up and spend the next hour talking to a Canadian couple who are here for two whole weeks on their
honeymoon. He is a very tall dark handsome Italian and
she is almost cute and very voluptuous and as she lies on
her stomach and he wipes her back gently with a towel I
wonder what she must've done to get this hunkster. She's

French and can hardly speak a word of English. They are both very tanned.

Two young men who work here at the Castle Beach Negril and are called social directors come along, wearing khaki shorts and white T-shirts. Yesterday the color must've been yellow, because Abby and the other woman who greeted me at the activities desk as well as the woman in the game room downstairs were all wearing yellow T-shirts and khaki shorts. They too are social directors and Abby explained to me that their job is to make sure the guests are happy entertained don't want for anything have all our questions answered before we have a chance to ask and to make sure we are having a great time which is why Norris and Gillette are on their way over here to solicit us for a game of volleyball. The Italian guy closes his eyes holds his long arm up pushes the palm of his hand against an invisible wall and says, "Not today, guys. I'm too hungover."

"Oh, come on, Ben, you can sweat it out," says Norris, who is a deep chocolate brown and oddly handsome, but could use a set of braces and perhaps a baseball cap to cover up that humongous oval head. "It'll be good for your body."

"I don't think I can," Ben moans.

The other fellow is parading further down the beach and I can hear him giving the spiel to other people. Norris is now looking at me. "Stella, you look like the athletic type. Come on."

"How'd you know my name?" He of course is wearing a name tag that says, as big as day, NORRIS.

"You met my friend Winston, and he told me he met a lovely American woman and that she was wearing braids in her hair. So what do you say?" And he holds his volleyball up on the tips of his fingers and begins to spin it. He is looking at me the way Quincy does when he's trying to sweet-talk me so he can get his way.

"Oh why not," I say.

"Oh what the hell," Ben says and struggles to get up. He's gotta be at least six five or six. "But when you see me tonight, Stella, please punch me as hard as you can if I tell you I've had more than two or three or four Beach Bomb Boombas, okay?"

"Why don't you ask your wife to do that, Ben?"

"Are you kidding me? Sasha's worse than I am. Look at her," he says, laughing. When I look down at her she is grinning but it is clear that she doesn't have a clue as to what we're talking about. "Play big fun," she says and drops her head back on top of her rolled-up towels.

We play for over an hour and it is big fun and I feel like I've lost at least five pounds of water. I'm also starving but can't help running back into the ocean to cool off. I dry myself, gather up the book I have not opened and my yellow tote bag with the monkey dangling from the zipper, and head to the dining room for lunch.

I set my stuff down on a table and go over to the buffet line, which is pretty long. I find myself looking around the place pretending that I'm not really searching for anyone in particular but I'm a little disappointed when I don't see him. I look at my watch. It's one o'clock. What time does he eat lunch? I wonder. Stella, stop it. Just what exactly is going on here? Well, I say to myself, he certainly is a pleasure to look at, what's wrong with looking with drooling a little bit for a change of pace I mean I don't want to touch just look but I would like for my heart to thump again which would make twice in one day and to be honest I just want to see if what I felt this morning was a fluke. Who the fuck cares? Where could he possibly be?

"Would you like to join us for lunch?" I hear Ben say.

"Sure," I say to him and his grinning wife.

I get some kind of seafood and a Caesar salad which they make for you right there and rice and beans and pasta and I'll never eat all this food I just get it because it feels free which of course it isn't it's just already paid for.

Ben interprets for Sasha during lunch and tells me how he has his own tile company in Quebec and how this is the first time in years that he has taken any time off. Even though it is his honeymoon and not a vacation it was really hard pulling this off trying to get away for two whole weeks because the tile business is tricky and you have to be there for your customers and when I'm not there things fall apart and since this used to be my dad's business and business has increased tenfold since I took over it is important for me to maintain my position because things are getting pretty competitive out there and if you lose your edge you have lost your edge. It occurs to me as I watch Sasha nodding in agreement that I haven't once thought about my job or the pile of work I left and how tall the stack will be when I get home. I don't care. It can all wait. My boss makes everything seem so urgent, as if the world will stop turning because we may miss an opportunity to make another dollar. I could sit out here and give myself heart palpitations if I think about my job for longer than three seconds but I am right now refusing to entertain the thought which is why I divert all my attention over to Sasha who is smiling at Ben and it is clear she is in love with this man. It is nice to witness. They are going to the pajama party. We agree to see each other there tonight.

The sun wipes you out—my afternoon nap lasts almost two hours. I decide to sit out on my balcony and read a little of *The Grace of Great Things* by Robert Grudin which sounded good when I read the book jacket in the store but it turns out to be too academic and deep and not exactly beach reading so I put it down after a half hour and pick up *Black Betty* by Walter Mosley which I've been meaning to read since I read and loved *Devil in a Blue Dress* but there's already a grisly murder on page two of *Black Betty* and I'm not much in the mood for death. I pick up the hardcover version of *Waiting to Exhale* by that Terry McMillan which I bought when it first came out and I've been meaning to read for a couple of years now and after reading like the first fifty or sixty pages I don't know what all the hoopla is about and why everybody thinks she's such a hot writer because her shit is kind of weak when you get right down to it and this book here has absolutely no literary merit whatsoever at least none that I can see and she uses entirely too much profanity. Hell, I could write the same stuff she writes cause she doesn't exactly have what you'd call a style but anyway I can sort of relate to some of her characters even though the main reason I didn't read this book was because from what I heard a couple of these women sounded too much like me although I'm not as stupid as a few of them. But I'm not in the mood to read about a bunch of woe-is-me black women. I sift through the rest of my books, skipping over *A Short History of God* and *The Between* which I heard was good but it's got some supernatural stuff in it and maybe this could work for me like at home but not right this minute and the author's name is Tanarive Due and she's young and black and from Florida because I heard about her from the *Miami Herald* when I was down there and there's *Moo* by Jane Smiley. I love everything she does—*A Thousand Acres* did it for me even before it won the Pulitzer—but I don't feel like going to a satirical college today and there's *Crossing Over Jordan* by Linda Beatrice-Brown though I'm not eager to take a little trip down memory lane all the way back to slavery either so I pick up something called *Going Under* by William Luvaas which sounds about right for some reason and this is what I settle on for the next two and a half hours.

I feel so silly going through my suitcase looking for a pair of pajamas to wear to a disco. But I search anyway. The only jammies I brought was my cotton number which is boring as hell but cool especially for someone who is going to be sleeping alone for seven more nights. I *did* bring one sexy number I got from Neiman Marcus last year that cost me a fortune but I wouldn't dare wear this because it looks like a slutty wedding gown and why did I pack the thing anyway oh yeah because Vanessa told me you should always pack at least one bewitching thing because you just never know and then I come across this almost but not quite sheer white cotton nightgown that has scalloped lace with little tiny pearls sewn in that fall right over your shoulder blades and it has a tiny little pink rose at the center of the neckline which is not too low and it also has a long sheer jacket to wear over it which has those pretty puffy sleeves you push up to your elbows. This is what I'll wear. It is soft and sensual in an innocent sort of way and not too revealing unless I stand in the light and like why would I want to do that?

I take another shower. My third today. And choose a frosty pink Marilyn Monroe halter sundress which of course requires no bra but the cut of the dress makes your breasts look firm and supple even though it is really just a double layer of fabric you are looking at and panties just don't seem appropriate for this dress so I don't wear any. At home I go through a can of Shower Fresh FDS in a few weeks because I cannot stand the way I smell down there when I perspire, the reason why, I understand, more men don't go down on women. Lord knows I wouldn't which is another reason why I douche at least twice sometimes even three times a month depending on how much attention I'm getting and I don't care what those gynecologists say about using up good bacteria and increasing your risks for infection because if that's true then why do women's bathrooms always smell like old fish? I'll be glad when somebody invents a twenty-five-cent douche or feminine wipes dispenser and puts them in all women's public restrooms and an automatic Lysol atomizer wouldn't hurt. I also have my little disposable cleansing wipes which I keep in my purse so that when I'm out and using the ladies' room I won't have to worry about adding to the smell. I mean, can you really smell too clean?

I let some of my braids or whoever's braids they are hang down in back and in that ponytail action back on the top. I slip on some low-heeled white pumps and don't dare put on any makeup since this suntan has given me my base and I just embellish it with some dark pink lipstick and a little eye pencil so I won't look like I've been embalmed. I lotion my arms and shoulders and then mist myself with some Calyx Prescriptives which I'm getting totally sick of because even though I discovered it almost two years ago and for the longest time it was my own little secret scent, now every other woman in America who shops at Macy's Neiman's and Nordstrom's seems to have discovered it, but I'm not in America am I?

There is no buffet tonight so I walk through the dining room to one of the three restaurants we have to choose from and I can feel people looking at me, especially some of those old white men with their fat wives who are wearing white pantsuits with silver and gold lamé and big wide shoulder pads and little gold sandals with miniature clusters of fruit overflowing on their big toes. Most of the black men here look like linebackers and as it turns out most of them are in the NFL and this must be the spot because there are at least twelve of them with their fine young girlfriends or wives, each more beautiful than the next, and some of them are really working it and I don't blame them—when you've got it like that do it like that and hell I give credit where credit is due. I am not envious of these young women with perfect bodies because I used to have one too and all I know is that after they've had a baby or two and they turn forty-two they better pray they look as good as I do.

I hope none of the people I met on the beach or that I played volleyball with and none of those social directors sit down at my table this evening because right now I just want to eat and listen to the band and decide if I really want to go to some stupid disco in a nightgown. The more I think about it the stupider it sounds. But in fact there is no band right now because all four of them are sitting at a table outside the restaurant where I'm headed and the drummer, whom I remember seeing last night, smiles and says, "Hello," and I say hello back and he says, "Having dinner with someone?" and I say, "No," and he motions with his hand at the empty chair and says, "Won't you join us?" and I say, "Sure," and sit down before realizing this is the third time in a single day that I have had companions and to think that my sister was worried about my eating alone! Maybe they were brought up to be extra polite in Jamaica I think as I sit down and listen to each of the young and not so young men introduce themselves. The drummer of course is the one who has his eye on me and the drummer of course is the least cutest of them all. I am tempted to give him some animal traits but I won't because I will probably be struck by lightning for thinking ugly thoughts about someone who is only trying to be nice. I tell them my name is Stella and they all first discuss then concur that they don't know anyone named Stella. The youngest of the bunch says, "You remind me a lot of a girl I know whose name is Zoleta."

"Really," I say and he is giving me the eye. I am almost ready to burst out laughing because I'm wondering if these young guys here have a thing for older women or is it that they're just all very friendly because I haven't been here twenty-four hours and already I've been in the company of more men who are paying attention to me than I have noticed in years. It is sort of refreshing.

"So what do you feel like?" the drummer asks.

"Excuse me?"

"For dinner, mon."

"Oh, I'm not sure."

"Could I recommend something?"

"Sure."

"Do you eat meat?"

"Sometimes, just not pork."

"Why don't you eat pork?"

"It's too disgusting."

"Not Jamaican pork," he says.

"I'll take your word for it."

"So how about some seafood?"

"Seafood sounds good. Is it spicy?"

"Everything in Jamaica is spicy, mon," and they all start laughing.

"Good," I say, laughing right along with them. "It's the reason why I came here."

"Why's that, mon?"

"To add some spice to my life."

"Yeah, mon," the drummer says and leans back in his chair and I suppose he's thinking he's the Spice Islands Man.

When the drink waiter comes I order my staple virgin piña colada and while I'm explaining to the band why I don't drink alcoholic beverages I smell that citrus ocean and as I turn around to look who but Winston is standing behind me.

"Hello, Stella," he says. "Enjoying yourself?" The band

members all look up, then back at me and back at Winston. All of a sudden this feels like a dick thang or something, I don't know.

"I'm having dinner with the band," I say.

"I see that," he says, stretching these three words out. "But we're still on for tonight, aren't we?" and he looks at me with those Phantom of the Opera eyes and I wish he would stop this shit because the blood is rushing to my face and I feel like I just had a shot of tequila which used to be my drink of choice and my God what *is* that cologne he's wearing?

"I'll be there," I say.

"Ten o'clock?" he asks.

"Ten o'clock," I say as he disappears inside the restaurant where our food is coming from and when I turn toward the band each of them is looking at me like what is this all about? But then they settle down as if they do know and once again I think this has got to be a dick thang but they really don't know what's up and it's not at all what they are obviously thinking. I am going dancing. That's it. "So what time do you guys start playing tonight?"

"In an hour's time," the drummer says. "But you are going to the pajama disco, I take it?"

"I'm thinking about it."

"It's big fun if you like to get crazy," says the young one who is staring at me like I've been reincarnated and have come back as this Zoleta person. "But you look like you like to get crazy," he says and winks at me. "Zoleta liked to get wild too. You remind me so much of her. You can't even begin to imagine how much."

"No, I can't," I say.

I slurp up my drink and they each have two or three shots of something and I sit there with them but every ten or fifteen minutes I turn toward the door to the restaurant secretly waiting to smell him again but I eat my entire dinner and pass on dessert and he never comes out.

Afterwards I move closer to the stage and listen to the band mostly to kill time even though they are really good but it is only nine o'clock and I am feeling a little restless and I don't understand this but the next thing I know I'm grabbing my little clutch and am on my way back to my room where I pick up the phone to call Delilah but realize I can't call her anymore. So then I think about Vanessa but change my mind because I don't know what I'm going to tell her except that as anticipated Jamaica is beautiful and blah blah blah and oh by the way I'm being pursued by or I am pursuing a twenty-one-year-old boy who has got me throbbing and shit and I'm entirely too old for this kind of shit and as a matter of fact I must be out of my middle-aged mind to even be tripping but how could he do this and where did he get this kind of power, I mean what the hell is going on here?

I change into my nightgown which seems a little on the long side because it conceals my knees and I put the jacket over it and push up the sleeves and I resemble some black maiden from the nineteenth century and this isn't exactly the look I was after but it'll have to do and then I spray on some more FDS and put on a pair of flat gold sandals with no fruit on the toes and to kill more time I watch BET music videos until the clock finally strikes ten and then I jump up from the bed and head out the door.

I feel ridiculous. I am still not wearing any panties and

now I'm wondering if you can in fact see through this thing and when I walk under one of the pathway lamps and look down you can indeed see the silhouette of my body which doesn't look quite as svelte and hourglassy as I believed it did just an hour ago when I was admiring myself in the mirror. But it's just too bad.

I arrive at the door that leads to the disco and standing outside greeting everybody are Norris and Abby. "Stella! You made it! We're so glad! Go on in! Have a ball!" They open the thick navy blue quilted door and when I walk in I am somewhat amazed at what I see. The room is dark but there is clearly a small dance floor which is filled with white couples all dressed in bustiers and garters and thongs and some of the men are wearing G-strings and boxer shorts and bikini briefs. The music is thumping and "Shy Guy" by Diana King is loud and then that beat starts pounding again and just as I'm wondering if he's in here I smell that smell and I hear a voice say, "I'm glad you made it," and when I turn Winston has my hand and is luring me out to the dance floor in slow motion. He is looking at me and smiling when he says, "This is my favorite song," and I say, "Mine too!" and we somehow know each is telling the truth and boy oh boy he's wearing black baggy shorts and a stark white T-shirt. His long legs look longer. Hairier. Leaner. His shoulders wider. As we begin to dance he is looking at me and smiling and then he says, "That's a really pretty gown you're wearing," and I say, "Thank you but how'd you get in here wearing that? Doesn't look like pajamas to me."

He laughs. "I came in in just my shorts with my shirt balled up and then I put it back on."

"But why?"

"I don't know. I'm kind of a shy guy," he says and I laugh out loud.

"What's so funny?" he says and he is in fact blushing.

I just shake my head and continue dancing until someone taps him on his shoulder and he turns to listen and then he turns back toward me and stops dancing. "What's wrong?" I ask.

He chortles. "I have to go change into pajamas because he doesn't know how I got in here dressed like this."

I laugh again.

"Look, I'm just going to run back to my room and change and it'll take me no more than five minutes. Promise me you'll stay here until I get back. Five minutes' time is all I'll be."

"Okay," I say and he is gone. I keep dancing by myself which in this crowd doesn't really matter. Ben and Sasha are here. She looks like I Dream of Jeannie and he looks like a tall Clark Gable in satin pajama bottoms and when the DJ puts on Montell Jordan's "This Is How We Do It" the whole place goes nuts and I see Abby who is wearing the hell out of those pink satin hot pants and a tight purple halter top grab a microphone and yell out, "You want to get crazy?" and the crowd screams out, *"Yeah!!"* and she screams out even louder, *"Then get crazy and take it off if it's too hot in here for you!!"* and on that last note I begin to see garters popping open and G-strings being pulled off stockings falling down thighs to the floor high heels tossed and in a matter of seconds half the dance floor is exposed flesh. I can't believe my eyes and when I look down my nightgown seems to be getting fuller and fuller until it feels like I'm wearing a crinoline slip and a suit of armor or something and I feel old and out of place because I can't imagine what would possess me to get naked in front of all these people and twirl and swirl my hips the way I normally do when I'm wearing clothes and as each second passes more people slip out of something else and I know in another minute or two their eyes will be on me which is the reason why I flee.

I run at seven this morning and even though it's not scorching like it was yesterday, it's still hot and balmy. Seal is plugged into my ears at a level I'm sure the fish can probably hear and makes me sprint for most of the two-mile stretch. I reach the end of the beach too quickly so I turn around and do it again. I need this rush. This feeling of exhilaration. I run because it makes me feel like I'm in control of my life. Like there is no finish line. I slow down to wipe the perspiration away that's running into my eyes. My shoulder blades are burning from the sunshine. My entire body is actually throbbing so I stop and stand there looking at the turquoise water. It is so clear and calm and beautiful that I take my sneakers off and run straight in because it feels as if I don't have a choice, like something is pulling me. By the time I walk out far enough to immerse my entire body under water, my skin tenses then tingles and accepts the coolness. My cotton shorts get soggy quickly and I feel them droop and cling but I do a few strokes anyway and float on my back until my body temperature has dropped and I get out only to realize that I don't have a towel and the only way to get one

is to walk over by the pool right in front of the entrance
to the dining room and I really don't want anyone looking at me sopping wet but I have little alternative and then
I think it's only quarter to eight now and not a whole lot
of people will be up.

But before I get my right foot on the top step by the
pool, Winston is standing there as if he's waiting for me.

"And good morning to you," he says, looking indisputably
alluring and tall and lean and what is he doing up so early?

"Good morning to you, Winston. What are you doing
up so early?"

"I had a bit of trouble sleeping last night."

He is looking at—no he isn't—yes he is looking at my wet
breasts and I can feel my nipples are hard and I wish they
would deflate but when I look at his face he isn't looking
at my breasts at all, he's looking at my feet, and I'm so glad
I got that pedicure before I came here but why am I even
tripping, I don't have to impress this boy!

"What happened to you last night? I came back and you
were gone. You said you would wait. Did I do something?" He almost looks hurt.

"No, Winston. It wasn't you at all."

"Then what?" he says, looking up at me now.

"Those people started taking their clothes off."

He certainly looks relieved and then he starts laughing.
"A lot of them do that. Some come over from He-do-nism
and they have a few too many drinks and you know. . ."

"I didn't like it."

He's nodding his head up and down as if he understands.

"But you didn't have to undress just because those id-
iots did."

"I know that, but I felt old and out of place."

"You shouldn't have felt like that at all. They're just wild," he says. "I came back looking for you and Abby told me she saw you leave and that you said you'd be right back so I waited and waited for over an hour but you didn't come." He is looking at me so innocently I accept the fact that this isn't some kind of a come-on. It is not quite as calculated or sophisticated as the brothers in America could do. Sincerity is written all over Winston's face and in the way his shoulders droop forward and especially in the way he tucks his lips inside his mouth as if to be saying, You said you could come out and play and then you didn't and my feelings were hurt and I felt silly standing around like that and I thought you liked me. Don't you?

I believe I am beginning to feel softer warmer easier-going inside and I would even venture to say subdued but hold it stop the cameras wait just a minute! Exactly what is going on here, Stella? I mean what do you think you're doing? Come on! Get a grip on yourself, girl. "I'm sorry, Winston. I didn't know what else to do, so I went back to my room."

"But I told you I was coming right back. I thought you wanted to dance with me." I realize I have in fact offended him.

"I *did* want to dance with you, Winston."

"Then couldn't you have waited for me outside?"

At home if some guy were bugging me like this I would've said: "If I wanted to dance with you I would've waited for you but I didn't so how many ways do I have to spell it out before you take the hint?" Winston is waiting for my answer and all I'm thinking is how much I would love to kiss him on those beautiful lips and put my arms around him but instead I say, "I would've felt silly just standing around in a nightgown, Winston, and why is it so important?"

He gives me this exasperated look, like: Don't you get it? and puts all his weight on one gigantic Birkenstocked foot and if I'm not mistaken his face is saying: Because I like you, Stella, but I'm trying to pretend as if I'm reading this expression all wrong because he's too young and I'm simply too old to be tripping like I'm in high school or something. "It's important"—he sighs—"because we didn't really get our chance to dance."

"Well, I'm sorry, Winston, it was rude of me."

"No, you weren't rude. I'm not implying that at all. I was just looking forward to seeing you and I was disappointed when you weren't there. That's all. It's fine. Really."

But I can see that it's not fine. He looks like I feel when I'm making love and my partner comes first and fast and then looks at me hoping I managed to get mine and I lie and say: "It's fine," but really I am frustrated as all hell and want to do it again until I get to fall over the edge like he did.

I am drying. "Well, look, I need to get a towel and go get changed."

He is looking at me in a curious manner out of the corner of his eye and if he only knew how sexy he looks but it's kind of nice that he doesn't. "Are you coming back for breakfast?" He asks as if he simply wants to know, but he is wearing a look of desire. It's all over his face. At his age he doesn't hide or doesn't know how to hide any of this stuff yet, he puts it all out in the open, and he is beginning to feel like a breeze coming through an open window.

"I think so. Why?" Now I'm sort of messing with him because I know deep down that this young man couldn't possibly be trying to hit on me. If I were say twenty years younger I could see it and he would unquestionably be my man of choice.

"I was just asking," he says. "I've already eaten."

Now why I am feeling let down all of a sudden?

"Have you tried any of the water sports yet?" he asks.

"No. But I'm supposed to go snorkeling later. How about you?"

"I don't like the beach."

"And you live in Jamaica?"

"All my life."

"How could you not like it?"

"Just never have. I don't like the sand."

"Okay. You have a right not to like the sand."

"So how are you spending the early part of your day?" he asks.

"I'm supposed to go horseback riding."

He nods. "You should go very soon if possible. The heat can be unbearable."

"Well, I'm scheduled to leave at nine-thirty."

"So maybe I'll see you at lunch?"

"I don't know, Winston. Maybe. Where are your friends?"

"What friends?"

"Norris? Abby?"

"They're working. I won't know until Monday exactly where I'll be, so I'm just sort of hanging around, helping them out here and there, but I've also put in applications at Paradise Grand and Windswept. Something should come up."

"Well, good luck," I say as I begin to walk past him, and the right side of my body accidentally brushes up against his arm and in that one second some kind of feverish current penetrates my whole body and in a perfect world or if this were like a foreign film I would just turn around and put my hand on the back of his head and pull his face to mine until our noses touched and I would brush my lips lightly across those thick beautiful lips of his and we would put our arms around each other like we'd been dreaming of doing and we would begin to slide to the ground and we would be oblivious to everything around us and simply make love right out here right this very minute.

"Well, have fun and maybe I'll see you later," he says.

Let us pray, I say to myself, and wave goodbye.

I am the only person on the van going to Issy's Riding Stable. The Canadians told me that I had better make my reservations early because sometimes it's hard to get in even two days ahead but it is worth the fifty bucks for the hour because you get to gallop all along the beach and ride up and deep inside the mountain and it is truly breathtaking.

I am not exactly impressed by the architecture of Negril as we drive past a packed and dusty marketplace with at least a hundred rickety wooden stalls filled with wooden objects and a kaleidoscope of cloth although red black and green dominate and then we purportedly go through downtown which consists of a bank and a small shopping center and we continue past small but brightly painted cement homes and cafés and outdoor restaurants and I was told that no building here is taller than the town's tallest palm tree which is an understatement. In fact there is not much to see in the way of sightseeing but Negril is where hippies-turned-yuppies have flocked, as they consider it a wonderful reprieve from the hustle and bustle of urban life in America.

I am dropped off at the bottom of a dirt road and am greeted by Issy's brother who's called the General, because Issy is a big shot and apparently doesn't do horses anymore, just owns the place. The General looks and smells as if he has been afraid of water for a long time and does not know what deodorant is. As we walk up toward the stable he says, "You got a smoke?" and I tell him I don't smoke and he is disappointed.

"How long do we ride?" I ask.

"Two hours. You get your money's worth, mon. I see to it. You'll love it. Not to worry."

The stable is ugly and stinks and looks like the set of *Bonanza* on a bad-ranch day and these horses all look anorexic; at least six or seven Rastas with long hot dreadlocks are sitting around playing some kind of card game and I can smell that ganja because it is hard not to. They hardly notice when I walk up with the General who has chosen my horse already and his name is Dancing Dan. I sign a bunch of forms and he asks me for thirty-five dollars for two hours and I thought it was fifty for an hour so I think it must be a black thang and I am impressed that they are so organized and businesslike with all the waivers even though nobody seems to be doing anything.

The General helps me get on Dancing Dan and off we go up a rocky red dirt trail lined with mango avocado and akee trees. Flowering bushes appear to be taking over the hillside and then we enter what looks like a real rain forest. The trees suddenly triple in size and density; their branches hang over the path so heavily that we often have to duck. At first it feels cooler and then it begins to feel like a greenhouse: sultry. I am also not exactly National Velvet and when the General begins to gallop I don't know how to lift my hips in unison to Dancing Dan's rhythm—they slap against that hard-ass saddle and not only does it sting but the breeze is causing all the General's funk to fly right into my face. "I forgot how to gallop," I yell out.

"No problem, mon," he says and turns his horse around. He explains to me how to do it and then says, "It's too bad you don't smoke, mon."

We lope along and I begin to see these tiny little square structures that look like shacks, some made of several different kinds and sizes of boards and wood just nailed on top of each other any old way. Most of these places have tin or aluminum roofs and maybe one or two little windows and I wonder why they're up here in these hills out in the middle of nowhere when suddenly I see children playing outside of one and then a woman hanging clothes on a line at another and then right in the middle of the trail a young boy about sixteen has two tin pans of water, one with soap in it, and he is scrubbing some type of clothing with his bare hands and he says hello to the General and asks if he has a smoke and of course he doesn't and it is obvious that they know each other. We saunter onward and some small children walk right in front of my horse and hold up an armful of red yellow and green beaded necklaces and I give them a twenty-dollar bill and they hand me all twenty or thirty of their necklaces but I shake my head no and take only a few because I don't want to exploit their craftsmanship and they look at me as if I'm nuts and then they run off squealing in delight and I put my other fifty back in my pocket twenty of which I had planned to use as a tip for the General because I believe in the power of tipping but only if he stops stopping and posing on his horse right in the line of fire of what little breeze there is.

"Do people actually live up here?" I ask.

He chuckles. "Oh yes, mon. For certain."

I am in a state of disbelief because it does not look like more than one person could actually fit inside some of these shacks plus they seem as flimsy as the little club-houses Quincy and his friends have built down by the creek near our house. It is difficult for me to accept the fact that grown-ups with children live inside these huts but I am trying not to pass judgment even though it looks like there might not be any running water or septic tanks or even electricity but I'm sure hoping I'm wrong. I mean even in Jamaica it is still 1995, isn't it?

As we pass one after another of these kinds of homes I find myself getting more and more depressed. This is how black people in the South used to live back in the twenties and thirties. I've got old photos of my grandparents sitting out on their front porches in front of rickety little shacks identical to these. I hate those pictures. My grandparents look worn out. Tired. Like they can't do any more have done enough and this is all we get for it, and as

Dancing Dan begins to pick up the pace all on his own I am so hot and sticky I wish I could get off this damn horse and sit down under a tree and find an ice-cold bottle of Evian or Crystal Geyser with lime. I pull on Dancing Dan's reins to slow his ass down because I can see the emerald-green ocean that appears to be a few miles down the mountain through a forest and that's when I ask: "General, when are we going to ride on the beach?"

"Beach?"

"Yes. Some of the people from my hotel said that they rode on the beach and I was wondering how much longer before we ride on the beach."

He laughs. "Oh no, mon. That's Sopher's Plantation, not Issy's, mon. We don't ride on no beach at Issy's. We give you the mountain ride, mon, so that you can see the *real* Jamaica, how the Rastas live."

Shit. Shit. Shit. "But I wanted to ride on the beach."

"You don't like to see mountain life?"

"Yes, it's fine, but General it's really hot up here and how much longer do we have to ride?"

"Well, you paid for two hours."

"I know but we can cut it short, I don't mind."

"No, mon. We give you your money's worth and a good deal at Issy's, right, mon?" He looks at his watch. "We still have well over an hour to go, but we stop for a drink soon, not to worry."

The General proceeds to point out a number of gardens filled with sweet potatoes and a slew of vegetables I've never heard of. As I look down at the dry red soil, the General explains why the plants aren't flourishing: everyone is waiting for the rain which will be here for sure tomorrow afternoon and all I'm wondering is what Winston is doing as Mr. Meteorologist is now proudly pointing out quite a few unfinished brick structures larger than those we've already seen and he says many of these are going to be big three-bedroom villas but I can't picture it. Every now and then he shows me what he defines as mansions which would not quite qualify as a Section 8 home in the hood at home and then I wonder something else. "General?"

"Yeah, mon."

"How do these folks get home? I mean we're like very high up here and these roads aren't exactly smooth and I have not seen a streetlight yet."

"Who needs light, mon? Everybody knows their way home. No problem, mon. We live 'ere. Some people have cars and some ride bicycles and others walk. Nothing will hurt you here. We've got Ja looking over us and who needs light, mon, if you know where you're going?"

Good point. I am ashamed for feeling the way I do but it is hard not to. We pass a bunch of children playing in a small meadow which appears to be in the middle of nowhere and then a little girl with a backpack stops to stare at me like I'm a freak and I'm thinking what is she doing out here all by herself? Further up are more kids, shabbily dressed but clean and chasing each other around and some are digging something up from the ground and one is chasing a goat (I think it's a goat) and they are all laughing and it suddenly occurs to me that these children look pretty damn happy like they are having big fun and I'm certain they don't have Sega Genesis or Super Nintendo or five-hundred-dollar road bikes or Lightning

Rollerblades at home and doesn't look like any crack houses or drive-bys or gang-banging going on around here and these kids look like they know how to amuse themselves, something we have forgotten, and I understand they are probably better off much better off than I thought.

"Would you like a Red Stripe?" the General asks as we stop by the fence of one of those little stores is what I guess they're called.

"I don't drink beer, but I'll take some water," I say.

To the right about a quarter mile up the hill I see an old black man sitting on a big rock and two little boys giggling. A pale gray horse stands right next to the man and all of a sudden the General yells out, "Hey Tanto!" and no shit, that horse starts galloping down that hill toward us and he looks like he's going to run into the fence but then when he gets close he makes a sharp right turn and continues on about his business down the trail we were on until we can't see him anymore. "How did you do that?" I ask.

"What?"

"Get that horsie to run down here like that—and where did he go?"

"He knows his name, mon. On a good day I bring an apple but he knows when I have one and when I don't. Come on in for a drink, mon."

Once again the local children stare at me and I smile at them and since there's no bottled water I get a green bottle of Ting which is a wonderful sparkling grapefruit drink that is ice cold which of course means that they do have electricity up here and I am very relieved. The General bums a cigarette from the man who apparently sells a lot of different items such as beer and soft drinks and fresh vegetables and fruit and candy and even some household items and toiletries from this little store. A girl of about sixteen stands in the doorway of the little shack that is connected to the store. She looks like she's going somewhere because her hair is greasy and slicked back and she is wearing freshly ironed old blue jeans and a starched white blouse and she reminds me of me thirty years ago. I remember that make-do look. As I take my bottle of Ting over to where the General is I can see another girl standing in her bra and panties inside the living room of the house, ironing something. Our eyes meet and there is something like disgust in hers for me. I sort of get it, but I go ahead and sit on a handmade wooden bench and drink my Ting while the General drinks two Red Stripe beers.

We have the most amazing view of the tip of the island and the view of the ocean is pretty much surreal—no one would believe this. I don't believe this. I am sitting on a live postcard. Miles of dark green clusters lead down to the blue-green sea, where I can see fishermen sitting in small boats, waiting. I see coral reefs shaped like navy blue states on a map of the U.S. The sky runs into the water. This is a good place to pray, I think. You would be more inclined to tell the truth from this altitude and someone might actually hear you up here I betcha. Even if I had remembered to bring my camera you would have had to be here to feel this to take it all in because a photograph even a video would not have the same impact. You always lose something when you try to recapture rename what you saw or felt and I am glad that I am here and I will remember all of this without a camera and when I tell people about it I just want to be able to recount enough of the beauty so that one day they will want to see it for themselves.

The General smokes his cigarette slowly and we sit there in relative silence for which I am grateful and as the two young girls come out of their home and take a tiny little key and put it in the tiny little padlock on their front door and disappear into a clump of trees, I'm wondering again what Winston might be doing. I guess I look a little perplexed because I hear the General say, "They're taking the shortcut to town."

On the way back I practice my galloping but it is still too hard to keep up with Dancing Dan and I'm too hot and I am tired of smelling the General and so when we get back to the stables I am anxious to give him that twenty-dollar American bill and he is happy as hell and I tell him to go buy himself some smokes and I want to say a can of Right Guard would be a good investment but instead I say, "I think I worked up a sweat so as soon as I get back to the hotel I'm taking a long hot shower so I'll not only feel clean but will smell fresh too."

"I don't blame you," he says and walks me down to the bottom of the road where the van is waiting to take me back to the hotel.

It is lunchtime and in fact I *don't* smell so fresh so I take my afternoon shower and put on my navy blue and white one-piece swimsuit and some white shorts over it and head for the beach. I decide to secure myself a chaise first and then come back and have lunch. I have to walk past the dining room in order to get to the beach so on my way there I look inside. The white tables are filled with two or three hundred people but somehow in the middle of all those folks I see Winston sitting all by himself and he is simply looking at me saying hello with his eyes. I wave but keep walking.

To my surprise I feel relieved to have seen him, and to be honest—be honest with yourself, Stella—I really am fucking ecstatic, because why else is my heart beating so fast, so irregular? I get myself set up and see a few of my favorite honeymooners sleeping and slurping and then head back toward the dining room.

His table is empty. My heart plummets and I am suddenly embarrassed because now I am totally aware of what is happening to me: I *like* this boy. I look around as if everyone has just heard what I'm thinking and I shake off the whole notion by piling my plate with pasta and seafood and forcing myself to eat every drop of it without once looking up from my table to see if he will reappear.

He doesn't.

I spend the next hour or so doing the back and forth sun and water thing and then I fall asleep under a palm tree for what turns out to be close to two hours and I wake up wet and hot and I run into the ocean right past a fuzzy-gray-haired black man who looks just like—I'm not kidding—the Creature from the Black Lagoon, without the scales and fins of course, and he is standing in water just deep enough to cover what appears to be a protrusion of extra skin in front of him and I assume he's blind because of the way his eyes are sort of crossing.

"Feels good, doesn't it," he says, and since I'm the only one in the water I assume he has to be talking to me.

"It sure does," I say and go on out a little further, do a few laps and my underwater ritual and then I head back to what is now clearly a deserted beach. It is siesta time for most of the drunks or people like me who get zapped from lying out in the sun all day. The old man is now sitting on the lounge chair right next to mine and I'm thinking I hope this motherfucker *is* blind and it would be nice if he were also deaf but be nice Stella he is old he could be your father but he is not.

As I come out of the water I can see now that he is not blind because his eyes are without a doubt now hungrily searching my body for some lost treasure or something. He should stop before I get sick. I grab my towel and wrap it around myself, hiding everything I can. I take another towel and begin to pat exposed parts dry.

"Hi, I'm Nate McKenzie and you are. . ."

"Stella Payne."

"How many days you here for?"

"Six and a half more," I say, gathering up my Walkman books towels.

"Me too. This is my eighth time here in the last three years."

I want to say, And am I supposed to care? Instead I just nod.

"Yep. Retired from the air force a few years back. Live right outside Pittsburgh but I love it down here."

I am reaching inside my tote trying to find my shorts because I don't like the way his eyes feel on my body.

"You been over to the nude beach yet?"

"Excuse me?" I say, turning toward him now. The first thing I notice are those bunions on his roosterlike feet and then that there is blood dripping down the front of his bow legs where he apparently has cut himself and I'm wondering if he's aware of it. "Do you realize you're bleeding?"

He looks down over his swollen stomach. "Yeah, fell off a bicycle today. It's all right. Have you?"

"No I have not been to the nude beach. Why? Have you?" What is he getting at? He reminds me of a dirty old man who probably has to pay for all the pussy he gets. As I look more closely I realize he's not really ugly but far from appealing and there is something vulgar about him. I think it's his mouth, which kind of looks like a fish's— like it stays wet and half open all the time.

"Yeah," he's saying like he's reminiscing or something, and then he comes back to the here and now. "This is my first time at *this* beach actually. You should come over to the nude beach. I think you'd like it."

"I have no desire to go to the nude beach."

"Why not?"

"Because I can't imagine getting any real gratification or pleasure prancing around in front of a bunch of white folks and dirty old men in particular with my clothes off and besides that I wouldn't want to give white men the pleasure of seeing my black body considering they used to rape us when we were slaves or did you forget about that little part of our history?"

He wipes his brow as if to say, Damn, you didn't have to get all deep on me. But then, being the whore that I guessed he was, he says, "Why don't you come over there with me?"

Before I throw up I say, "I have to return my towels and I'm going over by the pool to get a drink so maybe I'll see you later, Nate."

"Wait," he says, struggling to get up. "I'll have one with you."

Fuckfuckfuckfuckfuck.

When I get to the pool I am both delighted and relieved to see Winston treading water. He looks pleased when he sees me which thrills me even more. I drop my stuff on an empty chair and slide into the water before the old man can catch up. I can see him dragging his club feet through the sand and I feel bad for dissing him the way I have but not all that bad because he should find some young girl out here who needs a little extra cash to ring his bell and I am not that girl.

I am now about three feet away from Winston and I whisper loudly, "Would you do me a big favor?" and he swims closer to me gradually emerging from the water and wow he has hair all over his chest and his shoulders are broader and wider than I thought and damn his body looks quite a bit like a real man's and now his face is less than a foot from mine and I can smell that scent again and without thinking I say, "What is that cologne you're wearing, Winston?" and he says, "Escape," and I mumble, "I wish I could," and he says, "Excuse me, I didn't hear you," and I say, "Boy, does it smell good," and then I see the old man and I say, "Winston, would you just stand here and talk to me for a few minutes because that old man behind you but don't look is trying to hit on me." He turns to look anyway and then back at me and says, "I don't blame him," and I look at him like did you hear what you just said and I say, "Winston, please," and he says, "What?" and I look at him and he is looking into my eyes again like he could walk right inside them and it feels like I am moving closer to him but I really can't be sure because now his shoulders are somehow touching mine and this water is getting hot and I see the old man jump into the pool and head this way and I move closer to Winston which I can tell is a mistake because now I am beginning to feel as if I'm under the influence of something and whatever it is is pulling me toward this young man but I get a grip on myself and say, "What do you mean?" and he says, again, "Who can blame him?" and when I look at him he is looking at me for real like a man and I'm finding this all rather surreal and I say, "Winston, if I weren't in my right mind I'd swear you're trying to hit on me too," and he says, "And you'd be right." I let my head plummet under the water because I don't even know how to respond to this and so I blow air bubbles and then I see his face appear in the transparent blueness and he smiles at me underwater and nods his head up and down as if to say yes it's true it's true and it's okay it's okay and then we both come up for air and I wipe my face and catch my breath and say, "Winston, I know you can't be serious," and he says, "Do I look serious?" and I look at him and damn is he sexy and it doesn't seem as if he's trying to be, this is simply who he is, and he is looking at me not like that old man with the watering lips but so tenderly as if he would really just like to kiss me on the cheek or something and I swear this water is beginning to boil and I'm trying my hardest to digest what is happening here and then I hear myself say, "Hold it. Wait a minute. Stop."

"What?" he says again.

"You are serious, aren't you, Winston?"

"Very much so."

"Okay," I groan, since I'm in this now. "Let me ask you something. What's the oldest woman you've ever been with, Winston?"

"Twenty-four."

And I say, "Well, you'd have to turn those numbers around for me, sweetie," and he says, "So?" and I see he is somber, I mean there is this What is the problem? look on his face in his eyes, and I say, "Wait a minute. Let me get this straight," and he is smiling deeply at me again as if he knows what I am about to say and even I don't know what I'm about to say but he is clearly ready to respond and I take the first of a series of hyperventilated breaths and force out, "Are you saying that you would like to sleep with me, Winston?" and I look at him to see his reaction to that one and without blinking he says, "Absolutely," and he gives me a Don't look so surprised look, and out of the corner of my eye I glimpse the old man watching us and Winston pushes his right hand under the surface of the water and I can feel his long fingers just barely graze my waist and when I look into his eyes this time my body quivers and shudders and I can't believe it when I hear myself say, "Okay."

He is grinning fiercely and blushing at the same time and he says, "Really?"

And I look at him and say, "Really."

"You won't change your mind like last night, will you?"

"I don't think so, Winston, but I'll tell you something: I don't know what I'm doing and I can't believe what I just said to you—there's something illegal about this, isn't there?"

He is giving me a very comforting look. "There is nothing illegal about this and I don't quite understand what would make you say something like that."

"Winston." I sigh.

"What?" He sighs back, and he truly does look clueless.

"I'm old enough to be your mother."

"But you're not my mother."

"I know that."

"You don't look like my mother. You don't act like my mother. And you certainly don't feel like my mother," he says.

I must admit he is rather convincing. But this is totally scandalous, Stella, and you know it. The waitress comes over and sets one red drink and then what looks like my usual virgin piña colada down by us near the edge of the pool. Winston says thank you to her and offers me the glass. "When did you order this?" I ask.

"When I saw you headed in this direction."

"But how did you know I was going to have a drink with you?"

"I didn't," he says. "It was wishful thinking." He is looking in my eyes doing that hypnotism stuff again and in order to get myself together I turn my head a little to the left and I see old Nate staring at us his mouth watering with envy and I feel sorry for him all of a sudden and when I turn back toward Winston I cannot believe that this beautiful tall young man has said he wants to touch me wants to get close to me wants to make love to me and I am wondering what am I doing and did I really just tell this

boy that I would fuck him and yes Stella you did and well
if I do nobody really has to know it could be our little secret and I'm thinking he is so sweet and gentle and sexy I
really don't want to just *fuck* him I mean I can't picture us
like doing the nasty because I think I really want to make
love to Winston I mean I think I'd like to give him something tender something soft and warm and beautiful something that resonates so that afterwards the next morning
or next month or next year he'll have known what it felt
like to make love to a real woman and not like he screwed
me or I screwed him like these young hoochies out there
who fuck by numbers and think that the harder you do it
the harder you come which of course is not true so I am
surprised once again when I hear myself say, "So, Winston, do you think you'd like me to teach you something
or do you think there's something you can teach me?"

He takes a sip of his strawberry daiquiri and looks over
the glass and he is certainly not the least bit afraid to look
me in the eye, that much I do know, and he says, "Probably both," and I almost choke because now I can't wait I
want to do it right now in this pool.

"Will you have dinner with me and then could we go
dancing for real tonight first?" he asks.

"Is that how you want to do this?" I ask, shocked because with one of his older counterparts we'd be on our
way to my room like ten minutes ago. This is—he is—certainly
refreshing.

"I like you, Stella, and I want to spend as much time
with you as I can while you're here."

"But why, Winston?"

He sighs again. Shifts his body weight and rubs his

hands over the top of his head and down to the nape of his neck. "I like talking to you and I find myself smiling so much when I see you and I like the way that feels."

"But Winston." I sigh.

"What?" He sighs back.

"Are you sure you want to do this?"

"Why is it so hard for you to accept the fact that I think you're pretty and nice and I can't help it if I'm attracted to you and ever since I saw you walk into the dining room yesterday the whole place kind of came alive or like the fans started going faster or something but all I can say is you made my day when you spoke to me and you should not be worrying at all about my age or your age because they are only numbers and don't worry I won't disappoint you," he says, glaring at me in such a way that I believe him.

"I'm not worried about that, Winston."

"Then what are you worried about?"

"Me," I say, and set my drink down and start heading out of the pool. I reach for my towel and while I stand on the edge old man Nate is clearly looking at my ass and I want to say watch that young one down there and see how it's really done but instead I look at Winston and say, "What time is good for you?" and he dives under the water like those dolphins who perform at Marine World USA do and when he comes back up to the surface he grins at me and says, "You tell me."

I hold up seven fingers.

He holds up six.

Maybe they accidentally put some booze in my drink is what I'm thinking as I stagger back toward my room. I feel like I've jumped inside somebody else's dream. I mean I know I'm in Jamaica. I'm in Negril. I think I just got here day before yesterday but I can't be sure because a lot has happened since then and when I'm at home weeks months can go by and nothing worth noting happens. But yes. I am walking up the path at the Castle Beach Negril and I have just told a twenty-one-year-old that I will have sex with him tonight. Yes, that seems to be what I've gone and done. I press both hands up to my face and cover my eyes and cheeks and sort of sink at the knees and I can see some of the workers wondering if I'm off my rocker so I remove my hands and smile and continue to walk or float toward my room because I still do not believe I've consented to something this reckless. But then again, I'm not planning on marrying this boy. I'm just going to have sex with him tonight. And that's it. It's that simple. Do it and send him on his way. I've got a whole box of condoms. So what is the problem, Stella? I mean he is a consenting adult. He *wants* to do it. But why does he want to do the nasty with me? I wonder. Because I'm old. That's why. He's never had any old pussy before. That's it. He wants to do a comparison study. Does old pussy feel as good as young pussy? I can't answer that question and I don't want him to answer that question but he didn't act like he simply wanted sex, I mean he did ask me to have dinner with him, didn't he? And then dancing afterwards, didn't he? Isn't that like sort of what's called a date? But why am I even tripping? Why am I going this far? The bottom line is that he is tall and fine and sexy and young and I'm a good-looking middle-aged woman from America and he's game and I'll give him something to remember and if I work it right maybe I'll get off and I hope the boy can kiss because it would be a shame if God gave him those thick juicy beautiful luscious lips and he doesn't know what to do with them and I hope he's not one of those sloppy wet tongue-wrestling kissers that make you think you're really in the dentist's chair and I hope he knows how to move because I can help guide him some of the way but rhythm is something you either have or you don't have and it cannot be taught but I'll do my best and I hope he understands the importance of a woman's breasts but probably nobody's shown him how to handle them yet so I'll give him a five-minute demonstration and since he's young he should catch on fast and God just the thought of those smooth lips over my breasts okay change the subject Stella because I still have—I look at my watch—three whole hours to go. Lord what am I going to do for three hours besides go crazy? I feel like I want him right now but I am not going in that room and masturbate no way José I am going to save all of this for him and I feel sorry for him really because I hope he's up for this. I wonder what kind of music I should put on none of that let's-do-the-nasty music or any begging and pleading or that whining lovesick stuff but then again I don't want anything too funky and upbeat which means I'm back to Seal again but I also don't want to go completely off and act like I'm setting up this monumental seduction performance because that's like so tacky but I do feel kind of silly when I turn around and walk back to the gift shop pretending to need only a *USA Today* when in fact I purchase four of those round scented candles that look like kaleidoscopes on the outside which I place in subtle places around my room like on the headboard on the coffee table out on the balcony and in the bathroom. I feel like I'm cheating, like this was all premeditated and not at all organic or spontaneous, but then again this feels like the smart thing to do. Besides, he's probably never had so much ambience. Which is why I feel like I sort of owe him this.

As I stand in front of my closet trying to choose the most flattering dress I realize that I am not twenty-one years old that the clothes in my closet reflect this and when I look in the full-length mirror it is obvious that I am not even close to looking twenty-one years old that I haven't been twenty-one years old in twenty-one years and suddenly I'm wondering again why this young man really wants to sleep with me. I mean what is the attraction? What is his real motive? I know! He's probably heard the rumor going around America that single women over thirty and black women in particular will fuck anything, since many of them are on that slow track. They used to count how many weeks had gone by since they'd been laid but now it's gotten up to how many years has it been and they're all freaking out because they're super-lonely and in their quest to find Mr. Perfect for years and years have yet to come to the realization that he does not exist. We who have labeled ourselves Ms. Fucking Perfect Personified have not caught on yet that our perfection is merely a figment of our very own distorted imagination and I should know because I'm in that forty-and-over club for Emotional Subversives in Denial About Everything.

What I do know deep down although I keep it secretly secret is that I am terrified at the thought of losing myself again wholeheartedly to any man because it is so scary peeling off that protective sealant that's been guarding my heart and letting somebody go inside and walk around lie down look around and see all those red flags especially when right next to your heart is your soul and then inside that is the rest of your personality puzzle pieces and they're full of flaws and in your grown-up years you have just finally started to recognize them for what they are one by one. You're trying to resolve some of these issues but you're only up to say number four and the list is too long to get into here but the mere thought of being emotionally naked again is frightening because you remember how fucked up it got the last two or three times out there. Since the world is now aware that women like us are trying to beat the clock, some of us have built this invisible fence around our hearts like those that people use to keep their dogs inside the yard—if they go past that invisible wired line they get shocked until eventually they get tired of getting electrocuted and so they sit there and watch cars and other dogs go by and sort of just stay put. This is pretty much where I am: putting, and lots of my girl-friends are too because this is the big easy that I hope Winston hasn't heard about but then again I'm sure if they get BET down here they must get Oprah too.

The only thing I'm hoping is that if he is on this kind of sympathy mission, he realizes women like me are not really desperate. Getting laid is hardly a problem—almost any man'll take some free pussy—but getting laid by some-body you want to get laid by is an entirely different issue. When we finally meet somebody we do want to lie down with we aren't feeling desperate—what we're feeling is vul-nerable, nervous and scared. Big difference. Big big dif-ference. But once again, Stella, you are like getting far too deep here for somebody who is planning to have a little sexual encounter with a boy for one single evening so like could you spare me your philosophical sociological rant-ings on the status of women and black women in particu-lar in America, okay, and let's just get us some nuggies and hope it's good and get on with this vacation? Can we do that?

Okay, so this mental masturbating kills a whole hour. I decide that reading is a good time-passer so I pick up a book without looking at the title and begin to read the words one at a time instead of in groups like I learned to do years ago in that Evelyn Wood speed-reading class that never quite worked for me except the grouping stuff. It is not working now. I lay the book down and decide that the best thing for me to do is rest since I'll be expending and I hope consuming a great deal of energy tonight.

I call the operator and ask for a wake-up call at five just

in case I doze off and I get under the covers and everything and start thinking about oh my God what if people see us what are they going to think and say? Shit. Oh so what, Stella! This is America. No it isn't America. Okay. This is the nineties and oh go to sleep girl and then I turn my attention to those waves that are still at it outside my window and I push my face deeper and deeper into the soft white pillow and close my eyes for a few minutes and when the phone rings I am startled. The operator claims it's five o'clock and when I look at my watch it is.

May as well put the video camera on fast forward because that's how quickly I jump out of bed take a shower shave my underarms and legs douche pumice-stone my heels elbows knees brush my teeth pluck a few hairs from my eyebrows put some Visine in my eyes pull my cool braids to the other side of my head and rub my Calyx lotion everywhere on my body that's brown. I do that minimum makeup routine again because to be honest I can't stand all that mess on my face and the other reason is because I always want a man even a young one to know that what he sees is what he gets.

I stand in front of the closet again since I never did decide on what to wear and realize I have quite a few Marilyn Monroe—type dresses and that I am not a reincarnation of Marilyn thank the Lord and yet I also don't want to repeat myself and plus I don't want to look like I can't wait to get out of this dress but I also don't want to look like I'm a chaperone at my son's prom either not that I brought anything like that so I choose a soft yellow linen shift that has a low neckline in front and back and comes right above my knees but it fits snugly and makes

me look like I have a real figure even though I really don't
well what I have is narrow hips and a firm set of curvy
glutes aka a big ass which runs in my family and I'll tell the
truth I don't want to lose it ever. I put on my twenty-two-
dollar strapless bra I finally found in Macy's that fits my
own personal breasts without smashing crushing them
down or upping them two sizes and it actually gives me
that ever-so-light touch of cleavage I'm seeking but only
if you look from the side.

I slip on my mustard sling-back pumps some gold hoop
earrings and when I look in the mirror I think I've got it
going on, to be honest. I just hope he thinks so too. I
hope he hasn't changed his mind. What if he's changed
his mind? What if he's come to his senses and is hiding in
his room and I go out there all dolled up and don't see
him and I'll feel stupid? This is the reason why I often
hate men. They're all alike. You can't depend on them for
shit. They're weak. I do not for the life of me understand
why God even gave them balls when most of the time they
act like they don't have any. I can see that this weak-acting
shit starts at a young age, doesn't it? Well, I am making a
mental note right now to teach Quincy how to grow up
and flex his balls as much as possible, to jump into the fire
to take risks and even if you're scared do the shit anyway.
I don't want him to act like a little pussy like this Winston
like his daddy like so many of these fellows running
around in the world who don't deserve to be called men.
What some of them most of them a lot of them really need
is a month or two at a dude ranch run by women. We're
the ones who can show these simpletons how to be men
because we raised them and for some reason perhaps they

are all suffering from ADD because they have apparently forgotten most of the necessary valuable constructive stuff we taught them as young boys which is why most of them are in dire need of a refresher course today.

I pick up my little clutch and walk to the dining room with a serious attitude because I am preparing myself for disappointment and if I happen to run into him and he's like say with some young hoochie I will just give him my vampire look like I'll get your ass later when you least expect it for setting me up like this and what exactly did you think you could do for me anyway? You probably have never even had any *real* pussy, have you, Winston? Probably never even spent the night out except at a sleepover, huh?

There he is. Sitting on the bench outside the dining room. And he's alone. He stands up when he sees me and heads my way and wow does he look more handsome this evening or what and ohmyGod he's wearing that Escape again and I am so glad I didn't wear panties which is becoming a habit for me down here but maybe I should've this time because where will this stuff go that's trickling down my leg oh shoot but thank God I have my little wipes in my purse so right after he says "Hi" and smiles I say, "Hi, Winston, can you excuse me for a second, I need to go to the ladies' room," and he says, "Are you okay?" and as I amble away like they do in the movies I say, "I'm fine, just had a little accident but it's nothing really," because I surely don't want him to think I'm on my period because he's so young and everything and he probably no way would want to do it the very first time if I'm on my period even though I know men who will go down on you when you're bleeding which I think is disgusting and I can't even bear to watch them when they do it and don't come up here acting like you want to kiss me now no way go brush and floss and Listerine and then come back and let me smell your breath first and we'll consider another kiss then but not until then.

I am ashamed of myself for getting so worked up so fast and I feel kind of slutty but I also kind of like this feeling and I'm thinking I wish I could call Delilah to tell her what I'm up to—she would probably just say, "Go for it, girl!" Don't want to call Vanessa because she'll probably make me feel even sillier than I already do and Angela would probably scold me and tell me I'll be struck by lightning for even thinking about doing something like this so I clean up my act and come out of the stall and blot my lips and say, "To hell with both of you," and since nobody's really looking I actually giggle as I head back out where Winston is still standing in the very same spot.

His hair is jet black shiny and brushed back on top and I can see his scalp on the sides where it's cut very close and he has a gold hoop in his left ear and he's wearing a real button-down-the-front shirt that's not at all tropical-looking but looks as if it could've come from like the men's department of a major department store and not where the hip-hoppers shop either and I can't tell if it's purple or brown in this light but it has some kind of speckles on it that look like the solar system or galaxies and I'm so glad he has on blue jeans because I love the way he looks in them like he doesn't care that they don't exactly fit but they certainly look good on him and God his legs just go on and on and he is wearing these black suede bucks and I like his style his taste the decisions he's made and damn is he beautiful but what's weird is that he doesn't carry himself like he's all that handsome; he stands moves as if he's just sure of himself as if he knows who he is but he just doesn't know his own power yet. I am so glad.

"Is everything okay?" he asks with real concern in his eyes.

"Fine," I say.

"Are you hungry?" he asks.

"Not really. Are you?"

He smiles blushes and shakes his head from side to side. Hey. He's got dimples! When did he get those?

"We should eat though don't you think?" I say.

"We can at least try," he says and then we both start laughing almost uncontrollably and I think we both know why we're laughing.

"Winston?"

"Yes," he says and there he goes looking at me again but this time it's like real laserlike desire is emanating from his eyes and boy is it penetrating this little area in my chest that feels just like my heart and I wish he would like stop this.

"Did you just have to wear that cologne?"

"I thought you liked it."

"I do. That's the problem. It's making me feel dizzy."

"Did I put too much on?" he asks.

"No, I don't mean it that way."

And he looks at me again as if he doesn't get it.

"Never mind," I say.

"You feel like eating some pasta?" he asks and I kind of crack up because he says it like "pesta."

"Sure," I say and we walk through the dining room, where Norris and Abby and all the rest of the social directors and all the honeymooners and the folks from the van and the ones I lie out on the beach with including old man Nate all wave to us as we walk by. I should not be doing this out in the open, I think.

"Why are you in such a hurry?" Winston asks.

"Am I?"

"Yes, you sort of sped up for some reason. What's wrong?"

"Nothing," I say and sit down at an outdoor table.

"Tell me what it is," he says, leaning forward, and when I look into his eyes I can't remember what I was going to say but then I remember: "Winston, are you sure you want to do this because if you want to back out if you want to change your mind it's okay you won't hurt my feelings because I'm a big girl a grown-up really and I'm used to disappointment so if you're having second thoughts we can just eat dinner and maybe dance a little bit and say good night and be done with it no hard feelings."

His eyes are wide and he looks like he can't believe what I just said. "Could you repeat that word for word, please?" And he leans back against his chair and waits.

I am embarrassed no end. "You know what I meant."

"Stella?"

I cannot look at him.

"Stella?"

"What?" I say but I'm still not looking at him. I am feeling like I'm in fucking high school when in fact I could be the damn principal.

"I haven't changed my mind. I have been unable to

think clearly this entire day because you have taken up all the space in my head. I am not afraid, Stella. I am not afraid of you. I am not afraid of what is happening. I am not afraid of what might happen. And I will be honest with you. I haven't been this excited about a woman in . . . well, never."

I can hardly swallow even though I have nothing in my mouth to swallow because my mouth is past dry. "I'm really flattered, Winston."

"I'm not saying it to flatter you. It's the truth."

"I'm still flattered. And I'll tell you," I say and sigh, because I hear myself say, "Winston, even though I think this is kind of ridiculous I want you to know how much I like you too and—"

"What's ridiculous?"

I'm trying not to let my eyes roll up in my head. "Do you want me to say it again?"

"Are we back to the age issue?"

"Yes. Winston, I just want you to know that I've never done anything like this before in my life."

"What do you mean by 'anything like this'?"

"Well, a few things. First of all I've never gone on a vacation and picked up a man that I don't even know."

"You haven't picked me up, Stella."

"You know what I'm saying."

He is beginning to look a little offended so I decide I better clean it up because I didn't mean that I was picking him up like some prostitute or something. "Well, you know, what I really mean is this, Winston. It's the nineties, the age of safe sex, and folks don't usually go jumping into bed with strangers anymore."

"Do I feel like a stranger to you?"

"Well, no. But I just met you yesterday, Winston, and that's what's also kind of weird."

"I'm more than willing to tell you anything you want to know about me. Just ask me."

"Okay. Tell me about your parents."

"Well, my dad's a surgeon in Kingston and my mom's an RN. I have two older sisters. Both are married. I grew up outside Kingston and went to private school and have done two years at the University of the West Indies in Kingston where I was studying biology but I did not like it which is why I took a course in food preparation and am considering perhaps studying hotel management or becoming a real chef I'm not sure even though my dad doesn't want me to do either. There. So now you know everything about me."

When I heard him say "my dad" I was tickled enough to giggle but I decided it would be in poor taste and plus I shouldn't hold his age against him. It isn't his fault he's only twenty-one years old. Is it? And the fact that he thinks he has told me everything about himself is downright touching. "Well, thanks for sharing, Winston."

He doesn't get it. "What else did you want to tell me?" he says.

"Well, Winston, I can't seem to remember now, which means it's not all that important."

A waitress appears and gives me a go-girl smirk and I look at Winston and realize that we are like out in the open and Lord what am I doing? "Do you know what kind of pesta you want?" he asks me and I spot something on the menu and point it out to our waitress and Winston says he'll have the same thing and she takes our drink order and of course I ask for my virgin piña colada and Winston who also does not drink orders his virgin strawberry daiquiri.

"So what should I know about *you?*" he asks and leans forward on his elbows.

"I like your shirt," I say.

He smiles. "Thank you and I'm listening. I mean I have shared my deepest secrets about my personal being with you and now I'm waiting to hear yours."

"Well, I've been divorced for three years."

"Do you presently have a boyfriend at home?"

"No."

If I'm not mistaken he actually looks relieved and then he looks at me like he's on his way to another level or something.

"Why not?"

"Because it's hard to find one I like."

"Why is it so hard? You're quite attractive. I would think men would be swarming around you."

"Swarming? I don't think so, Winston. First of all, looks can only get you so far and, well, I'll put it this way. I'm also kind of picky. Maybe too picky but I do date and may I continue, sir?"

He is smiling and nodding at me. He looks almost edible.

"I have an eleven-year-old son whose name is Quincy and whom I love dearly and he's my best buddy."

"That's nice to hear," he says.

"And I turn tricks for a living."

"Tricks? What kind of tricks?"

"I'm just kidding," I say. "I'm an analyst for a securities company."

He looks confused and who can blame him? "It only sounds good but in essence my job doesn't make a whole lot of sense and I wouldn't be surprised if in the next few weeks computers will have taken over."

"And what exactly does an analyst do?" he asks.

"It's kind of hard to explain but basically when people or I should say in my case businesses and cities and universities and the like want to invest their profits to make more money I basically analyze all the different areas and avenues and give them advice on where it looks like their money'll grow the fastest and the safest."

"Ohhhhh," he says, nodding his head up and down. "And do you like doing all this ana-lyzing?"

"I used to, but the thrill is gone. Been gone. It's okay, though. It's a living."

"And you studied many years to learn to do this?"

"Yep. New York University. Bachelor's and master's." I don't even want to mention my M.F.A.

"Right." He sighs as if he's putting this all together and then he looks me in the eye and says, "Well, it seems to me that if one goes to college for so many years you'd at least end up working in some field that you derive a great deal of pleasure from. Don't you think?"

"Of course I do, Winston, but sometimes your attitude changes, your needs and values change, as you get older, and what used to excite you doesn't anymore."

"So do you have this same attitude toward people when your attitude changes?"

"What do you mean?"

"I mean when you get bored or someone wears out their welcome do you treat them like you would your job? Do you just kind of settle in or do you look for a new one?"

Damn. I take a deep breath. He certainly doesn't sound or think like he's only twenty-one. And he's not fidgeting or acting hyper and as a matter of fact I'd say he's more poised than I am. I'm even more surprised by what he's saying because it means he's measuring what he sees, he's trying to see if all the pieces fit, and this is refreshing. "Well, I'm the type that sort of hangs in there until I've exhausted my resources and when I realize I've given it my best shot I move on. But this can sometimes take a while."

He's nodding his head when they bring us our pesta and salad and we both instinctively seem to want to lighten up a little bit so we simply eat tiny morsels of food and chew heartily as if we're actually tasting it and then we lay our forks down and it's only a few minutes after seven and it's obvious we are both nervous but trying to pretend like this is a normal date but we know it is everything but that and maybe we should've stuck to seven instead of six because the disco doesn't open until ten but what we do is basically sit outside the dining room and listen to the band. Of course that drummer is staring at me and Winston from across the dining room because I can see his beady little eyes glisten and the other one, the young guitar player as he turns out to be, is looking at me like I'm still a reincarnation of his old girlfriend but Winston and I go and sit on a chaise by the pool and listen to the waves and the music and just talk about Jamaica and America and then we go for a walk but not on the beach because those stupid sand fleas are out there and even though they are invisible they bite you in groups and particularly your ankles and especially if you're wearing perfume they love perfume they bite you so hard you don't feel it until moments later when you begin to scratch and then it is uncontrollable and you really could cry but you think that if you just scratch hard enough it will go away but it doesn't and all you see is red and it is blood and so you have to rub that cream on and it doesn't help all that much which is why Winston and I agree to walk over to Hedonism where they are having a Hunk Show Contest and we sit there in their open dining room/bar and watch twenty young men from all over the world model suits shorts and swimsuits. They are all gorgeous and buffed and I am surprised that people have their clothes on because it's not what I was told they did over here and of course and under normal circumstances I would probably be screaming at these guys like everybody else is but they just don't seem to have the finesse and poise and grace and beauty that Winston here has and he's not at all an exhibitionist and he certainly could be which is why I feel like the lucky one I really do.

On the walk back he takes my hand and places it inside his and really grasps it and I am not kidding I am getting chills and goosebumps all over my arms and they seem to be running down my back as if somebody's tickling me but then his hand becomes warmer and I seem to be squeezing it tighter and we walk back onto the grounds of the Castle Beach Negril and the band is packing up and so we go into the disco and the DJ is playing some pump-to-the-bump music and Winston and I don't bother to sit down but head out to the crowded dance floor where we will dance for the next two hours and where I will get drunk watching how suave and smooth he moves, unlike some twenty-one-year-olds who are rather wild but not him he moves in an unrehearsed way as if he is feeling the music and it is what is dictating how he moves and he watches me swing and sway and I don't do so bad myself I just don't do the latest dances because I don't care but then the DJ plays this hold-me-in-your-arms kind of song and in slow motion Winston sort of like automatically pulls me close to him and puts his arms around me and we rock in one small spot and I go ahead and put my arms around the small of his back and he is nice and narrow and I feel like I'm really starting to spin the way that girl does with John Travolta in that *Staying Alive* movie and Winston smells so good and his chest is firm and his arms are so long and they are making me feel like I'm inside something good something warm safe go ahead and relax enjoy him Stella it's okay and his shoulders are so wide and I am looking at this hair sticking out above the V in his shirt and he smells so good and he feels so good and I hope this song lasts for at least another hour and I swear when I feel his hands squeeze my waist and he pushes me out and away from him a little bit and looks down at me and smiles and then kisses me on my forehead I feel like I'm on some kind of drug that causes euphoria because I am like floating right now but when he starts to pull me back against his chest and holds me as close as I can get but as softly as he can I finally realize that Winston is not at all a boy that he is not my toy for the night he is in fact a real man.

It is now about twelve-thirty and the dance floor is

empty with the exception of me and Winston. I think we not only have enjoyed dancing together but have both been stalling because we are kind of scared. But scared or not, the place will be closing soon and we have to get out of here and besides I'm not *that* scared really I want to do this so on a Warren G song I take Winston by the hand and say, "Are you ready to go yet?" and he says, "I've *been* ready I just thought you wanted to dance more," and I shake my head back and forth and we both smile and he takes my hand as we walk through the game room and out to the path that leads to my room and when we get there I open the door and walk in first and then I really feel like I'm in high school because I can't remember what I'm supposed to do next.

My heartbeat is way over my heart rate zone and if I had my monitor on it would've been beeping for like the past two hours. I am not a stranger to seduction it's just that I'm used to being the seducee and not the seducer but I can do this I can show him what to do, so after I press on Seal of course I turn to him and say, "Have a seat, Winston," and he sort of walks over to me all tall and everything and puts his arms on my bare shoulders and bends down and says—not whispers—in my ear, "You are really beautiful," and before I can answer I feel something warm and heavenly land on my lips but this can't be right this can't be oh God what is he doing he is pressing his lips against mine so softly that I am feeling like one of those velvet paintings and oh no he's not supposed to be able to make me feel like oh God he is kissing me like he has been wanting to do this for a long time but he is not frantic he is not pressing in hard and now his lips are whispering they are just barely brushing mine and please don't stop Winston I have been waiting a long time for a man to kiss me like this like he means it and who taught you how to wait a minute hold it stop I say in my head and push him away for a minute.

"What's wrong?" he asks.

I want to say don't you get it? You are like kissing me like you know what you're doing you are like kissing me like you know where my weak spots all are and your kisses are reducing them to nothing I am losing my strength but please kiss me again because you feel like what I need what's been missing like I've been waiting years all my life to have your lips touch mine like this, but all I say is, "Winston, your kiss is. . ."

"What?" He looks worried and I realize I am overreacting.

"I didn't expect this."

"What?"

"For you to be such a good kisser."

"You're the good kisser."

"No. You're the good kisser and it's making me weak. I wish I could but I can't lie about it. Look at me," I say and I feel like he must surely be able to see steam coming from my entire body or at least he can see how I'm disintegrating into a vapor.

"Feel my heart," he says and places my hand over it and sure enough it's pounding away. "It feels you," he says.

"I want you to take advantage of me," I hear myself say.

And he looks at me as if to say you've got this all wrong it is not about taking advantage of you and then he kisses me again and I am turning into mush inside and I haven't felt this in a gazillion years since maybe college and I feel like I could cry because I've been waiting to feel this magic I've forgotten how the magic feels and I've been waiting for him I have read about the power of a kiss but when he puts his tongue in my mouth he is not frantic he is slow-dancing with mine he is sending me a message and I'm getting it he is telling me a story and I am loving every word and when he holds me tighter he is telling me he wants to be closer can I get closer and so I wrap my tongue around his as if I'm trying to protect it from something and I move in deeper and I want him to know that it is not just the kiss that is moving me it is you the kisser the man behind the kiss and I have no choice I shift my shoulder blade under his armpit so as to feel like we are inside each other but he already knows that I can't get close enough to him and because he is helping me find a position where we will be able to blend once and for all and because it is impossible in what feels like slow motion we begin to search explore chins ears elbows eyebrows arms fingertips wrists but always back to our lips where something passes from him to me and me to him and we are spinning now and my lips feel like a hot peach between my legs feels like a hot peach and Winston please don't stop because I don't care that it's a cliché but I feel like a butterfly and I don't want you to stop making me flutter but he kisses me on my cheek and I kiss him on his cheek and he rubs his cheek-bone against my cheekbone and he says, "Are you okay?" and it is difficult for me to answer that question because I am trembling now I mean really trembling and I can only nod and he says, "Are you sure?" and I say something stupid like, "Isn't it hot in here to you?" and he takes those hands and brushes over my braids and holds me again until like three more Seal songs play and I swear I'm about ready to cry for real and if I knew him better I would and when I feel him unzip my dress I am scared but he does it so delicately so gently that I don't even realize I'm standing there in my strapless bra and no panties and he holds me to him again and rubs his hands up and down the back of my body and he says, "You certainly don't feel like I'd expect any forty-two-year-old woman to feel," and I say, "But I am," and he steps back and looks at me and I feel like Cinda-fucking-rella and he says, "And you don't look like any forty-two-year-old woman I've ever seen," and I say, "But I am," and he says, "Well, you feel better than any twenty-year-old girl," and I say, "But I'm not," and he says, "I know and I'm glad and you are so sweet and so lovely and Stella if we just stand here for a while would that be okay with you because I love the way you feel like this and I just really want to take you in," and I am really slipping away here by the second but I say in a little tiny voice, "Okay," and he holds me even closer so that I feel a heartbeat in his belly I can feel the hair on his belly brush against sink into my belly if that's possible until somehow it is minutes or it could be hours later and we are lying next to each other on the bed and somehow we have gotten his clothes off and he is kissing my nose and shoulders and he is still moving so very slowly and I'm so very glad that he's not rushing and if I'm not mistaken it feels as if he knows exactly what he's oh my God those lips are on my breasts oh God he's kissing them the right way and somebody please help me where did he come from please don't stop and oh please do stop before I scream but now his mouth is back against mine and I hear him unwrap his condom and he whispers in my ear, "Is it okay now?" and I'm thinking he is so polite he is certainly a considerate one and my answer is a light kiss and when he finds his way in he helps me glide and he guides me to his beat which is so slow and undulating and I feel him hold on to me until we are moving like those waves outside the balcony and I am lost at sea until I feel him squeeze me as if I'm falling overboard and he whispers, "Oh Stel-la," in my ear and I find myself succumbing surrendering to him and I say, "Win-ston, what are you doing to me?" and he sighs and whispers, "Oh Stel-la, why are you doing this to *me?*" and I say, "What?" and he moans, "Stel-la," and I am feeling like hot foam and I moan and sigh, "Win-ston," and we both squeeze each other as if we have been looking for each other for a long time and when we rest our heads against each other's wet skin the only thing I think we understand is that this is where we've always wanted to be and now we are here.

When I wake up his aroma pervades not only my pillows but the whole room. He was definitely here, I think. It was not a dream. No. It was real. He was real. I shower in lukewarm water and decide on thick white running shorts and matching top which I put on in slow motion. The foam soles on my sneakers are a nice cushion as I jump two and three steps at a time and head toward the beach. This morning I seem to float along the shore, as if my feet don't feel the sand at all. The sun has just barely risen and yet the sky is already royal blue and there are absolutely no clouds whatsoever. The ocean is serene, no waves. I can't believe it as I walk into the water with my sneakers on and see a society of silver fish swimming around my ankles. They are so beautiful that I stand there watching them for a long time.

I can feel the heat from the sun on my shoulders as I walk back to the beach, take my sneakers and socks off and sit down on the sand. I am the only one out here. It is my beach. When I look out at the ocean where it drops off and disappears it feels as if I could run on top of the water to the very edge and what I would find would probably be a waterfall. This is how weightless I feel right now. As if somehow in the middle of the night my soul was visited by something divine something—I don't know—but whatever it was and whatever happened I feel different today than I did yesterday. Lighter, as if a breeze could go right through me. Amazing.

And then I think I smell him. I turn to look and he's not there and I can only smile. And to think. I didn't have to teach him anything. I told him so before he left. "I didn't have to teach you anything, Winston," and he sort of chuckled and said, "Oh yes you did," and I said, "What?" and he said, "I've never felt such tenderness before, and boy," he said with a sigh, and he was about to say something else but he just rolled me back over on top of him and I kissed him gently and said, "I could kiss you forever," and he kissed me back and said, "You can, you should, I would like that," and then I heard myself say, "Do you have a girl-friend?" and he said, "No," and I found that a little hard to believe and so I said, "Why not?" and he said, "Because I haven't met anyone I really like," and I said, "Come on, Winston," and he said, "What? I'm serious," and since he sounded like he was I said, "Okay, so what qualities are you looking for in a girlfriend?" because I was just curious and I wanted to know if he'd really thought about this and he said, "Well, one thing I know for sure is that she'll defi-nitely be older," and I sort of picked my head up and looked down at him and once again he was wearing that I'm-not-kidding-you look and I said, "But why does she have to be older?" and he said, "Because girls my age are silly. All they're looking for is someone who has a nice car and lots of money and is willing to spend it all on them."

"Well, that's true of a lot of older women," I said, laughing. "At least in America. But I'm not one of them."

He laughed too. "In Jamaica money and status are everything."

"How so?"

"Well, where you live and what kind of house you live in is very important. It matters. A great deal. And the women here? A lot of them don't work. They stay at home and mind the children and cook. The husbands earn the living."

"Well, I wouldn't want to be in that position. I can and do pay my own bills," I said.

"I know. You're different," he said and I found myself kissing him again and it wasn't like I was even trying.

"So what else?"

"I don't know." It felt like he didn't want to talk about it anymore, as if I was doing too much talking, but then he said, "But I hope she'll be a lot like you."

"Me?"

"Yes. You. You're outgoing and I would have to say very brave because you came to Jamaica all alone and you didn't know anyone here. You seem smart and you don't act as if you're playing games because you came straight out and told me what you wanted to do and here we are and it's kind of nice, you know, not to have to play any games."

"What kind of games have you played before?"

"None really, but I've watched other people. Then again, there are some girls, you know, they pretend to like you but they really don't."

"You ever been in love, Winston?"

"I don't think so."

"You don't think so?"

"How would I know?"

A fabulous question. "Well." I sighed, because I'd never actually told anyone what I thought being in love feels like and it required some thought. "I'd say it's when you sort of crave being around a person because he makes you feel extraordinarily good and your adrenaline seems higher and everything moves at a faster rate and you can't seem to get enough of that person."

"Nooo, I've never felt like that."

"Have you ever been hurt?"

"My feelings have been hurt. Yes. Sure."

"You have any pets, Winston?"

"What?"

"Pets? You know. Animals that hang around your house and you give them a name and perhaps feed them in their very own dish."

He laughed. "Yes. I've got two dogs of no special breed and four lovebirds."

"Would you consider yourself an animal lover?"

"Yes."

"Have you ever lost a pet that you loved?"

The expression on his face changed. "Yes. I had a horse for six years and it got some kind of disease and had to be put to sleep. That kind of messed me up."

"You had your own horse?"

"Yeah. My parents own ten of them, but Simeon was mine."

"So you're a good rider?"

"Used to be. I'm not as fond of horses as I once was. What about you? You look like an animal lover."

"Well, my son and I have a dog, a cat and some fish." There was now a sudden silence. "So," I said.

"So," he said. "What are your plans for tomorrow?"

"Parasailing," I said.

He nodded and kissed me again. He could be habit-forming, I thought, as I looked at him. If only he weren't so damn young.

"What about afterwards?" he asked.

"Why? What are you gettin' at, darlin'?" I said in a southern accent, and he cracked up.

"Would you like to have dinner again?"

"What exactly do you mean by 'dinner'?"

He looked confused. "I mean we could go into town. Get away from Castle Beach. I'd like to see you in another setting. Under different circumstances. This place is beginning to feel closed in, no?"

"Yes. But you know what, Winston?"

"What?"

"I think we should do *this* again. Don't you?"

"Definitely," he said with a smirk and then we both burst out laughing as he squeezed me tighter and I pushed my fingers through his hair over and over and over until the back of his head was resting in my palms.

"So let's skip dinner."

"Are you sure?" he asked.

"Yes. *You* can be my dinner."

He chuckled. "So does that mean *you'll* be *my* dessert?"

"Absolutely," I said. "Absolutely."

"All right," he said and we lay there awhile longer, but because I was a guest at the hotel and if anyone saw him coming out of my room it could ruin his chances of working here, he got up in the middle of the night, put his clothes on and gave me another of those luscious please-don't-go kisses and left quietly. I looked at the cold candles and giggled out loud because I was glad I hadn't needed them after all. I then buried my face as deeply as I could in the pillows and sheets so I could smell him all over around and through that white cotton until I started feeling all marshmallowy inside and then it hit me that if I wasn't mistaken I'd been turned out by a twenty-one-year-old boy!

And now, as I gather up my wet socks and sneakers and head back toward my room, I am shaking my head in total astonishment. And who do I pass? Old man Nate. He looks better, like he should always get up early and do something.

"Hey, good-looking," he says.

"How goes it, Nate?"

"Not as good as you, I can see that. What—you been out here running and got your shoes wet?"

"Sort of."

"Having a good time?"

"Oh yes, I'm having a great time."

"Un-hun," he says like he's been a Peeping Tom or something.

"You going to Karaoke Night tonight in the piano bar?"

"I'm not sure. I hadn't heard about it."

"It's always fun."

"But I thought you just got here, Nate."

He chuckles proudly and I can't help but watch that fat gut of his writhe. "I told you, this is my eighth time down here in the last three years. I was one of their first guests after they built this place. I love it here."

"I do too," I say and begin walking. "Maybe I'll see you later," I say.

"Well, if you're going to the beach today, better get out here early. It's supposed to rain. Maybe even have a little thunderstorm today."

I simply nod even though I'd love to say: Excuse me, Mr. Weather God, but this is Jamaica. Not America. It is early July. It is summertime here. Not the rainy season. Nate doesn't know what the hell he's talking about.

After my shower I change and go to the dining room and this place is beginning to feel like home. I see the familiar faces and some new ones as I stand in line to get my Belgian waffle which the young brother who cooks them seems instinctively or predictably to know I want as I approach the long table and pass right by an assortment of other foods which I totally ignore. I look around for an empty table and do not see Winston anywhere and then I chuckle because I'm thinking he's sleeping in because he's young and still growing.

I eat my breakfast alone which is kind of nice and then I gather up my towels and head for the beach. I find my chaise and put my tote with all my junk in it underneath and one of the workers says to me, "When are you gonna snorkel with us, mon? You look like you love the water every day, come on and snorkel with us today."

"What time?"

"Nine-tirty and one-tirty."

I look at my watch. It's nine-twenty. "Maybe later, or tomorrow morning."

"I'll be looking for you, mon. And wear that bathing suit."

He laughs as he drags the boat out into the water. I lie there for the next hour or so and though it is so hot so early it's hard to believe when I slide my suit down that I am again two shades darker. I turn over on my back and fall asleep. What wakes me is the volleyball game. It is eleven-fifteen. Ben the Canadian sees my head pop up and he yells, "Stella! Get over here! We need you!"

"I'm coming, I'm coming," and I get up.

I play hard and well. The members of the other team, who weren't here the last time I played, are automatically assuming that because I'm a woman I'm going to play like one is supposed to play and I guess a woman isn't supposed to be strong or athletically inclined however athletic she may look, so they do not expect me to serve or hit the ball as consistently as I do. They probably thought the first couple of times were a fluke but when our team kicks their butt thanks to a few of my very own Monica Seles—like serves, a major statement is made and I think registers clearly on their little weenies.

We play until twelve-thirty, at which time I go back into the water, and as I'm standing there something hits me. I did sleep with a twenty-one-year-old boy last night, didn't I? And I did immerse myself in him like he was a real man and I have been thinking about him all morning and I did ask him if he would want to do this again tonight, didn't I? I did. You did, Stella. Yes, you did. What if he wakes up this morning thinking, Oh my God what did I do last night with that old woman? Why did I say I'd meet her old ass again tonight? All I wanted was some pussy and now she's like wanting to see me again and this is a resort and there is no way for me to hide or get away from her which is why I'm staying in my room until I know she's come in from her jog and had her breakfast and I will eat lunch before she finishes her volleyball game or parasailing. That's what he's probably thinking, I think as I head toward the dining room.

Well, not to worry, Winston. I'll let you off the hook. It was good and everything but I'll get by without getting some again. I think. One more time would've been nice but hey, you're young and footloose and fancy-free and you don't need some old broad coming down here on vacation treating you like some gigolo or something, so I can like back off, no problem, mon.

I see him sitting at a table, a hundred or so white ceiling fans spinning high above his head, and I notice the mountain of food on his plate and laugh. If this stuff weren't free would he be eating so much? He seems to be looking around the room and when he spots me he smiles and I smile because to be honest I was thinking that if he didn't see me I could pretend that I never saw him and maybe take my plate outside and let him completely off the hook and then this evening I just wouldn't show up and since I never told him my last name he wouldn't have to phone and wouldn't just show up at my room, at least I don't think he'd do something like that, but I wave to him and he motions me to come over so I do.

"Hi, Winston," I say, standing behind a chair.

He is looking at me kind of strange, as if something is

behind his eyes, some kind of story, but it's clear that he is trying to figure out how to tell me that even though he had a good time last night he can't come tonight, so I'm like ready for this.

"Would you join me for lunch?" he says.

"I'm really not that hungry," I say.

"Well, would you sit down for a few minutes?"

I hesitate for a minute, thinking, Oh he wants to tell me this shit sitting down, well hey no problem mon, but I do not take my yellow tote with the furry monkey from my shoulder.

"Are you all right?" he asks. He looks worried.

"Sure. How about you?"

"I'm fine," he says. "Fine."

"Good," I say and start looking around the dining room.

"You look like something's on your mind," he says. "And it doesn't look good. Did I do something?"

"No, you didn't do anything."

"Were you not so satisfied last night?"

I want to say, Are you crazy? Satisfied is putting it mildly. How about ecstatic? How about jubilant? How about calling me Ms. Fucking Enchantment? But instead I say, "Yes, I was thoroughly satisfied last night. What about you, Winston?"

He puts his fork down and looks at me all serious and says, "I have never had such a good time with a woman before in my life."

"And what does that mean?"

"It means I had a splendid time with you, Stella. You made me feel something deep and rich inside. Spicy." He is looking at me from the corners of those black slits he has for eyes and nodding his head up and down as if he is agreeing with himself.

All I can think is, Spicy? I guess I like spicy as long as he doesn't mean like jerk chicken spicy. "I'm glad to hear that, Winston, but . . ."

"But what?"

"Well, I was thinking. I mean I know we had a good time and everything last night and I know I surely did but it's daylight now and I just wanted you to know if you have like come to your senses and don't really want to do this again tonight you can just tell me and it'll be okay."

"Are you serious?"

"Very."

"I can't wait to see you again tonight. I couldn't wait to see you this morning. Do you know how long I've been sitting here waiting for you?"

I am like totally fucking touched. This kind of honesty is exactly what a woman wants needs to hear from a man. But why couldn't he be at least thirty-five? Shoot, thirty. I mean really. "Really, Winston?"

"Really."

"Well, can I ask you something?"

"Sure."

"What's your father like?"

"What do you mean exactly?"

"I mean does he look anything like you and is he happy with your mom or what?"

He looks offended and I can't believe I even said this. "My parents are very happy. Why do you ask?"

"I didn't mean it the way you think I meant it."

"Yes you did."

"No I didn't."

"I just don't want you to think I'm like taking this too seriously."

He looks even more offended now.

"What do you mean by 'this'?"

"You know."

"No, I don't know. Do you mean the sex or do you mean me?"

I can see that I'm not saying the right thing and what I am saying is being misconstrued but then again it isn't but all I'm doing once again in my life is protecting myself from what? A twenty-one-year-old or my own feelings? Which one is it, Stella? "Winston, I'm sorry. I'm just a little nervous because I really enjoyed being with you last night. I enjoy being with you period and it's just that I'm— let's face it—I'm so much older than you are and I'm on vacation and you really made me feel totally beautiful and sensuous and like a floating lily pad last night and I could kiss you right now and hug you which is why I'm feeling totally ridiculous and can you understand my position?"

He is smiling. "Not to worry, Stella. You should relax and not make everything so hard for yourself. I'm feeling very good about you and this day can't go by fast enough, you know?"

I believe him.

"So are you about to go parasailing?"

"Yep. What about you? How are you spending your afternoon?"

"Oh." He sighs. "I'll probably watch TV all day."

"*All* day?"

"Yes. I don't have any special plans, so why not?" He hunches and then drops his shoulders.

If I'm not mistaken it looks as if he was hoping I'd join him and he also seems a little disappointed that I'm going parasailing or that I didn't invite him but if he liked the beach I would love him to come with me but I'm not about to ask him if what he really wants to do is watch TV all day because it could very well be that he does in fact have other plans and he just doesn't want to tell me about them so I'll just go on about my business like I planned.

I stand up and readjust my tote on my shoulder. For some reason he suddenly looks lonely sitting there.

"So what time is good for you?" he asks.

"I don't care," I say.

"Stella, I don't want you to feel obligated."

"Winston, I don't . . . Look, I think we're both just tripping about this whole thing, and let's just have some fun, okay?"

He nods in agreement.

"Can I tell you something else?" I say.

"Sure," he says.

"Last night I made love to you without forgetting that you were a twenty-one-year-old boy."

"Really," he says.

"Yep. But tonight I'll make love to you as if you're a thirty-five-year-old man."

"Meaning?"

"Meaning I'm going to ignore our age difference and treat you like a real man."

"I wasn't aware you thought of me any other way," he says.

I just give him a look.

"Okay, I get it. So what time?"

"You pick the time," I say.

"Now," he says and starts laughing. "Forget about that silly parasailing. But if you must . . . I liked six o'clock yesterday. Would that be all right with you today? We would have lots of time."

"Six is fine, Winston. But I have a question."

"Shoot."

"What is it you want to do with me that will require lots of time?"

He begins to blush. He is so cute. He is so sweet. God, I could just eat him up right now. I could I could. "You'll see," he says. "Let me surprise you."

At that I push the chair all the way under the table and we give each other these glowing smiles. I walk away headed in the wrong direction and feel as if I'm on one of those magic carpets and that I'm like iridescent or something and when I get back out onto the beach I drift down to where the parasailing boats are and I notice that there are thick gray clouds forming in the sky and I hear this rumbling noise above my head and then I feel these little drops of water fall from the sky and I say, "Shit," and as they begin to gather up momentum I head toward rush back to my room.

By the time I fall across the bed to catch my breath it is pouring so hard I can hardly see the ocean at all and I hear this crackling noise and this is really beautiful I think as I open the doors to my balcony and lie across the bed, where I can no longer smell Winston because the maids have changed the linen which kind of pisses me off but when I close my eyes and go back to last night he is right here next to me with his arms around me and I can smell him oh yes I can and I inhale him over and over again and it is so peaceful in here and it feels like the kind of afternoon when you turn on the TV and watch *On the Waterfront* or *Casablanca* or something with Jimmy Cagney or Sidney Poitier in it and you curl up between crisp white sheets and forget the TV is even on and if he were here we could pretend we are in love and that we are made for each other and regardless of what is and what isn't I'm so glad I came here to this island to vacation and nobody has to know that I am already secretly craving this young man but I can like keep this to myself which is why I close my eyes tighter because I wish he were really here on top of or underneath or beside me but pretending is not quite the same that's for sure which is why I want the real man not the dream and in a perfect world he would be here and it would be fine and we wouldn't have to worry about anything except how we feel no age no whatevers.

I hear a knock on the door. I sit up and I look at my watch and it is three o'clock. It must be the housekeeper but they've been here already and I am naked for no particular reason and I grab my bathrobe and walk to the door and say, "Who is it?" and I hear his voice and I sort of fall against the built-in dresser because I cannot believe that I have willed him here and when I open the door he is standing there so brown and wet and handsome and those lush green banana plants and fuchsia flowers are framing his tall body and through his T-shirt I can see his skin the curve of those shoulders. The hair on his legs is smooth and slick. His toes glisten inside those blue

Birkenstocks and I am like turning into a believer again but all I can think of to say is, "Hello, Winston," and he says, "I'm sorry for coming by without phoning but I left my watch here last night and I just realized it and I didn't know your last name because you never told me and Stella, I've got some bad news."

I don't like the sound of those last words.

"Well, it's not really *bad* bad news but I have to leave Castle Beach today in an hour's time."

I feel like I am being harpooned or something but I can handle this I knew he was full of doo-doo and I say, "Come on in, Winston."

Coming in the door he ducks and he shouldn't be what he is who he is whatever he is and I shouldn't care what he is who he is but I do and I wish I didn't and I wish I could stop this just turn everything to the Off position. He sits down on the edge of the bed and I walk over to the television and spot his watch on the table right next to it. I hand it to him. He is looking at me very strangely. As if he thinks he knows me from somewhere else and he's trying to place me or something.

"Were you napping?" he asks.

"Sort of."

"It's raining pretty hard," he says nervously.

I change my voice to a no-nonsense let's-cut-to-the-chase tone. "So what's going on, Winston? Talk to me."

He is trying to get his watch on and having trouble so I help him and he looks at me and says, "I got hired at Windswept you know the resort right down the road a ways and they want me to start on Monday and I have to go home right away to gather up all my things because I'll be living there and I'm going to be assistant to the head chef and it's only until September but it's a start and sooo," he says as his voice drops two octaves, "I have to leave today, Stella, and I was really looking forward to our time together tonight but I have to go home."

Fuck you, Winston, I'm thinking. This is the best one I've heard yet but I am a grown-up a big girl a woman actually and I didn't come to Negril Jamaica to play any silly childish games with a boy so I say, "No problem, Winston. You do what you have to do."

He can tell I'm upset I guess because when he puts his hand on my shoulder I jerk away as if he's poisonous.

"I'm sorry," he says.

"Me too, Winston. Look," I say and move away from him until the wall prevents me from going any farther. "I hope this isn't a game you're playing because you're having second thoughts or you got cold feet about being with me tonight because I told you earlier that I was trying to let you off the hook if you didn't have the guts to come right out and tell me."

"Stella, I don't have cold feet and I'm telling you the truth. Believe me. I'm probably more disappointed than you are but this position is hard to come by and it is important and I'm sorry that I have to leave even though I wish I could be in both places at once but my parents have sent a car for me and it'll be here in less than an hour. Can't you understand my dilemma?"

He looks like he's pleading with me to understand, like he is in fact telling the truth, so I take a deep breath and decide that maybe he is, but still, where does that leave me? "Good luck in your new job, Winston. It's been very nice meeting you. And I'll look you up if I ever come back to Jamaica," and I head toward the door.

He sits there on the edge of the bed for a few more seconds and then stands up. The rain is really coming down now. This is feeling like I'm in the middle of a Saturday matinee movie and my man is about to go off to war and I'm about ready to say, "Be careful sweetheart," and "Please come back to me," and then I'd like break down which is why I am not enjoying this silly role and I wish I could like turn this channel to like Nick at Nite or something maybe even Annette Funicello when she was a little girl a Mouseketeer on the Mickey Mouse Club or how about Barney whom I have hated from day one but that's what I could use right now Barney singing I love you You love me We're a happy famil . . . no, to hell with Barney too, because all of you, you are all into ranting and raving about so much love all the fucking time and it is enough to get on anybody's nerves when there is no love in your world so just fuck you Barney just fuck you Annette and fuck you too, Winston!

He is standing in front of me now and he is so lanky and he has that Escape on of course just to bother me and I am not inhaling it right now period and I wish he would like hurry up and leave and stand outside to say whatever it is he has left to say, so I sort of put all my weight on one leg like I'm about to kick his butt or like I'm not even worried or concerned about what he has to say if he has anything else to say that is. So I'm like waiting for him to move. "I want very much to see you before you leave, Stella."

"Oh, really."

"Yes, really."

"And just how are we supposed to do that? Am I supposed to like run down to Windswept and wait around in the kitchen for you?"

I am hurting his feelings I can see that but this is not fair but life has never been fair has it Stella stop acting like a spoiled rotten little brat when you are in fact forty-two years old and you are simply on vacation and you have slept with a twenty-one-year-old boy who has—tell the truth—turned you completely out and now he is leaving and you like cannot deal with this.

"I'll have some time off during the day and I'm serious, I would like very much to see you before you leave."

"But why?" He's getting somewhat agitated, I can see that, so I try to clean it up before he has a chance to answer. "I mean look, Winston, you're just starting the job. How do you know you'll be able to get away?"

"Because we get two hours of free time each evening."

"Wow. Two whole hours."

"It's all I'll have," he says.

"I leave on Thursday," I say.

"Well, I'll be working twelve to fourteen hours and my first day is Monday but I'll make every effort to be here then, but definitely before Wednesday."

"And what if you can't?"

"I will," he says. "I will."

He bends down and kisses me puts his arms around me and holds me like he loves me or something and I kiss him and squeeze him run my hand up and down the small of his back like I love him or something and then he smiles at me and I see him walk out into the rain and in that split second as he vanishes from my eyesight and I close the door I realize that I am right this very moment already yearning craving longing for him and it also dawns on me that the last time I felt like this I *was* in love and I wonder could I do I love Winston but I couldn't because I don't really even know him and he is entirely and unquestionably unequivocally irrevocably too young and I am simply on this exotic island and maybe this is an oasis or something or maybe I'm under some kind of Jamaican spell because I am already aching at the thought of not seeing him again which is what feels like is going to be the case because I can't count how many times I've wanted something so much and didn't get it and I can easily count how many times I've loved a man and couldn't have him couldn't keep him for one reason or another and I can't count how many wishes fantasies dreams desires hopes I've had that have never come true because if I have learned anything in my forty-two years it's this: whenever things feel too good to be true it's usually because they are.

Okay. So when it stops raining I get dolled up for dinner like I've been doing and I go to the dining room and fill my plate up with something anything and the Canadians come to my table and Ben says, "Stella, are you going to karaoke tonight?" and I look up at them in the somnambulant manner which seems to have taken over my whole being since this afternoon and I say, "What time?"

Sasha is smiling as usual and looking more and more like I Dream of Jeannie because her hair is in a ponytail perched on top of her head and hanging down in these long blond swirls and Ben is ogling me like say yes and then she says, "Come, Stella. For fun," and I'm thinking, What the hell, I have no date tonight no plans nothing except this, so I say, "Okay. But what time does it start?"

To my surprise Sasha says, clearly, "Nine o'clock," and her husband gives her a big squeeze.

"She's getting better every day," he says, and there she goes again with that plastered smile.

After I fill up on whatever it was I ate I head toward the game room and play the slot machines for about twenty minutes and then Norris comes over.

"Hi, Stella," he says. "So I guess you know that Winston's gone," he says, and gives me this satisfied look.

"Yes, I know," I say. I've been wondering all along but didn't want to think too much about it but I wonder if Norris is gay because he is almost too sweet for my tastes and now it seems he's a little too concerned about my interest in Winston.

"It's really great he got the job, don't you think?" He looks at me out of the corner of his eye as if he's hoping to find evidence of disappointment in mine.

"Oh yes. I think it's great. A great opportunity."

"He won't be back," he says.

"I know that, Norris."

"You guys were hitting it off there though for a while, hey?"

"He's a nice kid," I say.

"Yeah, well, anyway you're coming to the disco after karaoke?"

"I don't know, Norris."

"Oh come on, Stella. It'll be fun. Karaoke is always fun and Bevon the DJ has already told me he will play 'Shy Guy' and 'Crazy' by Seal just for you."

"How sweet," I say and realize I have used up all my coins, that it's hot as hell in here and I have not won anything.

I go back to my room and remember I have not talked to my son in quite a few days and that I have also not thought about him all that much if at all until now and as I reach to pick up the phone I realize I cannot call him but I decide to leave a message on his dad's answering machine anyway and all I say is that I am in Jamaica and I am having a wonderful time and I miss you and I hope you will be able to bring some fish home but if not we can always get some from Safeway.

I decide it's time to call my sisters and I just pick up the phone and dial a number and wait to see which one answers. "Hi," I say.

"Girl, what took you so fucking long to call me I'm like been worried about you and shit thinking maybe your plane crashed or you got kidnapped or something but since you didn't what's up? You having fun got any yet are the men fine or what?"

"Vanessa, stop it. First of all, Negril is gorgeous and I'm having a great time. I needed this vacation in a major way. Have you been feeding the fish, Dr. Dre and Phoenix?"

"Yes, I've fed the little critters but Paco's been doing it too so if they're like waddling or floating on top of the water all puffed up and shit when you get back don't blame me. So what's going on, Sis? Tell me something good. Tell me something nasty!"

"You won't even believe it if I tell you."

"What what *what?*"

"Girl, I slept with a twenty-one-year-old boy."

I can hear her laughing uncontrollably into the phone. She finally gathers her composure and starts to chuckle, and then I join in, and when we are finally out of laughter she says, "Hold up a minute. Now repeat that again. Please."

"I said I did it with a twenty-one-year-old, and it was good and he was rather amazing but he got a job and had to leave and I kind of liked him, Vanessa."

"You can't *even* be serious? Wait a minute. No. I like the part about fucking him. Let's go there. What was it like, tell me all the details, but what do you mean you 'kind of liked him'?"

"Well, I didn't like just *fuck* him."

"Oh, don't tell me you guys like *made love* and shit."

"We did. That's exactly what we did."

"You fucked him, Stella. Get real. Is he Jamaican?"

"Yep."

"So is the rumor true or what?"

"I don't know."

"What do you mean you don't know? You didn't see it? Well, you had to feel it."

"No I didn't see it and yes I felt it and all I can say is that it felt—what difference does it make what size it is? That is not the point I'm trying to make here."

"Yeah, well, just what point might that be?"

"The point is that he is very nice and manly in more ways than in bed."

"Are you gonna get some more or not because Lord knows your dead ass could use as much as you can get. So are you like turnt out, girl? Did you have to go all the way to Jamaica to get your groove back on by a . . . how old is he again? Did you really say twenty-one?"

"Well, actually he won't be twenty-one for a couple of months."

"Wow. Like there's a big fucking difference, huh! Anyway all I can say is *You go, girl!!!*"

"Vanessa?"

"What?"

"Don't tell Angela. She won't get it."

"Get what?"

"She's so . . . you know."

"Say no more. I know how to keep my mouth shut but you know she's worried as all hell about you, so you should call her for a hot minute."

"I will after I finish talking to you."

"I need to ask you a big favor, Sis."

"What now, Vanessa?"

"Don't say it like that, damn. You have the right to say no."

"First tell me what it is. You're already driving my car."

"Can I borrow a thousand to fifteen hundred until I get my income tax refund?"

"Would it be an invasion of privacy if I asked for what?"

"No problem. I'm behind in a few bills."

"What else is new, Vanessa?"

"My car insurance is about to lapse."

"So I shouldn't even ask why you're behind, should I?"

"Same old same old. Checks don't stretch but so far."

"You said when you get your income tax refund. Now tell me something. Is it July?"

"I filed late. I'm good for it, Stella. Just let me know if you'll do it so I can write this check."

"Wait till I get back. But you know you still owe me close to six hundred from Christmas, or did we forget?"

"We haven't forgotten."

"Don't, Vanessa. I am not a bank. Got it?"

"Got it. Now," she says, sounding relieved, "are you like blacker or what?"

"About four shades. You could say I'm bronzed. How's Chantel?"

"Too grown. But she's fine."

"And work?"

"Motherfuckers still dying left and right. I'm about tired of working in ER really. All these gangbangers killing each other and shit is getting old. I can't take too much more of it. I'm serious."

"Well, lots of their stupid-ass parents are baby boomers like the majority of adult Americans which means they should've been hip to Malcolm and Martin and they should've had sense enough to teach their kids—especially their sons—what's up and if they had've these kids probably wouldn't be out there blowing each other's brains out stabbing each other like death is a joke like they're going to get a chance to do this again and if they like made an audiotape of *The Autobiography of Malcolm X* required listening—since they won't *read* anything—in say third grade maybe these kids would know that the war is outside not inside, don't you think?"

"I love you, Stella. You should've been an evangelist in a church for the fucking profane. But anyway, Sis, I've gotta go. Gotta clock in. Send me a postcard and enjoy that young man!"

"I will," I say but just as I'm about to hang up I hear her yell out: "Take one little vacation and in a matter of days you turn into Sally the Slut!"

"You go straight to hell, Vanessa." I try to wipe the smirk off my face. "And I love you too."

I stare at the phone because I am not in the mood for talking to Miss Tiddledywinks but she might be on the verge of a nervous breakdown or probably just itching to call 911 in Jamaica so I dial her number praying she's at like Target or Strouds or the Price Club picking out new eyelet comforters or something but when she answers I change my tone. "Angela?"

"It's about time you called. Why didn't you call when you first got there so somebody would know you arrived safely? Are you all right?"

"I'm fine. Damn. If you didn't get any telegrams, that should've told you I arrived safely."

"Forget it, Stella. It's simply called consideration. That's all. Are you having any fun or what?"

"I'm having a ball."

"Have you met any interesting people?"

"Yes."

"With or without clothes?"

"Well, both. Sort of."

"You didn't, Stella."

"Yes I did, Angela."

"What is with this Jamaican business that makes undressing so compulsory?"

"Don't let it worry you, Angela. I just wanted to call to say hello and let you know that I'm having a ball."

"Well, have you done anything in the water yet?"

I wanted to say, If I get lucky again, but instead said, "I've been parasailing scuba diving snorkeling water bicycling and Jet Skiing."

"Damn. And it's only Saturday. All this in three days?"

"When it's already paid for, you do as much of it as you can."

"So how are the men?"

"What men?"

"The Jamaican men."

"They're mostly American and they're all in the NBA or NFL and they're all with their wives or girlfriends."

"So that means you haven't met a soul who's available?"

"Nope."

"I told you you shouldn't have gone by yourself, didn't I?"

"But I'm still having a great time, Angela."

"Yeah, right. The signal you're probably sending out is: Hey, I'm alone and I like it this way. I'm off limits, out of bounds, and I don't need a man. I'm just fine by myself thank you very much."

"That is ridiculous. I do not emit any such spray of any kind."

"It's your body language, Stella. You can be hard, you know. Well, maybe hard is too harsh a word. But you can be very businesslike, downright cold. No eye contact whatsoever and I've seen you carry yourself in such a way that no man would even dream of approaching you. To be honest, I'm beginning to wonder if you don't prefer being single."

"Sure, I want to spend the rest of my life alone."

"Whatever you do, just please do not come home telling us about some tropical fling you've had with some Jamaican guy and you're in love and what have you. Those island romances don't count because they're not real. Those guys all want to become citizens, so they'll sweet-talk you if they think it'll get them to the States. Just keep this in mind if you even come close to warming up to somebody."

Skip the subject, Stella. "Is Evan coming home for the summer?"

"No. He's interning with a sports recruiting company.

He'll be home for a week before school starts, sometime in mid-August. Why?"

"Just curious. Be nice to see him."

"You just saw him at Easter."

"I know. Does he still have that same girlfriend?"

"Don't ask me about her, okay?"

"I just did."

"She's pregnant."

"Again?"

"Yes. But this time she's keeping it."

"No!"

"I'm three minutes from flying there and snatching it out of her. This was all planned. And Evan is too stupid to realize that he's been set up."

"How many months is she?"

"Would you believe four?"

"Whoa. She's on a serious mission, huh?"

"Evan wants her to move on campus with him and get married."

"Can we switch to another topic? I can't handle this right now. I am on vacation and I don't even want to believe that the words you just uttered about my one and only favorite nephew are even close to being true."

I can tell Angela is crying. I'm wondering if it's due mostly to those pregnancy hormones kicking in. "Angela, are you all right?"

"Yeah. I'm just so fucking angry at Evan for being such an idiot. I don't understand how he could fall for the okeydoke like this. Jennifer is such a manipulator and . . . oh forget it. This will be handled, and I'm sorry for ruining your mood."

"It's okay. But look, Angela, tonight's karaoke and it's starting in a few minutes."

"Oh, wow, now *that* sounds like fun. But before you hang up I want to tell you that the babies moved."

"No shit!"

"No shit. It's so weird feeling two of them."

"It's been so long I can't remember what one felt like," I say.

"You're the one who *should* be having a baby, Stella. It would be good for Quincy to have a little brother or sister."

Oh please, not this baby business again. Especially under the circumstances and all. I am really getting tired of listening to these unsolicited opinions and I'm especially sick of watching these over-forty women having their first child and acting as if the world is like supposed to stop. I do not would not dream of could not even fathom changing another pissy poopy Pamper or getting up in the middle of the night to a screaming I-need-a-bottle baby. No thank you. Angela wants to repeat herself and she'll remember soon enough how hard it is, especially when she watches her husband curl up into an even tighter knot each time she jumps out of that bed to go bond with the little crumb snatchers. I did my baby number. I love my son. But you couldn't pay me enough money to get pregnant at forty-two years old and if I did, when it was born I'd probably already be its grandmother. "As soon as I get home and find a brand-new husband we're going to get right on top of things so to speak and start working on adding to our family at our earliest convenience. How's that suit you, Angela?"

"You go to hell, Stella. But seriously. Have a great time and try to stay out of trouble."

"Not to worry," I say.

"What did you say?"

"Nothing," I say. "Bye, Angela. And I love you too."

Boy, and I thought my life was sad.

It is time for karaoke and I drag myself down the pathway and say hello to the night workers and go upstairs to the piano bar and sure enough it is filled to the brim with people mostly white people and they are singing up a storm and the words are on the white wall and they hand me a book and say pick a song and I am not at all into this. I go downstairs and find myself walking into the empty disco where Bevon the DJ is testing out his selections for tonight and I ask him if he'll play Diana King's "Shy Guy" and he says sure and he does and I stand on the dance floor by myself and dance and then he plays one of my absolute favorites by Seal, "Dreaming in Metaphors," and then "Groovin in the Midnight" by Maxi Priest, "Open Your Heart" by M People, and after "I'm Ready" by Tevin Campbell I have swerved swayed and swiveled until this sadness this hollow feeling overwhelms me and I say thank you and get out of there until I find myself taking a shower and putting on my cotton pajamas and sliding under the covers which do not smell like anything at all and I spend hours trying to shut down my brain and heart to rid them of him his image his scent those fucking kisses until I guess I finally fall asleep.

I am running on the beach this morning but my feet feel like lead and why is it that this beach seems longer and it's already hot too damn hot and why does it have to be so hot so early in the morning? Huh? I pass quite a few people on the beach, two of whom to my surprise are black women. They say hello and give me the thumbs-up and I think it is nice to see yourself outside yourself sometimes and it is also a nice feeling when black people acknowledge each other.

I continue with my normal routine after I run. I do the breakfast thing but Winston does not appear and I pretend that I'm not thinking about him but I have to make myself blink sometimes because it seems as if I see his translucent form walking right through these tables and heading in my direction. The two women I saw on the beach stop at my table with their trays. "Mind if we join you?" the taller one asks.

"Not at all," I say.

We introduce ourselves. The tall one's name is Tonya and although I guessed that she's a model it turns out she's a surgery resident at Massachusetts General Hospital in Cambridge. She barely looks old enough to be a candy striper. Patrice is an anesthesiologist at St. Luke's in Manhattan and she looks Puerto Rican or like she's mixed with something; her skin is flawless, a smooth creamy shade of brown, and her hair is long and thin, bone straight and black, and as soon as they start talking I'm sure they're both from the South somewhere but it turns out to be Chicago and they've been friends since elementary school. I tell them I'm from Chicago too but I grew up in the burbs and so did they and we like bond immediately because of the strong geographical factor. I tell them what I do for a living and once we get all this over with we sort of feel like, well, like three girls on vacation. "What made you guys come to Negril?" I ask.

"Well, we wanted to get away from our husbands," Tonya says and they laugh. Tonya is pulling her hair back into a ponytail. They are in great shape: Patrice has one of those *Shape* magazine bodies and Tonya looks like a few more crunches a day and she'd be a runner-up for the cover. Neither of them has any children and they're both thirty-one years old.

"You guys didn't come down here to get in trouble or anything, did you?"

Patrice blushes and says, "Not really. We love our husbands even though they get on our nerves sometimes, but we've both been working so hard these last eight or nine months and we hardly ever get to see each other anymore so we decided to take a girls' vacation and leave their butts at home. That's all."

"That sounds healthy," I say.

"Did I mention that I'm two months pregnant?" Tonya says.

"No," I say. "Congratulations."

Tonya says, "And what about you, girl? Where's your man?"

I feel kind of flushed. "Well, I came alone."

"You go, girl," she says, and they give each other a high five.

"So. Have you gotten in any trouble?" Patrice asks and they both lean forward so all four of their combined breasts rest on the table.

I am blushing harder.

"Tell us, girl, tell us! Curious minds wanna know!"

I lean forward and now there are six breasts sitting on the table. "Well, since I don't know you sisters I guess it's safe to tell you but I should be ashamed of myself even though I'm not but I slept with a twenty-one-year-old Jamaican guy."

"No you didn't!" Patrice says.

"Yes I did," I say.

"So what was it like doing it with a kid?" Tonya asks.

I don't like the sound of that. "He's not a kid."

"Whatever," she says. "What was it like?"

"Yeah, tell us. *How* was it, girl?" Patrice asks, bending even closer.

"Well, he moved like butter for one thing and I'm here to testify that I have never been kissed so good in my entire life."

"Get outta here," Patrice says, looking envious.

"A kiss can do it to you sometimes," Tonya says.

"Tell me about it. I was like totally shocked. I mean here I am thinking I'm gonna teach him a few things, turn this young boy out and blow his mind and hopefully make him think he's on fire and, well, do you see flames coming out of these braids or what?"

"It was *that* good, huh?" Patrice groans.

"I'm not even talking about the sex, you guys. It was some other stuff going on that I can't put my finger on. But all I know is that I'm messed up. Fucked up really. Because he's gone."

"Damn," Patrice says and takes a sip of her lemonade.

"Where'd he go?" Tonya asks.

"Well, he got a new job working down the road at Windswept so he had to go home and get his stuff which is like a four-hour drive from here because when he comes back he'll be like living there and everything."

"So go visit him," Patrice says. "My husband and I stayed there for our honeymoon. It's a beautiful resort, for couples only. Girl, go on down there and get your man," and the three of us start laughing.

I shake my head back and forth. "Can't do that. Don't know him well enough and I could scare the daylights out of him. Nope. I just wish I could stop thinking about him."

"This is too deep for me," Tonya says. "Girl, forget about him. Look at it for what it was: a one-nighter. You're on vacation. On a tropical island. It's called a fling. Not to be confused with the beginning or blossoming of a new relationship. The guy is exotic and goes with the island. It's not like something like this could lead to marriage! Find yourself a new victim tonight, girl, and you'll get over this little infatuation before you even blink."

"Would you shut your mouth, Tonya," Patrice moans and now all of us sit up and I feel like I've just reenacted the last episode of *I'll Fly Away* or something and we are all gathering our composure and trying to step out of that zone. Patrice seems to be totally identifying as if she's been here done that she can relate, girl, when Holly, this sexy tall lithe young social director with short curly hair whose breasts are so voluptuous they make all three sets of ours look weak and who has apparently been ill for the last two days flops down at our table and announces herself by saying "Hello" loudly in a British accent.

We each say hello back to her, and she sings, "Don't let me interrupt you. Carry on," and she taps the tabletop with her palm.

And so I do. "Anyway I *miss* my new boyfriend."

And Holly says, "Boyfriend? What's his name there?"

And I say, "Win-ston," in a Jamaican accent.

And she says, "You've got to be kidding. Not tall skinny homely Winston with the big lips?"

Patrice and Tonya are doing that tennis-watching thing with their heads and I say, "Yes, he's my friend. Why, what's wrong with Winston?"

Holly makes a yucky face and then pushes the air with her hands and says, "He's been after me for so long now he's getting on my nerves."

All of our eyebrows go up, but looking at her with her flawless sienna skin perfect white teeth round cheekbones curly eyelashes long shapely legs that tiny waist those curvy hips—she could easily be a high-paid runway model—I totally understand why Winston would be persistent in calling her. The fact that she does not take my "my boyfriend" at all seriously even though I was trying for facetiousness (although deep down inside I liked the sound of it after I said it) is kind of like a reality check and is somewhat heartbreaking for me at this moment in time and space. "You mean you don't find Winston attractive?" I ask, trying not to sound defensive.

"He's kind of cute but far too skinny. He really needs to gain some weight and he has no money and he's far too passive."

"Passive?" I say. I want to say, I beg to differ with you, sweetheart, but I don't, and as I'm thinking this Patrice and Tonya both give me the eye but Holly keeps right on talking.

"Yes, passive. He's kind of slow actually and besides I'm

sick of Jamaican men. They have no money, hardly any class at all, they can't dress, and I'm hoping to meet an American man one of these days."

"Is that why you have this job?" Patrice asks.

"No. It's just a job," she says, looking around the dining room, perhaps for a prospect. I'd really have liked to tell her that young men rarely go on vacation alone because they don't know how to entertain themselves and basically because they're, well, stupid and they don't want to bet on getting lucky when they can just pay up front and bring all the luck they need with them. So the chances of her actually meeting somebody who would forget about the Miss America runner-up he brought with him and go off in her direction would be slim indeed and she should save up her money and just like get on a plane and fly to the U.S.A., though her chances of getting lucky there will probably (but I don't dare say this to her) be even slimmer because there are millions of pretty women in the United States hoping and praying they get lucky too.

Holly taps the table again with her palm and jumps up. "Well, gotta go. Enjoy your breakfast. Are any of you ladies interested in a game of volleyball today?"

We look at each other. I say, "Maybe," and Patrice says, "Maybe," and Tonya says, "Maybe," and then we all laugh.

"She was cute," Tonya says.

"She was phony and knows exactly how cute she is, but forget about her, we want to hear more about Winston," Patrice says.

So I go back to day one and tell them everything and by the time I finish we are lying out on the beach on our respective chaise longues and Norris comes over and says,

"Ladies, are you going to play volleyball today?" and we all gaze up but I can see he is clearly looking at me and he says, "Did you know Winston stopped by this morning to drop off my key? You *do* know he was sharing my room?"

And I say, "No," and he smiles like the bitch he is and says, "Yep," and turns around and struts away like Naomi and Cindy do on those runways. I hate him.

"Who's Miss Thang?" Patrice asks over her sunglasses.

"I think he has a crush on Winston," I say.

"That's pretty obvious," Tonya says and rolls over.

"I don't want to play volleyball," I say.

"Me neither. We just got here last night and we're tired," Tonya says.

"Yeah," says Patrice. "I'm volleying right here."

We basically ignore Holly and Norris and when we hear the sound of drums and cymbals and "The Star-Spangled Banner" we each pull our sunglasses away from our eyes and turn to see where the noise is coming from.

We simply do not cannot believe what we see coming in our direction: a parade of red white and blue painted people. And there are about fifty or sixty of them! "They must think today is the Fourth of July!" I yell.

"You ain't never lied," Tonya says.

And we sit there until these naked patriots march right by us, their bodies painted interpretations of the American flag. Lips are red. Hair is blue. Black bodies are rendered iridescent white. Stars are painted across bellies and behinds and an old man's penis is red white and blue while a woman who has not had the liposuction she needs has miniature flags covering her private area and glued to each of her huge breasts. They are blowing trumpets singing up a storm and waving as they walk past us. We watch the heat from the sun melt the blue red and white but we are too stunned to comment and we just stare until they turn around and walk by us again and then we just sort of lie there and it is obvious that we are all thinking the same thing: did we just see a parade of painted naked people marching along the beach? We think we did we think we did we think we did.

To our complete astonishment, the volleyball game has continued uninterrupted. We shake our heads back and forth and drop them against our towels, which are rolled to form pillows, until we get so hot we run out into the water and swim for a while and then I guess we eat lunch and then I take my afternoon nap and then I eat dinner again and walk into the empty disco and it is boring and I go to my room and wonder what Winston is doing if he is thinking about me at all and I am thinking it is only Sunday and I still have all of Monday Tuesday and Wednesday left to go and why on earth did I have to stay so many days what am I going to do here on this stupid island without him? I mean I like Patrice and Tonya but they are not quite as stimulating company as Winston is and as I look out at those massive waves crashing against the big rocks again and I press Seal On again and I stand out on that balcony and breathe in the ocean air again and look out as far as I can but don't see anything at all except the world looking as if it ends somewhere out there and I step back inside and close the French doors because I'm tired of all this beauty all this water all this whatever, because it feels like this tropical fever has broken and now I just want to go home.

66 **I**'m really beginning to wonder if maybe I'm under some kind of spell or something," I say to Tonya and Patrice. We are lying on our stomachs oiled down and glowing on our chaise longues on the beach and of course I am drinking my third virgin piña colada of the afternoon and they're on their fourth real piña coladas.

"Girl, you sound like you're lovesick," Patrice says.

"That's impossible," I say.

"Why is it impossible?" she asks.

"Because he's a child," I hear myself say. Stella, come off it, girl, you know deep down inside you are totally smitten with this young man and you are the one who keeps tripping on his age when in fact is it really just his age that's causing you so much discomfort or are you uncomfortable because of your discomfort, which is basically a reaction to the high-yield comfort level he generated inside you, and because he happens to be young you have made that a negative and as usual chosen the negative as your focal point instead of the good stuff? I mean isn't it a much cooler cop-out to trip on the fact that he is young and therefore somehow unacceptable, but what if he were like white or Jewish or Asian or even a woman—I mean if you keep saying too young you can like use this defense for the benefit of who, Stella? If he were thirty-one or forty-one, what would the issue be then?

"Winston doesn't sound like any child I've ever met," Patrice says. "He's six foot four, living on his own, working full time, and he certainly approached you like a grown-up and he sounds *very* much like a man to my mind."

"Seriously," I say, "they *do* do that kind of stuff down here, don't they? Don't they have like conjure women who work their mojos on you for a nominal fee?"

"I've heard of them," Patrice says, nodding.

"He probably had this all planned from the beginning. He chose me. Or she probably chose me *for* him and he just went along for the ride. Maybe he's under the spell too."

"Girl, you're tripping too hard." Patrice rolls over on her side.

I sit up and look down at my thighs and legs and realize I am now totally bronzed and boy I wish I could keep this color. I stand, about to walk into the water, when running down the beach heading straight toward us looking like one of those men in a Calvin Klein ad is a very real bronzed statue and it is moving faster and as he gets closer I/we see that he is absolutely gorgeous!

I look over at Patrice and Tonya and they both pull their sunglasses down over their noses and we simply watch him as he approaches us and he is not wearing any shoes or shirt just dark nylon running shorts and he looks like a wide receiver because he is tall and muscular but his neck is not enormous his body is not puffed up and bulky like most football players' but his thighs legs shoulders triceps biceps are perfectly formed and now that I can see him closer he is the color of espresso and his mustache is thick and flourishing and his hair is cut close and look at those cheekbones and the hair on that chest and those pectorals pushing out from under it and when he looks directly into my face and smiles showing off those pearly whites and in a British accent says, "Hello," and then he turns to Patrice and Tonya and says, "Hello," and we are totally awestruck, can just barely manage a weak "Hi" but the three of us say it pretty much in unison.

He runs over to the outside shower which is close to the grassy area and I don't realize it but I'm like staring at him as he pulls that silver chain down and the water forms a silver waterfall over his body and the now-chocolate water bounces off his shoulder blades in little droplets that splash against the concrete and he turns his face up to the spray and I'm thinking as I notice that his waistline is probably smaller than mine that he should do some ads for Calvin (I might call Calvin when I get home to tell him that I've found his man for real) and then I hear Patrice say, "Go on over there and get him, girl."

Then Tonya sits up and says, "Something that looks that good should be illegal. Dang. Where did *he* come from?"

"I don't know but God must've sent him here for a reason," I say and finally I push my feet into the white sand and then into the water. I walk out until I'm up to my shoulders and when I turn around I am positive that that man is looking at me and if he's not he is looking in my direction and then when he waves and smiles I dunk my head under the water. This is unreal. I mean damn, here I am suffering from an enormous all-encompassing sense of heartache and now this black knight comes out of nowhere and where is his horse is what I'm thinking as I try to focus my eyes to adjust to the thick wetness to see if I can spot any fish families but I can't seem to see clearly today and when I come up for air he is gone.

I walk run through the water back to the shore where Tonya is now reading some medical journal and Patrice is reading *In Search of Satisfaction* by J. California Cooper but when they see me they drop their respective books in their laps and this time they take their sunglasses off.

"Girl, did you get a good look at him?" Patrice asks.

"I did," I say. "But where'd he go?"

"Up there," Tonya says, pointing to the second floor of the beachfront rooms that're right behind the volleyball area.

I pick up my towel and dry off. "If I knew it was gonna be raining men I'd've come down here a long time ago," I say.

"Well, it must just be in the stars for you, girlfriend, because we've been here two days now and the most play we've gotten is from little short guys or really old guys and all they say is, 'Hey, mon.' These wedding rings scare folks off, which is just fine with us. I *love* my husband," Tonya says.

"And I think I'll keep mine around a little longer," Patrice says. "But you, girlfriend, you ought to have as much fun as you can while you're here. You are single. And Winston is gone."

"Byeee, Winston." Tonya sighs, waving to the air. "When you snooze you lose, baby."

"How many days do you have left?" Patrice asks.

"Three," I say.

"We leave in two. But three days is plenty of time to do some damage," Tonya says.

Later, Tonya asks me, "What are you doing for dinner tonight?"

"Eating," I say.

"Funny. You want to go to Rick's Café with us?"

"I've heard of that—it's in one of my brochures or something."

"It's fabulous. It's about fifteen minutes from here near the tip of the island and some white guy named Rick owns it and it's outside and there are these cliffs adjacent to it and you can sit outside and eat lobster and watch these fools dive off."

"You're kidding," I say.

"I kid you not, but it's also known for the best sunsets you'll ever see anywhere, so you wanna come with us?"

"Sure, why not," I say.

When our taxi driver picks us up, he looks like he has just been told a good joke. I sit in the front seat because there is no room in the back after Tonya and Patrice get in his little Subaru. We pay him forty American dollars and he will wait for us outside Rick's Café until we are ready to leave. He is blasting this reggae station so loud that the bass actually hurts our ears.

"Can you give us a break on the bass, brother?" Tonya asks.

"No problem, mon," he says, still grinning his ass off. "So are you married?" he asks me and puts his left arm across the back of my seat and his right hand is on the steering wheel, which is also on the right.

"No," I say.

"No? What a pity."

"Are you?" I ask.

"Yes, but you are no less beautiful because of it."

"You better keep your eye on the road."

I can hear Patrice and Tonya cracking up in the back.

"I'm keeping my eye on you," he says.

"Do you have children?"

"Yes, two."

Without thinking I take my hand and whop him upside the head. "Then think about them and stop flirting with strange women or I'll get your name and number and call your wife!"

He immediately puts both hands on that steering wheel and begins to laugh and we all laugh as the car continues rocking because this narrow road is bumpy as hell and it seems as if everything and everybody are out this evening. Lining the road are hundreds of what look like workers leaving hotels. They are gathered in and breaking up from large groups and all are dressed in the same brown purple or green uniforms and many of their arms are out-stretched hoping to catch a ride and our driver is honking and waving at lots of them although he doesn't stop because he has a fare. Then there are these anorexic-looking dogs and the spookiest-looking cats I've ever seen, standing in the middle of the road as if they're waiting for us to go around them which the driver does and then there are goats and cows tied to trees with rope that doesn't look strong enough and they walk right to the edge of the road and simply stop.

I can tell we are going uphill but I don't know how high we are until we get out and walk out onto the patio of Rick's and we are up high all right. There are two or three hundred people here already but we are able to get a table and when I glance over at the rocky cliffs it kind of looks like a small section of Rome even though I've never been to Rome but I've seen enough pictures to know what a small section of Rome looks like and this could be a small section of Rome. This is really an inlet, a cove with jagged rocks leading to the top, where there is a herd of trees just standing there and a sign that says big and bold: "Beware of the Dog." These young Jamaican boys whose little chests almost look caved in jump like a hundred feet into the air like seagulls with their arms spread out and they really look like they're soaring as they cut through the dark turquoise water with hardly a splash.

I am like totally amazed as we sit there and watch the sun beginning to set and at first it is as yellow as a yolk and then it turns tangerine and then burnt orange and then ruby red and then a deep purple and at least five hundred tourists have their cameras and camcorders out and I'm wondering how do you videotape a sunset? These are the type of home videos people show when they come back from vacation that make their friends and relatives want to go outside to smoke a cigarette or a joint. These kind of people stand there and reload the VCR and pretty much forget your ass is even there because they are like reliving that moment remembering exactly what they were eating, like I am about to do with this lobster right now because my mouth is watering and it is so beautiful here and I am glad I'm not thinking about Winston and yet I'm curious I wonder if he's ever been here and jumped off this cliff he had to because he said he was on the swim team but when I look back out to the highest edge I see a grown man jump off backwards and do a double flip and my heart almost flies out of my chest and hundreds of people are applauding and yet what he wants are American dollars and preferably not ones from what I gather and then I notice that right down below us is a crowded lower platform from which tourists with common sense are jumping off and this is where I can picture myself plunging off too. Next time, I think. Next time.

I wear my peach jogging shorts and matching sports bra with matching socks and I'm beginning to think I look too much like those girls on those exercise videos and I vow to mix and match tomorrow. It is only seven o'clock and the beach is mine again until after I finish my run. I am doing my stretches against one of the sailboats when I hear, "Hello again," in the sexiest voice I have heard in ages with the exception of James Earl Jones and Wesley Snipes and when I turn around it is Mr. Espresso himself in those short shorts again but now he is wearing one of those muscle shirts with a trillion little holes in it and I realize how rare it is that I hear a black man speak with a British accent.

"Good morning," I say and am glad that I wore this little Jane Fonda outfit after all. I do however wish that my legs were not so thin and short and that God could also have made them more shapely and that my inside thighs could be firmer since I've been doing that inner-thigh exercise now for about a year and maybe I should've gone ahead and got those silicone implants before they took the shits off the market because then all I'd need to complete this look is a peach sweatband to go around my forehead. Even though I don't want to lift my other leg and rock forward I feel like I have to in order to not feel imposed upon by his presence so I lean over which is supposed to stretch out my quads and I can feel my glutes pulling which is apparently what he is looking at because I bust him when I turn and say, "Are you about to go on your run?"

He smiles at me like he is already imagining making love to me and for some reason I can picture myself doing it with him and I sort of have to shake this image off by pushing back on my hamstrings because I am worried that maybe I am turning into a real slut down here and he says, "Yes. And you just came back, I see."

"Yes."

"We should run together," he says.

"That sounds good."

"Could you run again now?"

"No way," I say. "I wish I could, but I'm not in that great shape."

"You look like you're in pretty good shape," he says, giving my body a once-over. Now if I was at home in America I might be tempted to cuss his ass out for looking at me this way but why I am flattered and not offended one iota is escaping me and I decide not to question it any further so I simply say, "Thank you."

He holds out his arm to shake my hand and says, "I'm Judas Germaine Rozelle," and all I'm thinking is who? but I extend my hand and say, "I'm Stella."

"Stella what?"

I cannot fucking remember my last name for the life of me. But then I suddenly do but I decide I don't know this man and I didn't tell Winston my last name and this guy's like a complete stranger and he might not even be a registered guest at this hotel and he could like actually be a rapist or a serial killer who jogs and also happens to be fine as hell so I just say, "Stella'll have to do for now." You are a slut, I think, because I say it like I'm flirting with him which I guess I kind of am.

"So," he says with a smiling sigh, "what brings you to Jamaica?"

"The sun the beach the island air," I say.

He's nodding in agreement. "And you are from . . . ?"

I want to say guess, but I don't feel like playing games and besides I have to go to the bathroom really bad. "California."

"I see," he says. "Los Angeles?"

"No way," I say. "Northern. The Bay Area. Forty minutes outside of San Francisco."

"It's very nice there," he says.

Now I'm nodding like a total idiot. "And you're from. . . ?"

"Born in Senegal, grew up in London, but live in Atlanta."

"Atlanta?"

"Yes," he says and God certainly knew what He was doing when He was passing out sexy smiles. Judas must've been second in line, right after Winston, but of course it had to be by quite a few years. . . . But stop it, Stella. This man certainly looks like he's of legal age although I can't tell really how old he is but at least I know he can buy liquor. "I've been in America since I was twenty-two."

My eyebrows go up. "And you're how old now?" I ask and then realize it is a totally stupid and inappropriate question but I know precisely why I'm asking it.

"I'm thirty-four. Why do you ask?"

"I don't know, really, I didn't even mean to ask. What brought you to America?"

"Well, years ago I played rugby while at Oxford and then I came to America to finish my studies in civil and structural engineering at Emory University, which is in Atlanta, of course, and I basically never left."

"Why Atlanta?"

"Why not? I love Atlanta. There are so many black people there and it is a great place from which to operate."

"What do you mean by operate?"

"Well, I'm a developer and I plan and design business parks—you know those kinds of complexes: office buildings, shopping centers and others—both in America and abroad."

"Really?" I say.

"Yes, really. And you? What do you do for a living and before you even answer I know it is something probably very fascinating."

"Actually it isn't. I'm a securities analyst," I say and leave it at that. He should know what it means.

"Fascinating," he says and seems to mean it. "So are you here with someone?" He is stroking his chin and smiling at me and appears to be looking right through this jogging outfit like he can picture what I look like without it and if it weren't obvious and if he weren't so good at it and if I were like at home or say in Oakland I'd probably ask him what the fuck he is staring at.

"Well, actually I came alone."

"I love it," he says, gleaming. "You are my kind of lady. All the way from America without a companion, hey?"

"Yep."

"Marvelous. You are very independent and high-spirited. I can tell."

"How can you tell all this?"

"A man knows. I knew it when I saw you playing volley-ball yesterday."

"You saw me playing volleyball?"

"Indeed I did. You couldn't see me because I didn't want you to see me staring, but you are very athletic and you gave those guys a run for the money."

"I played volleyball all through high school."

"Well, a lot of people did but they are not necessarily good at it and you are so strong, I love it," he says and actually giggles.

At home this kind of talk would almost certainly be on the verge of getting on my nerves and I can't understand why it's not now. "What about you, Judas? Are you here with your wife?"

"Me? Nooo, I have no wife. I brought a dear friend and she is only a friend," he says significantly. "She has recently been in a bad automobile accident and had to have her left arm amputated and she has been very depressed about that, so I brought her here to cheer her up.

As a matter of fact, there she is," and he points to this huge woman in a muumuu whom I had to look at twice because from here she looked like she could be his mother, but I should talk! Instead I just say, "That's very nice."

I have long since finished my stretches and can't even fake another one and I am about to cross my legs, so I say, "Look, Judas, it was very nice meeting you and maybe I'll see you later but I have to go to the bathroom something terrible," and he laughs and says, "Go go go, but what time do you anticipate having lunch?" and I say, "About one o'clock," and he says, "I'll see you then," and I say, "Okay," and run toward the hotel.

I go into the ladies' room which smells like raspberry Bubblicious bubble gum for which I am totally grateful and after I am relieved I go over to wash my hands and I look at myself in the mirror and all I'm thinking is: What in the world are you doing down here in Jamaica, girl, except getting yourself in nothing but trouble?

I see Judas at lunch with that woman and when he comes over to me she doesn't look happy about it. "She's not feeling very well. I'm going to take her to her room so she can rest and I'll be right back," he says.

I say something like okay but I am not about to sit here and wait for this African hunk. I mean African men scare me because I've heard how like if you kiss them once and do the nasty besides they want to marry you and then expect you to stay in the kitchen and cook and clean and to be a passive obedient child like all those Japanese and

Chinese and Muslim women and they want you to have
baby after baby (except for in China of course) but a lot
of the women in Africa don't even have a clitoris thanks to
the men who are the ones who get to enjoy sex with as
many women as they can squeeze in and I'll be glad when
these women get hip and just say no you are not cutting
off my daughter's clitoris and if you touch her I'll cut
your penis off how about that for a change of pace or they
should go get their bachelor's and master's and get a job—
no, a career—and have a nanny and a housekeeper to clean
the house and then they should rip off all those garments
and those hot-ass veils and just let their hair down because what does all this really have to do with religion
when you think about it? How do the clothes you wear
limit or prohibit your ability to express your spirituality,
your beliefs and love for a Higher Power anyway and hey,
who was it that decided that women should hide their
bodies their faces their hair? Shall we take a wild guess?
Let's try men! Why don't *they* hide? Why don't *they* wear
wigs and veils? And when I think about it why isn't the
mother of Jesus ever really mentioned all that much except for at Christmas? I mean why doesn't Mary get more
play, because Jesus is always simply referred to as like the
son of God, well, what about Mom and I mean let's get
real even though I have heard recently how they are
rewriting the Bible again to make it politically correct
which is a crying shame when I think about it but these
women should get a room of their own a life of their own
like Virginia Woolf did because times have like totally
changed and it is like the fucking nineties all over the
world. Then again I think that African men only try to

capture and lure you into matrimony when they want to become American citizens. Well, don't they all? But this Judas here already told me that he is an American and proud of it but it doesn't matter right now because I've had it with waiting for guys this week and so since I have not only gotten my groove back but also gotten my nerve up I decide that today is the day I will finally go parasailing for real which is exactly what I do.

I see Judas with his friend again at dinnertime and he comes over to me and says, "You disappeared this afternoon, but why?"

"I wasn't feeling so good," I say.

"Are you feeling better now?"

"Yes. Much."

"Good," he says. "Are you running in the morning?"

"Yes."

"Would you like to run with me?"

Would I? I think. "What time?"

"Whatever is convenient for you," he says.

"Won't your friend be upset?" I ask.

He turns to look at her and then back at me. "No. She's fine. Don't worry."

"How about seven?"

"Seven is fine," he says, smiling. "I'll see you then."

Right now it is Tuesday evening and even though the hotel is quieter than it's been since I've gotten here, Tonya, Patrice and I eat at the fancy-smancy French restaurant here on the premises and it was well worth the wait and then we dance by ourselves in the empty disco as if it's full of people and I tell them all about Judas and how I need to get my rest so that I can get up and run and when I walk into my room I am hoping that my message light will be blinking, that Winston will have called, that somehow he will have gotten my last name and he will tell me that his job is working out but he certainly misses me and he can't stand it and even though he doesn't get off until like twelve midnight would it be possible, would I mind and not take it the wrong way, but could I just come over and like kiss you good night or something.

My phone light is dead red. It looks as if it has never blinked, it will never blink. At least not as long as I'm in this room under the influence because I am truly acting like some lovesick cheerleader who has fallen hard for the quarterback and fucked him in the backseat of his Mustang and he was really just testing the water because his *real* girlfriend is at another college and he has never even tried to fuck her because he respects her, loves her too much and she is the girl he wants to marry.

I slide under the sheets and inhale as many times as I can until I can finally smell Escape and that is what allows me to sleep.

This Judas is exactly what I need, I think, as I put on a pair of white shorts and a No Fear T-shirt that says "If You're Not Living Close to the Edge You're Taking Up Too Much Space" on the back, and I pick out a pair of ugly white ankle socks, leave my Walkman on the built-in dresser that's right by the door along with my stack of tapes, because as I close the door and head out toward the beach I have a strong feeling that I'll be doing quite a bit of listening and talking.

He *could* turn out to be a very good distraction. I'm just hoping he can keep me distracted for the next two days when I'll be like outta here because I'm really getting tired of this hurry up and stop waiting shit.

Judas is standing near a boat that's parked at the shore. He looks as good today as he did yesterday. (You blew it, Winston.) When he smiles at me I'm thinking he could be one of those African gods or something who was sent here to bring me back to reality. Maybe he is the one I was supposed to meet here if I was in fact supposed to meet anybody here and maybe that's why God saved the best for last. I'm feeling lucky to be alive as we say our good mornings and begin to run down the deserted beach.

"How often do you run?" I ask him.

"Well, when you've been an athlete all your life you sort of get used to training so I've just never stopped. I run an average of five miles a day, depending on my schedule," and he says it like "shedjule."

By the time we reach the end where I usually turn around he has pretty much told me his life story which is very interesting but not as interesting as say looking at his body and I guess you could say we've bonded but we are both also sweating up a storm. I am feeling like Bo Fucking Derek in that movie *10* even though like most black women in America I hated Bo's guts for stealing our braids and having the nerve to put extensions and beads in and for thinking she was all that. We were like, Can't we have *anything* to ourselves? and of course when white women imitate us they are considered ultrabeautiful and can get on TV and sell cars but since we are just being our black selves, what do we get? Anyway when Judas walks into or on top of the water I find myself following him as if I'm sleepwalking and I walk right up to him and press my breasts against his chest and then I turn my head to the side and stare at his beautiful chocolate lips and then I lay my lips across his because I can tell he is hoping for a kiss and he kisses me tenderly and strongly and I'm like shocked because until very recently the only man who has kissed me like this has been Winston and I am like, Damn, maybe there are more of them out here than I ever imagined and so when he puts his arms around me and I feel everything on him rising and pretty much pushing me out of the way I am like amazed and my breasts are throbbing and I want to know how it is possible to throb for one man on say a Friday and then throb for another on what day is it now?

I am sinking low. I am losing my morals down here on this island and yet I am enjoying every single minute of it. But then I suddenly feel weird about this whole ordeal and when I open my eyes and realize that he is not Winston I say, "We should stop," because I think maybe I'm just doing this on-the-rebound stuff to appease my achy breaky little heart. I feel stupid for thinking about Winston out here in this ocean with this fine-ass man but I also feel as if I'm misleading him and once again misrepresenting myself but then again he does feel good and I am on vacation and I am single and he is single and we are here and Winston is gone so as we head back toward the hotel I relax a little bit and agree to go dancing with him tonight after dinner.

*　　*　　*

It is not the same. He has no rhythm and as someone from Africa he really should be ashamed of himself. I am actually embarrassed for him and embarrassed to be out here on this dance floor watching him move like some white boy. It occurs to me that I am not so old that I don't care if a man isn't a good dancer. Winston is smooth and sort of glides whereas old Judas here is doing some kind of quivering and jerking number and he's looking at me as if I'm like edible and when they play "Shy Guy" I look at him and he is not Winston and then I feel overwhelmed all over again and I say to Judas, "Would you mind if we leave?" and of course he's all game and everything and we go outside and sit on a bench and he talks some more and I simply am unable to hear him and yet I respond like I'm checking off answers in a box.

He is not a very good substitute. In fact he is rather boring. He represents all that I am trying to get away from. Despite his sexy accent he reminds me of my ex-husband because he is so impressed by how much he appears to be impressing me with his impressive credentials, and it is dawning on me as I sit out here next to these banana trees that belong to Winston that one of the things I like about Winston is that he has no skills and told me so and he did not try to impress me or pretend he could do more than what he does which is basically cook. He is who he is and I like who he is. I realize this as I look over at Judas who should really think about changing his fucking name which at first I was trying to overlook but now I realize that perhaps it's appropriate because obviously he merely wants to fuck me and for that reason and that reason alone I find myself taking him by the hand and leading him to my hotel room just to see for sure and sure enough he thinks he's a real Don Juan or somebody because he pulls me close to him immediately and he is like as hard as a cannon and before I know it he is kissing me and snatching my clothes off like in some porno movie instead of like in a romance novel which is what I prefer if I have to make the choice, and then I simply hand him one of my condoms and he is banging me very hard and he thinks he is really rocking my world but it's only the bed he's rocking. When he says, "Say fuck me Judas!" and then starts slapping me on my ass like I'm some stallion and he's trying to get me to giddy up I look at this motherfucker like he's losing his mind and I get up and grab my bathrobe and stand in front of the door and fling it open and say, "Please leave," and he says, "I only wanted to please you, Stella, and if I was too rough I can do it softer slower because I can see that you are the type who likes it softer and slower," and he sits there smiling and not budging and I say, "Judas, this was a mistake. I'm not really this loose."

"Well, I like loose," he says.

"I would appreciate it if you would leave *now,*" and he gets up slowly and walks toward me with his big black penis standing straight out and as he walks into the bathroom the tip of it hits my arm and I am about to throw up if he doesn't hurry up and Winston where are you? I think as I look out at his banana trees and our fuchsia flowers and then I hear the rustle of material as Mr. Jesus Traitor slides into his pants and slips on his shirt and he takes his time putting on his shoes and he walks up to me and says, "I'm sorry if you are offended in any way and I would very much like to make it up to you. Here is my card," and he hands it to me. "If you are ever in Atlanta, please look me up," and I say, "I don't really like Atlanta," which is a total lie, and he says, "If you come to visit *me* I will change your mind," and I want to say, Sure, in my next life, and he is winking at me as I step back to avoid what appears to be an oncoming kiss and now he is smiling as if saying, I'll get you next time, and I close the door and go sit on the edge of the bed like an old tired whore.

I feel bad. Maybe I was too hard on Judas is what I'm thinking after I wake up this morning and get ready to put on my jogging clothes then change my mind fast. I'm tired of running on the beach. This is my *last* day here. I have run on that beach every single morning I've been here and besides I do not want to run into him this morning. In fact I don't want to see Mr. Freak of the Week for the duration of my stay if it's at all possible.

I order room service and afterwards walk down to say goodbye to Tonya and Patrice, who are leaving in a few hours. We exchange numbers and all that and give each other hugs and then I come back to my room to consider packing but it's too drab in here and I still have the whole day so I decide to go snorkeling since I haven't really done much of the free or I should say paid-for-in-advance activities that have been readily available to me.

I snorkel snorkel and snorkel some more. The fish are beautiful and the coral reefs are unbelievable which is of course why people snorkel. I see every color and shape of fish imaginable and even when I snorkeled in Maui it wasn't quite this intense immediate close-up pretty. I want to touch the plants because they are swooning and swaying and look as though they are reaching up to the surface of the water but we are not supposed to touch the coral because some of them, most of them, are still alive and could die from being handled by human hands and I think it's pretty fucking amazing that you can touch something so beautiful in a lovely way and it could like just die. My ears feel like they're plugged with foam and it seems like the water is holding me together in one piece and when I look down at a thousand purple-and-yellow baby fish all headed in one direction I want to follow them but I feel as if I am cutting through their backyard without permission so I steer my body away and flap my fins back and forth until I see the rudder of the boat I came out here on. The water is quite warm and really only ten feet deep even though we are a mile or more from the shore-line. I could stay out here for hours I think as I take my mask and mouthpiece off and accidentally swallow a mouthful of salt water but I don't really care because I am like totally buoyant.

Instead of going to the regular beach, for some strange unconscious unknown or unplanned reason I find myself heading toward the nude beach and I tell myself that it's mostly to avoid Judas. I have on my one-piece blue plaid bathing suit. Whenever I think plaid I think ugly, like parochial school plaid, but this is a pretty hot bathing suit, though the cheapest of the bunch, and it does wonders for my figure even without any Wonderbra features inside the cups.

These people really ought to go somewhere and hide instead of flaunting all this flesh out in the open is what I'm thinking and I stop dead in my tracks before my foot even touches the sand. They are all mostly pink though some are darker than I am and there are plenty of large firm breasts in the air but I try to ignore all these people as I pass them even though I can feel them staring at me wondering why on earth I am wearing this plaid one-piece bathing suit and when I see old man Nate sit up I am afraid to look at him too closely but see patches of brittle gray hair all over his spotty chest and his arms are a pretty reddish-brown and he is looking at me and waving and I simply wave back and stop at a chaise that's about thirty feet away from him and about ten feet from an old fat slovenly white man who is sucking on a cold pipe. His wife who was probably a knockout in her younger years is reading a Jude Deveraux paperback and wearing a big floppy straw hat and she is as naked as everybody else out here and her breasts are the same size as her stomach which suffice it to say is humongous and she has these purple veins running all over her body like a map of major interstates or something. I sort of stand there for a minute and look out at the ocean which looks exactly like the ocean around the bend where everybody is wearing a bathing suit and I find myself sliding my straps down and then stepping out of my suit and the sun feels good on my ass and breasts and shoulders and I walk toward the beach with both hands covering my breasts and then I turn around and face the folks on the beach and for no reason at all I squeeze them and smile at that white man. Yes, you will go back to your room with your fat and fluffy wife who is gazing at me too as if she once looked even better than I do right now and then there is old man Nate who is like salivating and this tiny section of the beach is gaping with their so-called liberated and we-don't-think-of-you-as-naked little eyes and it is not really because I am all that gorgeous. The deal is that I am the only black woman on this beach because most black people only run around butt naked in Africa where we are in front of our own people and where it is the normal thing to do and nobody really gives a shit.

I stay in the water for just a few minutes and when I get out Nate is heading in my direction but I run to grab my towel before he gets close enough for me to see his elephant-size unit which is rather atrocious and scary-looking. I would never need this much dick is what I'm thinking as I cover myself.

"Now why you have to go and do that?" he asks.

"Don't come over here bothering me, Nate. I'm not out here to be hassled."

"I'm just glad to see you here," he says, standing there ever so proudly.

I look down. "You don't seem to be as glad as you say you are," and I begin to walk away.

"Why you leaving so soon and you just got here, girl?"

"Because I'm tired and this is boring."

All he can do is nod.

I eat lunch with the Canadians and even though they still have almost a whole week left to honeymoon they are clearly becoming either bored with each other or tired of hangovers, this island or captivity at the Castle Beach. I tell them how much I have enjoyed them and I Dream of Jeannie smiles at me and tells me, "So much meeting you fun, Stella!" Ben says he can't wait to get back to work because he misses laying tiles and cutting marble and granite and limestone and just for the hell of it I ask him what Sasha does for a living and he says she is a dancer. What kind of dancer? I ask and he blushes and makes swirling motions with his hands in front of his chest and rolls them down underneath the table and I say, Nude dancing? and he says, Well, actually she's a stripper, and my eyes go big and when I turn to I Dream of Jeannie she is nodding and smiling and says, "Yes, very much so!" I want to tell him that this girl should go back to school.

I take a taxi into town and spend hours at the marketplace, where almost everything they sell seems to be black red and green or made of wood but I buy a small sculpture hats skirts T-shirts shorts more T-shirts bracelets gold earrings Jamaican cookbooks at least twenty Jamaican CDs and postcards from the local merchants to show my support for their entrepreneurial endeavors on this island which I recently discovered is still mostly owned by the British.

I have a hard time getting all this stuff to my room but I manage and when I get there and take everything out of the bag I put on a Maxi Priest CD called *Fe Real* which they were playing this afternoon in the dining room when I found out Sasha was a stripper. I wasn't paying much attention at the time but they were playing it in the store when I walked in which apparently means that it had a subliminal effect on my psyche and I am like sick of Seal and Maxi is my new flame. As I drag all my clothes out of the closet and put them on my bed I realize I don't know where or how I am ever going to get all this shit into my suitcases.

I decide to write out my postcards so at least they are postmarked from Jamaica and not Miami which is where my plane has to stop for a two-hour layover, and I choose the one from Rick's Café where two young men are caught in midair jumping off the highest cliff and I decide to send this one to Quincy. I write something motherly and sweet and downright corny and then I come up with something else for everybody else's postcards—Angela's, Vanessa's, a few close friends and one person and one person only at my job—and then the phone rings. It startles me because I haven't actually heard it ring in days.

"Is that Stella there?" the voice that sounds like silk is asking.

"Winston?" I say and all of a sudden my heart is beating a thousand beats per minute.

"Helloooo," he sings. "How are you?"

"I'm fine," I say. "And you?"

"Fine. Working very hard. But say, are you still leaving tomorrow?"

"Yes. Early." I drop the postcards on the bed.

"Well, I would really like to see you to say goodbye before you leave, Stella."

I want to say, Fuck you, Winston, why haven't you called me until now, why call now, you little creep! but instead I hear myself say, "When?"

"Well, I have one and a half hours coming up for dinner."

"A whole hour and a half, Winston?"

"Well, I actually have two hours but—"

"Well, aren't I the lucky one."

"What's wrong, Stella?"

"Nothing, Winston."

"I just have to shower and then I could come right over."

I look at my watch. It is four thirty-five. "And what time might that be, because I'm supposed to have dinner with some friends this evening."

"Do I know them?"

"I don't know, Winston. What difference does it make?"

"Are you all right, Stella? Did I do something?"

"No, Winston, but I'm just really surprised to hear from you because your friend Norris has been saying you've been by here and he's been making me feel really silly about ever meeting and spending time with you."

"I came by once to drop off his key but I was only there for a few minutes and I asked him if he'd seen you around anywhere and he said no and I didn't know your last name and the front desk wouldn't give it to me and Norris said he had no way of finding out so finally I called Abby and asked if she would get it for me and she did and I've been calling you since yesterday but you're never in your room."

"Why didn't you leave a message?"

"Can we talk about it when I get there, because I have to be back by six."

"Okay," I say and feel foolish for sounding like his mother.

"I'll need a pass, as they won't let me in the front gate without one," he says.

"Not to worry," I say, imitating the island jargon.

"Can you meet me at the front gate at five past five?"

"I'll be wearing bright yellow in case you forgot what I look like," I say, laughing.

"That's my whole problem," he says. "I've been trying hard not to remember."

"And?"

"It's not working. I'll see you soon."

I pay sixty dollars for a pass so that Winston can come through the gate of the Castle Beach Negril and spend what will probably amount to only forty-five minutes. But I need to see him. I want to see him. If I don't, I feel like my trip won't have any real closure. Of course I know I want to sleep with him again but not under these circumstances because I would feel cheap and I don't want him to think for a minute that that is the main reason I want to see him and that that is the only thing I can think of to do with him when all we have is forty-five minutes. I already value him for more than sex, this much I do know as I stand there in my yellow shorts and yellow top, and when I see him come around that hedge in a deep pink shirt and those long purple shorts and he is wearing thick black sneakers with white socks he is so beautiful and he is already blushing and I can smell him before he gets close enough to touch me and he looks at me like he's dreaming and bends down out in the open and kisses me and I am never going to be able to forget him, that much I know already.

"You look very nice in yellow," he says and takes me by the elbow and I am feeling like he has made it back safely from the war and now I'm on my way to a convent or something.

"Are you cooking up a storm?"

"Not really," he says. "Mostly chopping and cutting, slicing and dicing. You know?"

"I think I know."

And we walk up that path for what is going to be the last time and it is weird and the fuchsia hibiscuses look sad, his banana trees look as if they are drooping today, and when I look up at him he looks as if he has many things on his mind, is suffering in some way from something, and I wish I knew what it was so I could help him out but by the time we reach my doorway and walk inside with all the things strewn all over the bed he leans against the wall and just looks at it all.

"So you're really leaving, huh?"

"Yep."

Maxi Priest is singing something lovely and mellow about keeping promises or breaking them, one of the two, but all I know is that I can't believe Winston is really standing here in my room until he comes toward me and stops and looks down and says, "Stella, I want you to know how sad I am to see you leave," with the utmost sincerity and I am afraid to look into his eyes because I might actually cry and I am too old to be crying over some young guy I just met on some island and I am feeling all mushy inside because I may never see him again and the mere thought of that is making me ache but I gather my composure and try to act like a real grown-up.

"Well, I'm certainly going to miss you, Winston."

"Really?"

"Why are you so surprised?"

"Why would you miss me, Stella?"

"You really want to know?"

"Yes, really."

"Because I like you, Winston."

"In what manner do you like me?"

He is serious about this. I can see it all over his face. "I like you the way a woman likes a man."

He seems satisfied with this answer and then he sighs and stands up real tall and says, "I'm here because I had to come, not because I wanted to. Because I *had* to."

"And what does that mean?"

He looks down at the floor and then over at a blank wall and then through the curtains out at the waves and then back at me and says, "It means I have these feelings and I don't know what to call them but I do know that they are unusually strong and I've never felt this way before."

"Join the club," I say.

"You feel it too?"

"Do I ever."

And then we both sort of sigh a sigh of relief and he bends down and rubs his cheekbone against my cheekbone and sort of just holds me for the longest time and I hold him and we merge again for the second time and then he kisses me deeply and slowly so slowly and his lips are so warm and my lips are so warm that they become sympathetic toward each other until this moment begins to feel sacred and no way can I leave this man on this island, and I drop my face down and press it into his chest and I say, "Winston, I wish I could fold you up and put you in my suitcase," and he rubs his big hands up and down my back and he says, "I wish I could fold *myself* up and jump inside your suitcase."

And then we just sort of stand there and rock back and forth for what apparently is more than a few minutes because I notice my clock says it is five forty-five even though he just got here.

We break away from each other and I say, "So, Winston, what do you want to do?"

"I hope to be able to see you again."

"I'm not so sure about that," I say.

"Why? You can come back, can't you?"

"I could, one day, but I have a job, Winston, and a son."

"I know. I could come visit you and your son."

"You just started a new job, Winston."

"That is right, isn't it."

"Yes, it is. But we can write to each other for starters," I say.

"You can write to me in care of Windswept."

"Windswept." I sigh.

"May I have your address?"

He is so polite I think as I walk over to get my checkbook out of my purse and tear off a deposit slip with my address on it and hand it to him. "Feel free to make as many deposits as you wish."

He is blushing again and I'm not so sure he knows what he's saying when he blurts out, "I want to make as many deposits as I can with you," and then he starts laughing and says, "I didn't mean that the way it sounded."

I am laughing too and I want to keep on laughing but we stop. We stop basically to hug each other again and I say something really stupid like, "Winston, I wish you were, say, at least thirty. This would make so much more sense."

He lets me go and looks as if I've wounded him with some blunt instrument. "Well," he says, "I'm not thirty and I won't *be* thirty for nine whole years, so what exactly am I supposed to do about that, Stella?"

"You know what I'm saying, Winston."

"No, what *are* you saying, Stella?"

"I'm saying that even though I feel like I'm totally smitten by you and everything, and if this were a perfect world we could do this, even take this to another level for real, but the world is not perfect and Winston you are too young for me and I'm too old for you and that's the reality of the situation."

He sucks on his lips. I would like to kiss them one more time for the road but that would make things even more hazardous than they already are. "Well, we can still be friends, right? Does that fit into your imperfect world or what?" he asks.

He is still weighing my answer the way I am weighing his question and I wish it weren't like this but it is and what would I, how would we, how could we, we couldn't, and so I say, "Winston, I'll walk you out to the gate if you want me to."

"You don't have to," he says at first and goes over to the door and then he turns toward me and he looks dejected and remorseful and I realize that truly I am not the only one who has fallen over the edge I am not the only one who has got it bad and so I say, "I know I don't *have* to."

"You look kind of busy. Packing and everything," he says.

"Would you like me to?" I ask.

He looks me dead in the eye and says, "I'd love you to," and I kiss him lightly and say, "Okay, but I want you to know that I'm not good at goodbyes so after we say it, when I say 'run' let's both just run, okay?"

"Are you serious?" he says, laughing.

"I'm serious," I say.

"That's one of the things I like about you, Stella."

"What's that?"

"You're always serious but you still make me laugh."

So we walk down that path again and Winston has his arm around me like I'm his woman and not his mother and we walk out toward the front gate but on the way we pass his friend Norris who looks like he is in shock to see us as if his scheme not only failed but actually backfired and like a lady I do not throw this in his face I simply smile and Winston and I both say hello and then we pass old man Nate coming out of the gift shop and he pretends he doesn't see us even though we almost bump into him and then we seem to run into every-fucking-body else who's staying at the Castle Beach Negril and Winston doesn't seem to mind and when we walk out that front gate when we cross that invisible wire fence I do not feel like I am being electrocuted until I kiss him and turn to run back across it.

I cannot bear the thought of that two-hour van ride on that bumpy road back to the airport, which is why I am up here in the sky with twenty-seven-year-old Nigel, the pilot, who doesn't look old enough to drive a car. This four-passenger airplane that will take approximately fifteen minutes to get me to Montego Bay International is giving me a panoramic view of this part of the island. Now I know why they call them the Blue Mountains, because they are so green they do actually look blue, and in some places the water is emerald green and right next to it like turquoise. It looks unreal but I have swum in that water. I feel as though I could actually come here every summer. As we descend and the tires screech down the runway, I decide that if things continue the way they have been for me at work I might just buy some beach property here, and as I get off the little plane and wait to get my boarding pass and pay my departure tax and sit and wait sit and wait sit and wait to get on that 727, I think I will.

Someone up here is wearing Escape. I look around. I can't tell who it might be. I close my eyes and remember that Quincy will be home in a few days and think how much I'm looking forward to seeing my son. I like being away from him but I sure love it when he's there. If I had to be anybody's mother I'm grateful to be his. I'm hoping I feel this way when he's like fourteen which I've been told is the age that you begin to want not only to disown them but to kill them as well. One of my girlfriends told me that they should just dig a gigantic hole somewhere at the end of the earth and bury every single teenager in the world until they're at least twenty and then let them out to get on with their lives.

We land in Miami in less than an hour. I really despise this airport. It is like a zoo. People from all over the world look like they're not of this world and no one seems to be able to speak English and everybody looks confused and you simply cannot find a free telephone and they are well hidden anyway. Customs is a total drag and I lie and say I spent two hundred dollars when in fact I spent more like two thousand but who can remember everything and filling out that form takes forever and as I'm walking through the airport I notice on the counter of the duty-free shop bottles of cologne and I walk in and ask the East Indian guy if they have Escape by Calvin Klein and he says yes but you are American so you cannot buy it and I say I just want to smell it because someone told me about it so he gets the bottle from a glass case and looks at me suspiciously as I take one long whiff and yes it smells just like Winston and I say May I? pointing it toward my wrist, and he nods Go ahead, and I press the top down and the mist lands on a big patch of my arm and I tell the man thank you and on the flight from Miami to San Francisco I sleep for three hours with my wrist placed close to my nose.

*   *   *

Even though it's ten o'clock at night, my house looks bigger and better. I don't get it. It's the same house. Phoenix can't seem to stop wagging that big brown tail, he's so happy to see me. I rub his ears briskly and pet him. Dr. Dre is blocking the doorway so that I have to pick her up before I can even think about walking inside. Our cat is a she but we didn't find that out until three weeks after Quincy had named her.

The very same driver who took me to the airport last week picked me up and is now carrying all three of my bags, which are even heavier than they were. I give him a forty-dollar tip because he will probably need the money to pay for the pulled whatever he'll get thanks to my Jamaican shopping spree.

I open all the windows in my bedroom and turn on the ceiling fan. It is pretty in here. I painted it a pale salmon because I wanted it to feel warm especially when it's cold outside. I have twenty-six messages so I sit on the bed and fast-forward through all of them, jotting down a few names and numbers and erasing all but five which I save and am now listening to as I unpack. One of them is from my so-called boss. "Stella, you need to call me at home as soon as you get back from vacation. There's a bit of a problem and it needs to be resolved right away." He leaves his number. What kind of fucking problem? And why is he calling me at home? I haven't even unpacked and already the bullshit is starting.

"Hey, Stella, this is Maisha calling. Girl, I hope you haven't forgotten about my gallery opening. Remember you promised me, Tiger and Rudy that you'd be here. Tiger's expecting Quincy. So be there or be square."

"We'll be there," I say to the machine. I love Maisha. I love Rudy and I love Tiger. They are a family and a happy one. Maisha and Rudy are one of the few couples I know who've been married for like a trillion years and are still very much in love. They still make each other smile and they each brag about how smart and talented and wise and tender the other one is and how lucky each is to have met the other and they actually look happy and if it's a front then I say both of them deserve Academy Awards for their splendid performances. Whenever I'm around them or couples like them—which is not very often—I watch their spirits their amiability their genuine affection and respect for each other emanate from them and permeate the entire room and my faith is kind of restored for a little while until, say, I come home and hear a message like the next one.

Leroy was the person I used to call when I needed sex. We had this understanding. We tried to be there for each other in times of need. Leroy had forgotten how to love and show affection and wanted me to teach him. He was a slow learner in this area though in fact he is a genuine genius and has an IQ of like a thousand or something. He knows a lot about everything, which is sort of his problem. He's too smart and has no real outlets in which to channel his energy. I was one of the recipients of this energy for a while and Leroy fascinated me because for a change I'd met a man who could talk about something besides himself. I haven't called him in centuries because he stopped satisfying me quite a while back when I discovered by accident that he was an alcoholic, which explained why it took forever for him to get off and when he did, Look out, Stella! He had me chafed and raw, running to the doctor with a bladder infection from being banged and jabbed; he behaved as if he hated me instead of wanting me and finally I decided why even bother?

On my machine, he is slurring, and I guess when you're drunk you don't know you're slurring and you don't even suspect that other people know you're drunk. He manages to get out: "Stella, this is Leroy. Where are you? Why haven't you called? I've been thinking about you so much these past couple of nights, Beverly, and I'm in the car going over the bridge and, Debs, can I stop by just for a few minutes? Are you going to be home in say the next half hour? Oh, shucks, you have no way of telling me that, do you? Oh well. It's been nice talking to your machine anyway. Call me at the office. Bye."

And I yell to the machine, "Take your drunk ass home to your wife!" I feel sorry for her, to be honest, but then again I don't. She knows he fools around and yet she tolerates it because they are—or he is—filthy rich since he owns every kind of franchise you can think of and he thinks because he's rich and handsome he is totally irresistible which is not true because he does not know when to stop. Doesn't know that life is not one big rush. It should be peaceful sometimes. Should be a whisper and not always a scream. Leroy believes that love can be purchased if you can afford to pay. He buys his wife anything and everything she wants and has for the last twenty years and it is so sad to me that in this day and age women still depend on a man to determine the quality of their lives and are still subjecting themselves to humiliation just to keep driving those fancy cars living in those humongous houses with rooms no one ever enters and is it really worth it? It is downright pathetic if you ask me but nobody *has* asked me and I am like talking to myself so get a grip, Stella.

"I know you must've lost your mind or something, Stella, because Vanessa told me that you slept with a teenager in Jamaica and that you actually like him. You must be going through some kind of midlife crisis; that's what you're probably going through. Well, shoot, I know a lady you can talk to about this, so call me."

Fuck you, Angela! I'm going to kill Vanessa!

"Stella, don't be too peeved at me but I accidentally slipped and told Angela about what you did on your summer vacation. It just sort of rolled off my tongue but to be honest I think the hussy needed to hear something to liven up her dead-ass world and I just really wanted to fuck with her cause I knew she couldn't handle this so let me know if any of your animals are dead and when can I like come over and pick up me and Chantel's gifts and souvenirs and I hope you didn't just send us a stupid postcard. I also have something to tell you. Byee. And by the way: welcome home."

Nothing like sisters, I think as I begin to unpack, and as I hold up different articles of clothing I wore when I was with Winston I feel myself getting woozy and it is then that I realize for the umpteenth time that he was not is not a dream a mere fantasy, that he really did generate something pure and deep inside me that is still circulating now that I'm home, and even though I am in my very own bed-

room and there are no waves outside my window and no
rocks and no banana plants or hibiscus, I can smell the
flowers hear the waves feel the sand between my toes and I
sort of have to shake my head back and forth to stop myself from hearing his knock on my door from seeing him
standing there in the rain from feeling his lips against
mine and as I pull more clothes from the suitcase, sepa-
rating soiled laundry from things that need to go to the
dry cleaners, I know for a fact that this longing this yearning I'm feeling is because I am missing him.

"Yes, Isaac, this is Stella calling. What's going on?"

"Well, first of all, how was Jamaica?"

"It was great. Negril is a beautiful part of the island."

"When'd you get back?"

"Late last night."

"That's good," he says. "Glad to hear you had a great
time. I've always wanted to see Jamaica. Been to Aruba,
but haven't had a chance to get to Jamaica yet. Ah, look,
Stella, there's a reason I called you at home."

"What's this all about, Isaac?"

"Well, I could have waited till you came back to the office and we could talk face-to-face, but I thought I'd fore-
warn you. A lot has happened since you've been away."

"Would you get to the point, Isaac, and stop beating
around the bush?"

"Well, Stella, you know there's been talk for some time
about downsizing and reorganizing your department, right?"

"Of course. Everybody knows that. It's no secret."

"Well, Fred has been replaced by Michael Javitz—"

"Javitz from our Los Angeles office?"

"Yes."

"And?"

"He's set on starting his department with a new team."

"Wait a minute, Isaac—are you saying what I think you're saying?"

"I didn't want to do it like this, Stella. I mean you and I go way back. . . ."

"So are you saying I'm out of a job?"

"Well, I guess that's what I'm trying to say."

"You've gotta be kidding me."

"Javitz feels that he really can't justify your salary."

"Oh, really! As much revenue as I bring into the firm, he can't justify *my* salary?"

"Stella, you've had the same accounts now for some time and we're trying to grow. New clients are just as valuable as long-standing ones."

"I don't believe this."

"You know how things can get at this level."

"And what level is that, Isaac? What level is that?"

"We're offering you a great severance package. A year's salary plus a bonus and most of your benefits. You can even keep your profit sharing."

"So are you saying I have to accept this?"

"Well, it's what we're offering."

"I'll think about it," I say. "And Isaac, thanks for sharing." I hang up and stand there looking out the window for so long that the tears I didn't want to fall finally condense. I do not have a job. I am unemployed. I have no income. After all these years of making what I thought was an investment, it turns out there is no return. *Poof.* Just like that. The ride is over. Do not pass Go. But I don't know what I'm supposed to do now. How I'm supposed to feel. And who can I ask? And even if I did, what difference would it make? I am going to have to start over. Somewhere else. Start over. Start all over. Again.

I drop the portable phone right there on my office floor and wander out of the house without realizing that I don't know where I'm going but the mailbox is waiting there so I open it and it's obvious that Vanessa hasn't been here in a few days because it's packed tight with white and brown envelopes magazines and as I begin to tug and yank to get all this stuff out and some of it lands by the curb I gradually begin to move slower and slower because for some reason I do not cannot even begin to understand or explain, right this minute I feel lighter and my head is clearing up like clouds that evaporate on those special-effect commercials and I realize that what I am feeling is relief and as I pile up all the mail and head back toward the house I am weightless and my legs are light and I can hardly feel the concrete steps under my feet and after I close the door I am on the verge of giggling because somehow and for some reason it feels like a gigantic burden has been lifted from my shoulders. In fact as I go through the mail most of which is junk and then dash upstairs to the laundry room and begin to throw all my running outfits into the washer I cannot wipe the smirk off my face because I am now rather ecstatic that I no longer have a job because all I know is that shit happens for a reason and maybe I'm being given another chance maybe this is really an opportunity to venture out in a different direction which is why I am going to pay attention this time out because what I am certain of is that for the first time in like seventeen years I am totally and unequivocally free!

"Come home," I say to Quincy.

"Mom! Where are you?" he asks.

"I'm home."

"You are? How was it?"

"Beautiful. And how about your vacation? Are you still having fun? Did you catch any fish?"

"Well, first of all I've been sorta having fun but Dad goes to bed kind of early and he took me to the arcade a few times so I could play Mortal Kombat Three and it was pretty cool and I caught six fish but they were too little so we had to throw them back."

"Oh, that was nice. So your plane gets in next Saturday at noon, right?"

"Yep."

"I'll be standing at the gate with open arms."

"Please don't, Mom. It's not necessary to have your arms open."

"Goodbye, Quincy, and tell your daddy I said hello and I'll call him after you get home."

"Wait!"

"What?"

"Mom, did you bring me anything from Jamaica?"

"Yes, I brought you lots of things."

"Like what?"

"Surprise surprise surprise," I say and hang up.

* * *

I am really home. I have just been fired from my job. And Jimmy crack corn and I don't care! If it wouldn't make me look so stupid I would call Winston right now. But I'm not going to. What would I say anyway? I just got home and I'm still thinking about you? I dreamed about you all the way home on the plane? I am already trying to figure out how I'm going to teach myself to forget about you? Because what this really was—according to an article I read on the plane—is called a "fling." A fling is when you go on vacation and get wild and crazy with someone you don't know and have the best sex and everything is so euphoric that you wish you could feel this way forever but because there are usually geographical problems and maybe language barriers and major cultural differences and say a vast disparity in age do not—repeat: do not—take this shit seriously because when you get home it's like over good-bye hastalavista baby no I probably won't see you next year but it was like steaming hot and I had a fabulous time and I hope I get as lucky when I go to Brazil next year, you know? However, on some rare occasions when you get home and days go by and you can't seem to get this person out of your mind and then you actually like find yourself calling him or her on the phone and writing little notes weeks later, then maybe just maybe this could like turn into a real relationship. For the most part, however, play it safe and forget about him.

Which is what I basically decide to do.

I go to Home Depot specifically to buy some long-bed boxes of zinnias and petunias and chrysanthemums and some bigger pots for my ficus and schefflera and some huge bags of potting soil vermiculite and peat moss, a few pairs of those gardening gloves and then I'm like out of there with my cart, which I push out to and get everything easily into the back of my truck.

I am in the backyard on my knees digging holes in the ground and poking little flowers inside each one and the soil is soft and cool even through these gloves and deciding which flowers to put where and how to group them becomes important to me and I get up from time to time to stand back and look at the pattern or lack of pattern these tiny bouquets are beginning to make and I enjoy how much livelier the yard is looking already. I don't even realize that I have been out here now for more than two hours until I hear what sounds like the engine of my car pulling into the driveway and the phone ringing at the same time. I walk over to the outdoor table and pick up the portable.

"Yes yes yes," I say.

"Your lovely sister and favorite niece are in your driveway and we are here to collect our gifts and I hope a check too and I've got some good news and I've got some bad news so come out to the garage and tell me which you want to hear first."

I hang up and walk through the garage and the two of them are in the front of my black BMW which is an M-5 racing car which I did not need but I bought anyway because I could afford it and liked it and it goes fast.

Vanessa is standing next to the car. She walks over and gives me a hug. She could be Pepa's sister of Salt-N-Pepa, at least that's what Quincy's friend Dexter thought the first time he was over and Vanessa walked in the door and his eyes got big and he said, "Pepa?" and she said, "Who, sweetheart?" and that's how he knew it wasn't her. *"What up, cradle-robber?"* she yells.

"Don't even start, Vanessa."

Chantel finally gets out of the car because apparently she was listening to something on the radio, probably some nasty sex-oriented gangsta rap song because she likes just about all of them. She and Quincy are the same age and often when I take him somewhere I take her too. She's sort of like the daughter I wish I could have had but never had and never will have.

"What are you doing?" Vanessa asks, putting her hands on her big hips.

"I'm planting flowers."

"Since when did you start planting flowers?"

"I've been meaning to do this for the past couple of years, so I'm doing it like now. Got a problem with that?"

"You look cute," she says. "Different. Like you kind of got like this little . . . I don't know. I can't put my finger on it."

"Well, I am four or five shades darker, Vanessa."

"Hi, Auntie Stel," Chantel says. She is my blossoming little cookie dough niece. Last year she was as thin as paper and this year she's actually got curves.

"Hi, honeybunny," I say and she runs inside the house, as if she's trying to get away from something. "Okay, cut the bullshit. Your bad news can't be any worse than what I've just gotten."

"What?"

"I am no longer employed."

"Get the hell out of here?" she says, looking around the truck to make sure Chantel is inside the house.

"Yep. They pulled this shit on me while I was gone."

"Can you sue 'em?"

"Everybody always wants to sue somebody. I don't have the time or the energy but I'll be getting what's mine. I'm not even worried about it."

"Wow, this is like totally fucked up, Stella. What a way to come home from vacation."

"I'm not really all that upset about it if you want to know the truth."

"I'm checking you out. You seem too calm, at least that's what I think I'm hearing in your voice. Are you on something?"

"No, I'm not on anything. Spare me. Now tell me what your bad news is."

"Promise you won't be too mad at me?"

"What is it, Vanessa?"

"Wait up. Did you write the check already?"

"I said I'd lend it to you. Now what is it?"

"I had a little accident."

I look over at the car. "Where?"

"The rear end. Left side. Taillight."

I walk back and look at it and sure enough it's cracked and there is a little dent on the side. "What happened?"

"This stupid son-of-a-bitch wasn't even looking where he was going when I was trying to back out of this parking space and like *pow!* I tapped him."

"No problem."

"You mean you're not pissed?"

"It's just a stupid little accident. Did anybody get hurt?"

She looks as if she doesn't quite believe this because I do have a reputation for being high-strung, for "going off," but only if I'm provoked, and occasionally for not being the most understanding when it comes to sensitive emotional issues. Or at least that's the word out on the street.

"No. Nobody got hurt," she says very slowly. "Girl, what has gotten into you? You ain't tripping and I know you're crazy about this car."

"It's just a stupid car. It can be fixed. What's the big deal?"

Then she starts laughing. "That young boy musta really done something to you. Look at me, Stella."

After she says this I can't because I feel myself blushing and I can't hide it with these dirty gloves on so I drop my face and then Vanessa runs over to me and lifts my chin up and says, "What has happened to you?"

I try my damnedest to wipe the smirk off my face and I say, "Nothing. And your check's on the kitchen counter. Go get it."

"You didn't go down there and fall in love with a twenty-one-year-old, did you, Stella?"

"Are you crazy?"

"No. *I'm* not crazy. Are you?" And she is staring at me like she hasn't seen me in twenty years or like I've just cut off all my hair or dyed it some outrageous color and she is giving me a serious once-over. "Something is different about you, Stella, and I'ma tell you something. You look better now than I've seen you look in a long time. I'm not kidding, you actually have like a twinkle or something in your damn eyes."

"I do not have any twinkle in my eyes. I'm just darker. I went on vacation and apparently it worked."

"That's not even what I'm talking about and you know it, Stella. You did fall in love with him, didn't you? Tell the truth."

"Would you stop it, Vanessa. You don't even know what you're talking about."

"Well, answer me this. How do you feel?"

"I feel good, as James Brown would say," and I start laughing.

"Cut the bullshit, Stella. Tell me."

"Okay, I feel something. I don't know what it is, but all I know is that I feel good inside, lighter, better than I have in years. I feel like, like I could plant every flower in the world in my backyard today."

She is smiling at me. "Whew." She sighs. "Well, just keep this to yourself. Let it be your business."

"I am," I say. "Now what's the good news?"

"Oh. The good news is that when I had the accident you know I was on my way to Reno with my girl Cassandra who I work with and to be totally honest I had my mind on my money and my money on my mind but I won three hundred and sixty bucks playing the slots!"

"That's your good news. Where's mine?"

"What's mine is yours, isn't it, Sis?"

"No. And we're not even going that far," and I turn to head toward the backyard.

"Wait a minute, girl! Take those stupid gloves off. We came over here to collect," she says and pushes me in the other direction. "And you better not hadda bought us no cheap shit and I hope you've got some champagne in here cause it's hot as hell out here and not only that but it's summertime and the living is easy and I want you to tell me all about Jamaica and this young man of yours. I'm serious. I want to know what a twenty-one-year-old boy can do for a forty-two-year-old woman that would make her look five years younger in a single week and she comes home and not be pissed after hearing that her sister has wrecked her sixty-thousand-dollar car and she still lends her a thousand big ones and she finds out that she is fired from her megabucks job that I certainly wish I had and yet she is still as cool as a cucumber. I want to hear it all," she says and puts her hands on her hips. "Blow—by—blow."

So I tell her.

I t ain't nothing but a meatball," I say to myself as I begin to pack up three of those stupid computers that have taken up so much room in my home office which while I'm at it I decide to redecorate repaint in fact I should like move altogether and just build a-whole-nother house! This notion flies right out the window of course because now I have no job and thank the Lord my mother taught me how to save my allowance for a rainy day which has been reincarnated and come back as tax-free municipal bonds and it was one of the few things Mama told me to do that I actually did and I am also grateful that years ago I made some solid investments in a now-famous coffee company and a very popular consumer shopping establishment that I frequent myself but do not get any special discounts at and thanks to Leroy who despite whatever shortcomings he may have physically emotionally and spiritually does have mucho business savvy and didn't mind sharing some of it with me. In fact he urged me implored me to become partners with him which against my better judgment I went ahead and did but only after he promised me that even if I stopped sleeping with him that shouldn't stop us from making money together which made perfect sense to me and he kept his word so I am like a major shareholder and part owner of a number of thriving fast-food soft-drink enterprises which I prefer not to name.

Plus I'm also not stupid. One of the primary and most important lessons you learn in securities is how to cover your own ass first. Why would I spend all my time and energy showing other folks how to make money if I didn't myself? My mentors always stressed the fact that as soon as you make more than enough to earn a living, start making a living. Put a small percentage of your income somewhere it'll grow faster than the speed of light and just like playing in Vegas take a risk but never risk more than you can afford to lose and then take some of that hard-won money and put it in a safer sure but slower-paced place so you don't have to stress over how it's performing but the goal is to have all of your investments spread out over into everything from umbrella insurance policies to stocks so that if you ever lose your job or even die your bills are covered your ass is covered your children are taken care of and so I took their advice and if I were to say die today or something my portfolio is set up so that after everything is paid off whoever inherits my property and possessions won't even have to pay any inheritance tax. So unlike some of these hotsy-totsy movie stars athletes rappers and rock-and-roll stars who spend all their money on expensive cars clothes mansions and go bankrupt from excessing, I will not. Over the past five years or so I followed my own tips which basically means that I can afford not to work for the next two and a half to three years without freaking out.

I will however verify and confirm this with my accountant my broker and by reviewing my own portfolio.

I don't know why this never occurred to me before, that I have actually been in a position not to work, but I guess it's because I've just always worked and besides I always thought what I was doing meant something to somebody, that I provided a valuable and unique service of some kind, but apparently what they say is true: you can always be replaced. But you know what? Fuck 'em.

I am also very much aware that I don't have a clue as to what I'm going to do to take the place of my job. What I do know for certain is that I am not walking through any more revolving doors with a suit on, gripping an attaché case. To hell with corporate America where people don't count but revenue has a pulse and all they do is watch it on an EKG. I give. So the search is on to find a place where I can be me and still make a living even though the truth is I don't have very many if any "marketable" skills except for designing and since I no longer have a job to distract me perhaps I'll pay closer attention to what used to give me pleasure in a major way.

My back and front yards are full of flowers and the roots of my indoor plants now have more than enough room to breathe. I feel like I'm coming down with something, like a cold or maybe even an ulcer, so I take an Advil and sit around and wait for it to kick in but when it does I still feel the same way: like I'm getting sick. I am folding the rest of my vacation laundry and beginning to put the last of the shorts and T-shirts into their respective drawers when I find myself dropping them on the bed and calling long distance information and getting the number of the hotel and for fifty cents they connect me and when I hear a Jamaican accent say, "Good afternoon thank you for calling Windswept this is operator Jasmine speaking how may I direct your call?" and I ask to speak to Winston Shakespeare and I'm thinking what a name what a man to have such a name and what a fool I am to be calling him and just as I come to my senses and am considering hanging up I hear his voice say, "Winston Shakespeare here," and I say, "Hello, Winston," and let out a sigh.

"Is that you there, Stella?"

"Yes, it's me," I say, feeling and probably looking pretty much like Jim Carrey in *Dumb and Dumber*. Da. Da. Da.

"How are yoooou?" he sings.

"I'm fine. I'm home."

"Yes, I know."

"I just called to say hello, Winston."

"Can you hold on a minute while I change to a private phone because I'm having a hard time hearing you in here. I'll only be a second. Don't go anywhere please."

"Okay," I say and stare out my kitchen window and all of a sudden I really feel stupid because what am I going to say to him: Winston I can't seem to stop thinking about you and I am one step away from buying my very own bottle of Escape for Men and spraying it all over my pillows and sheets so that I can just inhale you at night and I miss you so much it is driving me crazy and I'm just wondering if you're feeling anything close to what I'm feeling I mean were you like as affected as I was I mean are you like having trouble thinking and connecting the dots unless you are the dots and what am I what are we going to do about this because you and I both know this is ridiculous I am too old for you and you are too young for me and it would never work how would could we do this to make it work oh it would never work so let's just forget it?

"Stella, are you still there?"

"Yes, I'm still here."

"I sent you a postcard just today."

I am touched. "For real?"

"Yes, and you know I've been feeling very strange lately and I seem not to have any pep in my step if you know my meaning and everybody has been saying to me, 'Winston, man, what's wrong with you?' and I didn't know at first what they were talking about but then it dawned on me that I am feeling very depressed and it hit me that I didn't start feeling like this until after you left. Sooo, I'm telling you that I miss you, Stella."

My heart hurts. It is sinking and burning and dropping fast into the cave of my stomach and then all of a sudden I simply feel hot. I am coming down with something for sure and it's on the other end of this phone. That much I have figured out. "I miss you too, Winston," I say. "More than you will ever know."

"And how much could that be?"

"A lot. It's rather ridiculous really."

"It's not so ridiculous, Stella."

And then there is like this silence and then some more silence and then he says, "Stella?"

And I say, "Yes?"

"I want you to know that I had the best time of my whole life when I was with you."

"I'm glad to hear that, Winston. But we didn't really

spend that much time together when you really think about it."

"Precisely."

I hear him breathing and I believe I can smell him through this telephone and for certain I can see his lips move when he says, "I really hope I can see you again, Stella."

My shoulders drop my chest collapses my whole torso falls forward until my face is dangling close to the floor, and I hear myself whimpering, "I feel the same way, Winston." This is like too pathetic and I'm glad nobody can see me hear me in here behaving like I'm seventeen.

"Mine feels rather urgent, though."

"Mine too," I say. Dork. Dork.

"And I was thinking."

"What?"

"I was thinking that maybe in three months' time I can take a sick leave and come to California to visit you for a week or two. How does that sound?"

Here? He wants to come here? I like this idea a lot. I like it a whole lot but three months is a very long time and a woman could shrivel up in three months when she is like craving something and can't have it but then again I am trying to learn to be a more patient person and what a way to test myself and besides the most important thing right now is that I am not in this alone. It is not just me who has been bitten thank the Lord it's not just me.

"I'd really like that, Winston," I say. "You don't know how much I'd like that."

"I'm going to look into it," he says.

"Well, do you like your job?"

"It's good. I'm learning more and more each day. I could become a head chef after perhaps a year of apprenticing although it would do me good to get more training, but this is fine for right now as I'm gaining experience."

"What about your living quarters?"

"Well, it's okay. I sleep on a twin-sized bed and I have a roommate. He's okay but it's kind of cramped, you know, but it'll have to do as this is the way it is at every resort when you come on board like this."

"Do you have a TV?"

"No."

"Stereo?"

"Are you kidding?"

"Refrigerator?"

"No."

"Then what?"

"I told you," he says, laughing. "A twin-sized bed and a place to keep your personal belongings and that's it."

"So it's sort of like living in a college dormitory."

"Exactly," he says. "And your son, how is he?"

"He's still visiting his dad."

"And where is he again?"

"Colorado."

"In the Rockies, is he?"

I giggle. "Yes, sort of. He comes home Saturday morning and I can't wait to see him."

"It's nice having a son, hey?"

"Very. At least I like the one I have."

He laughs. "I hope to meet him soon."

Wow. The thought of Winston meeting Quincy kind of

wigs me out for a minute because what would I say to my child: "Quincy I want you to meet Mom's new boyfriend who cannot vote or buy liquor in America and no he's not going to be your stepdad but how about thinking of him as say more like a big brother and please don't ask me about his age but yes he will probably be willing to play Sega and Super NES with you, no problem, mon!

"You'd like Quincy," I say for lack of anything better.

"So what have you been doing since you've been home?"

I want to say getting fired and constantly thinking about you, but of course I don't, and instead I say, "Well, I've been planting flowers and making some career decisions."

"What's that again?"

"I'll write and tell you all about it."

"Will you?"

"I will."

"It feels good to hear your voice, Stella. You just don't know. Can you tell I'm smiling?"

What is so weird is that I actually *can* tell but what's even weirder is how much I know I must sound like some teenybopper. I have to cover my mouth and yank on my cheek to get that humming electricity out of it and then and only then am I able to say, "I'm smiling too, Winston."

"So you will write?"

"I promise," I say, and when I hang up the phone I am like ga-ga-ga-ga and I think about that stupid article I read on the plane and I guess we are sort of passing by the fling stage because we are speaking to each other on the phone and he has already written me a postcard and he has just said he wants to see me again and Lord what I wouldn't pay to feel those lips see those eyes stand within a foot of him and smell him again and it hasn't even been a week and that article claimed the so-called cutoff period to determine if your fling was turning into something serious was two. I feel like I should drop the author an I-beg-to-differ-with-you note.

I don't really mean that. I am not *even* thinking about any article when I lie on the bed stare up at the ceiling fan spinning and spinning until it feels like my heart is spinning and spinning in the opposite direction until I realize that I am feeling suspended comforted soothed as if I have been endorsed. As if for the first time in a long time someone has just said to me I like you because you are you and that's it. It's just that simple. He hasn't asked me where I live or what kind of house I live in or how much money I make or what kind of car I drive none of that bullshit that I am almost always asked by legalized grown-up men and it gets on my nerves every time. It's funny too that Winston hasn't once mentioned his or my age and I wonder if he's pretending that I'm not forty-two years old. Maybe he's forgotten. But what about when he remembers? Oh who cares. Shit. I like him. He likes me. And I'm happy about it. That's what I know right now. And right now it's enough. As a matter of fact it's good and plenty.

For some reason (and I *do* understand the reason because I'm not completely dense) I get this surge of energy and put away all my clothes in like one-two-three and then I head for the mall where I plan on buying Quincy a pair of sneakers that fit because his feet have grown again and that new CD by Monica with that song "Just One of Them Thangs" that I absolutely love and Mr. Shaggy Boombastic who is of all things Jamaican and oh yes TLC *CrazySexy-Cool* which I will buy two of because Quincy and I cannot share CDs ever since I bought him his own miniature stereo system for his room after he all of a sudden started watching MTV like it was going out of style and even I like Beavis and Butt-head every now and then and I'm not all that worried about my child being badly influenced because he knows from whence he came. And even though the word "fuck" is like my favorite curse word of all time and I use it as like all parts of speech my son has never and hopefully will never hear me use it oh I forgot that time when I was PMSing and he was fixing his go-cart and he had all the tools sitting on top of my car which scratched it and put a dent in it and it cost $2,300 to get fixed and I did go off on him and use the F word but he has not even come close to doing anything so costly again without thinking about it first and so I continue to use the F word privately because I use it more for personal reasons like for processing and digesting thoughts for use in front of dear friends and close relatives who also seem to favor its usage.

It seems like it was only a few weeks ago that Quincy was watching Nick at Nite and then all of a sudden like overnight switched to *MTV Jams* hosted by Bill Bellamy which is why he knows what's up with the latest music and keeps me well informed but he has been begging for TLC and he says he thinks the one with the patch over her left eye is cute and when I told him that she burned down her boyfriend's house all he said was So I still think she's pretty cute and I like her, Mom, and all I'm really grateful for is that this is the first evidence I've seen of him even noticing girls and I give him credit for having good taste buds and he is like starting from the top and even though I know it may be racist and sexist and I should be ashamed of myself but the fact that she is black kind of pleases me and the fact that she is a she pleases me even more so no problem, mon, is what I'm thinking as I turn into the mall parking lot and hell I might as well go ahead and get him a few new T-shirts that I'll hide in his drawers to save so he can "have it going on" at least during his very first week of junior fucking high school.

I hadn't planned on buying Winston anything so I am as surprised as anyone when I find myself in Foot Locker buying Quincy two pairs of size ten Airwalks and without thinking twice asking the guy if he could bring out a size thirteen of these Nike Airs which are hot off the press. I know not what I'm doing but then again I think maybe I do. The old wives' tale is that if you buy a man a pair of shoes he will most likely walk away from you. I want Winston to walk away from me. That would be the safest thing. It would also be the smartest thing. This much I do know.

But then I go a little crazy. When I go into the music store to get Quincy's CDs I begin to pick out CDs that I know Winston likes but probably doesn't have because he doesn't have any money and I must buy about six or seven of them for him: some hip-hoppers of course and some

rap and I throw Seal in for good measure and Mary J.
Blige and when I get outside the store it occurs to me that
he doesn't have a CD player so I decide to get him a
portable one with headphones and once in the store I figure I could use one on airplanes but now that I'm out of
a job how often will I actually be flying but then I could
also use it at the beach or outside in the backyard and
Quincy could use one too when we're driving up to the
mountains and I want silence and he wants Monteil Jordan so I get him a cheap one because he will drop it lose
it something and so now we all have CD players.

Of course the same thing happens with the T-shirts. I
go No Fear crazy too. I get Winston four and Quincy five
because after all he is my son. When I see those Kipling
backpacks in Macy's, I remember that Quincy needs a new
one so I pick a forest green for him and grab another for
Winston, just because. I am walking past the Sunglass Hut
and I see those cool mirrored glasses that wrap around
your face that all the young guys are wearing and I am
whipping out my Visa card once again but I am like totally
enjoying this, this business of doing something for somebody else. I mean Winston has like nothing, and this
might make him smile, let him know that someone, that I
am thinking about him. I will let it be a surprise. But. On
the other hand. What if he thinks I'm doing this to impress him or maybe I'm trying to buy his affection like
that old lady in that Richard Gere gigolo movie. I'm not
that fucking old, so why would he think that, Stella? And
besides, this stuff doesn't even add up to my car payment.

*   *   *

Angela is sitting on the side porch as I pull into my driveway. She looks upset about something. "You have gone and just completely lost your mind, haven't you?"

"What are you talking about?"

"Don't play dumb with me, Stella. You must think you're Diana Ross or Cher or somebody—is that what this is all about?"

"Look, it's hot as hell out here can I at least go inside my own house and get a glass of ice water while you rant and rave?"

"I didn't come over here to rant and rave whatsoever," she says, following me inside. "What did you buy? What's in all these bags?"

"None of your business," I say and push all four into the pantry. If she had a life she wouldn't be so nosy.

She sits down at the kitchen table, turns her chair so that it faces me, spreads her legs open and says, "Stella, you aren't serious about this boy?"

"Who said anything about being serious? Damn. Why is everybody making such a big fucking deal about this?"

"You're apparently the one making a big fucking deal about it and apparently your neighbors are all asking questions."

"How do you know what my neighbors are asking?"

"Because Vanessa said that the woman who lives across the street from you whose daughter is in Chantel's class told her that her mother told her that you've got a new boyfriend and that Quincy might just have a new dad."

"You're shitting me."

"Look, Stella, tell me for real what the deal is."

"I just like him, that's all."

"Do you realize what you're saying?"

"Yes."

"Do you realize how simple you sound?"

"Yes," I repeat and I'm trying hard not to laugh, because she's not with me, not even close.

"You're not taking this any further, I hope."

"What do you mean by 'any further'?"

"You're not planning on seeing him again?"

"Not anytime soon."

"What!"

"I said not anytime soon."

"I cannot believe my ears. Okay. Let's try this. Let's say for instance that you are serious. And answer this honestly. What can he possibly do for you?"

I am pretty much inclined to walk over to the door and open it and just ask her to take her Miss Goody Two-Shoes pregnant ass home but I also want to say you don't get it because you don't get anything. If it doesn't add up then it's a negative to you. But you know what? This *doesn't* add up. And I really don't give a flying fuck. Which is the whole point. All I know is that right now I feel good and this young man is responsible for it. He makes me feel like I'm in flight, he makes me feel like a rainbow, for lack of a better fucking cliché. "What did you just ask me?"

"What can he *possibly* do for you?"

"He's already done it." I sigh.

"Oh has he now. And just what is that? Can you give it a name?"

I am losing my patience with her about now so I storm over and put my hands on my hips and I say, "How about this: He makes me feel like I've been doing lines of coke like I've just smoked a good joint had a few drinks run a ten K had a deep tissue massage skied fifty miles per hour down KT-22 at Squaw Valley had a double espresso and a Xanax all at the same time. How's that?"

"You are tripping *so* hard."

"I haven't *done* anything! I'm not marrying him! I just slept with him and hope I get a chance to do it again and plus I happen to like him. What is so wrong with that?"

She is calm. "Haven't you heard about this stuff? It's called tropical fever or something. I mean think about it. You went to an exotic place that from what I hear is pretty close to paradise and you meet this fine young boy who of course any woman in her right mind would want to screw and then you do, but most people would just do it drop it and come on home. Get on with their normal regular life. Why can't you just do that?"

"I am trying to! I've only been home a few days and you're making it seem as if I'm about to elope!"

"I'm worried about you. You're acting too giddy."

"What do you mean by that?"

"Vanessa said all you've been doing is giggling."

"So?"

"We're not used to seeing you like this."

"Like *what?*"

She's searching for the germane word but I decide to help her: "Happy?"

"Yes."

"Oh, so is there a law out there somewhere that says Stella can't be happy if a young man is partially responsible?"

"I didn't say that."

"You and Vanessa have just gotten so used to seeing me feeling and acting beige instead of yellow, lonely and blue instead of excited and red hot, that now just because I'm acting like I'm alive or being a little daring and not just content being Lois Lane you can't handle it. Go on. Admit it!"

"Well, you don't have to say it like that because it's not true."

"It is true."

"You're the oldest, Stella. The one whose feet should be firmly planted on the ground."

"They are. I'm just kicking up some soil. I have a right to, you know."

"Stella." She groans as if she's losing her patience.

"What?"

"You know every young man's fantasy is to sleep with an older woman. Did you know that?"

"Not really."

"Yep. Evan slept with a woman thirty-five."

"He told you?"

"Of course he told me."

"And? Your point?"

"He slept with her quite a number of times. It was good for his ego, knowing he was able to satisfy a grown woman."

"And?"

"That's all it was. An ego booster."

"Look. You don't even know Winston, so don't compare my experience with Evan's little brush with lust."

"Like there's a difference?"

"I'd say so."

"Have you thought about the fact that this Winston is the same age as your nephew?"

That was low. "He's not my nephew."

"Well, just keep in mind that you are old enough to be his mother and think how embarrassing this whole thing could be for Quincy. I mean you do care about your child, don't you?"

"You can stop anytime now, Angela."

"Wait. Let me just ask you one last question."

"I'm listening," I say, exasperated.

"You did practice safe sex, I hope?" and she gives me this look.

"Fuck you, Angela," I say, but what I want to say is: Go home. Take a nap. Go put on an apron or something, go look for more emergency exits, since you seem to know where they all are, or go home and study your earthquake kit, because I've got tons of shit I need to do around here before Quincy gets home.

Now she's rubbing her hands over her mixing bowl belly more for effect than anything and she knows she has gotten on my nerves but she loves getting on people's nerves because it seems to be what confirms that she is indeed doing something, that she is in fact an active member of a real family and that she can do something that will make you actually respond. I feel like putting her in a high chair or a playpen and sticking a pacifier in her mouth. "Vanessa told me about your job."

"It's no biggie."

"I'd say it's a very big biggie and I hope you seek legal counsel so that you can get some kind of redress and you know Kennedy has all kinds of friends with expertise in this kind of situation."

"I doubt if it'll come to a lawsuit."

"You never know," she says, heading for the door hallelujah. "You can never be too prepared."

Oh yes you can, I think. And you're living proof of what can happen when you are.

My arms are stretched out as far as they will go when Quincy comes walking through the airport gate grinning his little buns off and runs into my arms like he's my baby which he is and one day I hope my sense of color and style will rub off on him and he'll choose his attire so that one thing coincides with or at least complements the other because right now he is decked out in a pair of brown plaid baggy shorts and an orange-and-green Phoenix Suns T-shirt and I'm not even going to mention the red Cardinals baseball hat which thank the Lord is on backwards. He is nevertheless still my chocolate chip.

"Hi there, bud!" I say as I squeeze him and can't help but notice that he has that same old skunkish smell that I thought we had like mastered. "Quincy!" I say and push him away. "Where have you been?"

"Oh Mom, don't start that skunk stuff again. So I smell a little bit. Everybody does. What's the big deal? I'm your son. Take me as I am."

I run. He takes off behind me and people are staring at us like what a shame, can't take them anywhere. But do we care? He rushes past me and I meet him in baggage claim because he is familiar with Oakland airport, having actually earned enough miles on a number of different airlines for a few free trips. As a result his name is circulating and has landed on some pretty impressive mailing lists and he has even been offered an American Express card a Diner's and a Hertz gold card. He begged and pleaded with me could he fill out the applications and I said, "Of course you can," and off he went with his pen in hand and the first question he asked me was who was his employer and I told him I was and the next one was what was his salary and I said you don't have one and he said come on Mom I have to put something in the blank so I said okay put five dollars in there and he said but they asked how much per month and I said you've learned multiplication this year figure it out and so he yells that's only twenty dollars a month who can live off that and I told him to get a life and leave me alone and then he asks how long has he been employed and I said ten and a half years, because that's how old he was when he filled the last ones out, signed and mailed two of them and I had to be the bearer of bad news that his income and his credit history weren't substantial enough and that he should try back when he's like thirteen or something. He has both denial letters in a special drawer in his desk and plans to send his new applications directly to the persons whose names are at the bottom on his thirteenth birthday because he is sure they will remember him. They have to, he says.

On the drive home he turns to me and says, "Mom, you look different."

"I'm darker," I say for the third time in the last few days as if no one really noticed.

"I can see that. I know what it is! You've got braids in your hair!"

"It took you thirty-five minutes to notice?"

"Not really. It's just that I'm telling you right now."

"So what do you think?"

"I like them. There are so many of them," he says. "Can I touch them?"

"Sure," I say and when his fingers touch the hair I growl and really freak him out.

"Mom!" and he is laughing.

"I'm happy to see you, Quincy."

"And I'm happy to see you too, Mom. Can we stop at McDonald's? My dad never took me to McDonald's because he's on a diet and he says it's too tempting so I like ate this weird food with him. Do I look skinnier?"

"No. But you look a little darker yourself, homie."

"Sitting out there doing all that fishing is what did it."

"And you enjoyed being with your dad?"

"Yeah, he's a pretty cool guy."

I nod, thinking I felt that way about him once too.

The dog and the cat block the driveway so that I have to honk to get them to move. Tails are wagging and Quincy gets out of the car and runs over to bond with them and I am like touched and this picture is like something straight off Nickelodeon for which I am grateful.

He runs straight upstairs to his room and then back down. "Mom, these are so cool!" he says, holding up a pair of red black green and yellow long muslin shorts I bought him that have a drawstring waist and which will probably not stay up anyway because my child is still going through that baby orangutan stage. "Thank you!" he says and disappears and then runs back out and says, "Wow! Mom! Look at this!" as if I too should be surprised at this stuff as if I am not the person who purchased it, but I say, "Wow! That's pretty nice, huh?" and we go through this, from the peace necklace I got at Macy's but he thinks it's from Jamaica and I don't bother to correct him, straight on down to the purple-and-black suede airwalks which of course he is now wearing with white socks pulled up to his knobby knees which also touch the bottom of his red black green and yellow shorts and he has somehow found a clammy cocoa brown Mossimo T-shirt which is supposed to be for school but does noticeably bring out the white etching on the peace sign dangling against that coral necklace and all of this together causes me to cover my eyes when he stands in front of me and says, "Thanks, Mom. You are so nice to me."

But this is not necessarily true, so I don't even get into it. I just let him run outside to show all the neighbors what I brought him back from Jamaica.

Quincy's been home now for three days and we're pretty much getting back into our routine although during the summer we don't actually have what would normally be considered a routine. What *is* becoming routine is that I hardly see Quincy because he lives outside with his friends and as soon as it gets dark and everybody is bored or tired I wait for the Big Question which is can Jeremy or Justin or Jason sleep over and then when I say yes they all come with sleeping bags and new Sega games. Though when his friends are here he has no real use for me except to ask permission to eat or drink something, and as soon as they are gone he is of course ready to bond. Even so the one thing I am grateful for is that no matter who's here or not here he always makes sure he gets his good night kiss and hug from me, except for maybe like one or two or three times lately.

He has finally told me all about his visit with his dad which sounded rather dull to me but I sat there and grinned the entire time trying to figure out when I'm going to tell him that I am no longer employed but he just got home he doesn't need to deal with any losses right now because after all it is summer vacation. While he rearranges his drawers I see him take three pairs of grungy dirty caked-with-hard-mud sneakers and a few pairs of straggly rough-and-had-their-day sandals and one pair of good church shoes that he's only worn once in six months and that no longer fit of course and he carefully and meticulously turns all of them on their sides so they are stacked neatly inside the bottom drawer of his chest and I watch in horror in pure amazement really but I decide once again just to keep my mouth shut because this is the child's room his private space and I do not want to impose my own mores and standards on him with the exception of personal cleanliness.

I have just barbecued some rib eyes and baked a couple of those microwave twice-baked Ore-Ida baked potatoes with cheddar cheese for him and chive and onions for me and I have made like this uplifting romaine salad with Japanese gourmet rice vinegar which has absolutely no fat and we are now sitting together bonding at the dinner table.

"So, Mom, tell me all about your trip."

"What trip?"

"*Mom . . .* Did you have fun in Jamaica?"

"I did indeed."

"What did you do?"

"Well," I say and I am grinning. "I spent a lot of time at the beach and you won't believe the water, Quincy, it's bluer and warmer than it is in Maui and do you know that when I got in the water schools of baby fish would swim around my feet?"

"No kidding? Right there at the beach, Mom?"

"Right there at the beach. And I went parasailing and snorkeling and the snorkeling was better than Hawaii too because the water is only ten feet deep and you don't need a life vest and I went Jet Skiing and it was just great and . . ." I get up and dash over to the kitchen counter and get a few extra postcards I failed to send or ran out of people I felt would appreciate receiving a postcard from me and I show them to Quincy who flips through them all with a vengeance until he comes to a duplicate of the cliff divers at Rick's Café that I'd sent him.

"Did you do this?" His eyes are open so wide he looks like a fool. But he is one handsome-looking little fool and I am so glad his looks are finally coming to the fore so to speak because I was having my doubts there for a while—a number of years actually—when everything on his face looked too big for his head or his head looked too big for those small features on his face except for those horse teeth that pretty much knocked those baby teeth right out

of the way but over the past six months everything seems to be blending and jelling pretty nicely if I do say so myself.

"Did you, Mom? Please don't tell me you did this."

"No, but I sure wanted to. Next time."

"Next time? When are you going back?"

"I don't know. Maybe next year."

"Gee, Mom, you always get to go to the best places and everywhere that's really fun and this looks so cool and you and I haven't even had our vacation together this summer and where are we going anyway, oh yeah, I forgot you said we're going to that dumb Martha's Vineyard wherever that is and you know I really wanted to go to Africa since I was like seven years old and you promised me we could go to the Ivory Coast and Nigeria but then you said not Nigeria because of all that political stuff going on there and some wars and stuff inside the city limits so then didn't you say we could go to like Senegal and if we had enough time and money we could maybe like hop over to Kenya and I know we're not going to Africa because you haven't brought it up once and so I'm begging you pleading with you: your poor deprived never-gets-to-leave-the-United-States-of-America-except-in-his-dreams-or-when-he's-On-line-America son is on his knees"—and he gets on his knees—"please Mom please can we go to Jamaica for our vacation instead of Martha's Vineyard?"

I sit there and stare at him and I am cracking up and he gets this phony pleading puppy-dog look on his face and then he exaggerates it even more so that he actually begins to look like a dog and then we both start cracking up and I hear myself say, "Okay."

He jumps up from the floor and says, "Really?"

"Sure. Why not."

"You're not kidding me, are you?"

"Nope."

He gives me a sloppy kiss on the cheek. "I love you, Mom," he yells. "You are the best mom in the whole world and as a matter of fact you're the best mom I've ever had!" And he runs to the telephone and dials a number before I can ask who he's calling and I hear him say, "Guess what, Chantel, we're going to Jamaica!"

He turns to me and says, "When, Mom? How soon can we leave?"

And I say, "I don't know. Soon."

"Soon," he says. "Probably like in the next couple of weeks if we can get a flight out." And just when did he become Mr. Jet-Setter? He then turns to me and says, "Mom, Chantel wants to know if she can go too."

"Why?"

"My mom wants to know why," and he is laughing because we always tease her like this.

"She says because she's never been to Jamaica."

"Tell her to watch more of the Discovery Channel instead of *Living Single* and maybe she'll travel all over the world."

"Mom, come on."

"Ask her why hasn't she ever been to Jamaica in all eleven years of her life."

"Come on, Mom. She heard you and she said she does watch the Discovery Channel, so can she, Mom?"

"Okay," I say. "Okay. Now get your butt back over here and finish eating."

"Mom, do I have to eat the asparagus?" he pleads after he hangs up.

"It is my duty as your loving caring considerate mother to make sure you chew swallow and digest something from the five food groups on a daily basis. Now sit down."

"There are only three food groups."

"Are not."

"Yes there are," he says. "Sugar, sugar and more sugar."

"Sit your little narrow behind down and eat everything that's green on this plate or you won't be going anywhere near Jamaica."

"Whatever you say, Little Woman," he says, winking at me. "And I love you too!" But in less time than it takes me to get a glass of water all five of those green stems are gone.

I can't believe I've agreed to do this but now that I've already opened my big mouth I feel as if I can't back out but then again I could lie and say we can't get any flights to Jamaica but the more I think about it the more I know not only that I want to go back but I feel like I need to because I need to see Winston one more time. To sort of finish this. Stop it or something. Get some kind of closure. Or if this is like a crush or an infatuation or even a fantasy or delusion, I can like register him once and for all in my brain and in one fell swoop erase him and then just get over it. He's probably going to freak out when I tell him I'm coming back to Jamaica and what if he doesn't want to see me this time, what if he was just faking over the telephone pretending he missed me and what if it was all just a front because he knew the chances of us ever reconnecting were slim to zero? Shit. Me and my big mouth.

The travel agent cracks up when I tell her that I'm thinking about going back but since I will have these children with me is there a nice hotel in Negril where I might be able to take them? She shows me a picture of the Frangipani Hotel which is pretty and peach and right next to the Paradise Grand Resort which is for couples only and where supposedly love is all you need because some friends of mine sent me a postcard from there once that said that and right now I am beginning to think that there is some truth to it. She makes a tentative reservation for the three of us in coach which I am already dreading because I am spoiled and don't do coach very well since my job always flew me first class and even when I travel on my own I usually upgrade to business or first but I am not spending that kind of money now because I am after all unemployed. I tell her I'll think about this and let her know for sure tomorrow, which will be Friday and which marks my two-week anniversary of being both home from vacation and jobless.

Quincy is in the backyard, swimming with nine little boys, and I am pretty much reading one of the books I started reading when I was in Jamaica. I am calm but at the same time anxious. I haven't heard from Winston even though I Federal Expressed his gift box along with a friendly letter wherein I basically told him how much I enjoyed his company and that this little package was an expression of my desire to put a smile on his face and how much I enjoyed meeting him spending time with him and how astonishing and powerful his kisses were. In fact I was totally honest and told him that they and he himself had a rather profound and lingering effect on me and that it is disturbing in a way because what in fact happened over there? Could he put his finger on it? and if not maybe we shouldn't question this maybe we should just pay attention and participate and not worry about it and I think I said something about passion being too underrated and how when you feel it deeply it resonates and you can't push it out away somewhere else and how innocent he felt to me how innocent he made me feel and I haven't felt this light inside in years and I thanked him for being Winston Shakespeare and wished him luck in the future and regardless of what happened I hoped he would stay in touch because who knows one day I might be at his wedding and then almost as an aside because I didn't want to give him the wrong impression that the sex was what has made me feel like this because it isn't, it just added to what was already beautiful what was already in progress, I told him how much I enjoyed making love to him the way he made love to me in such slow motion and that I get chills when I think about it so I try not to, but chills aren't bad once you get used to them—yes I did say all this. I also told him it would be perfectly okay if he called me collect to let me know when he got the stuff because I Federal Expressed it before I had a chance to change my entire attitude which seems to be fluctuating from one side of the color wheel to the other minute by minute and I am getting to the point now where I can justify any one of these opposing viewpoints aka emotions depending on my mood.

Right now I'm tense. Maybe I went a little overboard with the shopping. Maybe he'll be scared shitless. I decide that I should not be sitting here thinking about how some twenty-one-year-old is going to respond to a gift pack but instead I should be thinking about what I'm going to do with the rest of my life. However, I am drawing a blank and do not really want to go there at this moment in time and space so I don't.

I tell the children not to drown while I'm gone and that I am going on my run which I admit I lied to Krystal about because I told her that I'd run the day before but the truth is I've only been out twice since I've been home and I told her that someone had spotted some mountain lions up in the hills behind my house where I run and all she had to say to that was run a different way which made sense and so right now I am strapping my heart rate monitor around my chest and I put the watch portion of it on my wrist which begins to beep until I press the little button.

I am doing my stretches when I hear the phone and Quincy jets by me dripping wet. "Would you answer that, please?"

"Sure, Mom," he says and picks it up. "Hello. Sure. Who? Winston? Sure. Just a minute, please," he says and holds the phone up in the air. "Mom, it's somebody named Winston and he's got an accent."

"Is it collect?"

"I didn't hear the operator if it is. Mom, can we have some microwave popcorn and some Snapple, please?"

"Yes," I say and take the phone.

"Thanks, Mom!"

"And stop running through the house wet before you slip and break your neck!" I say but I cover the phone as I say it. My heart is pounding away, my heart rate monitor is beeping, which means I'm already in my target zone which normally doesn't happen until I've been out for at least ten minutes. This does not surprise me. "Hello, Winston," I say.

"Hello, Stella," he says and begins to laugh. "I have never been so surprised by something in my life."

"What are you talking about?"

"Come on. All those nice things you sent me. I don't understand. It was so thoughtful of you to think of me that way and wow, I don't really know what else to say, a huge thank you, I mean I am still in shock actually."

"It was only a few CDs a few T-shirts a pair of sneakers one pair of sunglasses and a little CD player."

"Easy for you to say that. No one has ever done anything like this for me before. Never. I can't thank you enough. It was so sweet of you, but why did you do it?"

"Because I wanted to make you smile."

"Well, it worked. It's working. I can't believe this. Everyone here is so envious because they had the box at the front desk apparently for quite some time and word finally got to me that I had a package from America and I knew it had to be from you and when I saw your name I felt so good it wouldn't have mattered if nothing was in the box really."

"Well, I'm glad, Winston."

"I'm not kidding. I really appreciate all of these things. It's like Christmas in July. Sooo, how are you?"

"I'm fine. About to go on my run."

"Guess what?"

"What?"

"I found out that I can get time off in three months' time and I loved your letter. You have a way with words you know and I have read it at least seven times already."

"You're kidding."

"I kid you not. . . . I sure wish you were here," he says.

I sigh. "Do you really mean that?"

"Yes, I do. I think about you so much it's starting to wear me out. Why? What's going on, Stella?" I can hear him laughing.

"Maybe I can arrange something."

"Are you saying what I think you're saying?"

"Yes. I'm coming back."

"You're serious?"

"Very."

"How soon?"

"How about two weeks from now?"

He's chortling. "Wonderful! This is great! You're not joking with me, are you?"

"Nope. But I'm not coming alone."

"And who will be accompanying you?" His tone is deeper.

"My son and my niece."

"Oh, fantastic!" he exclaims in a higher voice.

"So think about it for real, Winston. Do you think you really want to see me again?"

"Now that's a ridiculous question, Stella."

"You sure?"

"I'm sure," he says. "I want to see you again. Is that clear enough?"

"Well, we'll be staying at the Frangipani this time."

"I'll see if I can get two days off in a row. It might be tough since I just started and I have no seniority but I'll see if I can switch with someone. You are something," he says.

"And you're sure about this, Winston?"

"You're not listening to me. My only concern is if everything will be okay with your son. I mean I'm not sure . . . you'll have to tell me what you want me to do."

"He'll be fine. We've got a two-bedroom villa with an up- and downstairs."

"Sounds like a place I could live in," he says.

"You can for one night at least."

"You mean I can spend the night?!"

"If you want to."

"I would love to. What day are you getting in and what time does your flight arrive? I could try to meet you guys at the hotel."

I am tickled orange. I am grinning my ass off. I am happy. I am feeling like Mary Poppins, as if I could float right up through my skylight, I mean what is really going on here, Stella, I mean what is it that this young man does to you over the telephone no less that gets you all gaga and gooey? I do not know and I do not care I am just glad that my heart is ticking and he is helping me with the beats. "I'll let you know the exact day and time," I say.

"Stella, could you do me a big favor when you come?"

"What's that?"

"Would you bring me some junk food from America?"

"Junk food? What kind of junk food?"

"Oreos."

"As in Oreo cookies?"

"Yes." He chuckles. "And a bag of Lay's potato chips and any kind of candy but Skittles."

"You are serious, aren't you?"

"Very. These things are too expensive here in Jamaica. But only if it's not too much trouble."

"No trouble," I insist. "No trouble at all."

"And I am looking forward to seeing you, Stella. This is—all of it—everything is such a nice surprise. And I'll be glad to meet your son and—your niece, is it?"

"Yes."

"I'll cook something special for you while you're here."

"Something spicy?"

"Something very spicy." He groans.

We say goodbye and I am like fucked up all over again but I pull myself together and actually run for a whole hour without stopping, something I've never done in my life.

"Girl, are you on drugs or something?"

"Shut up, Vanessa. Please don't put me through this."

"Put you through what?"

"Why and how come and all that." I am sitting on the family room floor with my portable phone, flipping through interior design magazines as I am thinking about doing a little redecorating sometime in the near future and am trying to get ideas although I already have a few of my own that I like.

"Girl, look, I say go for it. I'm just glad you're taking Chantel. You'll be giving me a break. And hey, you should take whatever form happiness comes in when it comes your way. I mean hey, when you get right down to it, what is the big deal?"

"Are *you* on drugs?"

"No. I'm not the sister who has the problem with this young man. If everything you told me is true he sounds pretty mature and sincere if you ask me and I wouldn't worry too much about what anybody says. Shit, this is your fucking life, Stella, and besides, I haven't seen you this upbeat and happy since I don't know when."

"Thank you, Sis. I appreciate that."

"And check it out. Seems like ever since you got home all I see and read about are like older women with younger men and hey, you're not the only one taking a step back instead of forward, and you know what?" she says, sounding angry, and I'm not sure where she's coming from.

"What?"

"Men have been dating younger women for fucking centuries and does anybody say anything to them? Look at Hugh Hefner with his one-foot-away-from-the-grave ass. Didn't he marry that bunny who had just barely graduated from high school and hasn't she had like two kids by him?"

I almost spit out my cappuccino. "Yeah, but I do think she was in her early twenties."

"Same fucking thing. Anyway you should check out the statistics on this stuff. I say go for it and forget all the bullshit. Besides, did you know that I've heard that Marvin Gaye's first wife was like seventeen years older than he was?"

"Nope."

"Yeah, and Clark Gable too. They say that motherfucker married two women who were old enough to be his mama. So I wouldn't be tripping if I was you. I'd run and get some more of him if it's as good as you say it is."

"It's not the sex that's moving me."

"I didn't mean it that way—you're just taking it that way."

"I just want it clear. I like sleeping with him but I like *him* more."

"You made your point, now let's cut to the chase. You know my money is funny so I don't know how much spending change Chantel's gonna be taking over there to Jamaica. What's up with that?"

"Go to hell, Vanessa."

"Gotta ask," she says. "And how are you like in a position even though I know it's none of my business to be like the world traveler and you don't even have a job anymore?"

"Good investments. Something you'd know nothing about. So bye," I say and hang up.

"Quincy!" I yell.

I get no response so I run to the bottom of the stairs and yell louder: "Turn that mess off and come down here so we can bond!" He is listening to TLC again which is all he plays it seems and he has also started closing his bedroom door and Lord only knows what he might be doing in there but *I* don't want to know.

"Mom?" he says, hanging over the railing.

"What?"

"Can we bond up here in my room?"

"No. I said come down here right now and I'm your mother so do what I tell you to do or die."

"I'm coming." He runs down the stairs and we sit side by side on the bottom step.

"Will this bonding session take a long time?"

"So what if it does?"

"I'm doing a drawing and the paint is wet."

"I'm sorry. Then I won't keep you long."

"No, it's okay. I'm all ears."

"Well, that's certainly the truth," I say and he falls over against me which makes me fall into the wall and then I give him a big hug and I say, "Okay. Let's get serious."

He sits up straight and tall. "I'm serious."

"You know when I told you I had a lot of fun in Jamaica?"

"Yes."

"I also met someone over there."

"You did?"

"Yes."

"Well, it's about time!"

"Chill," I say. "Anyway his name is—"

"Winston. Mom, do you think I was born yesterday or what?"

"Yes. Winston."

"Too bad you had to go so far to find him, huh?"

"Be quiet, Quincy."

"So we're going to see him in Jamaica of course, right?"

"Right."

"I just want you to know that he is *not* my boyfriend, he is just someone that I like."

"I'm happy for you, Mom."

"There's a little problem, though."

"What kind of problem?"

"He's a little younger than I am."

"How much younger?" he asks.

"Well, he's not quite thirty."

"Mom, age ain't nothing but a number," he says. "Is that it?" he asks, standing up. "Mom?"

"What?"

"Are we finished bonding? I mean is there more you want to tell me?"

"No," I say. "But do you know what you're really saying here, Quincy?"

"I think I just said that age ain't nothing but a number."

"Where'd you hear that—on MTV or what?"

"It's on Aaliyah's CD. It's a cool song. You've heard it, Mom. They play it on Wild 107."

"But Quincy. Winston is not on that or any CD—he is a real person."

"Mom, what are you so worried about?"

"Who said I was worried?"

"Well, if you weren't, why'd you have to say it was a problem. It's only a problem if you make it a problem. Isn't that what you're always telling me?"

I want to pop him upside the head and hug him at the

same time. "Yes, it is," I say and feel like a little girl who's getting yet another lecture from her father. "Wait. One more thing."

"Yes?"

"Would you like some eggs for breakfast?"

"Mom, of course not. Don't you know that eggs are full of cholesterol and saturated fat and cause heartburn and are a hazard to your health?"

"No," I say, shaking my head. "I didn't have a clue."

I just know the plane is going to crash because I am having entirely too much fun this summer despite the fact that I have lost a job though it meant absolutely nothing to me emotionally and spiritually even if the money wasn't bad but I do believe that God works in mysterious ways which is why I don't have that job anymore and why I am feeling so much relief and, well, glee actually and I think it happened at this time in my life for a reason and yet somehow deep down inside I am feeling as if I will probably die very soon of some fatal disease which is why I yell to Chantel and Quincy to come stand over here with me in the first-class line where I am upgrading all three of us for a mere three thousand dollars because if I'm going to be dead soon my insurance policy will cover all my unpaid credit card bills. If tragedy does happen to strike while we're up inside the clouds my soul won't be all that far from heaven but it would certainly be nice if I could have another chance to press and seal my lips against Winston's just one more time which if God really is fair He or She would grant me a final pleasure before I go and if there's time an hour or two of some nuggies would be like frosting on the cake if it's not asking too much. That's what this is really all about: not the sex part, but the sense that for some stupid reason I am feeling like those emotionally handicapped women they write self-help books about who don't feel as if they deserve to be happy or that they're entitled to it. But if I were to dig a little deeper I'd know that this too is a bunch of bullshit because none of the logic applies to me. I mean here I am in the middle of my life which basically means I can look forward to even more than what I've already done which seems like a pretty good position to be in considering what the alternative is. So while I buy two packages of Oreo cookies a super-saver size Kit Kat one Three Musketeer a Butterfinger a PayDay three bags of Lay's potato chips—plain, barbecue and sour cream and onion—I add all this stuff up and I come to the conclusion that I have earned the right to some happiness and by golly I'm going to get me some.

The kids love the first hour of the van ride and how they manage to sleep through the second one fails me. When we pass the Castle Beach Negril my heart jumps. Those low lights are lining the driveway, illuminating the hibiscuses so that they look as if they are actually dancing, and in less than a minute we arrive at the Frangipani Hotel. It is peach and pretty even at night. Although it is only eight o'clock it has been dark since about seven. When we get to the check-in desk the kids are already heading toward the swimming pool which is lit up bright blue. A Jamaican woman dressed in a colorful African print dress with a tall gelé wrapped snugly around her head is singing a beautiful ballad and swaying her hardy hips back and forth on a big stage behind the pool and I can see that this is a lovely hotel and watching the long line of guests in front of the massive buffet suggests that the food is going to be good too.

"Good evening, Ms. Payne, welcome to the Frangipani," says a Jamaican girl with big black eyes who looks like she should be on one of those velvet paintings.

"How did you know my name?"

"We were expecting you," she says, making her lips form a little circle. She is so cute. "And by the way, we have a message for you that came in just moments ago. I'll get it for you."

The way my cheeks are tickling, I feel I have dimples. She comes back and hands me the yellow message slip and sure enough at 7:52 P.M. Winston Shakespeare called and "Please call me back asap" is checked off.

The bellman takes us down a winding sidewalk where we can feel and hear the ocean to our right but we can't see it and Chantel says, "Thank you for bringing me to Jamaica, Auntie Stell," and I squeeze her tight and then she takes off ahead where Quincy is already checking out the Ping-Pong. Our villa is right above another swimming pool and is pretty snazzy. The ceiling is made of whitewashed wood and A-framed and a white fan spins so fast you can't see the blades, but it is necessary in here and especially right now because the air is thick and hot. I see a little kitchen area with a refrigerator which I open immediately and there is a green bottle of Ting waiting for me. Stairs lead to where the children will be sequestered and it has twin beds and its own bathroom, thank goodness. My room, on the main level, is the same pale salmon color as my bedroom at home and twice the size of the children's room hallelujah and the bathroom is bigger and I can tell that we will like it here for the next week. The bellman puts our bags in their respective rooms and I hand him a ten-dollar bill but he refuses and then I give him a look that says, I'd take it if I were you and if you don't tell I won't tell, and he nods and smiles at me because he knows this is a black thang and goes ahead and slips it inside his back pocket.

I hear the kids running up the stairs.

"Mom, can we go swimming?"

"Yes, please, Auntie Stel, please?"

"But you just got here," I say.

"But we're on vacation!" Quincy says. "Isn't this what we're supposed to be doing?"

Good point. "Fine. Go." They run upstairs and I hear them squeal and then argue over who gets what bed and then to my surprise it appears as though they actually come to terms on their own without any intervention or threats and I believe that this could be a sign that they are maturing and just as I am getting deeply in touch with the beauty of what has transpired between these two they are charging down the steps with towels over their arms. "Slow down before you break your necks!" I yell. "Okay," Quincy says, and as he reaches for the doorknob I say, "Winston might come over to have a late dinner with us."

"That's nice," Quincy says. "But can we go now?"

"Who's Winston?" Chantel asks.

"He's my mom's friend who might be her boyfriend

but he's much younger than she is so you shouldn't say he's her boyfriend."

"How young is he?" she asks, looking at him. Chantel is on her way to becoming a serious chocolate fox and it should be only a matter of hours days months a year at most before she actually stops traffic. Vanessa and I are grateful that she doesn't know this yet, and as soon as she does, off to the convent she goes.

"About twenty-nine," he says matter-of-factly.

"Quincy, be quiet. You talk too much."

"That's not so young, Auntie Stella. Ready, Q-zart?"

She's just as ignorant as he is, I think, and I am grateful that they really don't know how to tell the difference between twenty-one and twenty-nine years old.

I want to call but I'm afraid to call but I call anyway. He is not there. The operator puts me on hold. Transfers me. Today is his off day. Puts me on hold. Comes back. We are looking for him. Hold. He's finishing dinner. He's coming now. Here he is.

"Yes?"

"Winston?"

"You made it."

"We made it."

"Good."

"Why are you eating dinner?"

"Because I was hungry."

"Don't have dessert. I brought you Oreos, potato chips and some candy."

"You didn't forget!"

"No, I didn't forget."

"I've been waiting for your call. Is this evening still good for you? You're not too tired for company?"

"No, I'm not that tired and yes, this evening is still good for me."

"When should I come?"

"How about right now?"

"Is fifteen minutes okay?"

"Take more time if you need it."

"No, I don't need more time."

"Okay. We'll probably be eating dinner at poolside so I'll look for you by the front desk."

"Looking forward," he says.

I hang up, feeling like a wind-up toy. I run into the bathroom and floss deodorize brush spray the works the usual. I change into a sleeveless denim dress and tie a bandanna around my head so that the counterfeit braids hang to the top of my shoulders and I push them behind my ears as I yell for the kids to come up now we must eat and yes you can go back in after we've finished.

These are obedient children because they know the price of all this so we are now choosing from a vast array of Jamaican dishes. Quincy picks mostly fruit and vegetables because he claims if he can't identify it he won't eat it. Chantel will eat anything and her plate reflects this and I get mostly pasta and fresh fruit, whatever won't cause me to have to floss in the next few minutes, something that will actually facilitate the cleaning of my palate as I'm expecting anticipating hoping praying for some version of a kiss.

I see him.

It looks as though he is the only living thing standing in

that lobby that is beautiful and should be noticed. He is looking around with his hands in his pockets as if he is about to start whistling and I put my hands over my belly to stop myself from cracking up because he is wearing one of the T-shirts I sent him, a peace necklace similar to the ones I gave Quincy and Chantel, the sunglasses even though it's night, and he's got the sneakers on too! This is so cute, I think as I feel my body lift from the chair and glide over to where he's standing and as I rise on my tiptoes and say, "Hello there," I can smell him of course and he turns and looks down at me smiles and I let out a sigh of relief as he bends over and gives me a soft really soft peck on the lips. His feel as if they just came out of the oven and I am pretty sentimental all of a sudden, like I could do a little whistling myself.

"Hello." He smiles. "Glad to see you." And I sort of just blush and squeeze his hand, go over to the front desk and ask for the evening pass which costs me sixty bucks and there is a different girl working here now and I can tell right off the bat that she's a bitch by the way her eyes are piercing mine and I can also see that she really thinks she's Ms. Thang because of the way her hair is greased back slick in a long flowing ponytail that hangs down to the middle of her back and she only has lipstick on her bottom lip which is really weird looking and she thinks she's really fine but her mannerisms are ugly. How she got this job I will never know but she hands me the form as if it is causing her some extreme level of discomfort and tells me to sign right there and drops a pen on the counter while she ogles Winston apparently vying for his attention but he isn't giving her any which seems to be pissing her off and

I can see that she's taking it out on me and I hope she like gets over it soon.

We walk to the table where the children are and I introduce them to Winston. Quincy is polite and shakes his hand and tells him how nice it is to meet him and Chantel simply says hello and then they go put their feet in the pool and pretty much ignore us.

"So you made it," Winston says.

"Yep."

"Your son looks a lot like you."

"If that's a compliment, I'll take it."

"Yes, he's very handsome and tall for his age, isn't he?"

"Yes, he is. Wears a size ten shoe."

"Really?" he says as he looks over at him.

"You're not hungry, I take it?"

"No. But you go ahead," he says.

"I'm finished."

"So what do you want to do?" he asks.

"I don't know. Not much. The kids want to swim some more."

"That'll be fine with me," he says.

"They'll be in bed by eleven."

"Are you sure this is all right, Stella? I mean my spending the night? I don't want to cause any problems."

"I've told them that you're going to watch a little TV with me this evening and if they want to go snorkeling in the morning, they have to be in bed by no later than eleven."

"What time is it now?" he asks even though he's wearing a watch.

"Nine-thirty."

He nods his head up and down and leans back on his chair.

"I like your shirt," I say and now I am ogling him.

He blushes.

"And where did you get that fancy necklace?"

"A very good friend sent it to me from America."

"She must be a good friend."

"Very. Although I'm hoping to get closer to her."

"How close?"

"As close as one can get."

I grin at him with my eyes and check my watch. It is still only nine-thirty.

He looks me in the eye and then leans forward, pressing his elbow then his forearm against the tabletop, and with his heated lips against my right ear he whispers, "Welcome back to Jamaica."

We are watching the kids swim and race and play games with six other children whom they apparently met here in the pool. It is now ten after ten. Winston shows them how they can improve their stroke, get more momentum and propel themselves forward better, demonstrating with his long hairy arms arching and cutting through the sticky night air. We can hear the reggae band all the way from here, which is a good five-minute walk from where they're playing. Couples and families sit out on their balconies and we can hear televisions on different stations as well as radio stations playing some jamming music that does not sound at all like reggae to me.

Since the pool is only five feet deep and there are quite

a few adults sitting around it watching their own children, I ask a couple if they plan on being out here much longer and they say at least an hour so I ask if they could keep an eye on my two and they say sure since "ours" are playing with theirs. I tell the children we are going to get a drink and will be back in ten or fifteen minutes. We walk slowly to the outside bar which is down the winding sidewalk and adjacent to the poolside restaurant where we ate earlier and I hop up on a barstool next to Winston and we order our usual beach drinks and even though the band is rocking nobody's dancing and then I see the woman with the Mister Ed ponytail sit down three seats away from us.

"Your son favors you a lot," she says, looking at Winston.

"No he doesn't," I say. "He really takes after his father."

"But he has many of your features." She stares at Winston, who turns to look at me as if to say: What are you saying and why are you saying it?

I pretend I don't see him.

"Well, maybe he does—I can't tell very much in this light. It's been a while since I've seen my oldest son."

"How long has it been?"

"Well, since his dad's Jamaican, he lives here with him and I see him mostly during the summers. We're divorced, you see."

"A lot of that going around these days," she says. "It's a pity."

"Yes, but it's worked out for the best because it's been, what, ten years now and I wanted my son to spend his blossoming-into-manhood years with his dad and he likes

living down here with the Rastas, but I'm so happy to see
him! Are you happy to see Mom, son?" And Winston
bends his head completely to the side and says, "Yes. This
is how happy I am to see you, Mom," and he gives me a
juicy kiss right on my lips and it looks like someone has
flashed a camera at Ms. Thang's eyes and she jumps up
from her barstool and stalks off while Winston and I sit
there and put our arms around each other and crack up.
"That was cruel," he says.

"It's what she deserves," and we take our drinks and head
back to the pool, where the kids grab their towels and say
good night see you in the morning to the other children.

Back at the villa, the kids take their showers and put
their pajamas on and come to the top of the stairs and
Quincy says, "Mom, we're tired so would you mind if we
went to sleep now?"

"What's wrong with you, Quincy?"

"Nothing," he says. "I'm a kid suffering from jet lag
and it's been a long day and Chantel and I want to give
you and Winston some space."

"Some what?"

"Space. You know. Privacy?"

Chantel comes out from behind him, nodding her
head in agreement.

"Well, maybe I'll see you guys again tomorrow," Winston says and then catches himself. "I heard you want to go
to Rick's Café and jump. Is that right, Quincy?"

"Yes! Will you jump too, Winston? Huh?"

"I'll jump if you jump," he says.

"It's a deal. See you tomorrow. Good night," he says,
and it appears as if these two have now bonded.

We are now sitting down here like two teenagers waiting for their parents to walk in the door any minute and bust them even though they're not doing anything. Winston is at one end of the couch and I'm at the other. "I don't bite," I say.

"I don't bite either," he says.

"Then make your move," I say.

"You make your move," he says.

"I don't know how," I say.

"Oh, I'm sure you do," he says.

"Help me," I say.

"How much help do you need?"

"A lot," I say, and he slides to the middle of the sofa and leans over in my direction and then I lean over in his direction and we merge.

"I can't believe I'm here," I say.

"I can't either," he says. "But you're definitely here."

"Are you sure you want to stay?"

"If you ask me that one more time, Stella . . ."

"Okay. Then up. I need to take a shower because I've been flying all day."

"So have I," he says. "But Stella, before you do, I have to tell you my bad news."

My heart drops. "What kind of bad news? I don't like bad news."

"I have to work tomorrow and I wasn't able to switch with anyone."

"So what time does that mean you have to leave?"

"About noon."

"That means you won't be going to Rick's Café with us, then, doesn't it?"

"If we went early, I could."

"You don't have to feel obligated to do something with my son, Winston."

"It's not that at all. I'd *like* to get to know him better."

"Why?"

"Because."

"Because why?"

"Because I like his mother," he says. "Now go take your shower."

I am Ms. Bubbles in there and come out smelling like I must've drunk a bottle of my Calyx and the first thing Winston says when I walk into the bedroom and I see the shape of his long body through the white sheets is, "Wow, you smell good," and I have put on this stupid summer nightie thing and as soon as I slide under the covers next to him and feel his warm body I decide that I am a grown woman and it's okay to take the thing off which I do.

I slide over to him and here he comes with one of his deep warm please-don't-ever-stop-kissing-me kisses and I put my arms around him his head his back and hold him as close as I can get which is not close enough and so I keep trying. He feels much stronger more sure of himself this time and I like what he is doing to me I like it a lot even though I can tell that we are both anxious. "You don't have to prove anything to me," I say.

"Yes I do," he says. "I want to prove how much I care about you by how I touch you," he says and lightly brushes his fingers over my hair. "I want you to forget about everything that's troubling you."

"How do you know something's troubling me?"

"Because I can feel it."

"Winston," I sigh, and he holds me closer and kisses me a little longer a little deeper and makes me feel safe like sympathetic magic and I guess he feels it too because he holds me squeezes me presses me up against his chest so firmly with such urgency and his arms and hands do not fall away from me until it is daylight.

When I bend down to kiss him he purrs and I tell him I am going for a run and he smiles and opens his eyes and waves as I put on jogging shorts and my sports bra which almost complement each other and then when I look at him for a few minutes lying in that bed with all his innocence and power I realize that I can run anytime so I take a condom out of the bedside table and place it on top and then I take off all this stuff and slide back under those sheets where Winston and I begin to bond in a major way.

"You could be addicting," he says afterwards.

"I bet you say that to all the girls," I say.

"What girls?"

"Winston." I sigh. "It's a figure of speech."

My head is resting on my pillow. His head is also on my pillow. "So tell me, Stella, where is this going?"

I sit up. "Where is what going?"

"Us."

"I don't know, Winston. Where could it possibly *be* going?"

"What's that supposed to mean?"

"You know what it means."

"You really do think I'm too young, don't you?"

"You are!"

"Too young for what?"

"I don't know. Me."

"Do I feel too young?"

"No."

"Do I look too young?"

I turn to look at him.

"Never mind, don't answer that," he says and we both chuckle for a second and then get serious again.

"Winston, look. I don't really know what I'm doing. All I know is that I like you more than I should."

"That's refreshing to hear. Look. What are you so afraid of?"

"I'm not actually 'afraid.'"

"Yes you are. You're afraid of what you feel because it's not fitting into your scheme of things, isn't that it?"

"Well, since you put it that way, yes."

"You know that American saying, I'm sure."

"What saying?"

"Shit happens."

Okay. That is true. Shit does happen. This has happened. I'll give him that. "What about you, Winston? What are you afraid of?"

"Nothing," he says.

"You have to be afraid of something."

"Honestly?" he asks.

"Honestly."

"Spiders and insects. All insects."

"I don't mean that kind of scared."

"Then what kind *do* you mean?"

"I mean, oh, never mind. Tell me, Winston," I say, looking at the fan swirling slowly above us, "what do you want out of life?" I'm thinking that this question should give him a little jolt.

"I want to be a good person, a worthy person, a strong man that people can depend on and know that my word is my bond, and I want to be charitable and loving and love a woman so deeply she won't ever want to be rid of me because I hope to be the light in her life. And making a decent living is pretty high up on the list too. How about you?"

"I feel the same exact way you do," I say, and swallow.

"Look, you asked me. And I'd like an answer as well."

"Well, I want to find my place in the world—at the table, so to speak. I want to give away warmth. I want to love a man so hard it feels soft and I want him to know that it ain't over till the fat lady sings. I want to see how far I can go alone and how far I can go with someone else. I want to be smarter. I want to be the best mother friend sister lover I can be. I want to respect other people's feelings as much as I can and I want to figure out how to make a living without actually having a job."

"But you have a job."

"Had."

"What happened?"

"I got canned."

"No kidding?"

"No kidding."

"When?"

"Right after I got back from Jamaica the first time."

"Why didn't you tell me, Stella? Are you okay?"

"I'm fine."

"And what are you doing back here?"

"What do you mean?"

"You don't have a job, Stella."

"But I still have a life," I say.

"So why did they release you?"

"Because they reorganized my department and I didn't make the cut."

"Do you feel bad about that?"

"Not really. What I really feel is relieved, if you want to know the truth."

"I can't imagine."

"Have you ever been fired?" I ask.

"No. This is my first job," he says.

"It figures," I say.

"Don't tease," he says. "Now let me ask you something, and be honest with me if you can. Do you have any particular plans for yourself?"

"Nothing too specific right now."

"So are you sort of searching?"

"It feels like I've got one foot on the path, yes."

"Would you let me help make your search easier?"

And all I can say is, "I think you already have, Winston."

"**M**om, where's Winston?" Quincy asks, leaning over the upstairs railing. I was beginning to wonder when they'd wake up. It's almost noon. I could tell they were both zonked last night and I was amazed that they admitted it. Now the Wicked Witch of the West appears behind him, white crust all around her pretty brown lips. Her hair is sticking out like a black halo and with her little pink nightgown on she looks like she's about to do that Peter Pan thing. "Good morning, Auntie Stella," she says in her high-pitched voice which she should pray at night she grows out of by her teenage years.

"Good morning, Chantel. Quincy, can't you say good morning?"

"Good morning, Mom. Where's Winston? What time are we going to Rick's Café?"

"Slow down. First of all, Winston had to go to work and he apologizes for not being able to come."

"Aaah, man!" he moans.

"He'll be back."

"Do *we* still get to go?"

"Of course. But I forgot we had talked about snorkeling this morning even though it's lunchtime now."

Quincy looks at his watch. "What's the time difference again, Mom?"

"Three hours."

"You mean it's already twelve noon here?"

"Looks that way."

"Mom, why'd you let us sleep so long!"

"Because apparently you needed it."

He runs down the stairs and goes over to the front door, opens it and looks out. "Wow," he says. "Chantel, come look. The beach is right there. Mom, can we go to the beach first?"

Chantel walks down the steps like a girl and saunters over next to him. She is still rubbing the sleep out of her eyes.

"Look, Quincy," I say. "Slow down, okay? First things first. This is the deal. It's our first day here, so let's do this. You two take your showers and then we'll get something to eat and how about we hang out on the beach and then go snorkeling at three since we missed the nine-thirty boat and we can go to Rick's tomorrow."

He looks over at Chantel as if he's waiting for her to concur but what neither of them realizes is that *this is* the plan and they will participate in it regardless. They give each other the nod and the spokesperson looks over at me and says, "That's fine with us, Mom."

"So let's get busy," I say.

"When's Winston coming back?" Chantel asks.

"Maybe tomorrow or Saturday. Depending on if he can get time off."

"He's cute," she says and has the nerve to blush.

She is too grown, I think, and I am wondering just how good she might look in a nun's habit.

After we eat a hearty lunch I begin my afternoon the normal way with my virgin piña colada. Some things remain the same, I think, as we pull our chaise longues close to the edge of the water. We can see our villa from where we perch ourselves and after I rub the kids down with number 35 sunblock off they go into the water where they will stay for the next two hours until it is time to snorkel and then we will snorkel and then they will come back to the beach until dinnertime.

I read, and I am somewhat bored in a way but not really. I love watching the kids romp and in fact as I watch them I realize how much I envy them. How clear of debris their world is right now. How long will it stay that way? I wonder. I hope to keep Quincy free of as much bullshit as I can. I want him to know it's out there but I also want him to know that he has the option of joining in or standing on the sidelines and letting it pass him by. He is a smart child. Quick. Which he got from me of course and I am hopeful that he will continue to be a dorky kid who happens to be a cute dork which is just fine with me.

"Are you Anita Baker?"

I look up and see a security guard standing above me. He is jet black and looks sort of like Wesley Snipes, which kind of throws me off for a minute but he is definitely Jamaican. "Me?"

"Yeah, mon," he says, lifting his policeman's hat up
and immediately dropping it back down.

"No. Afraid not."

"You sure?"

"Positive."

"What's your name, mon?"

"Stella."

"You got a last name, Stella?"

"Stella'll do. And you are?"

"Frisco. That's my name."

"Nice to meet you, Frisco."

I sit up because he is standing over me and I don't like
this feeling of him looking down at me especially since
I'm wearing my chartreuse two-piece with the Wonderbra
foam pads.

"How long you 'ere for?"

"A week. Just got here."

"Those your kids?"

"Yes," I say to keep it simple.

"Where's your husband?"

"Back at the Ponderosa."

"Where's that?"

"In Nevada near Reno."

"Reno?" he asks and I can tell he's trying to picture it
on the map but can't quite get it together.

"I'm sorry. It's closer to Las Vegas," I say.

"Oh," he says, smiling confidently now. "He couldn't
get away from the job, is that it?"

"Precisely. He owns a casino."

"You're kidding me."

"Well, he has partners of course."

"Wow, so you guys must do all right then, huh? But you have to if you're staying at this hotel, hey?"

"We fare pretty well, I guess. Well, look, Cisco—"

"Frisco. As in San Francisco."

"Okay. Frisco. I don't want to be rude, but I think I'm going to get in the water. It is a scorcher out here today."

"That it is," he says. "That it is. Enjoy yourself, now," and he tips his hat and walks over to a short palm tree where his bench apparently awaits him and he sits there and will sit there, watching the three of us in the water on a regular basis for the next several days. I will learn that Frisco works two jobs, that he is thirty-four years old and is looking for a wife, especially since he has been working hard and can now afford one. He will say he didn't want to get married if he couldn't pay for his children's education. I will ask him why the children that he doesn't even have yet will need to go to private school and he will explain to me that because the public school system is a farce the only way to guarantee that your children are well educated is to send them to private school which costs lots of money and Frisco feels that by the end of the summer he should have himself a wife even though he doesn't have any immediate prospects but he has a feeling she's headed his way and he's sure that sometime in the next year he will be a father.

Quincy is the first to jump off the cliff, of course, and it is befitting that my son, who is accustomed to begging, stands on the lower level of the lowest cliff, which is still some thirty feet above the water, and says, "Come on, Mom, don't be such a wuss. Jump!"

Chantel is standing next to me and in her Minnie Mouse voice she says, "It's really easy, Auntie Stell. Just jump!"

"I will in a minute, so don't rush me!"

I find it difficult to do anything when I have an audience, and behind and above us are about a hundred tourists with camcorders and cameras just waiting for fools like us to jump off this concrete platform that was built years ago on top of the rock that it's covering. Over to the left is the ledge where the real diehard fools jump down sixty or seventy feet. As I move out of the way for miniature human beings who are all under the age of ten to jump off this ledge I think fuck it and pinch my nose shut and then I simply jump.

Wow!

It feels like I'm flying and I have this feeling of nothingness and as soon as it registers I feel my feet legs thighs everything cut through the thick blue water and I go down down down then shoot back up to the surface where the warm wetness runs down my face and I feel so clean so healthy and refreshed and athletic and I want to do this again! Which I do at least ten more times with the kids. Side by side, we dive in. They swirl around in midair and though it doesn't work for me, what a rush I get when I slip through that water. Now I think I know how those Olympic divers feel. Well, sort of.

"Mom," Quincy says, standing next to me shivering. "Can I jump from up there?" He points to the sixty-footer, where a young girl has been standing off and on for the last half hour trying to conjure up the nerve to jump which she hasn't been able to do and as a result she is constantly moving out of the way for others.

"You must be crazy," I say.

"Mom," he whines. "I'm a good swimmer and you know it! Please, Mom."

"Quincy," I groan. "It looks dangerous."

"Mom," he says, gesticulating with his arms as if he's saying, Let's get on with the show. "Look at all those people who've already jumped. Do they look dead? Did any of them die? No. Are any of them hurt? No. Come on, Mom, please? You're always telling me to take chances. Now here's my big chance to take one. Please?"

"Oh, go ahead, Quincy, but just once. I mean it. You're going to give me a heart attack."

He's already on his way back up the thirty or forty cement steps we walked down to get to this level, and he's yelling, "Thanks, Mom!"

Chantel walks over and puts her arms around my waist. "Don't worry, Auntie Stell. I don't want to jump off that one."

"I wouldn't let you anyway. No way. Because I could not go back to California and tell my sister that her daughter broke her neck jumping off a cliff in Jamaica. So no. You won't be jumping. Quincy is a different species. He wants to jump, I've got to let him jump."

I stand there, my heart pounding away, and I'm thinking that this is the smart thing to do because I don't want my fears to become my child's fears and if he isn't afraid why should I make him afraid. And he's right, a lot of people have jumped and will jump off this cliff and it is pretty safe. It's just that it's so far down. There he is. He has a wide grin on his face and he doesn't even get his footing right before he is in flight and he looks like a human bird as he screams out something like everybody else has been doing and I look down and yes he makes it into the water and swims over to the side where he grabs onto the rusty railing and runs up the stairs to me.

"Mom, did you see me?"

"I saw you."

"It is the coolest feeling. Can I go again?"

"Quincy, please. I just had a stroke standing here and you want me to have another one."

"Don't look. Mom, it was so cool. It was great. You should try it. Well, never mind, but Mom, please. I'm still alive. Touch me," he says and grabs my hand and places it on his arm.

I snatch it back. "Oh, go ahead, boy!"

He jumps again and I can see he is having the time of his life and Chantel has made friends with some little blond girl from Switzerland and they are holding hands jumping off our little cliff together. After Quincy jumps about six or seven times, I think it's time for him to stop, which is what I tell him.

"But Mom, don't you understand? I was *born* to do this. Just three more times and I promise I won't ask any-more."

I'm pretty bored watching him at this point anyway because he keeps doing the same thing which is jumping since I told him not to even twist his mouth to ask me if he can dive.

We all dry off and the kids are in their zone I can see

and they are already a shade darker. We have lobster and crab legs for dinner at Rick's and get eaten alive by those invisible bugs and when we get back to the hotel room I do not have a message that Winston called. But it is okay. It is only Friday.

My message light does not blink all day on Saturday no matter how many trips I make into the room pretending to need a different tape for my Walkman a different book a different kind of sunblock a different pair of sunglasses. I am offended for sure by dinnertime and think who the hell does he think he is anyway?

The kids have befriended two black boys who are from New Orleans and as I sit and watch them play tag and a trillion other games in the pool I realize that I am feeling like a fool, like an abandoned fool. I am wondering why he hasn't called. I mean at least to say hello. Something. I mean I realize that he works fourteen hours a day which is downright shameful but normal procedure at all these resorts and everybody pretty much works six days a week which is also standard but very substandard if you ask me.

We get back to our villa around eight o'clock. My message light is blinking. I grab the phone and dial zero. "I'm calling for messages."

"One moment, please."

I am smiling already and when the operator comes back on she says, "Yes, Vanessa called and the message reads: 'Is my daughter dead or alive? Please call.' Do you need the number?"

"No," I say. "Thank you."

I am about to throw the phone across the room but I'm not going to go there. I am feeling like a child who cannot have her way. "Stop this, Stella," I say out loud. "For real. Stop it. He's a kid. He's a fucking kid. You are tripping. Don't do this. Please don't do this," I say and begin to dial Vanessa's number but get her machine and I leave her a message apologizing for not calling after we arrived and I just tell her that the kids are having a ball and that we will check back with her in a day or so. And not to worry.

On Sunday we snorkel at nine-thirty, Jet Ski at eleven, hang out on the beach all day, and the kids go snorkeling again at three. They like snorkeling and I like it when they are not within speaking range for at least a half hour to an hour at a time. I say hello to Frisco who is in his spot and I have read approximately eighty pages of *Laughing in the Dark* by this *Washington Post* writer named Patrice Gaines who used to use drugs and even went to jail and did all kinds of rough stuff and I realize that if she was able to pull herself up and get her act together then I should not be complaining one iota about the status of my life. But I resolve to try and give my life a little more scrutiny over the next few days while I sit out in this hot-ass sun and bake.

For starters, fuck Winston and fuck me for flipping over this handsome lanky Jamaican boy who wouldn't know what to do with a woman if he really had one. Let one of those teenyboppers try to turn you out, Winston. See if they rock your world to dust. See if they can make you soar. See how curious they are about how you feel what you think why you do what you do and how you do what you do. See if they can get under your skin inside the lining of your heart and grease it rub it warm it massage it and make it melt. See if they can do that for you, Winston, and next time some other woman comes from America who has an American Express card know that it does not mean she is an American Express and do not for a minute assume that because she is alone she is lonely and desperate because that is not was not the case. Nobody told you to bring your narrow ass over to my table. Nobody told you to flirt with me like a grown mature responsible adult man would do. Nobody told you to be so much man for your age and nobody for sure told you to kiss me and cause me all this anguish and stuff and I don't even know your fucking middle name which is probably something like Plato or Socrates but it should be more like Caligula.

I hope he doesn't call. That way I will be free of him. That way I can go back to my life the way it was before he entered it. I mean after all, I didn't come here to start anything, to get involved. I merely came to Negril for a little R and R, I came here to simplify my life not complicate it, and look what I get. No. I have been fired from my fucking job and do not have a clue as to where I'm going from here. I have not spent too much time thinking about it either and it is all this young boy's fault because he has messed things up so that I have expended most of my free mental energy thinking about him. Silly simple simpleton. What am I doing back here in Jamaica anyway? You didn't come here to relax, admit it, Stella! You don't know what you're doing, go on and admit that to yourself, Stella. Your heart led you back here and you know it and you can't stand the thought that you can't control the situation. Well, just fuck it! Fuck you for being such an irresponsible woman, who acted without thinking. You're forty-two, not twenty-two, girl!

Maybe I'm in the middle of a midlife crisis. That's what's happening to me. I don't know what I'm doing. Maybe I should just pack up and go home.

It is Monday morning and I hear a knock on the door. I look at my watch. It is only seven-thirty, so I know it's not the housekeeper. The kids of course are still asleep as they partied hard last night with their friends and I will watch Chantel like a hawk until we leave because she has already picked out her man who happens to be thirteen-year-old Tyrell and he is too old for her because she is only eleven and he is too tall and looks like he's more like fifteen and her mama should not have let her come here with that skimpy little orange flowered bathing suit which is showing off those two little olives beginning to protrude on her hard little chest.

I walk out and answer the door and it is a hotel employee holding three yellow message slips in his hand. "We apologize for any inconvenience, ma'am, but apparently your phone has not been in consistent working order for two days and you have these messages here which the gentleman asked us to bring to you as he says you have not returned his calls and he was very upset about that and we here at the Frangipani do apologize greatly for this."

I could hug him.

I tell him, "No problem, mon," but ask if the telephone is working now and he says it is being dealt with this morning. I sit down on the couch and flip through the messages. Two days' worth. I feel relieved and soft and a little girlish and I am happy. I am so very happy.

I decide to go for my run which I do and then come back and shower and then I go to breakfast and eat a waffle. I know I'm stalling but prolonging is probably a better word even though I don't know what I'm prolonging. When I get back to the room it's nine-something and I dial Windswept's number which for some reason I seem to know by heart. I am connected to Mr. Shakespeare's room as apparently he is not scheduled to work today until two o'clock. His voice is raspy, two or three octaves deeper, and his accent is more pronounced than I've ever heard. "Good morning, Winston."

"Stella," he says. "I've been worried about you. Not hearing from you and all that. Is everything okay?"

"Yes, everything's fine. I was a little worried myself to be honest, Winston, because I hadn't heard from you. . . ."

"I've been calling off and on for the last two days and you never returned my calls and I thought that since you were here and saw me again you had changed your mind about me."

"No, I haven't done that, I'm afraid."

"What happened?"

"The phone was broken."

"Oh, yes, mon! The phone was broken! And now it's

fixed. Stella. Stella. Stella." He sighs, sounding relieved. "Sooo, have you and the kids been having a good time?"

"Yes."

"Good. Can I meet you guys for lunch today? I'll bring over a few dishes I made for you to sample. If you don't have other plans."

"That would be great, Winston. But the hotel operator said that you start work at two today."

"Yes," he moans. "I'm not as happy about this job as I was at first. It is really beginning to take its toll on me, but I'll stick it out for what it's worth." Then he pauses. "Sorry. I don't mean to sound like a pouting child. So, how about twelve? I can only stay an hour and a half, if that's okay."

"That sounds good," I say. "Sounds real good."

When he gets here he is wearing a different No Fear shirt minus the peace necklace and he has on his very own Birkenstocks and a pair of long purple shorts. His legs are so hairy and he looks so handsome in the sunlight that I am tempted to tell him to forget about lunch, let's be lunch, but of course I don't.

The children are difficult to find but he and I sit out on the balcony and I taste his pepper pot soup which has some green stuff that looks like spinach floating in it and it is delicious and then I taste this orange potato which is a cassava and it is sweet and then he gives me this fish dish called escovich and it is real vinegary and full of carrots and onions and some other vegetable and Winston says it is served mostly at breakfast but he wanted me to taste it and it is different and then he gives me what he calls "rundown" which is salted mackerel simmered in coconut milk with tomatoes and onions and I would like to eat more it is so good. And lastly he brings me some pan-fried plantains, which I kiss him for and I do not worry about flossing at all.

We sit at the table looking out at the beach for a few minutes and then Winston wraps his hand around mine and squeezes it. "I wish I could stay." He sighs.

"I wish you could too," I say.

"I enjoy your company."

"Why?" I say.

"Because I feel comfortable around you. I don't have to pretend to be something that I'm not. I'm not used to it. But I could get used to it."

"It?"

"You. . . . My dad never talked to me about those birds and bees, you know. And my mom left it up to my dad. Sooo, this is all kind of new to me and I'm not sure what I'm doing or if I'm doing it right."

"You're doing it right, Winston, don't worry. And plus there is no right or wrong way. It's what makes you feel good inside."

"Oh, I'm feeling good inside, I'd say."

"You're going to make a great chef," I say then.

"We'll see. My dad always wanted me to go to medical school and he's a bit disappointed in me since I didn't."

"But this is *your* life."

"Exactly. But he doesn't understand that."

"Does he know you want to be a chef?"

"Not really. I'm not completely sure myself. It's what I've been given a chance to do and it seems okay."

"It's okay to be uncertain, Winston. I'm not sure how many people your age know exactly how they want to spend the rest of their lives so don't worry about it. You should talk to your dad about how you feel."

He shakes his head no.

"Why not?"

"We don't talk."

"Then talk."

"He doesn't have much to say to me."

"Then talk to him so he has to."

"I'll think about it," he says and turns his attention to the waves. We sit there for a few more minutes not saying a word. He squeezes my hand, then lets it go and stands. His shorts have slid down to his hips. "I would like to gain about twenty pounds," he says, pulling them up.

"I think you look fine, Winston."

"I'm too skinny. People tell me all the time."

"Don't listen to them. I like how lean and tall you are."

"Really?"

"I kid you not," I say, standing too.

He smiles a satisfied smile and takes his long fingers and grazes them softly over my braids. He looks like he wants to kiss me but then he bends down and puts his arms around me and just holds me for the longest time. I belong in his arms, I'm thinking, when we hear the children running up the steps and then they appear.

"Winston, you missed Rick's!" Quincy says.

"I know, and I'm sorry about that, Quincy. I had to work, mon."

"A man's gotta do what a man's gotta do," Quincy says, and of course this throws Winston for a loop.

"Hi, Winston," Chantel says. She is flirting, I see.

"Say, I brought you guys some lunch. Some of it's a bit on the spicy side, so be careful."

"Are you leaving again?" Quincy asks.

"I have to go back to work."

"Why do you work so much?" Chantel asks.

"I have to make a living."

"Good point," she says.

"So when are you coming back?" Quincy asks.

"I'm afraid my next big break won't be until tomorrow evening."

"Really," I say. "Well, I'll probably be packing."

"Tomorrow's only Tuesday," Winston says.

"We leave on Wednesday morning."

"Nooo. I thought you didn't leave until Thursday."

"That was last time."

He sighs. "If I'd known that I would have tried harder to get tomorrow off—they won't give it to me, Stella."

"It's okay." But it wasn't okay. Why do people always say that when they don't mean it?

"I'll have two hours for dinner tomorrow at eight. And I'll be here to say goodbye. Is that okay?"

"It's what you have to give. It's what we'll take."

He gives me a light kiss. Chantel, pretending to eat, is actually taking notes. I roll my eyes at her to let her know that she is busted. Quincy of course is busy eating, only the plantains—he says he loves fried bananas.

I am sitting out at the poolside restaurant, sipping on my virgin piña colada. It is eight-fifteen. Winston called at six to tell me he would be here for sure. I keep looking out into the lobby hoping to see him appear like he did the first night we got here but over the next half hour I get zingy watching the same empty spot hoping that he will walk into it. He does not.

At five to nine I say fuck him again. I don't need this. This is so tacky and inconsiderate. I put something in my mouth and cannot taste it. My heart is aching. Who the fuck does he think he is, standing me up? And what kind of sick little game is he playing? I didn't come here to get my fucking heart broken by some boy. I wonder if he's in a racket and I've been set up. But why me? He doesn't know anything about me. I didn't make him come here. I didn't beg him to. He volunteered. I feel as if every single tourist at this hotel knows I'm sitting here waiting for a man who isn't going to show up. This is what I get. For not playing it safe. For taking a risk. This is how and why you wind up feeling like a fool, because men—and I don't care how old or young they are—coerce you, get you to trust them, and then you start acting like a fool.

I'm glad the kids are having dinner with their New Orleans friends, whose mother was also kind enough to "babysit" while I have dinner with a friend and say my farewells. It is now five after nine and I can't take this much more. Fuck you, Winston, and thanks a lot for everything! I get up from the table and storm back to the villa, where I see the flashing red light on the telephone. I am afraid to pick it up but I do anyway and the operator tells me to call the front gate which I do and the guard tells me that he has Winston Shakespeare out front to see me.

I march through the parking lot right to the front gate

and I am so pissed I can't wait to tell him I don't know who you think you are showing up an hour and ten minutes late and am I supposed to be grateful to get fifty minutes of your precious time well don't do me any fucking favors fella and just who do you think you are anyway? Am I supposed to beg for some goodbye nuggies, or are you showing up late because you don't want any more of this old tired pussy, is that it? If that's it then why don't you just come right out and say so!

There he is, standing by the guard. He looks a little perturbed and distraught himself I think as I walk up to him stand on my tiptoes give him a peck on the cheek and say, "Thanks for coming. Goodbye. It's been nice meeting you."

"Stella," he groans and looks down. "I've been waiting out here since five minutes to eight but this time they wouldn't let me inside the gate and we've been calling your room and there's been no answer and so I said she's probably sitting in the dining area and if they could ring you there and they said they did but you weren't there and finally I had them try your room again."

"Really?"

"Yes, really. What did you think happened?"

"I thought you were standing me up."

"Why would I do that?"

"Because I thought you had come to your senses."

"I've never lost them," he says.

We are standing in the driveway entrance and the headlights from an incoming car force us to move over to the grassy area. Winston looks down at me and gives me a kiss.

"I am really disappointed that we weren't able to spend more time together."

"So am I," I say.

He looks down the road at cars that seem to be drag racing. "Well," he sighs, and then just puts his arms around me and begins to hug me. "I'm going to miss you, Stella."

"I'm going to miss you too, Winston."

"You know," he says and kisses me on my forehead, "I am afraid I have become too attached to you."

"What does too attached mean?"

"It means that I am finding myself thinking about you all the time and wishing I could see you."

"Join the club."

"Remember when you asked me if I've ever been in love and I said I didn't think so?"

"Yes."

"And remember when I asked you what it felt like and you said you sort of crave being around a person and how they make your adrenaline move fast and you can't get enough of them?"

"Yes."

"Well, I'm kind of feeling like that," he says and I slide my hands in his back pockets, where I feel a condom in the left one.

I am totally touched by his honesty. "Well, Winston, let me tell you a little secret."

"What kind of secret?"

"I do believe that I have like fallen in love with your young behind and it doesn't make an ounce of sense and

I'll be on a plane in the morning and five thousand miles away so I'll just have to like get over it."

"What?"

"You heard me right."

"Why do you have to get over it?"

"You know why, Winston."

He hugs me and kisses me and cars begin honking as they pass but it doesn't cause him to stop and I think my feet are sinking into the moist soil below this grass and as our lips show that they are not in the least afraid to love each other it occurs to me that I wish I could keep him. Tonight tomorrow and for a long time because I like the way he makes me feel and I'm wondering, as I take my hands out of his pockets and hold him as close as he is holding me, why can't we keep doing this? I mean is there a law against this somewhere? Are the love police out here scoping the area, hoping to bust us?

Winston breaks away from me and then puts his lips on my neck and presses down his warmth and we are making love with our clothes on out here on the side of this road with all this rushing traffic flashing by and I am racing too, so much that I know I can't take much more of this, I can't.

"So I hope to be seeing you real soon," he says.

"You're just saying that now, Winston," I say.

"Oh, so you think I'll say something different tomorrow or next week or next month, is that it?"

"Winston, I'm forty-two years old."

"I know how old you are."

"And next year I'll be forty-three and then I'll be forty-four."

"So?"

"So this doesn't really make any sense."

I can tell he is as tired of hearing me say this as I am of saying it, but it is the truth, any way you slice it. He squeezes me a little closer as if he's trying to reassure me that he is rejecting this whole idea and I can feel his heartbeat and then he lets out a long sigh. "Someone *your age* ought to know that anything that's good hardly ever makes sense," he says and then his weight drops and he takes two steps backward and looks down at me. "And if there's a law written somewhere that says it has to, then let's just break it."

"You just don't know when to stop, do you, Stella?"

"Angela, would you do me a favor. Please call my house before you come over here." I wish I could tell her how beautiful she looks right now but I can't. Her skin is a copperish color and she is all aglow. Her hair has grown out and she's wearing it in those thick dangling Shirley Temple curls. Her belly looks like a beach ball under her pink dress and she finally has some boobs.

"I haven't *been* calling before I come over. Why now all of a sudden? You're losing your mind, Stella. My God, he's a child and you went back to Jamaica to sleep with him again—what is it with you?"

If she weren't five months pregnant and my sister I would kick her ass and then throw her in the swimming pool. "Would you like some iced tea?"

"No, I . . . what kind?"

"Raspberry."

"Yes, I'll have a glass. So what possessed you to go back down there, Stella?"

"I wanted to swim with the baby fish and I wanted

Quincy and Chantel to jump off a cliff," I say, getting up and going into the kitchen. I look out at her through the blinds and she is a spitting image of our mother, and for the past year or so she's even been acting like her, which is where all this reprimanding must be coming from, I guess. But deep down inside, I know she's only interested in protecting me because maybe if I were in her shoes— and Lord knows I'm glad I'm not—if I were looking at this from her perspective, it does look a little foolish. But then again, Angela has always played it safe. She applied to twelve universities even though her GPA was so high she could easily have gone to her first choice, and when she was accepted at all of them her next dilemma was how close to home to be, but Ma told her to go on and go far, be independent. If the truth be known, even then Angela got on everybody's last nerve.

"Are the babies moving around a lot?" I ask.

"Yep," she says and starts that business of trying to get comfortable even though she's not all that huge yet. "So is this thing over now, I hope?"

"Why are you so concerned about it?"

"Because I think you're taking it too far and I want to know when are you going to forget about him and start thinking about what's real: like for instance your next job. Have you had any free time to devote to that minor issue?"

"Yes, I have."

"And?"

"And what?"

"Have you sent your résumé to any of those head-hunters?"

"No."

"And why not, Stella?"

"Because I don't want to go back into securities."

"Oh, so now—don't tell me—you've had an epiphany and you've decided that the corporate world is empty and offers no spiritual mental or emotional gratification so you're going to take this time to search deep within yourself until you find something say a little more creative and fulfilling, do I have this right?"

"Exactly."

"I do believe you are either having a nervous breakdown or you are going through a midlife crisis. Stella, you just don't throw away a career because you're dick-whipped over some boy who the only thing he *can* do for you is fuck you."

"You don't get it, Angela."

"Don't get what?"

"Something has happened to me. Winston is only partially responsible for it. I'm not rejecting the corporate world because I got laid real good. And for your information I've only slept with him twice."

"See, that says a lot right there. You're really screwed up if that's all it took."

"This is not just about *him.* I've been doing everything according to the book for so long that I didn't see how I've been living like I'm in a cocoon or something, like I've been in a walking coma."

"That's bullshit and you know it."

"You don't know how or what I feel inside! That's part of your fucking problem—you only look at surfaces and that's as far as you can see. Well, I've dug a little deeper and I realize I'm tired of missing out on opportunities for happiness that come my way. Sometimes you don't know what form it's going to come in but when it does come I'm learning that I should accept it."

"Oh, so you think God *sent* this boy to you?"

"Maybe. But I don't have God's toll-free number so there's no way I can like call and ask him or her, is there?"

"Him or *her*? See what I mean. Since when did you start being so politically correct?"

"Forget it, Angela. Look, my insurance guy's coming over here in a few minutes to talk about my car."

"You never did answer my question."

"About what?"

"This business is over, isn't it?"

"You mean with Winston?"

"Whatever his name is."

"No. I think he might be coming for a visit actually."

Those babies must be doing somersaults, because she grabs her belly and takes a deep breath. "You can*not* be serious!"

"Very."

"And just when is he supposed to be coming?"

"I don't know."

"And how long will he stay?"

"I don't know."

"And what will you do, buy him a ticket?"

"The thought had crossed my mind, but it's really none of your business, now is it?"

"And he probably calls collect, I suppose?"

"You know what? If I remember correctly, when you were chasing after Kennedy you paid for quite a few trips to go see him when he was in law school, now forgive me if I'm wrong."

"That's like comparing apples and oranges."

"Oh, is it really? You spent a fortune on plane tickets and called him on the phone two and three times a day if I'm not mistaken."

"So?"

"So what's the difference if I were to send Winston an airplane ticket and let him call collect?"

"The difference is that I was making an investment in my future. Kennedy's educated, smart and a good provider and we share things on an intellectual level that you couldn't possibly dream about with a kid who's barely out of high school. Come on, Stella! Wake up! What would your prospects be for marriage? And how about being a father to Quincy, have you thought about that? I mean, this could never become anything other than what it is: an island fling."

"You just don't get it, do you? First of all, you don't know what we talk about and I'm not about to waste any time telling you. And who's talking marriage here? Did you hear me say anything about marriage? And besides, I don't need a man to anchor my future. I own my own home. I own another home in Lake Tahoe. I have stocks. Municipal and tax-free bonds. I own the cars that I drive. What did you own in your own name before you said 'I do'?"

"That is not the issue. The point is I've got it now."

"The point is that I don't need a man for any of those reasons. What I need one for is love."

"You can't be serious."

"I'm very serious."

"Oh, so you think that all you need is some damn love?"

"Of course I don't, but I'll tell you one thing—I'm realizing that after coming up with my list of dos and don'ts and must haves: how tall he is and what he has to look like and how much money he has to make and all that kind of thing, it has dawned on me that no wonder I'm by myself, because it's hard to find somebody who can fill in all those fucking blanks."

"I found one," she says.

"Yahoo," I say.

"You really do think you're Diana Ross or Cher or somebody, don't you, Stella?"

"No I do not."

"Then why can't you act your age?"

"How am I supposed to be acting?"

"Like a forty-two-year-old woman."

"Meaning?"

"You know what it means. Acting responsibly. Forget it."

"Oh, you mean even though I feel pretty much like the same person I was at say thirty-two, even though I've seen and done a lot more since then because I'm like ten years older, I guess I'm just supposed to metamorphose into this middle-aged entity, this over-the-hill being, and reject anything that has to do with being youthful including having a youthful attitude toward life, and I guess because I still wear my blue jeans a little on the tight side with a bodysuit, because I don't happen to be fat and slovenly and out of shape, and because I get my hair braided and let it hang down and whatever—if this is what you're talking about—I mean you think that because I have a little zest and zing and break a few rules that I'm what, regressing? What am I trying to do, imitate twenty-two-year-olds? Is that it—you think that I don't like being forty-two, that I'm just doing all this because I'm suffering from nostalgia, that I'm having secret wishes to go back in time—is that what you're thinking?"

"I didn't say it. You did. Just be careful is all I have to say."

"Careful about what?"

"Does this guy know you have any money?"

"Not really. And so what if he did?"

"These guys from these foreign countries *all* want to find themselves a rich sugar mama so that they can trick you into marrying them so they can become American citizens. Everybody knows that."

"What I've *heard* is that those kind of marriages are usually prearranged by two consenting adults, that there's no trickery involved whatsoever. And like I said, who's talking about marrying anybody?"

"Well, you're acting like you're suffering from dementia, so who knows how far you might go? I'm just forewarning you. And you can get mad and take this any way you want to: but don't be a total fool and marry this boy without signing a prenuptial agreement, that's all I have to say."

With this I get up and walk Angela to the side gate and hold it open and my insurance man, Rodney, pulls up at the same time.

I say hello and then they say hello but I don't bother to

introduce them. Still in a huff, I shuttle him back through the gate.

"So, Rodney, what exactly is the problem?" I see Phoenix running toward us and lock the gate. I am not in the mood for being sniffed or for petting. Rodney is a giant. Used to be a linebacker, whatever that is, for USC in the early eighties but got injured and turned all his attention to security protection and coverage. He has his own office and can't be much more than thirty and his hair is a big mass of tight brown curls and even though his face is twice the size of mine his horn-rimmed glasses are loose. He's pretty close to being handsome.

I flop down a little too hard in a wooden chair and he basically leans against one of the posts that hold up the trellis.

"Well, this isn't really all that big a deal actually."

"You said over the phone it was sort of bad news."

"Hold on a minute, little sister. Okay, this is the real deal. A recent law passed in the state of California requires that whenever a licensed driver is operating someone else's vehicle and they have an accident the owner of that vehicle by virtue of their consent to the person they gave authority to drive that vehicle is responsible for any and all damages that may arise as a result of any accidents."

"Are you saying that I have to pay for this?"

"That's about right."

"You're not bullshitting me?"

"Wish I were. But it's not all that bad. I mean we'll take care of this, Stella, because the asshole she hit was driving a 1982 station wagon that isn't even worth what his estimate came to."

"Then let my sister pay him."

"That's not a smart thing to do, because if she pays him off, he can come running back next week or next month with some sudden debilitating illness and sue her."

"So we're just going to pay him and get my car fixed?"

"Yes, that's better all the way around."

"Then my sister's paying the deductible, but what does this do to my rate?"

"It may go up a few cents. But Stella, please try to slow down. You got three speeding tickets just in the past year!"

"I can explain," I say, chuckling.

"Don't explain," he says. "Look. Are you dating anybody right now?"

"Why, Rodney? Your girlfriend dump you?"

"No, I'm engaged. I've got this guy I want you to meet. He is the coolest guy. I play golf with him. He's a judge. In excellent shape. A great sense of humor. Good-looking guy, really."

"How old is he?"

"I don't know. I'd guesstimate Spencer to be maybe fifty, fifty-one. Somewhere around there."

I am already shaking my head no. The thought of going from twenty-one to fifty-one is making me nauseous. "He's too old," I say.

"You should meet him, Stella. He's not your typical fifty-year-old guy, know what I'm saying? I mean I told him about you, how jazzy you are, and I mean the guy works out, he lives in Alameda on the water and he's got like this boat and he has the best parties. His hair isn't even gray."

"I'll think about it," I say.

"Well, look. Would it be okay for me to like set up a lunch date where the three of us could get together? Totally innocent and out in the open?"

"I'll think about it," I say. "Fifty-one, you say?"

"That's not so old, Stella."

"It depends on how you look at it," and I walk him to the gate.

This is hard. I am spending so much energy trying not to think about him, and the harder I try the more it doesn't work. I wrote him a letter last week and mailed it off priority and then couldn't remember a word I'd said. But life goes on even when you can't get what you want because you think you need it. All I can do is learn how to deal with this yearning and pray that maybe it'll go away soon or that maybe I'll meet myself a wonderful man—say a thirty-four-year-old professional who's fun funny fabulous finger-licking good and who will rock my world ten times harder than Winston did. This could happen, I suppose.

I am taking Quincy to the mall where he will meet two of his friends and they will cruise the place for two and a half hours while I go see *Batman Forever* since Quincy's already seen it three times and even though he only has twenty dollars in his pockets with which to go on his shopping spree he will probably not be ready to go home after I come out (he swears that he does not come to the mall to look at girls).

"Quincy," I say, as he is pressing the CD button to change from Annie Lennox to Warren G one too many times. "Give me a break, would you?"

"Mom, we always listen to your music. Isn't it fair to let me listen to a personal song of my own every now and then?"

"Be quiet, would you? I need to tell you something."

He turns the sound down, which I think is pretty considerate, considering, and leans back in his seat. "I'm all ears and please no jokes today, Mom."

"I don't have a job anymore."

"Really?"

"Really."

"That's pretty cool, huh? Does it mean you can stay home during the day like Jeremy and Jason and Justin's moms do?"

"Well, not exactly. Sort of. Maybe. But not really."

"Which is it?"

"Well, their moms all have husbands. We don't have one in our house."

"Tell me about it."

"I didn't like my job all that much."

"So why'd you go there every day?"

"Because I used to like it and it helps us live the way we do."

"So did you like quit and just say, 'Hey, guys, I'm like outta here'?"

"Not quite. They basically fired me."

"You mean you got canned?"

"Yep."

"Awesome, Mom. I can't wait to tell Jere—"

"This is not something you go blabbing to your friends about because then they tell their parents and it's really nobody's business but ours, you got that?"

"Yes, Mom. But it's nothing to be ashamed about."

"I didn't say I was ashamed, did I?"

"No. So tell me, are we going to have to get on welfare?"

"No."

"I can get a job to help out with the bills if you want me to."

"Well, if you can find a job, that would help some. That five-dollar-a-week allowance really puts a dent in things."

"Mom, you hardly ever give me an allowance!"

"I give it to you in lump-sum payments, but believe me, I count the weeks and I make deductions when you don't clean your room or when I have to ask you to do something more than once."

"Don't remind me. So are you going to get a new job?"

"I'm not sure. I don't want to work for another corporation."

"So work for yourself."

"And do what?"

"I don't know. You always tell me that one day I'll be able to pick and choose what I want to do because I'm multitalented. You have lots of talents too."

"For instance?"

"Well, let me think."

I'm waiting. I'm hoping. Maybe he knows something I don't.

"You cook really great dinners."

"Go on."

"You can sing."

"I can't sing and you know it."

"You can paint."

"I cannot paint. You can't count painting old furniture. That's not a talent, it's just a hobby. I do it for fun and fun only."

"Well, we have lots of it in our house and I like it, and Mom, what about those weird earrings you make sometimes? And what about that thing you made out of that wire stuff? I mean you've got talents you don't know you have. Listen to your son! I speak the truth!"

"This is all very sweet and thoughtful, Quincy, and in a perfect world I could do like that Demi Moore thing in *Ghost* and sit home all day and just throw and spin clay and make pots and cups and somehow all the bills would get paid. I have enough money to last us a while, but I have to figure out what I want to do that's fun for a change, and something that'll make ends meet. Do more than make ends meet actually."

"You'll find it. Just take your time, as you always say. And Mom. Can I ask you something?"

"Sure."

"Can I get my ear pierced today?"

"Sure," I say.

His narrow butt jumps a foot up off the seat. "Really?"

"Why not?"

"You are the coolest mom. I mean it, Mom. I love you," he says and leans over and gives me a peck on the cheek. "And don't worry, you'll find something to do that makes you happy. I know you will."

And Quincy turns the volume way up, presses the button for disc 2 track 2 and now here comes Monteil Jordan singing "This Is How We Do It," and I'm hoping that I will soon find out how to.

I come out of the theater feeling disoriented. I didn't like *Batman* all that much, to be honest. It was really stupid, but of course I didn't go in in a mood that was ready for silliness. The sound track however is certainly slamming and I am on my way to buy it when I see Quincy and his little friends standing outside Foot Locker.

"Mom!" he yells and why he always has to say everything so loud I don't know. I hope this is something he'll grow out of. Soon. "Look what I bought. It is so cool," and he shows me his hand. On it is a silver ring that has a hand with silver fingers spread out across the top and inside the hand is an eyeball with a green pupil and it looks pretty close to real.

"What is it?"

"It's a ring."

"I can see that," I say. "But what is the point?"

"It's just cool. That is the point."

"Whatever," I say. "We have to go now."

"My darling Mom, would it be possible to—"

"No."

"You didn't even hear what I was going to ask."

"The answer is still no."

"Mom," he whines.

"Say goodbye to your friends."

"Goodbye, ladies," he says and starts following me, pulling on my sleeve, which I cannot stand.

"Let go of me," I say.

"Mom, if I could just borrow ten more dollars of my allowance from you I promise that I will clean Dr. Dre's litter box without your having to ask me and I will clean the fish tank today as a matter of fact and Mom, I just really would like to get this new CD for this movie that's not even out yet called *Dangerous Minds* or something but the CD is so cool, Coolio has the coolest song on it. Mom, please, I promise not to ask for anything else until Christmas!"

"Quincy, you are getting on my nerves, you know that?" but I reach inside my purse like a chump and hand him a ten and he jumps for joy and runs into the store as I stand around there wondering what Winston might be doing what the weather is like in Jamaica and if he could possibly be thinking about me.

"Thanks, Mom. You will love this CD."

"Oh look," I say. "There's a place to get your ear pierced. Want to?"

"Right now?"

"Why not? Are you scared?"

"Are you kidding?" he says. "I'm not scared of anything."

We go in. I pay eleven dollars, which includes his gold stud. The sound of that gun hurts me and within seconds it seems we are walking out of there and my son's ear is pierced and he now thinks he is like totally cool which he is.

I go to the mailbox and am flipping through it when I see a postcard with my name on it and in handwriting I have never seen before. It is from Winston. I stop and sit on the steps outside and read it so fast I have to read it again and again: *Hello there Stella. I can't tell you how much I enjoyed meeting you. I had the best time I ever had in my life. Never met anyone like you before. I miss you. Glad I met you. My job is all right. I am thinking about you a whole lot and I want to hear from you. When will you make me laugh again? And how about a kiss? Had any pesta lately? Hope to see you one day in the near future. Hello to Quincy and Chantel. Love. Winston.*

Without really thinking I go inside and pick up the telephone. I dial my travel agent's number. I tell her that I need a round-trip ticket between Montego Bay and San Francisco. She is a little confused. Says wait a minute. You mean you're going back? No, I tell her. This ticket is for a friend. Oh, she says. And when is he or she traveling? I'm not sure when he can. Leave the dates open. That costs more. I don't care, I say. Hold on a minute and I'll tell you how much. Is this for coach? I say yes. She comes back on and tells me that it is more expensive because of the open date business and then I ask her what the difference is between that fare and first-class and I hear her punching keys and she says only three hundred dollars and I say do it and give her Winston's name and she chuckles at Shakespeare and says, Wow, so this is serious, and I say maybe it is, maybe it isn't, and I say I want this on my American Express extended payment and when can I pick the tickets up and she says in about an hour and I tell her I'll be there and when I walk in she hands me the tickets and I slide them inside my Federal Express envelope which is already filled out and after I walk out I drive straight up to the FedEx drop-off box and push it inside and then I drive away slowly because I realize that what I have just done is irrevocable that I can't change my mind now, that I have made a statement a very large statement and when I feel my foot press down on the brake it is not because I am already regretting doing this, no no no, it is because I am proud of myself for doing something I really want to do without worrying about what anybody will think for a change, and the other reason I bring my car to a halt is because I am so excited I can hardly fucking breathe.

"One two, one two three! One two, three four five! Good morning!" I look over at my exercise trainer alarm clock that Krystal gave me for Christmas and I say, "Shut up!" and there she goes with that "One two, one two three!" business again until I press the cotton-candy-colored button on the top which causes her entire pink unitarded body to freeze with her foot caught in a kicking position and I am tempted to crack the plastic open and snatch off the little pink sweatband that's going around her blond hair and break her bony Barbie body in half once and for all. But as I struggle to get up I think, How would I ever explain to Krystal that Blondie had a little accident?

It is only seven o'clock but Quincy and I are flying to San Diego for the weekend to my friend Maisha's gallery opening and I want to get there in time to help her do any last-minute things.

The phone rings as I'm getting out of the shower and I hear that familiar drone of the AT&T operator and I wonder which imprisoned relative it is this time. But when I hear the operator say "Winston" I perk up and tell her that I will accept the charges.

"Stella?"

"It's me."

"I'm sorry for calling this way but the last two phone calls almost wiped out my paycheck and I won't talk very long as I know how expensive these calls can be but Stella, guess what I got today from Federal Express?"

"I can't begin to imagine, Winston."

"Airline tickets to California!"

"You're kidding!"

"Stella. I don't believe you. You are something, you know that?"

"No, I don't know," I say.

"You sure about this?" he asks.

"That's why I sent them."

"So when can I come?"

"You mean you want to come for real?"

"Absolutely."

"When *can* you come?"

"I've already asked for time off, but I'm not sure if they're going to give it to me being as I'm so new and all."

"How long would you like to come for, Winston?"

"I'm not sure. How long will you have me?"

"Don't ask me that."

"Stella, you want the truth?"

"Yes, Winston, I want the truth."

"I've asked for a three-week leave. How does that sound?"

I am too tickled. "Three weeks sounds wonderful."

"Are you sure?"

"Yes, I'm sure. Are *you* sure?"

"I'm positive. I can't believe you actually sent me a

ticket. No one has ever done anything like this for me before. Why are you doing all these nice things for me?"

"Because I like you, Winston, and I guess I'm nuts."

"No, I don't think you're nuts, but you're very kind and I will make it all up to you."

"You don't have to make anything up to me."

"Well, I think I might be able to come in a month's time. How does that sound to you?"

"It sounds great, Winston. I wish you were here now."

"I wish I was too. But I'll be there, Stella. Don't worry. I'll be there. Sooo," he says. "How are you?"

"I'm fine. On my way to San Diego."

"To the zoo?"

"No, not this trip. A friend of mine owns an art gallery and she's having a big opening this weekend."

"Are you going with friends?"

"What do you mean by friends?"

"I mean who are you going with?"

"Why do I have to be going with anybody?"

"I was just asking."

"Don't be so nosy," I say and start laughing.

"So are you?"

"Going with someone?"

"Yeah," he says and he has that worrisome tone again which I am kind of beginning to like hearing.

"Yeah. I'm going with this person named Quincy."

"Nice," he says. "Very nice. Well, will you call me in a few days' time, then?"

"Why?"

"So I can hear your voice."

"Maybe. Maybe. Maybe. I got your postcard, Winston."

"You finally got it?"

"Yes. I liked what you said. A lot."

"I like you a whole lot, Stella."

"Well, apparently I like you a whole lot too."

"On that note, let's say goodbye before you take this to that other place, okay?"

"What other place?"

"Goodbye, Stella. Love you."

"Love you too, Winston," I say and then I hang up.

Wait a minute. Hold it. Did he just say, "Love you"? and did I just say, "Love you too"? What is going on here, Stella? What is going on?

We are in the air.

"Quincy," I say and slide the earphones away from his ears. He is listening to his cheap portable CD player, which actually sounds better than mine. "We need to talk."

"Right now, Mom?"

"Right now."

"I'm listening."

"How would you feel if Winston came for a visit?"

"Fine."

"For like three whole weeks."

"Fine. I like Winston, Mom."

"You don't even know him, Quincy."

"Mom, I did meet him, remember?"

"Yes, but you didn't really spend any time with him."

"Well, I liked him when I was with him."

"So how would you really feel about his coming here?"

"Mom, if he makes you happy it makes me happy."

"Have you been watching Jenny or Oprah?"

"I like Jenny Jones, Mom. She did a show the other day on teenage pregnancy and it was very informative."

"Oh, be quiet, would you."

"So is Winston going to sleep in your room with you?"

"I think so. Do you have a problem with that?"

"No. I know all about this stuff."

"What 'stuff'?"

"Sex."

"And what do you know about it?"

"First of all that people like doing it and that if you aren't married you should practice safe sex and use a condom. Mom, are you practicing safe sex?"

I don't believe this kid. "Of course I am," I say.

"Good, because there are so many STDs out there it would break your darling son's heart if you were to get like AIDS or something and die and then who would be my mom?"

"Enough already. What else do you know?"

"What else is there?"

"Nothing," I say and pick his headphones up and hand them to him.

Maisha and Tiger meet us outside baggage claim, and Maisha is looking terrific as usual. Her dress is almost always colorful festive and reminiscent of the Caribbean and African designs which she somehow manages to effectively mix with designer jackets and the toughest shoes I've ever seen. Her hair is long thick dreadlocks which are tinged

with gray and at forty-five she is also in great shape because she believes in the E word too.

Maisha and I were both in the MFA program at Chicago
Art Institute but she actually used her degree. She strug-
gled for years trying to make ends meet but she stuck it out
hung in there held on to her dream and her giant of a
husband, Rudy, was behind her all the way all this time.

"Hey, girl," she says, giving me a big hug before we get
into their burgundy Saab convertible. Her son, Tiger, or
Tyson, who is a year older than Quincy and taller than I
am now, gives me a hug and he too is starting to dread on
top. Quincy hugs Maisha and accidentally steps on her
sandaled foot.

"Will you look at those feet?"

"What?" Quincy says.

"What size are you now?"

"Ten."

"I wear eleven now," Tiger says.

"So now that we've bonded, shall we?" I say.

Maisha giggles and the boys jump in the backseat. The
top is down even though it is foggy and pretty nippy down
here if you ask me but I don't say anything, I just lean forward close to the glass and think how beautiful San Diego
is and that if I ever left the Bay Area this is probably where
I'd move to.

"See, Mom," Tiger whines, "Quincy's got his ear
pierced."

"You do, Quincy?" and she looks in the rearview.

"Yep," he says and turns so she can see.

"Aren't you scared you'll mess it up when you're playing sports?"

"Nope. It's summertime now and by the time basketball starts it'll be healed."

"I'm playing football, and practice already started," Tiger offers.

"So you'll have to wait," Maisha says. "Thank the Lord."

Now she is looking over at me and grinning. I know why. Because I opened my big mouth and told her about Winston and she is waiting to hear all the details, and after we drop the kids off at an arcade and go down to her beautiful gallery to help get things set up, over the course of the next two hours I tell her every single thing that happened between me and Winston on down to my sister who thinks I've gone bizonkers and my sister who says if it feels good do it.

"I'm with Vanessa, girl."

"What?"

"Hell, I think you should send him a ticket. Get him here as fast as possible."

"Are you serious, Maisha?"

"Abso-fucking-lutely. How often does this shit happen? I mean what does his age have to do with anything?"

"A lot."

"Only because you're making an issue out of it. But seriously, you like him, huh?"

"I like him a lot, Maisha."

"Then I'd go for it, and don't worry about what anybody says. This is your life, girl. You're not going to get another chance to come back and do it over. Enjoy yourself. Hell, enjoy him."

"I sent him a ticket," I say.

"*That's fantastic!* Now that's the way to do it, girl. To hell with the do-the-right-thing shit. Besides, I really don't see any difference in what you're doing and what men have been doing for years. I mean if you were a man and you happened to have met some young chick on an island and she didn't have a career and all that bullshit and any money but she made him feel good and he sent her an airline ticket do you think anybody would be tripping? I doubt it. So fuck this double standard shit, girl. I mean really."

I am so glad she feels this way. Deep down I feel this way too but the world is still the world. I just have to learn to get over it. And so far I think I'm doing a pretty good job. Because after all, I did send the ticket, didn't I?

"Stella, let me ask you something else, though, girl."

"What's that?"

"So like what're you gonna do if he gets here and you guys hit it off and everything is still magical and you don't want him to go?"

"What do you mean?"

"What if you guys are like madly in love and shit and he doesn't want to leave and you don't want him to leave—what are you going to do?"

"I don't know. I haven't thought that far ahead yet."

"I think you should."

"How can I think about something like that?"

"Because it is a possibility, that's why. Shit happens when you least expect it."

"Yeah, but understand this, Maisha. I don't want to marry the man. The truth is I *am* old enough to be his fucking mother."

"But you're not his mother, Stella."

"I know that. But I'm not having any more kids. And it's not like we can plan this long life together. I mean there will be no wedding no babies no picket fences. None of that."

"How do you *know* that?"

"Fuck you, Maisha. Don't you get it?"

"Get what?"

"I'm not going that far with him."

"How do you know *that?* Who are you to predetermine how far your heart wants to go?"

"I don't mean it that way. All I mean is that I don't exactly know what this is but I do know that he makes me feel extra good inside and I miss him and want him here and if all I get is three weeks then I'll take three weeks of bliss versus three weeks of nothing."

"I hear you, girl, but I want to tell you something else. You know my mama has lung cancer, don't you?"

"No, I didn't know that." I groan. "I'm sorry to hear that, Maisha."

"It's okay. I'm dealing with it. You know me and my mama ain't never got along too tough."

"Well, yeah."

"Basically, she's a conniving wench. Always has been, always will be. She's got nine kids and out of all of us there's only three who even bother to call or visit her."

"But she's still your mama. Be glad you've got one."

"I know that, but the point I'm trying to make is this. She must be the most coldhearted person I've ever met in my entire life, and after she divorced my father some twenty-five years ago she has been one lonely miserable woman. My mother is seventy-three years old and I doubt if she has had so much as a date in all that time, not to mention sex and love, which is why she's probably so hard. She became very bitter after he left, and you know what, she'll probably die lonely and hard like this. Now, I'm going to be the one who takes care of her. I've accepted the responsibility and it's okay, I'll do it, but the point I'm trying to make here is that listening to her and watching her and knowing she doesn't have much time left on this earth in this world, Stella, if you can get ten minutes, ten weeks, or ten months of happiness, take it. *Anytime* you can get it, take it, cause some folks check out of here and don't even get that ten minutes because they were either too scared to open up to other possibilities or only saw problems as problems or made them problems instead of opportunities. You don't have tomorrow promised to you. You just don't fucking know."

"I know," I say. "But I'm really sorry to hear about your mama, Maisha. And you be sure to let me know if there's anything I can do, cause I don't have one to complain about or help."

"I know, baby. But hey. Let's get off this dreary subject. So anyway, you know what?"

"What?"

"Stop acting like such a fucking grown-up, Stella. Do you realize that as women we've been programmed to do the right thing since we were little girls and even when we were in our twenties and tripping hard with these fools we were in love with—remember when we were all doing drugs and hanging out partying?"

"Of course I remember. Well, sort of."

"Anyway, my point is: even back then when we were supposed to be footloose and free spirits and shit, who was the one in the relationship who made sure the rent and stuff was paid on time?"

"We did."

"Who made sure shit got taken care of in general?"

"We did."

"So my point is we've acted responsibly for so long that I think we could've had more fun than we did and in fact I believe we're entitled to a whole lot more so I think now is the time for you to enjoy what the fuck you missed."

"Never thought about it that way."

"Think about it. And think about this. What if Winston really falls in love?"

"And?"

"First of all, a lot of young men fantasize about being with an older woman because who better to learn the ropes from? And also, if they're able to please and satisfy you, then that's a feather in their ego cap. Some of them use this experience so they go out and trample all over these hot young girls, but some of them actually do like older women and some of them do fall in love."

"But I can't do anything about that."

"Just remember that this isn't just about you, Stella."

"I know," I say. "But stop, Maisha. I can't think straight as it is."

"This is one of the signs," she says.

When we get to her house, Rudy is there. He is a jazz musician. A saxophonist who has played with the best, including Miles Davis. He also teaches jazz theory and composition at the university. He is cooking and Maisha frowns when she sees him in the kitchen and shakes her head back and forth to me as if to say disaster disaster and when he turns around she smiles in pure delight. "Rudy! Making dinner again!"

"Yep. This is something special I had when I was in Brazil, if I can remember the shit right, but I'll know it when I add enough of these spices to it. Hey, Stella. What's the deal with all the hair?"

"Shut up, Rudy. I bought it."

"Yeah, and who had to die in order for you to get it?" He laughs. "Is everything all right down at the gallery?" he asks Maisha.

"Everything's ready to go," she says. "I was telling Stella here she ought to do some more of those tables and what is that stuff you use to make them smooth and brassy looking?"

"Gold leaf."

"Yeah. And what else have you made lately that you keep hidden in the garage?"

"Well, I made this thing which I brought down here just for you."

"You brought me something? Oh where is it, go get it, please, you give me the best gifts a girl could ever have. What is it? Earrings? Stella, you should sell those damn things. I could sell them from the gallery, you know. Come on upstairs."

We run up the stairs of this house that looks like something out of *Interior Design* because even though the furnishings are sparse the artwork dominates and what is in here is jamming.

I open up my garment bag and pull out something I call wearable art. It is a crop-top sweater made of copper thread that I have knitted together and bordered with rust-colored angora.

"Don't stand here and tell me you made this?"

"I am standing here telling you I made this. Started it over a year ago, finished it this spring—remember when I got that virus and was stuck in bed?"

Maisha nods though I know she doesn't remember.

"Anyway I didn't have anything else to do and to be honest I'd forgotten all about it until I was packing to come here."

"Girl, you ought to quit. This is beautiful! I love it. I want some more of them. Make some for the gallery. Please. Where did you come up with the idea? What is it made of?"

"Copper thread, sort of. Put it on."

"Are you crazy?"

"You can wear it, Maisha."

"Oh no, baby. I'm not wearing this. I'm putting this on my wall. No, I'm going to put it in the gallery. Today. Would you mind?"

"It's yours. Do whatever you want to do with it. I'm just glad you like it."

"Like it?" And she walks over and gives me a big hug. "You are better than you think you are, girl. And that is a good thing, but you need to wake up."

"Oh, guess what else?"

"What?"

"I got fired."

"Good," she says. "It's about time you got out of that

dreadful place. You did it long enough. So now I guess you can finally be the artist you were meant to be, right?"

"I wouldn't go that far."

"You'll see," she says. "You'll see how far to go." And then in the next breath: "Girl, I think Winston sounds wonderful and I hope you fall hopelessly in love and that he blows your mind because Lord knows you've been in a slump since your divorce. Enjoy yourself. So do you love him? Tell me the truth."

"I don't know!"

"Bullshit. You do know."

"I guess I do but it's kind of embarrassing to admit."

"What's to be embarrassed about, girl? He's a man. You're a woman. Whammo."

"All I know is he feels like the Lieutenant of Love and I feel resurrected or something."

"Well, girl, you sure look good and I can't tell if it's the hair or what but whatever works, work it."

"I'm trying," I say. "But Maisha, this is scary, you know."

"So what?"

"I know. But to be honest, don't think I haven't thought about what I'd do when he gets here and I can't stand the idea of his leaving. I mean what would I do?"

"Ask him to stay," she says. "Simple as that. Now come on, we need to go downstairs and pretend to eat Rudy's nasty dinner and girl just nibble on it and I'll distract him long enough to toss the shit out and then we need to get dressed."

*　*　*

Rudy's meal is fabulous and as a matter of fact we all take seconds. Maisha is so proud she hugs him twice. We all get dudded up and head for the gallery, where people are already trying to find parking spaces. Maisha has my sweater in her hand and as soon as she gets into her office she makes a tag for it and finds a small spot on the wall near the door to the garden, where long tables are filled with fresh flowers and cheese and fruit and wine. This show is a retrospective of about twenty African-American artists' work and within the next hour the place is swarming with two hundred plus people. Checks are being written. Credit cards are being whipped out. Little red dots are placed on pieces that hang on the wall or stand on the floor.

Maisha saunters over to me. In her pale yellow suit, she looks great, smart, funky. "Girl, eight people have asked me about your piece. We are going to have to talk some more about this. I mean it. You should pay attention, for real. Isn't everything just gorgeous?"

"Everything's gorgeous," I say and walk her over to what appears to be a very old photograph of a black family that somehow has been transferred onto glass by the artist Mildred Howard—and I look on my price sheet one more time—it's $3,500—and knowing I can't afford it, I ask, "Maisha, can you please put me on the friendly payment plan? I *have* to have this. These people could be *my* family."

She gives me a big hug and then whispers in my ear. "Girl, don't look, but that guy over there has been asking Rudy about you all evening and he wants to meet you, girl."

I turn to look and I must admit that if it's the one I think she's talking about he is rather splendid in appearance. "Is he the one with the baggy pants and white shirt?"

"Yep. He's a sculptor and those are two of his pieces over there. You want to meet him?"

"I don't know."

"Oh, it won't hurt. Just meet him. That's all."

"Okay."

I stand there feeling pretty naked. Maisha goes to get him and he is looking at me as he walks over. He is really distinctive looking, like maybe he could be a model or something, because his features are pretty much perfect. I am beginning to notice lips more than I used to and his are thick and smooth and shaped like they would be pleasant to kiss. He looks to be forty maybe and he is about six one and dark dark brown and his skin has almost a satin sheen to it and he has a zillion baby dreadlocks which make him look more like an African prince than What's-his-name I met in Jamaica who was actually from Senegal.

"Ralston, I'd like you to meet one of my longest and dearest friends. Stella, Ralston."

"Hello, Ralston," I say.

"Nice to finally meet you, Stella. I've been asking about you pretty much since I got here."

"Really?"

"Really. And I love your work. But why is there only one piece of yours in here?"

"It's a long story. I love *your* pieces. Wish I could afford one."

"I could make you a deal," he says and he seems to mean it. He is also looking at me like he's looking inside me with those beautiful big obsidian eyes and I am feeling a little weird about this so I turn away.

"I'm really on a tight budget," I say.

"Maybe we could do a trade sometime."

"Maybe we could," I say.

"And where do you live?" he asks.

"Up north. In the Bay Area."

"I do too. Where exactly?"

"Right past Walnut Creek in Alamo."

"I live in Montclair!"

Gee fucking wilikers.

"We should have lunch sometime."

"We should," I say.

"Would you mind giving me your number?"

"No, I don't mind," I say, which is a lie. I have already given my number to whoever I want to have it but I cannot say that to Ralston. "Just get it from Rudy or Maisha," I say.

"I will call," he says.

"I'm sure you will," I say. "Now if you'll excuse me, I want to take a look at the rest of the show."

"Go right ahead," he says, peering at me like he has made some kind of discovery. What he doesn't understand is that a prior claim has already been made.

I'm scared, worried and beginning to wonder if maybe I am going a little bizonkers. I'm in my truck, on my way to the grocery store. The light is red and I'm just sitting there thinking what have I gotten myself into? I mean what in the hell am I *really* doing? I mean did I actually send a twenty-one-year-old a first-class airline ticket to come visit me and he said yes and he's coming here to my home for three whole weeks? I mean, what are we going to do for three whole weeks? I haven't had a man in my house longer than twenty-four hours in almost three *years.* You mean someone'll finally get to use that other sink in my bathroom? But does this also mean I'll have to clear off that entire counter of all my fingernail polish lotions perfume and makeup? Where will I put this stuff? And what about drawers? Or will he keep his things folded up in his suitcase(s) and I wonder how many of those will he be bringing? And will he want to party all the time? Probably. I mean he loves to dance, and I don't do the town all that much—well, never, really—which means I'm going to have to do some serious investigating to find the best spots for dancing. But what else? What will we do all day long, since I'm home these days? Will I be carting him around everywhere, because he probably can't drive and if he can, can he drive a stick, and if so I know he won't be able to adjust to driving on the right side of the street and I wonder does he even have a driver's license? Should I do his laundry for him while he's here or just let it pile up? What if he gets on my nerves? What if I get on *his* nerves? What if after a few days I realize I don't like him anymore? That it was just a crush a lustful heated fascination an infatuation. That Angela was right and this was nothing more than a tropical apparition. That I only want him because he's taboo. I wonder if maybe I *was* lonely as hell, hard up, just grateful for some attention. No, I wasn't that fucking hard up and I haven't exactly been dying of loneliness. I can get a man if I want a man but finding one I really like and yearn for is a whole different brand of Snapple. So no, that's not it. What if he doesn't like American food, what will he eat? What if he dies while he's here? Or what if he gets a toothache or needs an appendectomy or is bringing some incurable tropical disease over here with him? And how about those fruit flies? Does he own a jacket or a coat with a lining in it? I mean the temperature is already starting to drop here and if it turns out that I happen to still kind of like him after he leaves it would be nice if he could like come back for say a winter visit since he will have had a fall visit and then I could take him up to Lake Tahoe and he could see some real snow and we could lie down and make angels and with those long arms, wow, what wings he could make. And Quincy could show him how to snowboard and I could show him how to fly downhill and do bumps. I wonder if he's ever seen snow? If he's ever touched anything so cold and soft.

Oh no. There's one of my neighbors. Shit. The neighbors! What about the neighbors? Who am I going to tell them he is because they will ask they ask about anything that looks new and Winston will be a new addition on the block and a tall handsome one at that and with a Jamaican accent and everybody knows I went to Jamaica this summer and they will think I probably bought him or blackmailed him or kidnapped him and how will I account for his presence? I mean *who* is he?

I hear someone honking behind me. "I'm moving!" I yell and jut forward put on my blinker and turn into Safeway and now I am smiling. I get a parking space right in front, which means there is a God, and now I'm laughing because I realize that the reason I'm having so much fun this summer is that for the first time in a long long time I am not all that worried about what anybody thinks, and so yes, I am acting a little irrationally, a little spontaneously, but hell, if I had known that acting silly and foolish felt this good I'd have been behaving like this a long time ago.

So to hell with the neighbors. I don't care what they think. Well, I sort of do because I happen to like my neighbors and besides, I forgot I do have this child who has to face their children on a daily basis, so I will have a little chat with Quincy about yet another deep anthropological philosophical spiritual issue to which I'm sure he will respond in his very own Quincyesque manner. God, I love that boy. Now what did I come here for? Oh yeah, groceries.

*   *   *

Quincy and I are bonding again. It is a Saturday night and we are sitting on the red leather love seat in our family room and the dog is at our feet. I wish someone were here to take this picture. We are watching the Discovery Channel, a show called *Shipwrecked*, which I didn't tune in to until Quincy had already been watching it about fifteen minutes, but when I asked him if he wanted me to sit down and bond with him, he said, "Sure, Mom. Even though you don't even know what the word means!"

We both laugh at that because we like to joke around with and use as much of the nineties slang as we can so we will remain among the hip hipper hippest of families ever to grace the suburbs. Not really. He throws the afghan across our laps even though it is rather warm in here and the French doors are open. We are watching what I assume are Australians on a gigantic boat out in the middle of some ocean doing something. "Is this Australia?"

"I'm not sure," Quincy says.

"Why don't you know?"

"Because they haven't said where they are."

"I bet they have said it and you just weren't listening."

"I have been listening."

"Well, where do you think they are?"

"In the sea."

I want to say, No shit—you are so deep, Quincy. But I wouldn't dare. "If they did say where they are and you just haven't been paying attention, you should be paying attention because you're going to be in junior high school in two weeks and your attention span is going to count for a whole lot and right now you are unable to answer a simple little question that I have posed to you in front of whatever this is but you know what?"

"What?"

"I still love you, boy!"

"I love you too, Mom, but if you hadn't been in the kitchen banging pots and pans so loud in the dishwasher maybe I would've been able to hear where they were!" and as he's saying it he slowly but steadily rises to a standing position.

"What are they diving for anyway?"

"Some kind of old ship or treasure or something," he says and flops back down in one kerplunk.

"Which is it?"

"Both!"

"How close are they to finding it?"

"Well, they've found some interesting stuff down there, but not enough to answer all their questions. And you know what's really cool? They don't have the right kind of equipment to do the kind of diving they're doing but they're doing it anyway and guess what, Mom? There're sharks down there."

"So are you saying that the sharks could like eat them or kill them?"

"Exactly."

I stare at the crew on the boat. There must be at least twelve of them. They are all men. They are all white. They are all crazy in my estimation because it is apparent as I watch them holding up their maps and plotting their course that there is no way I'd be out in the middle of a fucking ocean diving for some old ship that may or may not have any treasure on it while sharks down there could possibly eat me up. "Black people would not be out there searching for some sunken ship unless they knew for sure that it had at least a gazillion dollars on it and even if it did no way would they be diving down there with the wrong jumpsuits on that sharks could like chew right through. Black people don't like this kind of danger."

Quincy scrunches up his shoulders. "But Mom, this is *exciting* to these guys, you have to give them that much—come on."

I am shocked to hear him say this because he certainly is not as black as I was when I was his age. As a matter of fact, we would be dissing these people right now, calling them fools and yelling at the TV just like we used to when we turned our heads upside down on the floor so we could see under the skirts of those square-dancing ladies, laughing at them for not having anything close to rhythm, for looking ridiculous, and then during horror movies when the monster would come after the blond bombshell and she always fell down we would get mad and yell, "Get up, dummy!" and when she was too slow or broke her stupid high heel and we wondered what she was doing in high heels when she was at a picnic or at a campsite or when she finally fell into a hole or a ditch or whatever or was dangling from a branch or something we would stand up and scream, "Kill that clumsy dummy, Swamp Man! Go ahead, eat her bootie up!"

I sit here without once getting up not even to go to the bathroom which I really need to do but I made a promise to myself that tonight I would watch an entire show with Quincy. I've been trying to do this on a regular basis since we've come back from Jamaica, at least when I'm able to catch him.

The show goes off and of course the guys had put two and two together and realized that the ship had to have come from Saudi Arabia based on x, y, and z and shoot, after I studied the map and backtracked the route it led straight from the Indian Ocean on up to the Arabian Sea and I could've told them that but it has been very nice sitting here watching anything with my son who turns to me on this sofa and says, "Mom, I like it when we do this," and I peck him on his forehead and say, "I do too, Quin. And we've only just begun."

He is just about to hop up from the sofa.

"Wait a minute, Quincy. We need to talk."

"Again?" he asks and flops back down.

"Again."

"What did I do now?"

"Nothing."

"Is this gonna be a lecture?"

"No."

"How long will it take, do you think?"

"I don't know. Why?"

"Because *Ren and Stimpy*'s coming on in a few minutes and then *Are You Afraid of the Dark?*, and Mom, can I stay up until eleven-thirty to watch *The State*?"

"The what?"

"It's on MTV."

"Is it as ludicrous as Beavis and Butt-head?"

"Not at all. Ha ha ha, didn't think I remembered that word, did you?"

"I know you're smart, Quincy, but I just want you to keep proving it to yourself, because I'm already impressed. You see, I was generous in that delivery room and

I told the doctor to make sure you got some of my best brain cells and a few of your dad's and apparently you wiped out most of his supply but anyway I'm convinced that you're more intelligent than the two of us put together and ten times brighter than you think you are. You'll see. You know, I used to play a game when I was little."

"What kind of game?"

"I constantly tried to amaze myself."

"Meaning?"

"Well, first of all, being dumb was never a goal of mine. I knew a lot of ignorant people and I wanted to be smart, smart enough to live an interesting life when I grew up, so when I was in junior high school I used to pick a letter for the day like say B and read as much as I could in the B encyclopedia and I would circle words in the newspaper I didn't know and look them up and write sentences using them and give them to my mother at the end of the week."

"And?"

"And I'm all off the track. See what you made me do—you made me lose my train of thought."

"I didn't, Mom! You always do this and you know it."

"Do what?"

"Start talking about one topic and then end up talking about a different thing. You should stick to your topic sentence. I learned that way back in fifth grade, Mom. Stick to your topic."

"Okay. You know when Winston gets here some of the neighbors might be a little curious about who he is."

"Yeah."

"And they might not understand."

"Might not understand what?"

"Well, first of all that he's a lot younger than I am."

"Mom, remember: age ain't nothing . . ."

"I know, but some people don't feel that way."

"But you do, don't you?"

"I try, but our neighbors are pretty regular folks and they might not get it and they might want to ask you about Winston."

"But it's none of their business, is it?"

"No, it isn't, but we don't exactly want to come out and say that because it would be kind of tacky and just rude really."

"So what kind of questions do you think they'll ask?"

"Well, like who is he, for starters."

"And what should I say, Mom?"

"Well, I don't want you to lie. Say that he's our friend and he's visiting from Jamaica."

"That's the truth."

"Yes, it is. And when and if anybody asks you how long he's staying you can say just a few weeks but he might actually be coming back to go to graduate school here, you're not sure."

"What's graduate school?"

"College."

"Is he?"

"I don't know, Quincy."

"Mom, are you lying about this stuff?"

"No! And if anybody, anybody at all, happens to ask you where he's sleeping, what do you think you should say?"

He hunches up his shoulders, because he's not sure what answer I'm looking for.

"Just tell them he's sleeping with your mom which is why she's looking so good, whistling and smiling so much more these days."

"Okay, if you really want me to," he says.

"I'm just kidding. I wanted to see if you were listening. Turn that stuff down."

He presses the volume control on the remote a few times.

"Anyway it's nobody's business where Winston sleeps, and if anybody asks you you tell them to come see your mom."

"Sounds like a plan to me," he says.

We are silent for a while. I watch a few minutes of *Ren and Stimpy*. These are two sick puppies. "I wish he'd hurry up and get here." I sigh.

"Me too," Quincy says.

"Why?"

"Because I like hearing him talk and you just act a lot happier when he's around and plus I bet he likes playing Sega and Super Nintendo."

I don't touch this.

I haven't talked to Winston in four days. I'm kind of freaking out about it because now that we have decided to see each other on my turf my domain my soil it is dawning on me that maybe I was set up or something. Maybe he is a real gigolo like Richard Gere was in that movie, and Winston did conveniently sit down at the table behind me, didn't he? He'd probably been watching me waiting for me to do something that would prove I was some gullible middle-aged lonely broad from America who hadn't been fucked in months and would probably drool at the sight of a fine young man such as himself. Maybe he sensed it. Maybe he had his little friend Norris steal my records from the hotel files and he found out all about me, like how much money I made, where I worked and how well I lived. So maybe he already had the rundown on me when he gave me that sexy sneaky grin that day. And now that I think about it, he was sort of following me around, wasn't he? Everywhere I turned, there he was. And he certainly took to me quickly. Too quickly if you ask me. I know if some foreigner sent *me* an airline ticket I'd have to know every single detail about her before I got on a fucking airplane and flew to another country to see her. He must know somebody. He could be a fucking serial killer for all I know. I wonder what it is he really wants. I mean it's not like I could end up being his girlfriend or something. So what could he possibly want from me, a woman old enough to be his mother?

I'm tripping too hard again so I decide to go on and call him even though I don't like calling him so much because I don't want him to feel pressured and I want him to feel good about this whole thing in general. I've been waking up in the middle of the night lately wondering if I really did send him a ticket and if he really is coming and will I roll over and there he's going to be right next to me right in my very own bed. I get a little charge when I think about it but when he comes on the phone I hear a catch in his voice. I knew it I knew it I knew it. He isn't coming. I can hear it. I knew this was too good to be true. Knew it knew it knew it. "Is everything all right?" I ask.

"Well, sort of," he says.

"What's wrong, Winston?"

"Well, my parents are kind of giving me a hard time about this."

At the sound of "parents" I am reminded that he was still living at home before he got this job. Boy. When was the last time I lived with my parents? "A hard time about what?" I ask.

"About my coming there."

"But Winston, you're just visiting, not moving here."

"I know that."

"Well, what exactly did you tell them?"

"I told them that I met someone whom I really like and care about and that she is American and she sent me air fare to come visit and I'm taking a leave from my job and I'm going to California in five weeks' time to see her."

"And did you tell them how old this friend was?"

"Yes. Thirty-four."

When he hears me laugh he laughs. "Thank the Lord," I say and I do feel relieved because if he were my son I'd be a little skeptical about his traipsing off to America with a forty-two-year-old woman he'd only spent a few days with. Really.

"They're worrying if maybe this isn't some kind of scam."

"What do you mean, a scam?"

"Well, my mother in particular can't understand what it is you see in me."

"Oh, really?"

"Yeah. She says I have no money or anything so what could you possibly want from me?"

"And what did you tell her?"

"I didn't know what to tell her."

"Don't you know, Winston?"

"I think I do."

"And what do you think it is that I want from you?"

"Me?"

"That's right. But let me tell you something. This morning I made you out to be a serial killer! I'm scared too, Winston, and I've been worrying whether you're interested in me only because you have some sneaky self-serving reasons."

"Stella, what could I hope to get from you?"

"I don't know. Maybe a green card."

"But how would I go about doing that?"

"Never mind, Winston. Do *you* want to know what I see in you?"

"It would help."

"You really want me to tell you, right now?"

"Yes," he says and his voice is softening, becoming more at ease, more the Winston I'm used to hearing.

"Well, for starters, one of the things I find intriguing about you is that your eyes aren't stale yet."

"What do you mean by that?"

"It means you haven't been around long enough to have a warped and cynical view of the world and people or at least women and your way of looking at things is fresh and it is rubbing off on me and it is the way I used to look at things, at life, at people, and you're not scared of the future and I am sort of regaining my virginity, if you get my drift. You're still fascinated and overwhelmed by things and I find you refreshing and I'm glad I met you, in fact I'm grateful."

"I'm grateful to *you*, Stella. I mean you are the one person I can actually talk to about anything and you don't bite your tongue and I don't have to pretend to be something that I'm not with you and you make me feel really good about being who I am. And you make me laugh. Not very many people, girls, women, can make me laugh."

"I'm not finished," I say.

"No?"

"No. I like the fact that you're not worried about everything, that you're still unsure of yourself but not plagued by insecurity. And I think you're beautiful and I love looking at you with your clothes on and off. I love your voice. I think you're sexy. I love your smile your laughter your shiny black eyes your bushy eyebrows and those thick beautiful lips of yours."

"I've always hated my lips."

"I know. I've hated mine too. But look at how things turn out. The very things we were teased about as kids— these big lips and round cheeks and full noses and every- thing—have turned out to be our best features."

"You think so?"

"Well . . ."

We laugh.

"I love the way you kiss me, Winston, and I'll tell you right now that no one has ever kissed me as good as you have."

"I know that's not true, Stella."

"I speak the truth. And I'm not finished. I like the fact

that I don't know what you're thinking all the time. You keep some things to yourself. I like that mysterious stuff."

"Really?"

"Really. And I like the fact that you don't know your own power."

"What power?"

"That's my point."

"Are you finished?" he asks.

"Well, I like that even though you don't know for sure what you want to do, you're testing the waters."

"Yeah, because I'm not totally convinced that I want to be a chef, you know?"

"No problem, Winston. But take it from me, if there's ever going to be a time in your life when you can afford to take risks and chances and make mistakes it's now, when you're in your twenties, because you can always change your mind and go in another direction and the world won't stop if you err."

"See, that's what I mean. No one ever talks to me like this except you, Stella."

"And I like the fact that for some reason I don't understand, you seem to be overlooking my age, and that you like me and not what I represent."

"Your age is not an issue for me."

"Well, go tell your parents all this stuff."

And we burst into laughter again.

"They're really getting on my nerves, to be honest, and I don't understand why they're making such a big deal about it."

"Because they're your parents, Winston, and they love you and they have a right to be concerned. Be glad they are. But the real question is this: What's your biggest fear?"

"About coming over there?"

"Yes."

"That you might not like me as much as you think you do."

"Oh, really."

"Really."

"Well, let me put your mind at ease, Winston. I'm having trouble sleeping because I'm so excited."

"Join the club."

"I miss you a whole whole lot and it takes so much effort for me not to think about you I'm just getting to the point where I'm able to admit it openly."

"And what about your sisters, Stella? How do you think they'll receive me?"

"Well, Angela is pretty much on the same wavelength as your parents, but not to worry, you won't be spending much time with her. Now my other sister, Vanessa, she's got a nineties attitude, so she's all for this and can't wait to meet you."

"And Quincy?"

"He's geeked. He just wants to know if you'll play Sega and Super Nintendo with him."

"Sure I will, but tell him I'm not very good at it."

"It doesn't matter. But understand this, Winston. I don't want you to think I want you to try to pretend to be his dad or anything."

He snickers. "How could I when I'm barely ten years older than he is?"

Now I snicker.

"When does he start school?"

"In a few weeks."

"And how will he get there?"

"I'll drive him to the bus stop."

"Could I take him sometimes while I'm there?"

"Sure. But Winston . . ."

"Yeah?"

"Do you have a driver's license?"

"Of course I have a driver's license."

"Do you know how to drive on the right side of the street?"

"Yes. It's just like driving on the left side."

"And have you had any dental work done lately?"

"I have no cavities, Stella. What is this about?"

"What about fatal diseases? Any that you know of?"

"None that I can think of offhand."

"Ever had an occasion to kill anybody?"

"Only twice, but I served my time for those crimes already."

"That's good," I say.

"That should cover everything, I hope," he says.

"Wait. One last thing."

"What now?"

"Are you handy?"

"What's that?"

"Can you fix things?"

"I can fix a *lot* of things," he says.

"Name two things you know how to fix."

"Just two?"

"Okay, three things."

"Well, I can fix cars and bicycles and pretty much anything that moves, including you."

"Okay, Mr. Smartypants."

"So does that mean I can get clearance?"

"From me it does. I don't know about your parents."

"I'll deal with them."

"And what are you going to tell them now?"

"Nothing different really. They'll just have to accept the fact that this is my life, that I'm a man and I'm doing what I want to do. And that's it."

"Is there a chance they could cause you to change your mind?"

"I doubt it," he says. "I'll be walking through that gate at San Francisco airport on the thirtieth of September."

"That's five whole weeks away, Winston. What's a girl to do?"

"What's a *man* to do?"

"You could always take up embroidering or knitting or sewing or quilting."

"Look, Miss America, I'll talk to you again soon."

"Bye, Winston," I say.

"Love you," he croons.

"And I love you too, Winston," I say, and I say it loud and clear.

It is Labor Day weekend. Quincy and I are driving up to Lake Tahoe for five days. What I'm really doing is killing time, counting the weeks and days left until Winston gets here, but it is also an opportunity for me to spend some quality time with my son alone with no distractions before he begins a new life as a junior high school student.

Phoenix, the dog, farts in the back of the truck all the way up and I am tempted to give him some Pepto-Bismol tablets. I know he will eat them because he is stupid and will eat anything you give him. Vanessa begged us to let Dr. Dre come to a weeklong slumber party being thrown by their cat Milo, so we acquiesced, but only under the condition that the two kitties slept in separate beds. The Big Plan is to go Jet Skiing, fishing, rafting, anything we can do in, on or near the water.

Day one. "Do you want to go Jet Skiing today, Quincy?"

"Not really, Mom. I just want to sleep in."

"Okay."

He sleeps in. It is noon.

"Do you want to go anywhere, Quincy?"

"Not really. Can we just rent some videos?"

"Sure."

We rent some videos. I go to the grocery store. I buy some food. I cook some of it. We eat it. We go to sleep.

Day two. A repeat of day one.

Day three. Winston does not call. I gave him the number last week and he said he would call on Saturday and today is Sunday. I am not calling him. I cannot call him. We are too close to the beginning. I jog with the dog at six thousand feet and today the altitude is making me a little short of breath but I keep going. There are two-hundred-foot evergreens everywhere and the air is thin and crisp and I can see snow on the top of quite a few mountains. I love it up here. I feel healthy up here.

Quincy and I sit out on the deck and read for hours at a stretch. It is the most peaceful time he and I have spent together in at least two years. I used to lie on his bed for an hour before bedtime or on a Saturday afternoon and read to him and then when he graduated to books with chapters sometimes he read. I'd look over at him, at his entire body, which appeared to have grown in the last few minutes; his lips moved and his eyes danced and darted across the page and I'd think: My son can read; he can comprehend things, he is making discoveries and he will soon have even more opinions about the world. Sometimes when he felt me watching, smiling, he stopped reading and looked at me and maybe winked or grinned because he knew exactly why I was beaming and I'd lie there and imagine how much longer we had to do this, lie on his bed side by side and read aloud, my arms rubbing against his cotton pajamas.

And how many more times would I be able to ask him if he'd like a lift and he'd automatically put his book down and move down to my feet which I lifted and pressed flat against his chest and took his hands and lifted him into the air above me where he laughed and we did this over and over. At other times we'd just put on a Beethoven CD that Quincy liked and we'd read our respective books and eat popcorn and he'd drink raspberry Snapple and I'd drink kiwi strawberry.

Right now he's reading book number gazillion of R. L. Stine's "Goosebumps" series which is fine with me because he has previously finished *Congo* by Michael Crichton and *The Autobiography of Malcolm X* by Alex Haley and *Roll of Thunder, Hear My Cry* by Mildred Taylor. Back in June the school sent a list of twenty-six books, from which Quincy was supposed to choose four to read over the summer. Of course I bought *all* the books and he promised me that he would have them read by Christmas. Don't do it for me, I told him, do it for yourself. I've done sixth grade and it was good.

We take a nap. We go to the health food store, where I buy yet another bathing product because it is natural and smells good. We eat Mexican food for dinner and my stomach feels weird but we lock the dog in the garage, leaving a window cracked, and we drive to Reno where I win $225 playing the dollar slots while Quincy plays Killer Instinct upstairs in the arcade for two whole hours and then I drive home and we fall asleep and there was no phone call from Winston.

Day four. It is Labor Day and I wake up with sharp pains

in my side and my stomach is bloated and I feel nauseous. I call Vanessa to ask her advice since she works in a hospital and is used to pain and suffering in the larger sense.

"How do you know if you have cancer?" I ask her.

"What kind of cancer?"

"Any kind?"

"Well, if you have lung cancer you get short of breath and you're coughing all the time and there's a tightness in your chest. Why, are you feeling like this?"

"No."

"Well, then there's prostate cancer."

"I don't need to hear about that one," I say.

"Well, with breast cancer you have a lump in your breast of course," and I grab one but figure this couldn't be the kind I have because I had a mammogram earlier this summer and it was negative.

"If you had other kinds you'd just have pain and maybe some blood and stuff. Why are you asking me about this?"

"Because I've been having stomach pains since yesterday and I feel weird, like I'm pregnant or something."

"Get real, Stella."

"There's no way I could be pregnant. I mean first of all I had my period in August and plus we used condoms."

"So if it's still bothering you when you get home, make an appointment to see your doctor and get it checked out."

"I think I will."

"So what are you guys doing today?"

"I don't know. Maybe Jet Skiing."

"Well, have fun. You know what you've probably got?"

"What?"

"Gas."

"I would know if I had gas, Vanessa."

"You're excited about Winston coming and everything and you might just be stressing."

"Okay, if it turns out that I've got some kind of terminal disease and I'm going to be dead before Winston even gets here, I'll have you to thank for helping me get early detection."

"Bye, Stella. Call me back later if you think you're not going to live, okay? I just want you to know I've got first dibs on the BMW."

I hang up.

"Mom, is any member of our family lactose intolerant?"

"What?"

"Is anybody in our family lactose intolerant?"

"I don't know. Why?"

"I was just wondering."

He is lying on the couch now. "Quincy, I'm going to go down to the emergency room for a minute because I've got these pains in my stomach and I just want to get it checked out."

"Mom, are you sick?"

"I don't think so."

"Want me to go with you? I'll go with you," he says and sits up.

"No, Quin, stay here. I won't be long. It's probably nothing."

"You sure?"

I nod and nod and nod until he buys it.

* * *

I've been in here now for three hours. It is a holiday, they say, and it is busy. I see a guy come in who is bleeding from his eardrum and then a young mother has had an epileptic seizure while she was home alone with her brand-new baby and her mom is holding it now and there are at least four I-can't-look boating-related accidents where folks are coming in on stretchers and there is too much blood and this doesn't even include the heart attack victims so I just sort of lie here and read one magazine after another and wait for the results of some kind of tests they took almost two hours ago.

When the paisley curtain finally slides over the metal bar and I see Dr. Kildare appear in a light blue gown and he says hello while looking down at my chart, I feel like I need to put my hand over my heart to keep it in place, but I manage a meek hello and he says, "So you're not pregnant and all your blood work is just great."

"You mean you didn't see any signs of cancer?"

He looks up at me and smiles. "Afraid not. Sorry to disappoint you."

"It's okay," I say.

"Nothing unusual at all shows up, but I'll be happy to send these results down to your own doctor. Let me ask you something," he says, looking down at the chart. "Ms. Payne, have you been under a lot of stress lately?"

"Who isn't?"

"I mean have you been under any extra or added stress?"

"The truth?"

"Yes."

"Well, if you count the fact that I was recently fired

from my job and that I've fallen in love with a Jamaican man who is young enough to be my son and he's supposed to be coming to visit me in three weeks even though I haven't heard from him in a week now and one of my sisters is giving me a real hard time about the whole notion and my other sister is all for it and the fact that I'm trying to figure out if I'm a fool and how I'm going to spend the rest of my life, I guess you could say I'm under a little extra stress, yeah."

"Do you drink coffee?"

"Yes, I do."

"Strong?"

"Very."

"How many cups?"

"Three."

"Make it one."

"A day?"

"Sometimes coffee can be really acidic. But you know what this sounds like to me?"

"An ulcer?"

He chuckles. "No. Anxiety. Plain old nerves. Try lowering your coffee intake, blowing out more air than you take in and getting plenty of exercise."

"I do get plenty of exercise."

"Have you ever tried yoga?"

"Yoga?" All I'm thinking is that gee whiz I'm not dying thank you Lord but when I hear yoga being offered as a prescription instead of say Vicodin, I know I'm in California.

"Yes, yoga," he says.

"Nope. Don't do yoga."

"Then maybe you'll just have to wait and see like the rest of us."

"That's it?"

"Aren't you glad this is it?"

"Yeah, I guess," I say and I am glad I'm not dying but this waiting is excruciating and feels unhealthy.

When I pull into the driveway Quincy and Phoenix are kicking it on the deck again. Quincy jumps up and runs over to the railing. "Are you okay, Mom?"

"I'm fine," I yell out the window.

"Winston called," he says.

"He did?"

"Yep."

"What did he say?"

"Hi."

"Where did you tell him I went?"

"To the hospital."

"Why'd you tell him that?"

"Because it's where you went?"

"Did you tell him why?"

"I told him you had a pain in your stomach."

"Is he going to call back?"

"He wants you to call him."

"Okay," I say.

When I get upstairs I dial his number and the first thing he says is, "Stella, are you all right?"

"I'm fine, Winston. I just had a few little pains in my stomach and it turned out to be indigestion and anxiety."

"Nervous about my coming there?"

"Of course I'm nervous about your coming here, *if* you're still coming."

"Oh, I'll be there, Stella. You sure you're all right, now?"

"I'm sure."

"Well, look, duty calls and I just wanted to touch base with you, make sure you haven't changed your mind about seeing me."

"You can't get here fast enough," I say.

"If I could, I would," he says.

"That's a Seal song," I say.

"I know, you sent it to me, remember, and it's the only CD you played when we met and I'm not crazy about him but I play it because it reminds me of you."

"Everything reminds *me* of *you*," I say and kiss the phone.

"I don't want any more reminders," he says.

"I feel the same way, Win-ston."

"I want you to know something, Stella."

"Know what, Winston?"

"When I come there, I really want to see how deeply we can take this."

I get a lump in my throat so hard I can hardly swallow.

"What do you mean, Winston?"

"I mean I have never really felt this way about anybody before and I feel so clear and light inside and I just want to see how far we can take this. I want to show you how good I can love you. You know what I'm saying?"

Whew. "I think I do, Winston."

"It's just that—how can I say this?—it's just that it feels like when we're together there is something going on between us that has to do with more than love, you know, it's sort of like we have a similar intuition about things and I just want you to know that I'm open to exploring wherever this takes us. Does that sound weird?"

"Not at all, Winston. Not at all. I think we can work on this," I say.

"I'm serious, Stella."

"I'm serious too, Winston."

"I'm not coming there to play house or play games or to hang out at the disco every night."

"I thought you wanted to go to the disco."

"It would be nice but I dance enough here at the resort, and don't you have to be twenty-one there to get into clubs?"

"Yes, but you're twenty-one, so don't worry about that."

"I'm not twenty-one."

"What?"

"I told you I'll be twenty-one on my next birthday."

"And when is that?"

"Next month."

"Lord Lord Lord," I say.

He begins to laugh. "Don't tell me. I'm too young for you."

"Shut up, Winston. It just means we'll be boogying to the beat in the family room."

"Doesn't bother me one bit. I'm coming there to be with you, not all of dancing America. So is everything looking okay?"

"I bought you a toothbrush."

"You did?"

"Yep. It's plaid. Do you like plaid?"

"Not really, but if you bought it for me, I will like it."

"And what side of the bed do you want?"

"Left," he says.

"I like the left."

"How about top?"

"That sounds good," I say. "I'll be trying to figure out the best way to make sure you're as comfortable as possible up there, how's that sound?"

"Sounds real good, Stella. Now I better go before I have no job to come back to."

We hang up in our usual way and I sit down on the rug and when the dog comes over and sits on my right foot I am really surprised to hear myself whine, "Winston, don't you think you would like to do a little chefing here in America?"

"**D**on't bring him over here," Angela is saying.

"Don't you worry your little heart out any," I say into the portable phone that I'm shouldering from one room to another, expecting at any moment now to hang up.

"Are you sure he's got a round-trip ticket?"

"The only thing I am sure of is this, Angela. You need to take a big chill pill because all the stress and grief you seem to be experiencing over my happiness is going right through your bloodstream and straight into your amniotic sac and if your babies come out hyperactive, suffer from attention deficit disorder and are both evil as all hell—like those kids you always see who throw temper tantrums in public—you will only have yourself to blame."

"So where's he going to sleep?"

"In the garage with Phoenix or maybe I'll clean out the guesthouse and lock him in there until I need him for sex."

"And how does Quincy feel about his coming?"

"Quincy is excited."

"He's probably just saying that."

"Well, I'll tell you what. We'll see, Angela. Won't we? Now if you don't mind, I've got a ton of errands to run."

"There you go spending up all your money and he hasn't even gotten here yet."

"But whose money is it?"

"That's not the point. And speaking of money, what is going on with your job situation?"

"How many times do I have to tell you?"

"You haven't really told me anything."

"I'm not going back to work. At least not in the corporate sense of the word."

"And what is it you propose to do to make a living?"

"I think I'll sell pussy! Bye, Angela. And do me and your babies a big favor: stop watching so much daytime television and talk shows in particular because the people who host them don't know what the hell they're talking about and you sound like a talk show prodigy and my suggestion to you is this: get a fucking life, Angela, and stop passing judgment on people who aren't afraid to improvise, who aren't living by a prescription that doesn't fit your Little Miss Muffet image, because if you don't you're going to end up the mother of your husband's children who spent their wonder years at home making curtains baking cookies and carpooling and then at fifty you'll be trying to remember what else you used to do before the kids before the husband and why didn't I ever use my fucking degree. You'll be trying to remember what dreams you had that you put on ice when you are forced to go back out into the real world and look for a job or a lost career because your husband will have gotten bored with your dull ass a long time ago and he'll have gone out and gotten himself a newer more improved woman who reminds him of the way you *used* to be before you put that 'sold' tag on him and you will be angry and bitter and distraught and clueless because you weren't paying attention and, Angela, you will cry your heart out when you pull your lemon bars out of the oven and wonder where the fucking yellow went."

And I hang up.

I am finished with her for real for a while but then the phone rings right away. "Look, Angela, I'm tired of defending—"

"It's not Angela, sweetheart," Leroy says. Boy, talk about a blast from the past. And it's broad daylight so at least he's not drunk yet. He's calling from his car phone as usual.

"How are you, Leroy?"

"I haven't been able to catch you all summer. Where've you been? How've you been? What you been up to?"

"You do know who you're talking to, right?"

"Stella. Why wouldn't I?"

"Forget it, Leroy. I've been doing a little traveling this summer."

"Oh yeah. Where've you been?"

"Jamaica."

"Where in Jamaica?"

"Negril."

"So is what they say true about the men down there?"

"Only the young ones," I say to his vulgar ass and that answer should shut him up.

"Okay," he says and clears his throat. "When can we get together, Stella? I've been thinking about you a lot."

"I can imagine you're having a hard time sleeping."

"Seriously. I miss you."

"I'm kind of busy these days, Leroy."

"Working hard?"

"Nope. Hardly working at all."

"What's that supposed to mean?"

"It means I got fired."

"Did you get yourself a lawyer?"

"Nope."

"You should get a good discrimination lawyer. I know several I could recommend."

"It's already handled."

"And so where are you going?"

"Nowhere."

"No, I mean which firm's after you? I know there're lots because as soon as word gets out they're on you like white on rice."

"I'm sort of going in a different direction."

"What direction would that be?"

"Well, I might go back to school."

"For what? Not another degree, I hope. What do you have, three already?"

"I might just take a few art classes."

"Wait. Don't tell me: stained glass or like pottery or something? Come on, Stella."

"No. But you know, Leroy, you may very well have just given me food for thought. Look, I've really gotta go."

"Please don't go yet."

"But I have nothing more to say."

"Well, if you need a reference or anything, you know I *know* everybody. I can help you."

"Thanks, Leroy, but only if you know someone who might want to buy some furniture."

"I might be interested, depending on what kind it is."

"Well, you won't see anything like it in like say a Thomasville Macy's or even Levitz, your favorite store and mine."

"So when can we get together, Stella? I miss you. I haven't felt your smooth warm skin in almost five whole months."

"Leroy, get a grip, all right? I've met somebody."

"Oh hell." He sighs. "I was wondering when it was going to happen."

"Well, it's happened."

"Oh well. Are you happy?"

"I will be."

"What's that mean?"

"Yes, Leroy. I'm happy."

"Well, I'm happy for you, Stella."

"Thank you, Leroy."

"Let me know when I can see some of the stuff you're selling, okay? My wife loves all that weird shit, so if I can support a friend, might as well support a friend. I'll talk to you soon. Be good and stay in touch."

I hang up again. Even though on the surface he's a true Doberman, underneath he's still got a little calico left in him. If his wife cracked her whip every now and then, he'd be fine.

"So what's it gonna be, leg curls or lunges?" Krystal asks. We are in my exercise room. I am looking out the window.

"I don't really care," I say.

"Lunges it is then. Let's get your five pounders," she says and I reach down to pick up the purple weights. Krystal is a lifesaver. Thanks to her I didn't gain any weight after I quit smoking, which I was afraid of but which was not the main reason I started working out with her. I am lazy by nature and Krystal is and has been my motivator. We talk about everything and of course she knows all about Winston. She thinks the whole idea is pretty "neat," as she puts it, but has some reservations which she does a pretty good job of masking because she believes that you should try something before giving up on it but at the same time not lose sight of your goals in life which may in fact be a contradiction to what you're doing. Krystal is thirty-four and has been married to a really nice guy for the past five years. She is happy and still loves her husband and from what I've seen he still looks pretty smitten with her too. Unlike some personal trainers, Krystal actually has a master's degree in physiology and has already qualified for the hundred-meter race in the Olympics next year.

We do two sets of fifteen. I am sweating. She isn't.

"So are you getting excited?" she asks.

"Of course I'm excited."

"Has Angela cooled her heels any?"

"Nope. I had to go off on her."

"Well, I wouldn't be too hard on her if I were you. After all, Stella, this isn't something a person sees every day. She's your sister and she loves you and I think she's just concerned."

"I know," I say, pulling out my blue mat and pulling on the ankle weights. I get on my knees and with palms down push my bent left knee up and down until I feel it pulling in my butt which is the whole point. "I mean I don't really need her blessing, Krystal. I'm an adult, and I wish she'd give me more credit for having some idea of what I'm doing."

"I understand perfectly," she says. "Are you counting?"

"Fifteen," I lie.

"Let's take it to half range. Fifteen more. Anyway the reality is you like this guy and I think the fact that you sent him a ticket is fantastic and that he's coming is awesome and it's like an adventure and both of you guys know or have an idea that it won't likely lead to marriage and it's not like it's going to last forever, so I don't see anything wrong with it. Right leg," she says.

"I know," I say. But what about the whole notion of forever? When you get right down to it, how long is it? I mean why can't we just fall in love and simply love each other as hard as we can and see what happens, see how far we can go with it, what levels we can reach in terms of understanding being passionate compassionate honest hopeful. I mean how can we grow if we think we've already arrived at the end? I mean isn't life supposed to be this evolving thing, kinetic? I mean isn't this one of the reasons why we get bored, because once we reach the penthouse we feel like we've made it to the top floor but then there's a roof garden and if we keep going there are like clouds and then an entire whatever?

This is precisely what happened to me when I got married, and I don't want to go there again. I don't. I won't. Can't. I do not want to repeat that. Besides, I'm not a boring person, that much I do know. Rarely am I bored with myself and I don't like the idea of being a bore and I have no intention of boring Winston. I just hope he *gets* it. I hope he knows and I believe he knows that what we are doing is searching for the curve the arc the warmth the depth of field to live our lives in three-D and feel it deeper than that. That we want to jump that we are hunting for ourselves that we want to spread ourselves thin and split the layers because somewhere in all this somewhere under this shroud of hardness and pain and everything that hurts is something soft and supple something hushed and we know how to get to it, we know how to inch our way in because we have already started.

"Ready for crunches?" I hear Krystal ask.

"Can't wait," I say, and we both laugh.

By the time we finish with the upper body, Krystal says, "Well, one thing is for sure. He's not gonna find too many forty-two-year-olds in as good a shape as you."

"I'm sure he's been keeping track," I say, as we do a few cool-down stretches.

"The bottom line?" she says.

"What?"

"If it feels good, I say go for it. Follow your own heart and your own head and forget about what anybody says. This is your life, Stella, and no one can experience it better than you. Now are we on for Wednesday?"

"Can't wait," I repeat.

Quincy is walking down the stairs looking shiny and brand-new. In fact he is wearing his new brown plaid shorts that come to his knees, a hidden-in-the-drawer dark brown golf T-shirt, brown-and-gray airwalks, and he smells like he must've poured the entire free sample of Tommy Hilfiger cologne all over himself. His hair is about a half inch long now, very thick and black and kinky, because ever since we were in San Diego and he saw Tiger's dreadlocks sprouting, Quincy decided that the least he could do was grow himself an Afro. I'm all for it. It doesn't seem that long ago that I was wearing an Afro. Some things do repeat themselves. "Don't you look spiffy," I say.

"Thanks, Mom," he says and drops his backpack on the floor.

"And you're matching!"

"Mom, I've been matching for four whole months now."

"That's not true, Quincy, and you know it. Just last week you had on at least three different designs, prints stripes plaids, and a number of participating colors were going at it all at once on your frail little body, so I beg to differ with you, homie, because I'm afraid this *is* the way it was."

"Well, I know how to match now," he says.

"You're on your way, and you smell very good too."

"Thanks, Mom."

"But Quin, all you need is a smidgen behind the ears and maybe a tad on the neck and a dab on each wrist and that's it."

"Well, when I was taking that little plastic thing off it splattered all over me so that's what you're smelling—the splatter. That's not the part I actually put on my neck and arms. Smell," he says and holds out his arm.

I take a whiff. Maybe one day he'll be able to put it all together.

I go into the kitchen and take the biscuits out of the oven and set two on the table next to a plate of hot grits, a few slices of casaba melon and a glass of apple juice and I sit down to watch my son eat. We always eat breakfast together, at least when school's in.

"So are you excited?"

"Of course I'm excited, Mom. Wouldn't you be excited if it was your first day of junior high and you were going to a brand-new school? Think about it."

"Don't get cute, okay?"

"Sorry. I was just kidding."

"Well, put a cap on it."

"So are *you* excited?" he asks.

"About what?"

"Winston'll be here pretty soon, won't he?"

"Yep. And yes, I am getting excited."

"Do you love him?"

"What?"

"Do you love him?"

"What would make you ask that?"

"Well, you like him a whole lot. He's coming here to visit us and he's going to sleep with you and you guys will have sex again, probably a lot, and I was just wondering, that's all."

"I love a lot of things about him, yes."

"Would you marry him if he asked you?"

"I don't think so."

"Why not?"

"I don't want to. . . . . I haven't thought about marrying

anybody, Quincy, and besides, he's only coming for a visit."

"Yeah, but what if he really likes you and you really like him and you don't want him to go back to Jamaica?"

"I haven't thought about it."

"You should, Mom. You really should."

"And what would you do if he wanted to stay?"

"Be his buddy. Mom, what does loving somebody feel like?"

"Boy, I can tell you haven't had your coffee yet. Let me think for a minute here. Well, it sort of feels like there's a very warm bright light burning inside you and it's running throughout your entire body and makes you tingle."

"That's it? I feel like that when I Rollerblade."

"Well, that's just one of the ways it feels."

"Can you give me some better examples, please?"

"You know how you feel when you snowboard?"

"Yep."

"That rush you get?"

"Yeah," he sings. "Same as Rollerblading."

"The truth is, it's awfully hard to explain. It's just that you feel really good being around someone."

"Like who, for instance?"

"Well, maybe that wasn't a good one either."

"Try me."

"Well, try this: You haven't eaten all day and you've been craving praying for some McNuggets, a filet of fish with extra tarter sauce and super-size fries with a large Sprite. You know the feeling that comes over you after you take that first bite?"

"Do I ever!"

"That's how Winston makes me feel."

"Wow. That's pretty deep, Mom. What a good metaphor. You should maybe try being a writer."

"Thanks for the career advice," I say. "Anyway I just want you to know that the kind of love a woman and man feel for each other is different than the kind a parent feels for a child."

"How is it different?"

"Well, let me put it this way. I feel very protective of you. Everything that happens to you matters to me."

"Don't you feel like that about Winston?"

"Well, yes. But let me finish. When grown-ups really love each other they kiss and hug and touch each other and they *make* love which is a better more accurate way of saying they have sex but they also share all kinds of things like their feelings fears hopes and dreams even their frustrations and they sort of feel comfortable with each other and relaxed enough to know that they've got each other's back."

"I've got your back," he says, winking at me.

"I know, Quin. But you know the difference I'm trying to show."

"Of course I do, Mom. You get romantic with Winston and you get cuddly-wuddly with me but we both make you feel good. How's that?"

"That's good. That's very good. And I don't want you to ever worry that I won't have enough love left for you no matter how much I give to Winston or whomever."

"Do I look worried?"

"How silly of me to ask. Now hurry up and finish your breakfast before you miss your bus."

"Thanks for sharing, Mom, and I love you too."

* * *

I am getting out of the shower, looking at myself in the mirror. As I rub my body with Calyx lotion I seem to see gray hair everywhere and I'm wondering if he's going to be able to really handle this, if he's really going to be able to look at me and think I'm beautiful and not simply beautiful for my age. Because the bottom line is that I am indeed forty-two years old and I wish there were a way I could stay forty-two for the next twenty-two years so that Winston could catch up to me and then we could be the same age at the same time. But this is not true. I am proud to be forty-two and I'm looking forward to being fifty-two and sixty-two and so on and so forth and I don't even know if I'd be feeling the same toward Winston if he were my age. I think if I'm going to be honest with myself then I have to admit that part of what is appealing is the fact that he's not someone I should want or have, but the odds are working in my favor so far, aren't they, Stella?

It takes me forever to get dressed. I don't know for sure what to wear. What do you wear to the airport to pick up someone you love? I mean really. I stand in my closet for the next twenty minutes trying on skirts slacks suits shorts and T-shirts and put them all back on their respective hangers and decide on jeans and a lavender cotton and Spandex top that fits snug but I choose a mint green linen blazer I bought from a men's store to wear over it. Simple silver hoop earrings. No makeup except a little lipstick and eye pencil to highlight the corner of my eyes. I stand at the mirror to see if I look okay and I look okay, pleasant, like I might actually be a nice person, but I'm not so sure if I'd want to like run into my arms and kiss me. Maybe I should put on some more makeup, but no, I don't want to look too embellished. Besides, I am a woman, not an ornament.

I'm just about to take a step in the direction of Quincy's room but I remember that he's spending the night with Vanessa and Chantel, at Vanessa's insistence of course. "Girl, you don't need your son pressing his ears against your bedroom door or coming down with some ailment so he could get your attention. Anyway you need to enjoy the first night of this honeymoon alone. So I'll be over at six to pick the boy up." I am grateful to her and I'm also scared; Quincy is a great buffer, a great silence breaker, a great whatever.

I have done everything I could to spruce up this place. I went to Home Depot and bought two new large plants. I have bought new colorful thick thirsty towels and I have stacked them neatly right next to his plaid toothbrush. I have moved some of my clothes over in my closet to make room for his. Same goes for the shoes. My exercise drawer. Cleaned out. Empty. And in the medicine cabinet I have given him the whole bottom shelf for his toiletries. I am now hyperventilating, but it's okay. I know I'm just excited and scared and anxious and in a way I wish I could actually catch a plane to the airport and swoop him up from the runway and jet on home so that I could avoid that hour's drive over the freeway and over that long bridge and then parking the car and walking all the way to the gate where my heart will pound pound pound until he walks through.

*   *   *

I am surprised at how calm I am standing at Gate 83, waiting. The ride was totally smooth and I only did eighty. I feel like I floated here. In fact I feel pretty much the same way I did when I went snorkeling. I don't understand why I'm not bouncing off the walls. Why I'm not a nervous wreck. Why I don't hear any buzzing or hissing in my ears. I mean this man is about to walk off an airplane and into my life and even though it may only be for three weeks my whole life could very easily change in the next few minutes hours but as I stand here I realize that my life has *already* changed and regardless of how long he stays, no matter what does or doesn't happen, I have already discovered that there *is* another side you can go to, which is pure and good, that it is always there waiting for you to notice, that it is free but costly to find yet once you arrive, once you get there, you find you can bounce again skip again gallop again that you can recover from loss and pain and heartache that you can be repaired renewed restored without even comprehending what or how it has happened and you can simply blink and accept the fact that you are absolutely and unequivocally a new and improved version of your old self and no matter what happens from here on out you will not misplace yourself again you will not get so lost you can't get yourself back you will not let the dust pile up collect settle all over your heart, no siree, not ever again.

I blot my lips, glad that I wore a matte lipstick instead of the shiny kind. I'm still not sure what I'm going to say to him though I've rehearsed this greeting in my sleep a thousand times and there are only so many different ways to say Hi Winston or Hello Winston or You finally made it, Winston! or I'm so glad to see you, Winston! or Welcome Winston or How was your trip?

I wonder will he kiss me out here in the open but I know for a fact that I won't kiss him because it would be rather tacky and I don't really want to embarrass him so maybe if I like stand on my toes and give him a friendly peck people will think he is my son and we can do our real kissing once we get in the car. I sure hope he looks like he did in Jamaica but right now I have no image of him whatsoever in my head, it has just sort of gone blank and is now full of this gray space and I don't understand this so I turn away to look out the window and I hear his voice say, "Hello there, Stella," and when I turn around he is standing there so tall and beautiful and as he walks over toward me I smell his Escape and I feel my shoulders drop and when he puts his arms around me I feel so relieved so grateful that he is live and not Memorex anymore and I put my arms around him and clutch him tight because I want him to know how happy I am to feel him see him smell him and then he looks down and says, "I made it," and he presses those Easy-Bake oven lips against mine and I absorb them as long as I can stand it and then I back away and say, "Welcome to America, Winston," and he exhales and puts his arm over my shoulder and as we walk through the airport people are looking at us and we wave to them and once we get to baggage claim we are so busy laughing smooching hugging holding hands looking at each other, making sure we are really here, that it is not until we are the only two people standing here that we realize we are at the wrong carousel, but we don't care. We do not move except to hold on tighter. And all I know for sure is that he is here. That I am here. That I am happy. And we are going home.

"You want to drive?" I ask.

"Don't start on me already, Stella, all right?"

He is blushing. I am grinning. "I'm just teasing," I say, and of course he knows this. He puts both suitcases into the trunk. "Nice car," he says. "And black is my favorite color. What kind of BMW is this?"

"An M-5."

"Isn't this a race car?"

"Yep."

He is shaking his head back and forth as he gets in. His legs are longer than I remember but then again I've never been in a car with him before and I sit and watch him search for the button that slides the seat back. "Sooo," he says. "You didn't tell me you were also a drag racer."

"You mean I left that little detail out?"

"I don't recall your mentioning it, no."

"Well, I like to go fast," I say.

"This I know already."

"You got a problem with that?"

"Not at all."

I put the car in reverse.

"So is this sarcasm what I have to look forward to over the next three weeks?" I ask.

"Afraid so," he says. "You got a problem with *that*?"

"Not at all," I say, trying to wipe the smirk off my face. "Not even a teensy bit."

Winston is full of excitement as we zoom along the freeway and I tell him where we are what he's looking at and how much longer it'll be. I point out Candlestick Park, the Pacific Ocean, the fog, downtown San Francisco (particularly the pyramid building). I tell him how long the Bay Bridge is and why we have to pay a toll, and then we go on past Oakland. I tell him that I'm his happy tour guide and I'll answer any questions he may have but all he says is, "I'm just taking it all in," and "Pay no attention to me," and I say, "Ha!" and he says, "Ha!" and leans back in his seat until I turn off the freeway. When I finally get to my neighborhood I point out the grocery store. "That's where you'll be spending most of your free time, doing all the shopping for the next three weeks, and seeing as how you're going to be cooking breakfast, lunch and dinner, you'll need to remember how to get here, so pay very close attention."

It looks like he's actually making a mental note.

"And that's the gas station and McDonald's and the movies are right down there and across the street is a car wash which you won't be needing because I have some very nice rags for you to use and there's the cleaners and video store though you won't have much time on your hands to watch any home movies unless we're starring in them of course and that's the pizza place and then there's the hardware store that you will also undoubtedly be frequenting. Possibly we'll let you off on Fridays for good behavior."

Steadily shaking his head back and forth, he is still beaming.

I turn onto my street and he says, "You can't be serious, Stella."

"About what?"

"You can't live in a neighborhood like this."

"It's just a bunch of houses."

"But look at them. They're mansions."

"You want mansions? I can *show* you mansions. These are hardly close. Anyway not to worry—if I don't figure out what I'm going to do with the rest of my life in like the next twelve months, mine'll be up for sale and Quincy and I will be moving to the projects."

"What are the projects?"

"You never heard of the projects?"

"No."

"It's where you live when your money is tight or you don't have any and it's not the most comfortable or luxurious place to dwell and you don't necessarily want to raise children there if you can help it and they're usually right in the middle of the hood."

"I take it *this* isn't the hood?"

"Afraid not, but I can certainly take you there."

"I think I like it here," he says. "I believe I know what the hood is like. It's the ghetto. And we've got lots of them in Kingston."

I pull up to my house, which is sort of a contemporary white Mediterranean with a dark teal clay tile roof, and Winston is shaking his head again. My white Land Cruiser is parked in the driveway. "Is that *yours*?"

"Every woman needs her own truck," I say. "Now come on, darling. Let me show you to your suite."

Once inside, it's apparent that he's a tad overwhelmed by everything, I guess, and I'm trying to keep in mind that Winston is from Jamaica and even though he comes from a nice home and all maybe he's not used to seeing one like this even though the house itself really isn't that big a deal if you ask me. We are standing in the kitchen but he is looking into the family room at a table that is bleached bird's-eye maple and copper and stainless steel and it curves and slants and dips and I admit it is shaped rather oddly.

"Wow," he says. "Where'd you find a table like this?"

"I designed that about ten years ago."

"You mean you thought this up," he says, not really asking me.

"Yep. And had someone build it."

"And you're serious?"

"Of course I'm serious."

"But Stella, you said you made a few pieces of furniture here and there, that's all you said."

"And it's the truth."

"Yeah, but Stella, this isn't just furniture, not in the furniture sense of the word. It's like sculpture, art or something, don't you think?"

"Well, I see furniture as functional sculpture if it does what it's supposed to which is perform but if it can also add something beautiful or funky to a room, why not?

Most furniture is boring when it should be more like music, you know. Anyway that's how I used to feel when I did this."

He walks over to a little bench that is made of strips of suede burlap linen and leather. "It looks like it's alive," he says, and we both laugh.

"That's one of the pieces I actually made, but a lot of it I just designed and had built. You'll see."

"Stella. You never let on that you had *this* kind of talent. Why've you been so modest? Why didn't you tell me more about this?"

"What's to tell?"

He moans and gives me a look but it is obvious that this isn't the last we'll talk about it and I am pleased that he likes what I have done and I am pleased that I am finally paying attention to what pleases *me*, what has made me take a step back long enough to look carefully at things. I have chosen metal and wood and paint and fabric as my medium because I am interested in the texture of things, in creating harmony where there was none before, in making the impossible possible, reversing the irrevocable. It is in surrendering to this process that I can give in give it up and be who I am what I am where I am and when I blink hard and open my eyes, take it all in and *see* what I dreamed, *feel* what I dreamed and I have some evidence.

Winston has been walking around inside my dream and has just stepped out of it. "This house. It's rather amazing," he says, looking down. "What's this floor made of?"

"Concrete."

"Concrete. Inside a house. And it doesn't even look like a sidewalk."

I give him a tour and explain whatever needs to be explained and when I show him my bedroom he kind of freaks a little because it is one of the coolest rooms in the house (I wonder why). "We're sleeping in here?"

"Well, you could have the guest room down the hall with the daybed or you can sleep out there in the love shack next to the garage. See it? Wherever you'll feel more comfortable, sweetheart."

"I'll stay here. With you. What's the love shack?"

"It used to be a guesthouse."

"And what is it now?"

"Nothing."

"What do you mean by 'nothing'?"

"It's a mess. I keep junk in there."

"Do you mind?" he asks, and heads outside. I follow him. We stick our heads inside the little stucco building and it's not really in such bad shape, it's just got a wheelbarrow and hoes and gardening tools and tents and Christmas ornaments and more junk on top of more junk and it's dusty. My drafting table sits among the tallest of items and of course Winston notices it.

"So looks like I'll need to get some special cleanser from the hardware store in the morning to get this place fixed up and since you'll be using this," he says, pointing to the drafting table, "I should start with this, don't you think?"

I'm pretty close to crying and I don't remember the last time anybody made me feel this good inside, I don't remember the last time somebody "came through" for me. I'm just hoping I can give him half as much as he's already given me. "I guess it wouldn't kill me to put some rubber gloves on, but then I'll need to go to San Francisco to pick up some supplies at my favorite art store and do you think you'd like to go with me?"

"I'll drive," he says, and we walk slowly toward the house and when we get inside the door we both stop and sort of just stand there and look at each other and then we both get this dorky look on our faces like What do we do now? I really do want to make love to him but I don't want to act too eager like I can't help myself plus he should be tired but then again he's young so maybe he isn't. Relax, Stella. He's here for three whole weeks.

"I should get my bags," he says.

"Want me to help you?"

"No. They're heavy. Would you have any tea?"

"Tea?"

"Yes, you know, tea?"

"Sure, I've got all kinds of tea. What kind do you want?"

"I don't care, Stella. Any kind."

"Well, if you're going to be this easy to please, you can stay awhile."

"Don't tempt me," he says and makes his way out toward the garage while I boil water. When he comes back I let the tea brew and follow him back into my room, where I stand in front of the dresser.

"You can have these two drawers," I say.

"You actually cleared these out for me, didn't you?"

"Yes," I say, sitting on the edge of the bed. It is a simple platform bed and very low to the floor, so I am kind of leaning back on it. The sun is setting and is casting a sort of yellowish hue over the salmon walls, which is actually very pretty, and the room is beginning to turn the color of a ripe cantaloupe.

"This floor *is* purple, isn't it?"

"It is."

"And so is the one in the room next to it, right?"

"Yes, they are. This wood's from Africa and it's called purple heart and the stuff on my office floor is just plain old leather."

"A leather floor?"

"Yep. It's been done before. Believe me."

When I see him hold up a suit, I walk him to the closet and point to an empty area. "You can hang all your stuff there."

"All I brought was one suit. Will I need more?"

I smile. He is so sweet. "No, I don't think you'll need more than this one. How many suits do you have, Winston?"

"You're looking at it," he says and cracks up. "I don't go to very many formal affairs, you know."

"Not to worry, bud."

We stop in the bathroom. The ceiling is yellow plaster and curves like the top of a tunnel. "Boy, do you have unusual taste," he says. "I've never seen any of this stuff before. Ever. Aren't those sinks glass?"

"Yep."

"And are those seashells in the countertop or am I just imagining it?"

"No. They're there."

"This is some house you have here. I'm serious."

"Well, I'm glad you like my home, Winston, and while you're here, please live in it like it's yours, because it is."

"Thank you, Stella," he says and pecks me on the nose. "I'm just a little overwhelmed by it all, you know."

"That makes two of us."

"So can we like just stop moving for a minute or two?"

"We certainly can," I say, pointing to the door. "In or out?"

"Right here is fine," he says, and we lie on our backs on the bed and watch the ceiling fan spin and Winston's feet are touching the floor and mine hang over the edge and I feel my fingers walk over the puffy comforter squares and I take his hand in mine and hold it. We lie like this for a long time and it is so nice to share the silence with a man to meet one who appreciates the calm and then it seems like just as I am thinking how nice it would be to roll over into his arms Winston pulls me over on top of him and puts his arms around me and kisses me and I kiss him back and he says, "I'm so glad to see you."

And I say, "I'm glad to see you too."

"I can't believe I'm here," he says.

"But you *are* here," I say.

"Yes, I am," he says. "Sooo," he says. "Are you ready?"

"Ready for what?"

"An evening swim."

"You feel like swimming right now?" I ask.

"You got a problem with that?"

"Nope," I say and sit up.

"But let's swim in here first, if that's okay with you."

"No problem, mon," I say, and slowly prepare myself for a swan dive.

"**Y**ou sure your sister's going to accept me?"

"Winston, you can relax."

"I *am* relaxed. I'm just wondering, you know."

He is driving the truck and he is driving like he's been here all his life. I am impressed. We pull up in front of Vanessa's house, and Quincy and Chantel are in the driveway, chasing her two cats. "Mom! Winston! You're here!" Quincy yells, and runs to give me a big hug and then he actually hugs Winston, who hugs him back. Chantel imitates Quincy's moves.

"Where's your mom?"

"Right here," Vanessa says, coming out of the house with a bandanna tied around her head, looking even more like Pepa, and she is wearing tight blue jeans and supporting them rather nicely from every angle and the yellow print blouse is tied up front into a knot.

"Oh, hi, Cindy!" I greet her.

"Cindy?" She looks confused.

"Crawford, isn't it?"

"You know where you can go, Stella. Don't be so rude. Oh forget *you*. Now let me guess, you must be. . ."

He is blushing. "Winston."

"And you're from?"

"Jamaica," he says.

"You've gotta be kidding!"

He is still blushing.

"How you doing, Winston? I'm Vanessa. Stella's beautiful brilliant sister. Want to come in?"

"Not right now, babe," I say. "We're on our way to San Francisco."

"Well, Quincy can stay here."

"We want him to come with us," Winston says. "And Chantel as well, if it's all right."

Vanessa is giving me the eye of approval behind his back and then she does a thumbs-up and now she's making her lips pantomime, "You go, girl!" and I simply smirk. "Take her, keep her," Vanessa says. "I've got about six loads of clothes in here and I'm barbecuing some steaks later. Do you like barbecue steaks, Winston?"

"Sure I do."

"Then would you guys like to come back later for dinner?"

"Sounds good," I say. "We'll see you around fiveish."

First we go to the art store, where I don't even want to think about how much money I spend on supplies: times change, prices go up, is one thing I know for sure. But it's all good is what I'm thinking after we fill up the back of the truck, and I smile for a long time because it feels like Christmas and I can't wait to open these gifts.

We spend all day on Pier 39 and take the ferry to

Sausalito and skip Alcatraz and then we drive up and down San Francisco streets and after a couple of hours of this Winston says, "Stella, I don't have to see the entire city today. Aren't you tired?"

"Not really. I thought you wanted to see San Francisco."

"I do, but not all in one day. I can always come back," he says.

"I know. I just wanted to show you as much as I can while you're here."

"I want to see as much of *you* as I can while I'm here," he says, and Ms. Nosy is all ears and eyes, but Quincy is staring out the window counting Volkswagen Bugs and yelling "Punchbuggy!" each time he sees one so he hasn't heard a word we've said.

"I want you to see what's available," I say to Winston.

"I've already seen what's available. Why do you think I'm here?"

"You certainly are fresh in America, Winston Shakespeare."

"What?" he sings.

"Mom, can we stop at McDonald's?"

"No. Your aunt Vanessa is barbecuing, remember?"

"Oh yeah. But McDonald's would be much better— right, Chantel?"

"If I could get a filet of fish with extra tartar sauce, sure, but I like my Mom's barbecue. She makes the best sauce."

"Look. We are not going to McDonald's and that's the end of it."

"You tell them, Mom," Winston teases.

As we go over the Bay Bridge, Winston is looking around again. "It really is pretty here," he says. "I like the feeling I get from this place."

"And what feeling is that?"

"Peaceful," he says. "It feels really peaceful here."

Angela's station wagon is parked in Vanessa's driveway. I am almost ready to throw up, but she came and we're here and she asked for it but I make myself a promise not to act ugly in front of Winston because I would surely scare the man off and he hasn't even been here twenty-four hours yet. Then I kind of panic. What if she gives him the cold shoulder? Or what if she embarrasses me? Interrogates him, makes him feel uncomfortable? We'll just leave. That's exactly what we'll do if she gets out of line.

When we get in the house Angela is the first person I see because Vanessa is outside on the patio taking the steaks off the grill. Angela does not like to smell smoke.

"Hello," she says ever so nicely.

"Angela, this is my friend Winston. Winston, my sister Angela."

"Hello," he says, and walks over to shake her hand but of course I'd like to yell, "Don't touch her! She's got evil mean cooties and they might rub off!" "It's so nice to meet you," he says and gives her a warm smile.

Angela smiles back, which makes me very suspicious, but she's wearing her favorite navy blue Laura Ashley–type dress with the white Peter Pan collar which makes her look sweet and innocent but of course this is the reason why women wear these dresses in the first place and let's face it, you turn your back and close the door tight enough and you would be surprised to learn that many of them are the biggest sluts in town, but today Angela does look pretty even though I hate to admit it. "I've heard a lot about you, Winston, and I've really been looking forward to meeting you. Glad you finally made it here safely." She almost sounds sincere even though Vanessa is standing at the window making a Howdy Doody face.

He points to her big belly. "So I understand you've got two of them in there, hey?"

"That's right," she says. "Both boys."

"You know that already?"

"Yep."

"And when are they scheduled to arrive?"

"That's cute," she says, as if she is really capable of being touched, and looking at her she is rather convincing right this second. "Around the tenth of December."

"That's soon," Winston says.

"Barbecue's up!" Vanessa yells in the doorway, holding a platter of glistening rib eyes. We walk into the kitchen in single file and reach for paper plates, which Vanessa has stacked inside those straw holders.

Winston piles up his plate with a steak, baked beans, sour dough bread and a salad. "Would you have any Thousand Island dressing, Vanessa?" he asks.

"Who eats that mess?" Vanessa asks, frowning.

"I like it too," Angela says.

"Well, sorrreee. Ranch is as close as I can get. Come on, Winston, try something new. Get used to it, bud!"

Winston blushes and Angela walks over to him. "She's a little crude, so don't pay too much attention to her. She's known for having bad hair days."

He laughs. Pours some ranch dressing over his salad

and offers to do the same for Angela. She nods a thanks. "Can I get you something to drink?" he asks her.

"Thanks, Winston. I'll just have some of that lemonade," she says and walks out on the patio. Winston pours her a glass as Quincy and Chantel run downstairs, to eat in front of the television, I suppose.

Vanessa comes over to me with her plate of burgundy meat. "He's nice," she says as we watch Winston and Angela, seated side by side at the picnic table. "And fine as hell, I might add." We see Winston laughing about something. "Don't worry, girl. I don't think she's going to do anything stupid."

"I hope not," I say. "But I'm going out there just to make sure."

"Knock yourselves out," Vanessa says. "I can't take that hot-ass sun. I'm staying right here in my kitchen thank-youverymuch."

I go on out and sit down to face them and the sun is indeed blazing against my back. "Hi," I say for lack of anything better.

"Stella. Angela tells me she has a son in college."

I peer over at her. She has an affable look on her face.

"Winston was telling me he was a pretty good swimmer and volleyball player in high school and I was telling him that in America you don't see very many black swimmers or volleyball players and that Evan's one of the few black hockey players. Right, Winston?" she says as if she's trying to convince me that she has no ulterior motives. "As a matter of fact, he'll be here next week. How long will you be here?" she asks him.

"Three weeks," he says, looking at me as if to verify this.

"Three weeks is the plan," I say.

"Well, Stella, would you bring Winston over to meet Evan, have dinner and meet Kennedy?" she asks, giving me the warmest grin. I do not understand this.

"Sure," I say.

"So, Winston. What part of Jamaica are you from?"

And he tells her and then she asks him a number of questions about his family, his job, and he tells her about his aspirations for maybe becoming a chef, and it looks and sounds as if she's trying to or has actually bonded with him and if I'm not mistaken she also appears to be impressed for some reason I can't quite discern.

Finally, we all come inside and Angela says she has to get home. "Winston," she offers, "you know they have some very good culinary schools in San Francisco. Would you ever consider coming here to get your education?"

I am shocked to hear this, and Winston is sort of taken aback, and Vanessa, who is clearing the table, actually misses her palm and wipes crumbs right onto the floor.

"I don't know," he says. "I haven't given it much thought."

"You should," she says, and says goodbye to him and yells down to the kids. I walk her to the door and she asks me to help her carry a bag of something or other to the car and I do and once outside she says, "Look, Stella. I know I've been a little hard and everything and I don't mean to be. I just have had a difficult time accepting the whole idea of this and I just want what's best for you. I want to see you happy. See you get the love you deserve."

"I know, Angela."

"He's sweet. Nice. Very poised and gracious. And quite handsome. Doesn't carry himself like he's as young as he is."

"I know," I say.

"Meeting him makes him more real and not this apparition. I just thought of how immature Evan is and I assumed Winston would be the same, but talking to him . . . I guess when you're not from here . . . I don't know. Anyway he just seems to be more mature and worldly, to be honest."

"I'm glad you can see that," I say.

She lets out a sigh. "And you look good, Stella. You've got a glow I haven't seen in a long long time."

"You can see it too?"

She nods. "Who else has seen it?"

I blush. "Everybody."

"You know I'm the skeptic in this family," she laments, and I nod, and she says, "I just don't want you to be careless. Just try to take this slowly, that's all." She tosses a bag into the backseat of the station wagon. Then she turns and gives me a hug and her stomach is warm against mine. "But after all is said and done, you do what makes Stella happy."

"Thanks, Angela."

And as she gets into the car she rolls her window down. "I think Evan will like him too. See you later, Sis."

"Bye, Angela," I say and watch her drive off.

During the first week we act like honeymooners. We brush our teeth together we shower together we make love two and three times a day (well, actually we only pulled that marathon off once) and then there are those three evenings when we just snuggle up all night long in front of the fireplace which we believe has some real emotional value and we decide that we will do this more over the next two weeks. I have been nice and let him sleep on the left side and on top of course and it is working out.

He has taken Quincy to school instead of dropping him at the bus stop and insists on picking him up and I suppose they've been bonding in the car. Winston's been helping him with his math problems and listening to some of Quincy's existential essays; all of this happens right before dinner, which he has been cooking for us— Jamaican style—and we've been enjoying spicy meals and dishes and I have particularly loved watching him move around my kitchen touching pots and pans that I have touched and when we stand next to each other at the kitchen sink and put our hands in the same sudsy dishwater and our fingers find each other under that water and squeeze I realize just how much I like his being here.

At first I was really worried about what it would be like having another person invade my space, because no one has been in my space in a long time. But I like walking past him in the house, I like waking up and seeing him feeling him smelling him, I like taking baths and showers with him and drinking the weak coffee he makes for me. I like doing laps in the pool next to him and watching him clean and hose down the garage and turn the love shack back into my work space and fix Quincy's go-cart and put a new head on the sprinkler valve and stack an entire cord of firewood that was left all over the driveway. I like soaking in the Jacuzzi with him and he has actually asked me out on "dates," like tonight we are having a midnight picnic by the pool.

I think he is growing on me.

During week two we drive up to Lake Tahoe. He has never been in cold mountains before. It is fall up here and it is nippy, very nippy. We are sitting in the hot tub on the deck. It is ten o'clock at night.

"Have you ever read the Bible, Winston?"

"Not the whole thing. Have you?"

"Bits and pieces. It's too long, the language is so archaic, there's so many folks to keep track of and I think it's overwritten, to be honest. But I really appreciate the story. Do you believe in God?"

"Yes, lots of them."

"How many?"

"I don't know. You call on the kind you need."

"For instance?"

"Well, I called on the Love God when I was hoping that you would fall in love with me."

"And?"

"He came through, didn't he?"

"He did."

"And I called on the Courage God to give me enough courage to leave everything I care about behind to come here to be with you."

"Really? Any others?"

"Well, now that I'm here I'm soliciting a few of them, yes."

"I'm listening."

"Well, I'm asking the Perpetual God to help me maintain what we've started and I'm asking the Love God again to just visit us on a regular basis and I'm asking the Patience God and the Understanding God and the Perfection God and the Direction God to show me how to be more patient and understanding and not strive for perfection and to guide me in the right direction."

"You amaze me," I say.

"Then that means the Amazement God has come through as well."

He smiles at me and reaches out his hand. I take it in mine. It feels warm. It is a man's hand. It is big. He is rubbing my fingers and they are tingling so much that I move against him and look into his face and just smile. "I think we're both crazy," I say.

"Those would be the Crazy Gods that apparently we've both called upon, hey?"

"Afraid not. I didn't ask for them or this."

"But you got it, didn't you. You got me, didn't you. So now what do you want to do about it?"

"I wish you could stay."

"I wish I could too," he says.

"How long would you stay if you could?"

"As long as possible," he says. "As long as possible."

Winston has a cold one morning so I drive Quincy to school.

"So how is everything going?" I ask.

"Fine."

"You haven't been showing me your homework like I've asked."

"I will, Mom. And guess what?"

"What?"

"You remember when I told you I was signing up for computer animation for my flex class?"

"Yes."

"Well, remember when I told you there were too many kids who signed up and they put our names in a hat and I wasn't one who got picked?"

"Yes."

"Well, guess what?"

"What?"

"Yesterday the instructor told me that one of the kids dropped the class and guess who got picked?"

"Who?"

"Me!"

"But how?"

"Well, they put all the names in the hat again but this time they used *my* hat."

"You sly little rabbit," I say.

"Winston's got a bad cold, huh?"

"I think so."

"You should make him some hot tea, Mom. And take his temperature and make him put on his jammies and stay under the covers, just like you do me when I'm sick."

"I think I will," I say. "Quincy, are you enjoying him? You know, his being here."

"Very much. Aren't you?"

"Yes."

"Glad to hear it, Mom, because we're going Roller-blading when he gets better and he said he likes to fish too and I certainly like it when he drives me to school. He's a good driver."

"He stays in his lane?"

"Oh, all the time! Sometimes he wants to turn the wrong way but I just yell and say, 'No! Not that way, Winston!' but other than that, he's a great driver. Awww, Mom, I promised I wouldn't tell about those close calls, so please don't tell him I told, okay?"

"No problem, mon," I say when we pull up to the bus stop. "Now get out." He gives me a kiss and I give him one back.

It is nearing the end of week three. I feel like I'm PMSing because everything is getting on my nerves. Winston is getting on my nerves. He is leaving in a few days and I'll be glad when he's gone. I'll be glad to have my space back, to get my life back the way it was before he got here. I mean, everything has totally changed. He takes up so much room and even though I know my son is going to miss him, I told Quincy he can write to Winston and maybe we'll go back to Jamaica during the Christmas holidays or something, I don't know for sure, because when I think about it, Jamaica really wasn't all that exciting, I mean maybe there are some other islands we should consider.

Oh stop it, Stella. You are on your way back to that place you said you weren't visiting anymore. Admit it. You love this man fiercely and you are just afraid of what you're feeling you're afraid that you will miss him too much when he is gone and you don't even want to think about his not being here so you are trying to figure out what it is about him that you will not miss that you could absolutely not live with if he were to, say, stay. For example, at night when he pulls all the covers over to his side of the bed and you wake up freezing your buns off. I mean how long do you think you could tolerate that? And he snores like a goat and he has those sinus problems and he is forever blowing his nose honk honk honk every morning and I mean how many boxes of tissues would this add up to on a weekly, monthly basis? And how about the music issue? I mean let's face it, Stella, you like a little hip-hop and rap as much as the next black person but does he have to play the same song over and over again and do he and Quincy have to have a volume control contest? And then there's the bread problem. He does not like the crust and he eats the middle doughy part and leaves crumbs all over his plate, which really is unnerving. And he slurps. Everything gets slurped up with something else. Maybe this is a Jamaican thing, but it doesn't work here in America. And how about the way he gets things done. He is one slow-moving cookie and yes he does get things done but it's just that he never seems to be in much of a hurry to do anything. You are like a speed demon and he is constantly asking you what's the big rush and you get pissed because it is a difficult question to answer as you do not know why you are in a hurry sometimes. And then last but not least are the wet towels. Why does he have to put them in the hamper where they begin to mildew and mold and you have a hard time figuring out where that smell is coming from. And even though he is rather persistent in his dream of achieving excellence in domesticity he doesn't understand that one should measure detergent and it is not safe to put bleach in dark clothing and what

392 ■ Terry McMillan

else can you think of? Think harder because you haven't even left the tip of the iceberg yet and you know it. There is more. There is always more that you will not be able to tolerate, just watch. He's still got a few days left. You'll see. You'll be so glad when he's gone, I'm here to tell you.

I'll be so very glad when he leaves because that way I can get my drawers back (even though I can't remember what I did with the stuff that was in them) and I'll be glad to have the counter space back on that other sink so I can put all my nail polish and lotions and perfumes back where they were in the first place. And all my blouses and jackets that I moved for him, hey, I need that space because I haven't even done my fall shopping yet and I will need as much hanging room as possible. And the bed. Who needs to feel his warm body next to mine every single day of the week? I mean it has really become rather cumbersome rolling over in the middle of the night and early in the morning and feeling him, and plus making love on a regular basis is so time-consuming and my hair keeps getting all messed up and I am becoming tired of eating a plum or some kind of fruit to make sure my palate is clean when I wake up and I don't even want to think about all I've been going through to keep myself smelling shower fresh everywhere not to mention keeping the stubble off my legs and from under my arms and plucking my eyebrows and brushing three times a day instead of two. I mean I have really been going out of my way to make this man feel good and what have I gotten in return, what have I really gotten in return?

"Stella?" I hear him call. He is outside. It is too cold to be out there, maybe I shouldn't go out. I'll just stand in the doorway and answer whatever question he has. And he has certainly become Mr. Talkative since he's been here, I mean really. Downright nosy. Now he wants to know when am I ever going to come out to my new work space and I told him after he leaves when I can focus and he told me to stop focusing on him and I might be able to focus on my work and I flicked him off because I'm a very talented person this much I know and all I'm doing is waiting for the muse to strike because it's hard getting your groove back once you've lost it but he wasn't really buying this and neither was I but it was all I could think of and so I told him I was thinking about taking some design classes and if he were living here he could maybe take one too just for fun. He told me he'd already looked in our yellow pages and saw quite a few schools and the California Culinary Institute caught his eye and just for the heck of it he called and they mailed him their brochure and he said he basically wanted to compare what they had to offer here in the States to what was available to him in Jamaica and he said it should be here today or tomorrow but he wanted to save it to read on the plane ride home.

The phone starts ringing. "What is it that you want, Mr. Shakespeare?"

"After you answer that, come on out," he says. He is lying in the green-and-white-striped hammock I bought from Hammacher Schlemmer's mail order catalog right before I went to Jamaica. I've been afraid to lie in it because it makes me feel like I'm about to fall out.

"Why do you want me to come out there?"

"I want to talk to you, Stel-la."

"About what, Win-ston?"

"Come out and see."

I get the phone. "Yes?"

"Stella, how are you? This is Ralston."

"Who?"

"Remember I met you in San Diego at Maisha's gallery?"

"Oh yes. How are you?"

"Fine. Look. Wanted to know if we could get together and have dinner this weekend."

"Wish I could, but I'm kind of busy this weekend."

"Well, what's your schedule looking like?"

"Full."

"As in *full* full?"

"Yep."

"I hear you, baby. But you can still have a friendly dinner, can't you?"

"I guess I could."

"Cause I'd like to talk more about your work, my work, what we're doing and where we're trying to go with it, you know?"

"I'd like that."

"And hey, I'm still interested in doing some trading and I'd like to see more of your stuff. Think we can do that?"

"I think we could. Yes."

"Then cool. Don't be a stranger. Write my number down. And bring *him* too. Cause hey. This is a black thang, sister, I thought you knew that."

"I do," I say, and write his number down and right after I say goodbye there is a click. "Hello?"

"Is this Stella?"

"Yes it is. And may I ask who's calling?"

"This is Judge Spencer Boyle. Rodney Wolinski, your insurance broker, gave me your number and said it was all right to call. Is this a good time?" he asks, sounding like a senior citizen.

"Actually it isn't, Judge Boyle. I was just about to give my husband a bath."

"Excuse me?"

"I'm sorry. Did I say husband? I meant to say baby."

"You've got a baby? Rodney didn't tell me you had a baby."

"Oh yes, I've got a baby all right. And boy, what a big baby he is," I exclaim, and then I thank the judge for calling and wish I could've told him that his best bet would be to stop by the Rossmoor Retirement Condominium recreation center and maybe he'd have a better shot at finding himself a hot little number in there. I place the phone in the cradle and saunter on outside into the stinging night air and I stand over my baby. He stretches out the canvas of the hammock to make room for me and I just look at it. "I can't get in there," I say.

"Why not?"

"There's not enough room."

"I'm making room."

"I'll fall out."

"I've been in here for over an hour and I haven't fallen out. It feels like you might, but you don't."

"I don't like that feeling."

"You don't like the feeling of falling?"

"No."

"You mean you don't like feeling out of control."

I give him a how-did-you-know-that look and then switch to a you-think-you-know-so-much look.

"Come on. Get in," he says. "I won't let you fall."

And see, this is what I mean. This is what he can do that kind of bothers me. He makes me comfortable and I'm not used to feeling this comfortable with a man and the thing is I know it's stupid to resist but oh, Stella, get in the fucking hammock and so I listen to the woman in me and I get in and Stella knows what's best for me because once I feel my body drop down into against Winston's I know he's not going to let me fall anywhere but here.

"Are you okay?" he asks.

"I'm okay," I say as my nose brushes against the hair on his chest. "I'm just cold."

"How's this?" he asks and puts his arms around me.

"Better, but it's freezing out here."

"Okay okay okay. Don't move," he says and gets up and I feel like I'm falling for real as I roll to the center of the hammock and the sides roll up so that I feel like a piece of corn on the cob inside some husks but before I know it he's back with the down comforter from the bed and he slides in next to me and turns on his side so that his heart is against my back and God he feels good these goose feathers feel good and I am so warm I could sleep out here like this. "Now," he says.

"Now," I sigh.

"How are you feeling, Stella?"

"I'm feeling just fine. And you?"

"Not so good."

"What's wrong?"

"I'm having a hard time accepting the fact that I am leaving in a few days."

"I am too, actually."

"Well, you haven't said anything."

"I didn't know how to tell you."

"You could've said something like, 'Winston, I'm having a hard time dealing with the fact that you are leaving.' You could've said that."

"And how would you have responded?"

"Well, I would've said, 'Stella, you know I love you, I love being with you, I love what we are doing and how I feel, how you make me feel, and I don't want to leave. Ever.' "

"You would've said that?"

"Yes. And how would you have answered?"

"I would've said you don't really have to leave except that I don't want you to lose your job because of me."

"And I would've said but I would be happy to quit that job as it means nothing to me, not even one tenth as much as you do, and Stella, I can always get another job."

"You would've said that?"

"Absolutely."

"And what is it you would do in America if you had stayed?"

"Well, I would apply to school and work on becoming a certified chef with a specialization so that it would be easier for me to get work in this country and I would work doing anything until such time, as I am not the type of man who could tolerate being taken in by a woman, you know, I mean I would have to earn my own way and help out in the household, you know?"

"Yes, I think I do."

"And then if this woman that I loved would allow herself to not feel the need to be in control of *everything* all the *time* and just admit that she feels what she feels and if she is scared she should know that this guy named Winston loves her enough, that she doesn't have to worry, and she should tell him what she's afraid of and he will comfort her because even though he is not rich and probably never will be he cares about her so much and he hopes it will be enough and he would really like to be her most trusted friend and once she accepts this then maybe they could perhaps even get married."

"Married?" I ask and twist my body over so that I am now facing him.

"Yes, married," he says. "If she loves him as much as she claims and even half as much as he loves her."

"She does," I say. "She tells me all the time. It's kind of getting on my nerves if you want the truth, listening to her go on and on about how she can't believe she's fallen in love with this young man from Jamaica that she met on vacation, but her problem is that she is afraid of marriage because of what she's seen it do to love, how much you actually lose, for instance, like spontaneity: everything seems to have to be planned out in advance, and she does not always want to know what is going to happen next; and then how about passion: it gets pushed out of the way or maybe even shoved over and down to the bottom of the list of *needs* to that list of *wants* and is now considered superfluous, and where there used to be joy and laughter and warm smiles all of a sudden they cross over the picket line and everybody's pissed about something stressed out every day and so she feels that marriage is just so misrepresented, so overrated and not at all redeeming and plus it changes people and she does not want to be changed."

"But she would be marrying a different *kind* of man than she has grown accustomed to in the past. She would be marrying someone who shares her lust for life her enthusiasm her sense of wonder and he is excited by her independence. She would be marrying someone who appreciates the differences between them, who loves to disagree with her because he enjoys watching her get worked up because he gets a charge listening to her rant and rave and he is grateful that he has met a woman who is already a grown-up, one who thinks, who has opinions and does not go along with the program, but he also likes the fact that she is made of good stuff and she is smart enough to know that happiness is here for the asking and this could be their very own adventure."

"She appreciates hearing all this but she knows that even though Winston loves her right *now* he is too young to be thinking about marriage."

"He disagrees."

"That's too bad, because she believes from the bottom of her heart that if he were to marry her, in a year when she is forty-three and then when she is forty-four—if it lasted that long—he would regret ever doing this because her hair will be getting gray and she will begin to get those wrinkles."

"He knows that wrinkles and gray hair do not make her any less attractive and besides she will have earned them and plus she already has some gray hair in a luxurious place and she should know by now that he fell in love with what he saw inside her, not simply what he was able to see with his eyes."

"But he will look at younger girls."

"Of course he will *look,* but he will *love* the older one," he says and puts his face closer, right in front of mine, so that our nostrils are touching. "Are we finished?" he asks.

"I guess so."

"I'm serious, Stella."

"Winston. Okay. Let's say hypothetically speaking that we were to like get married. I mean really: how long could it possibly last?"

"I don't know."

"That's a good answer," I say.

"But who *does* know, Stella?"

"You're right. Who does ever know?"

"So," he says and wraps his arms snugly around me.

"So," I say and slide mine under his.

And then suddenly he just lets me go and it feels like I'm going to tumble out of this hammock but for some reason I really don't care, because I mean how far down could I really fall? I mean there's grass under this thing and then there's this moist soil beneath the grass because the sprinkler system comes on every morning and . . . "Stella?"

"Yes, Winston?"

"So will you marry me?"

I look at him for a few seconds and then I give him a deep juicy succulent kiss and then I take an even closer look into those sincere eyes and I say, "Are you sure you know what you just asked me?"

"Yes, I know what I just asked you."

"What?"

"I just asked you to marry me."

"Ask me again."

"Stella, will you marry me?"

I turn away to look over at the swimming pool for no particular reason except to maybe catch my breath and then I look up at the black sky that has absolutely no stars which is like totally perfect because they are not necessary and so I ponder this thought this notion this gesture this whole idea for a few more seconds and then I smile at Winston and press my lips softly into his and I do love this man I do I do but I look at him one more time to make sure he's like for real and when I see that he is I take a deep breath to make sure I am real and Stella girl accept the fact that you finally got something you wanted, that it's okay to enjoy him this moment go on and make this move feel this groove fool go ahead jump dive in deep fly swirl girl you have earned this you deserve this you can take this to the bank, so when I like hear all this advice and stuff being given to me by this mature in-the-middle-of-her-life woman who knows what day it is what time it is and whose name happens to be the same as mine I am like totally sold swayed convinced so I just go ahead and drape my arms around this beautiful man named Winston Shakespeare and I say, "Okay!"